The Rapture

By the same author

The Serpent's Circle

The Rapture

Patrick Harpur

MACMILLAN

The author would like to acknowledge his debt to the works of Bruno Bettelheim; to H. F. Wood's *All Over Britain with the Author*; and, not least, to his mother.

First published 1986 by
MACMILLAN LONDON LIMITED
4 Little Essex Street London WC2R 3LF
and Basingstoke

Associated companies in Auckland, Delhi, Dublin, Gaborone, Hamburg, Harare, Hong Kong, Johannesburg, Kuala Lumpur, Lagos, Manzini, Melbourne, Mexico City, Nairobi, New York, Singapore and Tokyo.

British Library Cataloguing in Publication Data

Harpur, Patrick
  The rapture.
  I. Title
  823'.914[F]   PR6058.A6876

  ISBN 0-333-40549-8

Filmset in Palatino by Filmtype Services Limited, Scarborough, North Yorkshire.
Printed and bound in Great Britain by The Garden City Press Ltd, Letchworth, Herts.

for Cary

PART ONE

Dark Sentences

ONE

RED ALERT. *The singularity activates. It's angry. Not stable. It boils in the blackness. It's in the hole, it's in the littlun. It's making its big grab. No, no. The singularity lets out its power, its beams plode the world splat crash. Mustn't, no, not ever. Mustn't blow up the bigun. The bigun shines away, light years away.* DANGER. *Oh, oh, the singularity drags the littlun down into the hole in the littlun. The littlun spins, spins, venting the horrorizon. The singularity pushes him in the hole, pulls him in the dark. Hang on, hang on. The littlun clings to the vent horrorizon, clings like grim life, hangs on for dear death. Hang on.* DANGER *he screams. The singularity burns, tears, pulling his insides out, pulling his outsides in, watch out, the hole, help help* PLODE *he screams Ah Ah Ah Ah splat crash plosion.*

Ruth watched the small boy intently. His knuckles showed white where they clutched the porcelain rim of the lavatory bowl. His ribcage jerked up and down, its bones jutting out painfully. Droplets of perspiration freckled his expressionless face. 'Danger,' he whispered. '*Plode.*' There was a faint splash.

Mikey suffered himself to be lifted off the lavatory. Ruth remembered not to flush it: the innocent act of pulling the chain provoked such terror in the boy that he flew into a frenzy of spinning to compensate for the loss of his excrement. She wiped his knotted little bottom

9

and picked up his clothes to dress him. It was still only nine o'clock and she was already exhausted.

Mikey had taken forty minutes to complete his complicated bowel movement. Most of that time was spent running in tight circles – he'd advanced at least from spinning on the spot – in order to make the lavatory 'safe'. Then there was the ritual of the slow removal of all his clothes, then more running, and finally the mad dash for the lavatory above which he had to lever himself by his skinny arms. It was too dangerous to sit. Even so, sitting was as nothing compared to the danger of defecation itself, from the critical 'Red Alert' condition to the terrible and final 'Plosion'.

After more than a year of such shenanigans, with precious little change, Ruth was ready to scream. One tiny gesture of recognition, a single glance, was all she asked. She felt that Mikey was doing something brutal to her, turning her into the inhuman convenience he treated her as. Worst of all, she could show nothing of her frustration to Mikey; the smallest rejection might set him back months. She stared into his pale mask-like face, imagining its blankness breaking into a smile. But if he looked in her direction at all he seemed to look straight through her. Be patient, Ruth, she said to herself; but her frayed nerves had no defence against the sting of his indifference and the dull throb of guilt at her inadequacy. I don't love him *enough*, she thought; but when did love ever cut any ice?

Attuned to every nuance of Mikey's behaviour, Ruth was about to pull his Incredible Hulk T-shirt over his head when she noticed that, although he was facing the door, his hand had strayed back towards the lavatory. The contradictory movement caused her heart to flutter. She grasped the vague hand, placed it firmly on the white rim, and waited. The boy stood absolutely still for five minutes. His naked body didn't register the cold, just as it was oblivious of heat; Mikey carried his climate inside him. When he put his other hand on the rim, the motion was detached and mechanical; he leant slowly over the lavatory bowl like a small automaton. Only the spasmodic rippling of his stomach muscles suggested that he was performing a prodigious deed of daring. His unfocused eyes gazed, as if across an immense distance, at his stool floating in the water below. Ruth was wary of her own sudden excitement. She had too often fallen prey to violent swings of mood – high hopes dashed to deep despair – which left her empty and strung up. She spoke to him softly, reassuringly. Mikey ignored her.

He reached down into the lavatory, poked the stool with trembling fingers and backed away. He seemed about to run in his panic-stricken circles. Instead, he returned to the stool and tentatively grasped it, like high explosive, in both hands. He moulded the excrement feebly between forefinger and thumb. His mouth worked, soundlessly at first, forming the syllables of forbidden words. He seemed to strain, pushing outwards, as though words were things to be expelled, like turds.

'The singularity ... will blow up the world. Its beams ... too strong. The littlun lets out the beams ... the light. Danger. The bigun must stop him. He'll plode. The light can't escape ... nothing escapes ... not ever ... the dark ... the horrorizon.'

The words were addressed to thin air, but the voice — or was it wishful thinking? — the voice seemed a fraction less toneless than usual. Certainly, Mikey had never before been so verbose in the context of the lavatory. It really did begin to look as if .... Ruth didn't allow herself any indulgent fancies. Instead she addressed herself to the new word: 'horrorizon'. What could it signify? All Mikey's neologisms concealed areas of particular sensitivity, but she had long since given up hope of deciphering all but a few of his apocalyptic utterances. She had learnt that she, and all adults, were 'biguns', while Mikey was sometimes the dreaded 'singularity' and at others the 'littlun' who lived in fear of it. Like all severely autistic children, his sense of a self was so diminished that he could no more say 'I' than a newborn baby.

'What is the "horrorizon", darling? Where is it?' She didn't expect an answer. Mikey lifted his hands and began to dab his chest with his excrement. Gradually he grew bolder until he had covered all the accessible parts of his body with long brown smears. The most perilous area was the mouth: he came no nearer to smearing it than a dab on the chin, preceded by a rapid rotation of his left hand to simulate in part the revolving of his whole body that warded off danger. Ruth was fascinated, her initial revulsion forgotten.

'Good, Mikey ... good ... I see you're covering yourself all over ...' Gently she encouraged and affirmed his unprecedented behaviour. 'That's it ... good ... you *are* brave ....'

Mikey abruptly finished and turned towards the door. Although he was nine years old, he was small for his age and still so emaciated that Ruth had no trouble picking him up. Puzzled but delighted, she carried him off to the bathroom in the dormitory wing.

The Unit was cheaply and compactly built on three sides of a square. The ground floor was the children's domain, except for Dr Frieling's office and a modest reception area. The west wing contained the two dormitories and bathrooms; the east was entirely given over to an airy, bright, all-purpose area known as the playroom. In between, a corridor gave on to the schoolroom and the dining room, with its kitchen tacked on to the back. There were toilets attached to both wings. The

11

floor above belonged to the adults. It contained Dr Frieling's two rooms and the bedrooms, communal sitting room, kitchen and bathroom of the resident counsellors. There were only three at the moment – Ruth, Carol and Adrian.

In the playroom a number of the Unit's other twelve children were playing pig-in-the-middle. Others could be heard in the schoolroom next door. Kevin the Wolf, a feral child so called to distinguish him from Kevin the Silent (who preferred to remain mute), was curled up under a table, fast asleep. Carol caught Ruth's eye as she swept through with Mikey, inert and filthy in her arms. They rarely spoke on duty since Dr Frieling insisted that all their attention be directed to the children in their charge. However, the sight of Mikey made Carol raise her eyebrows and smile.

In the beginning she had resented Ruth Maier. She suspected that Dr Frieling had given her preferential treatment by assigning her to a single child, while she, Carol, was responsible for three. She even suspected that the old man had fallen for this under-qualified 'mature' woman (Ruth was forty; Carol twenty-seven) to whom people naturally applied such old-fashioned adjectives as 'handsome', 'striking' and even 'voluptuous'. Carol would have liked to have added 'plump'. But she had to admit that Ruth's full bosom and hips were emphasised by the surprising trimness of her waist; the broad forearms were solid rather than fleshy, and the robust straightness of her back made her seem taller than she was. Her dark complexion and expressive features gave Carol the idea that she was foreign – there was an exotic suggestion about the cheekbones, the strong nose, the curly mouth with its wide smile, the close-set black eyes which Carol thought of as 'flashing'. Especially irritating was the hair, which Ruth neglected. Falling around her face in lustrous dark-brown waves, it always looked sensational.

Carol's resentment quickly vanished. When she saw how excruciating Ruth's task really was, she had to admit that she herself wasn't tough enough to crack a nut as hard as Mikey. When she at last confessed her envy of Ruth's hair, she was greeted by incredulous hoots – apparently, Ruth had envied Carol not only *her* straight fair hair, but also her exasperating slimness and scandalous prettiness. Moreover, Ruth claimed to be terrified of her competence, cowed by her professionalism, amazed by her patience, *awe*-struck by— They both collapsed with laughter. Carol omitted to mention that she saw in Ruth an ancient quality, met with occasionally in Old Masters, which combined the strength and resignation of a peasant with the

12

grace of a noblewoman. Nor did Ruth mention that, confronted every-day by Carol's goodness, she went to bed every night acutely conscious of her want of love.

Ruth returned her friend's smile and, wrinkling her nose, twisted her head towards Mikey. Carol made a sympathetic face and refocused her attention on the children's game. It never varied: each child always played the same role and the 'pig' always captured the ball on the fifth exchange. No one took the pig's place; the game – an optimistic name for it – merely started again to run its dreary inevitable course. But at least they recognised the ball, and each other. Some of them eventually admitted slight innovations into their obsessive patterns of sameness. Some even learnt enough self-determination to function outside the Unit, whose full title was the Unit for Disturbed Children. Though pleasantly untechnical, the name was nevertheless a euphemism. The children were not disturbed when they arrived. They were in fear of their lives.

I don't know what got into me. I'm a bit calmer today. Your coloured pills probably have something to do with it. They won't be necessary from now on. I'm pretty much myself again. Oh, no formality, please – just call me 'Harry'; everyone else does. 'Old Harry' is what the lads down the Invoice Office call me ... *used* to call me. I still can't quite get it into my thick skull that I won't be going back there after – what? – must be forty-six years not counting the war and that. There's no harm in the lads, no real harm, but I prefer to omit the 'old'.

In fact, I'm not so old. I was born in nineteen twenty-four. You a train man at all, Doctor? Ah. Pity. You see, I was born on the *very day* that the *Flying Scotsman* broke the record for the London-to-Edinburgh run. A little over eight hours, if I'm not mistaken, and I'm not. I sometimes wonder if the record run wasn't a sign and portent of things to come – not for my mother, of course, who was taken to God two days later, but for me. The fact that I was a biggish baby – still are, I hear you say, ha ha – probably did the mother no good. By all accounts I came out with my eyes open and the midwife had to thrash me black and blue – I was no fool – before I'd cry. 'He'll end on the gallows,' Father was heard to say, a thing he maintained right up to his last breath – he was a dry one, was Father – except that he always said 'gaRllows', being deaf as a pudding and a Scot to boot and thus confused in his pronunciation.

Is this the sort of thing, Doctor? I don't suppose it is. I can't remember when I last talked about myself. Yes, I can; it was during a Cornish thunderstorm in nineteen forty-five – how could I ever forget? – but

13

there were exten − special circumstances then. I dare say a man's got no business harping on his personal stuff, particularly a man in my position. However. Since you insist, I don't mind rambling on. I've no wish to be rude. But I've led a humdrum life, every day the same for I don't know how long, so don't say I didn't warn you.

Also, it's not going to throw any light on.... Well, don't get me wrong, Doctor − I'm not about to tell you your business. I'm sure the psychiatrics is no end of a benefit to people with disorders of the mind and passions − lust, concupiscence, etcetera − but you'll admit that the mind and passions and so on aren't everything, far from it, and that the spirit walks abroad in this world for better or worse whether we like it or not. And while I'm at it, if you'll forgive me, from what I've seen of the souls shut up in this place, a spot of the old exorcism might be just the ticket. Not in every case, mind − you don't want to go mad − no, just when you've drawn a blank with the old pills, electricity, etcetera. I know what I'm talking about. I've been threatened myself and might have gone under a number of times over the long years if I hadn't been delivered into the hands of the Lord, who has buffered me time and again from the onslaught of the Evil One, who exists in the world, contrary to the general consensus, and who will only be banished − God willing − in the Age to come.

It must be pretty plain to you by now that I shouldn't be in the loony bin − I beg your pardon, the psychiatrical hospital − at all. Don't get me wrong. I'm very grateful, and to take a rest is delightful; but, as for what I did, I rather think it's a matter for the police courts and a case of a couple of weeks in choky. I admit I did wrong; I'm heartily sorry for it, and I'd rather be punished than have to explain. I can't be *cured* of what ails me except by Christ, who will cure all the world's ills at His Coming.

I never raised a hand to anyone before now. It was a case of mistaken identity − on my part, I mean. Also, there were ... other circumstances, of which I cannot speak. I say this not in mitigation, but as *fact*. All I *can* say is that, although my guilt is not in doubt, I've recently endured enough to send anyone who was not stiffened by the Holy Ghost, as I have been to my pain and joy, clean round the bend.

'A girl's been attacked,' said Dorothy from behind the local newspaper. Rex was crouched next to his untouched coffee, pointing his video camera at Cassandra, who was staring manically out of the kitchen window at a starling. He didn't hear her above the blare of the television on which several pleased people, all dressed in what appeared to be golfing clothes, were sitting on large sofas and laughing.

14

'A girl's been *attacked*.' She hadn't meant to repeat it. She couldn't help herself. The item, sandwiched between council news and a wedding photograph, had shocked her.

Rex ceased trying to capture the play of morning light on Cassandra's fur and put down the camera. 'That's scarcely front-page news,' he remarked soothingly. 'Happens every day.' He smiled at Dorothy, his beautiful hands absently caressing Cassandra.

'Not here. Not in this area.' Dorothy couldn't keep a tiny tremulous note out of her voice. In spite of the suppressed irritation on her husband's face – he was so patient with her – she couldn't stop herself going on: 'It happened on the heath . . . just outside the estate. Less than a mile away.'

'Calm down, darling.'

'I am calm. I'm just saying that a girl's been attacked. It's not usual for round here. I thought you might be interested.'

Rex nodded slowly; his face was thoughtful, sympathetic. She really didn't deserve him. She concentrated on his hands stroking the cat. Women noticed hands almost before faces. She hadn't dreamt that hands like Rex's existed – at least, she'd never seen hands like them in Liverpool where, it was said, the men's hands were honest. Dorothy remembered them as callused, spatulate, contemptuous of women who could like them or lump them.

'It was horrible. The man wore a mask or something.' The cat blinked at her with smug malice. She hated the way Rex was fondling her fur.

'But she got away.'

'Yes, she got away. She was taking a short cut from the station. It was virtually broad daylight. We've been asked to come forward.' On the screen, a fat overwrought man in a satin kaftan was reading horoscopes and wriggling on his sofa. Out of habit, Dorothy paused to listen to Virgo, her sign. In the newspapers she always read Rex's sign before her own. Romance was in store for her, the fat man averred, squirming suggestively and letting out a girlish squeak; Dorothy shuddered.

'We?' Rex's eyebrows were raised patiently.

'We. The public. If we saw anything . . . suspicious.'

'But we didn't, did we?' Rex was faintly repelled by his wife's smooth made-up face. There was something almost unhealthy about the accuracy of her eyeliner at breakfast, about the bright red mouth pursed into a blob, when she wasn't even dressed.

'No. No, of course not.' Dorothy couldn't seem to convey how disturbing the article was in the context of the jolly little paper. She

15

wanted reassurance. 'It could have been me,' she said, hating herself for saying it.

'It could have been her,' Rex confided to his cat. 'Dorothy could have been attacked by a great big nasty hairy man, eh, pusskins?'

'It's not a joke, Rex.'

'Poor Dorothy,' Rex whispered. 'She never has any luck, does she, Cassie?'

'I don't like that cat. You love that cat more than me.'

'Oh, darling. Stop it. Please.' He turned to Cassandra and cooed: 'Of course Rex loves Cassie, but Rex loves Dorothy much more. And Cassie loves Dorothy, too, don't you, Cassie? We're one big happy family—' He stopped abruptly, pushed Cassie off his lap and switched off the television. Dorothy sipped black coffee. 'Family' was not a word they used. Unthinkingly, simply to take the edge off the uneasy silence, Rex said: 'I was attacked yesterday.' He glanced at Dorothy's stricken expression and bitterly regretted the remark. He hadn't meant to say it; it was a trivial thing. But too late.

'What on earth do you *mean*?'

'Oh, it was nothing. Not an attack at all really. I was joking. Some old drunk yelling in the High Street. Nothing at all.' But was it nothing? He was reluctant to admit it, but he still felt quite shaken.

'*What* old drunk?'

Rex shrugged. 'I don't know. He came up behind me, shouting some mumbo-jumbo. Two policemen grabbed him. It was quite funny. I'm not even sure he was shouting at me.' But Rex was sure. He had walked away as fast as he dared, without looking back. The man had pursued him, shouting; he had come near enough to grab Rex by the shoulder, to tear the sleeve of his light grey suit, before the policemen intervened. It was the randomness of the assault which unsettled him most. Why pick on *him*?

'Did you get him arrested? Press charges? He should be locked up.'

Rex forced a laugh. 'Good God, no. The policemen asked me that. It wasn't worth it. The poor bugger didn't know what he was doing.' In fact, Rex had simply wanted to get away from the scene as quickly as possible. He'd made light of the incident, laughing it off. He caught a glimpse of the culprit, sitting on the pavement with his head on his knees and a policeman standing over him.

'You should have followed it up, Rex. He could attack again.'

'It wasn't an attack, I tell you.'

'Why did you say "attack"?'

'Forget it, Dorothy. Please.' Rex found it difficult to forget. The man had cried out strange and frightening words. The familiar bustling street seemed suddenly accursed. 'I'd better go,' he said briskly. 'I'll be late.'

'What were you doing in the High Street on a Monday?'

'Hm?'

'Why weren't you in London? At the office?'

'Oh' — Rex gestured vaguely — 'lunch with Travers at the bank ... keep him sweet.' It was better to lie about the bank manager than worry Dorothy. He bent to give her a kiss on the cheek and noticed the face powder clogged in the larger pores under her eyes. It tasted slightly sweet on his lips. Dorothy sensed his faint distaste. Why, if he didn't like it, had he made a special point of disparaging women who looked a mess at breakfast? Left to herself, she wouldn't have bothered with cosmetics at all.

Ruth lowered Mikey into the warm water. Baths were occasions when he had shown the most progress over the past year. He seemed to like the water and the sensation of being stroked, quietly and rhythmically, while Ruth sang to him. Today the emphasis was on washing more than usual, but it seemed to make no difference. His rigid limbs became less dense and heavy — the properties of the 'singularity' — and more like human appendages.

'It hides everything. Nothing gets out,' Mikey whispered to the bath taps. Ruth guessed that he was answering her earlier question about the 'horrorizon'. She had discovered that his fear of human contact was so great, yet the need to test her fidelity so deep, that he often answered her questions hours later when he thought she might have forgotten them.

'I see. The horrorizon hides everything, does it? Tell me about it, Mikey. It's safe to tell me.' Ruth struggled to sound bright; Mikey's answers never made sense.

'A littlun can't be seen. He's just empty ... mess. A mass of mess. A littlun's too messive for Earth. He drops through. Earth is just mist ... white mist ... zillions of miles ... away.'

As ever, Ruth failed to grasp the topography of his private world which, from any other point of view, was indistinguishable from hell. She had sworn to join him where he was, to penetrate his world so that she might retrieve him, but a tremendous effort was needed simply to concentrate on him for moments at a time; like a stone, there was nothing personal about him to arrest the gaze. People didn't notice him in a room; he was, as he claimed, invisible. His cloak of invisibility was spun by rotating his body or running in circles. Designed to protect him, it threatened to extinguish him. Somewhere inside it, Mikey was clinging to his own self's precipice.

'I can see you, Mikey,' Ruth assured him. 'You're here with me . . . safe with me. I won't let anything bad happen.'

'The vent horrorizon hides the light. It disappears with spinning. It'll never disappear. It goes round the singularity. Nothing gets out. A littlun has to spin faster than the sun. Nothing goes faster than the sun. A littlun can't be seen ever. Time stands still . . . at the vent horrorizon. It goes backwards inside the hole. A child of nine knows *that*. A littlun is alone . . . in the dark . . . he's all plosion . . . plosion and mess mess mess.' Like himself, the enigmatic statements were self-contradictory and self-defeating.

All at once Ruth saw clearly how, in a perverse way, she *had* joined him in his world. Day after day she fed him, dressed him, undressed him, washed him, looked after his every whim without recognition or response. Tortured by perpetual anxiety over him, she had no life of her own. He was sucking her down. She could no longer tell whether his new faecal behaviour, his unusual amount of talking in the bath, signified real change or whether she was imagining it.

She fished Mikey out of the water and held him tightly while she pulled out the plug. He was terrified of dissolving and disappearing down the plug-hole. Together they watched the water spiralling away. 'Plode,' Mikey murmured, betraying his agitation. Bathing, eating, sleeping, shitting – the most basic functions were sources of intolerable anguish to him. In many ways it would be better to be dead; in some ways, he was.

'There'll be times when you'll want to do away with yourself,' Dr Frieling had warned her when she first applied for the job. She hadn't believed him then. He was sitting on the floor of his office, mending a wooden wagon and looking so shabby and dispirited – so like her father in his grey cardigan – that he wrenched her heart. Drawing on her own abortive psychoanalysis, Ruth was critical of what she saw as the doctor's old-fashioned Freudian basis of the children's treatment.

'Believe me, Miss Maier, I agree,' he had surprised her by saying. 'Even an old witch-doctor like Freud is of precious little use to these children. I know this. But what can I do?' He spread his hands in a familiar helpless gesture. 'His model of the psyche is the only one that comes close. "The child is father to the man." Freud said this, in effect, and he was right. Unfortunately, he did not say why one infant's milk is another's poison. Take two children with identical upbringings – one becomes a saint, the other takes an axe to his parents. Why? We don't know.' Again the helpless gesture. Ruth blushed now to remember his forbearance in the face of her amateurish theorising. He listened quietly and seriously, blinking behind his round spectacles, turning over the pieces of broken toy in his expressive hands.

'You are right, Miss Maier,' he sighed at last. 'I'm an old man. I fall back on Sigmund because I find him comfortable, like this old worn-out cardigan. Besides, he wrote so eloquently. But we all have our little psychologies here at the Unit. Like secret vices. We use them to comfort ourselves, not to cure the children. Try to understand. My children, in a sense, precede psychology. Not one of them will leave here *cured*. But we are their only hope for some kind of life; we have nothing to lose. Any small shelter serves in a whirlwind. Are you a religious person?' Ruth admitted that she was not, despite a flirtation with the Roman Catholic Church as a child.

'Neither am I,' said Dr Frieling. 'But it hasn't stopped me from falling to my knees and praying for one of the children. And who's to say it doesn't work as well as one of old Sigmund's spells? You have a kind heart, Miss Maier, and that's worth more than Freud and God put together. I intend to offer you the job. The pay, as you know, is negligible and it will be nothing but trouble. Will you take it? Think before you answer,' he warned. 'You will have to develop virtues, Miss Maier, or you'll go horribly mad! Humility, patience, love — these are the tasks of counsellors at the Unit. And when you have exhausted them you will find you have hardly begun. There will be times when you'll want to do away with yourself. Then you will come to me and we'll talk — about psychology!'

Ruth started the job on the spot. She was to help Dr Frieling assess a candidate for the Unit who was waiting outside. He was called Mikey Ballantine. Carol carried him in, and Ruth knew right away that he was for her.

Patting Mikey dry and dressing him, Ruth wondered if she ought to go and see Dr Frieling now. She had done so before when the boy seemed about to make a breakthrough and it had proved a false alarm. Besides, the old doctor would probably scold her for working too hard. She herself knew that it was irresponsible and self-defeating to work the equivalent of a double shift. A nervous wreck was no good to Mikey. But whether out of love or stubbornness she could hardly bear to be parted from him for more than a few hours. She used to long to get away for an evening, to take a train to Town, for instance, and see a show; now she only felt at ease among the kids and counsellors who knew her. The outside world wasn't safe.

Mikey didn't mind walking to the playroom. As soon as he was installed in his chosen spot — a giant bean-bag in the corner — he withdrew into total inaction. The morning's exertions had taken their toll on both of them. Ruth sat with him, cuddling him, telling him she accepted him as he was, unconditionally, as she had done for months. Mikey lay like a lump in her arms, his eyes blank and dead. It was worse than usual somehow after the earlier excitement. Ruth asked Carol to keep an eye on him and, wrapping up warmly, went out for a breath of air.

TWO

RIGHT-O. I'll begin.

I live here in Wyebridge, at number one, South Road; you probably know it. Oh, well, it's not a mile from here – you turn left at the end of Station Road and it's on the left before you reach the new council houses. I say 'new'; they've been there twenty-odd years now, but if you live all your life in the same house everything around seems new. I remember when this place was a private house and that's going back a bit .... Sorry? *Personal relationships?* Ah. Let's think. I suppose you mean Father. Oh yes, we got on famously. By and large. When I think back to the hardships he suffered with his deafness and that, plus no helpmeet to care for him or to cleave to, then I'm bitten by remorse that he should've been burdened with such a useless son. He couldn't work, so we had next to no money, bar his pension, until I became a wage-earner. No, it wasn't his deafness – it was his leg or, rather, his lack of it. He lost it on the railways as a young man. Never said how, didn't like to be asked, made him irritable. He always said he'd had it blown off by Jerry in the first war. A great joker, was Father. He had this wooden one instead.

Actually, it got him in the papers once, the wooden leg. You see, Doctor, when they installed the first moving staircase down the underground railway in nineteen eleven or twelve – Earls Court it was – they thought people would find it hazardous. So, just to show folk how easy it was to use, they paid Father to tramp up and down this escalator for a week. With his wooden leg. Must've done the trick because they caught on after that, the escalators. That was the last job he had. Sorry. I didn't mean to wander off the point.

I suppose I was just putting off telling you about *relationships*. What you mean is relationships *with the fair sex*, don't you? I may be unmarried, but that doesn't mean I haven't had my moments. Personally, I think you're barking up the wrong lamp-post with this *relationships* business – my work is the main thing, the heart of the matter, so to speak. Not the office. I mean my *real* work. Still, I dare say we'll get around to that. Meanwhile, since you've been kind, I don't mind telling you about – well, *you* know. I've been pretty lucky on the whole, even though it's not easy steering clear of people, which is necessary for my work because, of course, a man can't serve two masters.

There was a moment in primary school that still lights up my mind. It was a history lesson with the Terrible Pie. Short for Shepherd's Pie. His name was Mister Sheppard, you see; I didn't get it, either, at the time because I'd never had Shepherd's Pie, never even *heard* of it. I was running through my brain the names of the stations from Wyebridge to Waterloo (I recited them once to the great joy of the children of Israel; but I mustn't get ahead of myself). It was my ambition at the time to be a guard on the trains. I knew it was futile to aspire to driver or footplate man – I'm so clumsy I'd probably wreck the engine. As it turned out, even guard was a foolish dream. Anyway ...

When the Terrible Pie asked me a question, I blurted out 'Hersham' – that's the station after Walton-on-Thames – instead of 'Hastings', and everyone split their sides. No one believed that I knew the answer really, although I mentioned it to some of the boys after school; but they only chanted 'Poor old Harry got killed at the battle of Hersham' until I was angry enough to do them some violence, but could do nothing in fact because of their pointed faces and sharp, laughing teeth. (You see, Doctor, I was 'old Harry' even in those days, at the age of seven.) But you mustn't think that I'm liable to such feelings now: I've long since trampled my anger down. I was young and unregenerate at the time, and knew not the ways of the Lord.

But I learnt something that day which I've often found to be true, namely that every cloud has a golden lining. Because, after I'd made a muck of the answer and the laughter had temporarily died down, Poole, the boy who was put next to me as a punishment for writing 'B——' (I won't say the word) on the blackboard, passed me – wait for it – a *sweet*. Well, you panic in situations like that. I didn't know *who* to pass it on to. I mean, I'd had the odd note before, listing some of my many shortcomings, but never a *sweet*.

It was passed to me, it turned out, by of all people Jean Macintyre, who was sitting six desks away staring hard at her pencil-box with two red patches on her cheeks. Some of the boys called her fat, but I never saw it myself. She was just big for her age, like me, with a long neck and dark hair that would've done credit to the Daughters of Zion. But altogether without their wantonness, of course. Naturally I couldn't, you know, *speak* to her for fear of Father finding out, especially as the other girls used to shout 'Jean loves old Harry', which words were bitter gall to me for her sake but also ravishing because of the thought that they might be true .... I determined to defy Father and *speak up*. But it was too late. Jean Macintyre moved away in the middle of term. To Ashford in Kent, I heard.

Verily I believe that this business of Jean Macintyre might have come to something if I had spoken up sooner; but, as it is, I'm un-married and likely to remain so now. Unluckily I had none of the other boys' distractions, for I was such a muddler that I couldn't kick a football without falling over. And as for cricket, I was in mortal fear of a hard ball, a fear which I retain to this day. So I went to the station and booked engine numbers. Also bogie-block, four-carriage train sets and train destinations. It was hard work, and frightening too, because of all the numbers. I was good at composition, but numbers terrified me. But I fought them. One of the things I had to do at the station, for example, was copy out all the timetables and *calculate the average speeds*.

I kept the sweet until nineteen forty-five, as a matter of fact. It was a gobstopper. I don't know if they still make them so big and with so many beautiful different-coloured layers. I sucked those layers off from time to time over the years. The last but one was yellow, the colour of Jean Macintyre's pencil-box, and then it was just a tiny white ball. The person I gave it to never said what happens after white.

Ruth strolled through the line of tall firs which screened the Unit from the main building. In the distance vague figures could be seen moving like hallucinations through the mist that the green lawns exhaled under the thin yellow sunlight. They passed unhurriedly up and down the gravel paths, nodding to one another like guests of some great per-sonage taking turns about the grounds before luncheon.

Sitting on a bench underneath a beech tree, snowdrops bunched at her feet, Ruth imagined herself in a more gracious age until the mist dispersed and she saw the figures more clearly – grey shades jerking and muttering to and fro, absorbed in their private compulsory sor-rows. She was used to the inmates now, connected to them like a distant relative. Some worked at the Unit as cooks and cleaners, to free

23

the counsellors from donkey-work so that they could devote all their time to the children. To free the counsellors – that was a laugh.

Ruth closed her eyes and, willing herself to relax, rested her mind on the image of glittering snowfields, blue sky, dazzling white peaks stretching away into infinity – an image which normally never failed to relieve her tension.

But today her mind wandered. She remembered the moment when Carol appeared in the doorway with Mikey in her arms. His emaciation made the eyes in his bony head seem very large and dark and blank. His mouth was half-open as if frozen in the act of speaking; the lips were dry and cracked. Long dark hair framed his face, accentuating the pallor of his delicate skin beneath which blue veins were visible.

'This is Mikey Ballantine. Go and say "Hello" to Dr Frieling,' said Carol, putting him down and leaving the room. Without any sign that he had heard her, Mikey moved obediently towards the doctor. It was pitiful to watch: he dragged his stiff leaden legs across the floor like a deep-sea diver on dry land. Yet no flicker of exertion disturbed his impassive face. As he approached the old man, he stopped and began to revolve, grinding round like a millstone at first and then slowly gathering momentum until he was spinning like a top. His arms wrapped themselves around his body, and his body became hunched and shrunken before their eyes. Faster and faster he spun in a stunning virtuoso display until it seemed that he must fly out of control. Instead he cried out piercingly: 'DANGER.' Moisture was trickling down his face, but still it remained unmoved. 'RED ALERT.' The face flashed past like a pale beacon. 'PLODE,' he screamed, 'PLODE.' Even in a scream his voice was weird, toneless, rather like a deaf person's voice.

He stopped as suddenly as he had begun. His arms dangled at his sides, his head dropped forward; he was not in the least dizzy, only limp.

'Well, Miss Maier. What do you think?'

'Astonishing' was all Ruth could say. She leant forward and, smiling gently, addressed the boy. 'Mikey ... Mikey, are you all right?' There was no response.

'Don't smile,' said Dr Frieling sharply. 'You're smiling to make him think you're a nice person. Only smile when you're invited to. *Your* emotions have no place here; they distract your attention from the child.'

Ruth nodded. She went up to Mikey and, instinctively bracing herself for a great weight, picked him up and sat him on her lap. He was as light as a feather. She stared, fascinated, into his face, speaking softly, coaxing him to reply. His eyes flickered once in her direction, revealing a tiny spark of interest before they went dead again, fixed

24

on empty space like a famine victim who has long since ceased to cry for food.

She was seized by the irresistible impression that inside the little boy there lived an old man, mortally tired of living. When at last he spoke, the words came from a great distance and were expelled with enormous effort. Ruth had to bend her head to hear what he was saying.

'Empty ... black ... heavy ... black ... empty ... hole.'

The despairing adjectives made her go cold. Dr Frieling shook his head.

'An interesting case. We can't take him, of course. He's too old now to do much with.'

'He's not even *nine* years old,' cried Ruth.

The doctor turned his palms upwards. 'You tell me you've read the literature. Then you'll know that in such acute cases we have to begin very early if we want to achieve anything approaching normality.' In defiance of his vast experience, Ruth mentally scanned what little she knew about autistic children.

'He speaks, Dr Frieling,' she said. 'Despite everything, he has hung on to language. Surely we can build on that? He hasn't given up on life yet – we mustn't give up on him.' She was as surprised as the doctor at her own vehemence. She saw by his face that she had scored a telling point.

'True, Miss Maier. You've done your homework. But it is also plain that Mikey is not speaking as we understand it. He's not ... communicating. His words are at best addressed only to himself. It could take years to bridge the abyss between our world and the private world to which his words refer. By that time, the damage ....' He stopped.

'That's not a reason for abandoning him.'

'So. You're prepared to take him on? Be careful. Your sentence will be a long one. Think.'

'I don't have to think. He'll die without proper care. It's obvious.'

Dr Frieling nodded. 'Welcome to the Unit, Miss Maier. I suggest that Mikey moves in on Monday. That will give you a chance to read his reports. They are a bit sparse. The best were compiled by an enlightened nursery-school teacher of his, a ... Miss Wickham. After that, you will interview the parents' – he lifted a significant finger – 'that is where the trouble began. If I had my way, I'd abolish parents. If they agree to our conditions, Mikey will be in your sole charge from then on.'

Unconscious of the critical decision being taken above his head, Mikey remained insensate in Ruth's arms. She clasped his hand. He received it without pleasure or protest. He was a million miles away.

25

Although the sun's rays were methodically sweeping away the mist, it was still cold. Ruth wound her scarf more tightly around her neck. The high, sprawling hospital, once the grandest house on the St Michael's Hill estate, threw its shadow over the patients who were still exercising in front.

'It's not their fault,' she said aloud. She was referring to Mikey's parents. She had to remind herself at frequent intervals that they were not to blame for their son's condition. 'Not *all* their fault,' she added. In an attempt not to judge them too harshly, she had thought a lot about the causes of autism before she came to interview them. She had not got very far. The causes were obscure; they occurred at a very early stage of the child's development, probably at least as early as the breast-feeding stage. The result was that the child was deprived of the elementary plankton on which the whole oceanic economy of the personality depends.

The only certainty was that at some crucial point Mikey had felt, rightly or wrongly, rejected by his mother. This alone could not explain his condition: all children feel rejected at some time – whenever their need to be fed is not immediately satisfied, for instance. But, in a few rare children such as Mikey, the experience was devastating. Even so, he might still have adjusted to normal growth had not some specific trauma convinced him that he was liable to be destroyed at any moment. Ruth had hoped to discover what this catastrophe might have been when she spoke to the parents.

Meanwhile she had struggled to picture the unimaginable world of the autistic infant: the tiny blob of inchoate sensations and needs entirely dependent on the goddess Mother. Bathed in the glow of her love, nourished by the blissful breast, wholly absorbed into her warm power, he is suddenly cut off – exiled from Eden to the freezing wastes beyond. The deep yearning to return to paradise is stymied by the equally intense fear of renewed disappointment. Weeping with frustration, he ricochets between extremes of longing and terror; the weeping deepens to screams of fury; the screaming stops. Now there is only the brooding rage against the mother, himself, the world; a rage so deep that it is too dangerous to express – or even to *feel* – in case it unleashes a flood of destruction or provokes horrific retaliation from those who arouse it. The more violent the infantile anger, the more it must be suppressed, until the child is buried in a black fire of despair for which he is the stoker, the furnace, the flames and – finally – the ashes.

In more abstract mood, Ruth conceived of the autistic dynamic as a vicious spiral: longing and fear turning to anger, twisting to despair, returning to longing – with each turn screwing the child deeper into

26

withdrawal and self-absorption. And the bitterest part was that the child was, after all, only conforming to what he had interpreted as his parents' wish — the wish *that he should not exist.*

An adult in mortal danger may resort to fight or flight; with these options blocked, the autistic child plays dead. Either he withdraws into catatonic emptiness, allowing himself no experience; or he withdraws into a solitary, self-created parallel world. Over the months, Ruth had changed her mind about Mikey. She no longer saw his withdrawal as being of the first kind. She suspected that he inhabited a private world with its own strict laws, the key to which lay in his bizarre behaviour and vocabulary. She was certain that his spinning, for instance, was ambiguous. On the one hand it shut out the normal world and, on the other, it was an attempt to maintain contact with it. But it didn't prevent him from sinking, in his own terms, into a dense black empty hole.

Ruth's reverie was disturbed by the sound of a bell from the hospital. Some of the distant inmates suddenly became agitated; others froze in their tracks. One of them went flapping across the grass like a tent torn from its pegs in a high wind.

'Troubled spirits,' sighed a voice beside her. Ruth looked up sharply. A big burly man was standing next to the bench. It was difficult to tell his age — about the mid-fifties, she guessed. He stooped slightly as though he wished to appear smaller. He wore an old but carefully pressed dark suit, a dark blue tie under a stiff collar and heavy black shoes. Underneath his cap, she could see sandy hair faintly gleaming with fresh hair oil.

'Yes,' she said carefully. He was surveying the patients with a proprietorial air which made her think that he must be a doctor or male nurse. But she couldn't be sure. Once inside the asylum's iron gates, nothing was certain. However, although he must have been ten or fifteen years older than she, he cut a handsome figure. Ruth was conscious of having neglected her appearance lately, not bothering with her hair or face and eating too many sweet things out of anxiety. She felt uncomfortably *lumpish.*

'Your name isn't ... by any chance ... Jean Macintyre?' the man asked. He smiled wistfully and with such charm that Ruth was a little dazzled.

'No ... I'm afraid not.'

'Ah.' He paused, and then gestured tactfully towards the hospital. 'Are you ...?'

'No,' said Ruth quickly, realising she must look even more of a fright than she thought. 'No, I work in the Unit. Behind the trees there. With the children.'

'Children?' He smiled again and turned his face towards the sun thoughtfully. His strong, angular profile reminded Ruth of a gamekeeper or, more precisely, a gillie. 'They're lucky to find themselves in a beautiful place like this ... we all are,' he mused.

'Yes. I suppose so.' Ruth hadn't looked at it quite like that.

'Many of us will live in lovely houses in the New Age.'

'The new age ...?'

'The Millennium. When Christ comes in glory to claim His own.'

'Oh. I see.' How could she ever have thought him handsome? The man was as mad as a hatter.

'As a matter of *fact*,' he remarked, 'we haven't got much time. The last days are upon us.' Ruth fiddled with her coat cuff, concealing the fact that she had instinctively looked at her watch. 'I think that bell was calling us to lunch. I must be off. The food here is excellent.' He smiled. Ruth saw clearly how the smile couldn't possibly be charming, only daft. Or was it, she wondered, that he smiled a second later than expected, as if at some private second thought? 'Well, miss, I hope we meet again before, you know, the last day. *And* after, of course,' he added seriously.

'Yes. I hope so,' said Ruth, feeling foolish. She watched him walk off, in a shambling ungainly way, across the lawn to his lunch. Then, realising that she'd been gone longer than she intended, she hurried back to Mikey.

Mikey had deserted his bean-bag and was standing near the playroom door, gazing vacantly at the wall. His apparent disinterest indicated his desire to go and eat in the dining room; but despite the entreaties of the other counsellors he would not move until Ruth returned. She promptly led him by the hand to his familiar place at table and put a plate of ravioli in front of him. He glanced at it once, furtively, and rotated his left hand rapidly over the food to neutralise its destructive properties.

'The singularity ... drags matter in. It's all gravity,' he announced. 'Matter' was Mikey's word for all food. Ruth was grateful that the early-morning spell of talking had been resumed. 'It pulls matter in,' he went on. 'The hole is ... never ... filled. The hole gets more ... empty more ... dense more ... heavy. The gravity pulls matter in ... *fast*' – whereupon he began to shovel the ravioli into his mouth at great speed. 'Plode,' he gasped between mouthfuls. 'Plosion.'

Ruth forced herself to concentrate on his words. It was clear that 'gravity' partly expressed the dislocation between him and his body; he didn't swallow – food was pulled down mechanically by an inner magnetism. The hateful singularity was behind it all, of course. She tried to think of a way to overcome this misconception.

In the early days, eating had been so traumatic that Mikey could only ingest with the help of frenzied bouts of spinning, which in turn made eating extremely tricky. Ruth recalled with horror how she had on one occasion been blowing on a bowl of scalding vegetable soup to cool it while he rotated, only to have it snatched from her hands during a brief pause in Mikey's revolutions. With a cry of 'Red Alert!' he had downed the entire contents of the bowl in four enormous gulps. He registered no pain at drinking the burning soup, let alone any enjoyment or disgust: he was completely disassociated from the act of eating.

As Mikey continued to waste away, Ruth had consulted Dr Frieling.

'I'll *have* to feed him myself. By force, if necessary,' she wailed.

The doctor was shocked.

'You'll do no such thing. Mikey's whole life has been subject to force, real or imaginary – it makes no difference. The whole point of the Unit is to create an environment completely different from the one the child abandoned in the first place. We must *prove* to him that a world exists which he can enter as he is, unconditionally, warts and all. How *else* will he trust us enough to leave his own sad empty little world?' He could be very stern when his passions were aroused.

'But he won't listen to me when I tell him it's safe to eat,' Ruth countered hotly.

'Of course not. If it were safe to eat, he'd *eat*. Eating threatens his life. I've seen it time and again. Nothing must intrude into the mouth because the mouth is the first thing we use to explore the world. *Suck*. That's what we do, starting with the delicious all-nourishing *breast*. Don't cast your eyes to heaven, woman. Take my word for it, the whole hoo-ha begins at the breast. Mikey got nothing from it except, possibly, milk. Milk without love is poison. So, of course, he's not going to risk putting things in his mouth again even though he longs to. It would mean admitting that there's another world out there. Obviously it's more than his life is worth to do *that*. All we can do is surround him with a world of nourishment and, with luck, he will enter it of his own accord, in his own time. Nothing else will do, least of all the slightest coercion. Is that clear?'

'Yes, yes. But he'll *die* if he doesn't eat.'

'Yes. He will die. Is that so bad? Wouldn't he be better off?'

'You're a monster. I won't let him die.'

'Good. Then think of a solution.' Dr Frieling's eyes twinkled behind his glasses. Ruth burst into tearful laughter. He linked his arm with hers and walked her around the office. 'We'll think together,' he said. 'You can't feed him. You can't stop him spinning. Therefore you must spin for him while he eats.'

'But that won't work. He's the one who has to spin.'

Dr Frieling removed his arm from hers and pulled out the typist's chair from behind his desk, bidding her to sit down. Slowly he began to turn the revolving chair in a clockwise direction. Ruth gave a scream of delight and, leaping up, hugged him. The old man spread his hands modestly.

For several months Ruth spun Mikey around in the chair, slowly enough for him to be able to eat from a plate in his lap, fast enough to ward off hostile forces, until he had enough confidence to sit at table and content himself with a circular waggle of his fingers over each mouthful. All his food remained liquid, semi-liquid or cut into tiny pieces. He could not bite, chew or lick. His mouth stayed half-open, his lips dry and sore despite Ruth's efforts to moisten them with Vaseline. Like teeth and tongue, lips were part of a taboo area, too dangerous to acknowledge because of the enormity of whatever trauma had metaphorically smashed his mouth during the oral stage of his development. Rather than fail all over again to satisfy his heart's desire through his mouth, Mikey preferred not to use it. All feeling, physical as well as emotional, was withdrawn from the mouth by a monumental effort of repression. Fortunately, his teeth were in good repair: some children chose to endure a mouthful of rotting teeth and exposed nerves rather than suffer the insertion of dental instruments.

Ruth refilled Mikey's plate with ravioli. Her instinct alone told her that Mikey was ready to sustain the bold stroke she had decided to inflict on him. As soon as he had finished twiddling his fingers over the plate, she whisked it away and put it on the floor. Then, grasping Mikey firmly by the legs, she turned him upside down so that his head and arms were in reach of the plate. Mikey dangled from her hands, unmoved and unmoving.

'Can I help you at all, Miss Maier?' Dr Frieling had strolled up unnoticed and was watching her manoeuvre with interest. Ruth blushed. She was always a little unnerved by the doctor's assiduous formality with members of staff, matched only by his complete informality with the children. He had her father's way of looking at her in a sidelong quizzical way while his eyes smiled behind the solemn spectacles.

'As a matter of fact, you can,' she answered rather defiantly. 'You can hold him like this for me.'

'Certainly.' He grasped Mikey's legs and held him an inch off the floor like a prize fish.

'Now, Mikey,' said Ruth, kneeling next to his head, 'listen to me. If you want more food, you must eat it upside down.' She took a spoonful of ravioli and held it in front of his mouth. He opened his lips a bit wider to allow her to ease it in. 'Now swallow, Mikey. Swallow.' She looked up at the doctor. 'I'm trying to persuade Mikey that it's *he* who holds the food down and not his so-called gravity.'

'Quite.' The doctor was noncommittal. They both stared at Mikey's head. He swallowed his mouthful. Ruth fed him several more spoonfuls, repeating each time that the food did not fall out because *he* was holding it down, not 'gravity'. He did not react to this information but, restored to an upright position, merely remarked:

'Australian singularities have the same gravity.'

'I'm afraid he's right,' said Dr Frieling. 'Gravity isn't affected by turning the world upside down, as any child knows. You'll have to get up earlier in the morning to outwit Mikey!' He gave a loud bark of laughter and strolled off.

Although Dr Frieling reminded Ruth of her father, he was far more robust than Papa, who had been a thin austere man, forever old – more like a grandparent than a parent. His white hair, the dry skin stretched over fine bones, his dreamy expression, all made him seem ethereal. He taught piano and flute at a girls' school, a convent which reluctantly accepted other denominations to meet its costs. Ruth herself was educated there from the age of eight, with a welcome discount on fees. A music teacher's salary was not substantial but, if there had been any struggle to make ends meet, Leo Maier and his wife Anna carefully concealed it from Ruth, who was the beloved daughter of their advanced middle age. They were both dead now.

In 1946, the year Ruth was born, the Maiers lived in a small north London semi-detached, cramped by their sombre old-fashioned furniture, which seemed to be infused with the aroma of Mama's rich stews, savoury broths and fragrant baking. From her kitchen citadel, in which she subjected raw food to alchemical transmutations served in ceremonious meals, Anna exerted her occult influence throughout the house. She was a dark taciturn woman, squarely set on strong legs. Her plump face was shiny from the heat of the kitchen. Her answer to Ruth's asthma was to feed her, and Ruth responded by eating ravenously throughout her childhood, growing strong and rounded under her mother's approving eye. Papa's appetite was less healthy, and he had to enlist Ruth in a conspiracy against his wife. 'Quick, quick,' he'd exclaim in panic, heaping food on to her plate from his while Anna was out of the room.

Meeting the parents of her friends at primary school, Ruth was amazed at how young and lively they were, and struck by their unusual accents. When she realised that it was Leo and Anna's German accents that were odd, she felt a twinge of shame and looked at them for the first time through the eyes of a proper, perhaps slightly priggish, English schoolgirl. She noticed Papa's sloping, rather rounded shoulders, his two fingers stained with nicotine from incessant smoking, the shabbiness of his grey cardigan. She wondered why Mama neglected her profuse dark brown hair while insisting that Ruth brush her own identical hair until it shone. But she wouldn't have swapped them for the world: Leo and Anna were devoted to each other and to her. Their love was as plain as the nose on her face. For her sake they did not talk about pre-war Austria – they didn't even speak German. They severed themselves from their roots without sentimentality so that she would grow up an Englishwoman. The only hint of their sacrifice occurred when Papa would retire moodily to the attic and paint watercolours. They were always variations on the same scene: a river with a bridge, a field full of flowers and distant snow-capped mountains. He always pretended that he had made the scene up.

The only occasion she could recall hearing her parents speak German was one night soon after she had gone to the convent. She was woken by the sound of their raised voices. Sitting on the dark stairs, clasping the balustrade, she was frightened by the strange guttural language being spoken behind the half-open parlour door. From their occasional lapses into English she realised that they were arguing about her. 'Anna, Anna,' her father had cried despairingly, 'this iss not a medieval ghetto – this iss England!' 'You heard for yourself, Leo,' came her mother's stubborn reply, 'no girl could play like that. She has a dybbuk.' 'Of course she hass no such thing . . .' and they returned to German. Ruth no longer cared to listen in any case. She tiptoed to the kitchen and cut herself a comforting slab of fruit cake.

They were referring to an incident earlier in the evening. Ruth had been practising a Schubert tune on the parlour piano. As she became absorbed in the music she found herself playing faster. The simple melody began to develop extra notes and extraordinary trills, started to assume a sinister baroque quality that was certainly not in the score. Her small fingers flew over the keyboard so nimbly that she couldn't keep up with them. Her hands had taken on a life of their own. Ruth was alarmed. Her breath grew shorter and shorter. Something black and wavy flashed from left to right just above her line of vision. Her lungs wheezed with the sound of an old rattlesnake. She broke away, gasping, from the piano. Her parents were standing in the doorway, bemused by her sudden virtuosity. As they coaxed her out of her asthmatic attack she saw them exchanging glances.

After much difficulty with the spelling, she found 'dybbuk' in the dictionary. The oddness of the word, hard and primitive like a crocodile, had stuck in her mind. It meant the soul of a dead sinner who transmigrates into the body of a living person. A Yiddish word, apparently, meaning 'devil'. 'Yiddish' was itself a funny word; funny ha-ha, like 'peckish'. Ruth played the piano less often after her experience, and soon didn't play at all. Instead, she joined her young schoolfriends in their passion for Elvis Presley.

Leo encouraged her interest as he encouraged her in everything, paying deep attention to her smallest caprice. He was persuaded to buy one of Elvis's long-playing records, the envy of her friends, but which he could ill afford. He would listen to it with her, the same look of grave concentration on his face as when he listened to his pupils playing their flutes. Sometimes he would call out to his wife, busy among pans in the kitchen:

'Anna! Come and hear Elvis Pressley. He hass a fine voice, yes?'

'A good-looking boy,' Anna would concede. 'Plenty of flesh on his bones.'

Although Ruth knew that Leo was sincere in his praise, she felt uncomfortable — even resentful — that he should have taken her enthusiasm for Elvis at face value when it was his gorgeous swept-back hair that she admired more than his music. After a while, she begged her father to put some Brahms or Mozart on the old Dansette record-player instead, and vowed never again to be thoughtless or false in her professed interests. But long after the craze for Elvis had passed she was reminded of her insincerity — and of the expense of the LP — by Leo's private rendering of 'Heartbreak Hotel' in the bath. His accent and his gentle, melancholy tenor voice infused the lyrics with a poignancy that even the Pelvis couldn't match: 'Since my bebby left me, I am sitting here on my own ...'

It dawned on Ruth that her parents belonged to another, possibly extinct world. When her friends discussed boys, for instance, she would find herself blushing violently, not for herself, but for a father who was scandalised by girls who smoked in the street and for a mother who was shocked by skirts that came up to the knee. She protected their innocence fiercely and nearly bit off her tongue when she inadvertently referred to a television programme the other girls had been discussing. 'Anna!' Leo immediately called out to his wife. 'Anna, why do we not have a television set? Such marvellous things we're missing, such a lot to learn!' Ruth had terrible trouble preventing him from buying a television set the very next day.

THREE

'He was a good child,' Mrs Ballantine had said when Ruth interviewed her and her husband. She had cast a listless fastidious glance around Dr Frieling's cluttered office. Ruth felt fat and unkempt in her presence. Dorothy Ballantine was so slim and chic, perfectly composed in her pastel silk and cashmere. Her meticulous make-up enhanced every delicate feature of her pale, pretty, symmetrical face. Her dark glossy hair, cut in a neat page-boy style, gave her an almost boyish appearance, younger than her thirty-one years. Her grey eyes were lighter than Mikey's, or seemed so, but when she opened them wide she looked startlingly like him. 'Such an obedient child,' she murmured. Ruth waited for her to continue, but the words seemed to have exhausted her. Finding out about Mikey's past was like getting blood out of a stone.

'Not at first, darling,' prompted Rex Ballantine. 'Or later,' he added, flashing a shy smile at Ruth.

'No, not at first,' Dorothy agreed. She seemed to have trouble concentrating on the questions.

Rex smiled again, apologetically, and said: 'I'm afraid I was rather busy in the early days, Miss Maier. Setting up my own business, actually. But I did notice that, to begin with, Mikey cried a lot of the time.'

'All the time,' said Dorothy.

'Fortunately he stopped, quite suddenly, and rarely cried at all after that. I think it was the strict feeding schedule that did the trick, don't you, Dorothy?' Mrs Ballantine didn't find it necessary to reply. Rex leant forward in his chair, tilting his curly hair closer towards Ruth. She was grateful for his attentions. Perhaps he hadn't noticed how bulky and flustered she was compared to his elegant wife. His beautiful pale-blue eyes held hers, thoughtfully. He looks just like Paul Newman, she thought.

'How strict was the schedule?' she asked Dorothy.

'Every four hours. Without fail. Just as the paediatrician advised,' she added defensively. 'He was no trouble for some time after that. He was a good child.'

Behind the words, Ruth glimpsed a picture of a baby hungering for care and attention as well as for food; a baby crying and crying and never being *heard*. With the advent of the feeding schedule, Mikey was not even fed when *he* was hungry but only – cry as he might – when it suited the powers that be. Tears of hunger turned to tears of rage, the more virulent for all their impotence. He stopped crying for fear of drowning in tears. He had to adapt, to become a function of the schedule which administered his food. He gave his body over to the regular processing of intake, gave up the craving to be listened to, and loved. He became as obedient as a machine. He became good.

Ruth had to resist a powerful desire to sink her fingers into the smooth swath of Dorothy Ballantine's hair and shake her out of her lethargy. Instead, she studied the report on Mikey compiled by the perceptive nursery-school teacher, Jenny Wickham, who specialised in backward children. It was she who had instigated the tests for organic brain damage. They had shown that Mikey was not only physically sound but also unusually sensitive and intelligent. He was tentatively diagnosed, for want of a better word, as 'autistic'.

'Jenny Wickham says that Mikey had more or less given up talking by the time you sent him to nursery school,' said Ruth.

'Yes. After all we did for him,' sighed Dorothy.

'But she managed to coax him back into speaking.'

'Did she? Yes, I suppose she did.' Dorothy was bored.

'She says that Mikey often mentioned someone called ... "María". Who would that be?'

'A Spanish girl we had. A sort of au pair,' said Rex. 'Mikey had become a bit of a handful by then so we tried to get some help for Dorothy, didn't we, dear?'

A slight frown ruffled Dorothy's mask of indifference. Her fingers began to work on each other in her lap. She said: 'He wouldn't do anything for himself.... He had to be waited on hand and foot. He treated me – he treated us all – like *dirt*.' She looked Ruth in the eye for the first time. 'He never *once* called me "Mummy".' Her face blanked out again; her fingers were tightly interlocked.

'María wasn't altogether suitable,' Rex went on. 'She was a bit scatterbrained. Inclined to spoil the boy. When she left we decided to try him out with Jenny Wickham.'

'So he stopped talking when María left . . . ?'

'Yes. It was the last straw.'

'Mikey seemed to have thought that María died or was killed, according to this report.'

'That was one of his fantasies. He had several. For example, he claimed for a long time to be from another planet.'

'So Miss Wickham says. She also says that he had an astonishing grasp of scientific things, technology and so on. Apparently he could recite list upon list of facts about the planets and stars—'

'I think I can take some credit for that,' smiled Rex. 'I've always been keen on science myself, especially astronomy. Mikey was fascinated by the telescope I bought him. Even before he could read, his nose was always in some picture-book about the universe. I seem to remember a drawing he made of a nuclear reactor – copied from a diagram, of course; he didn't bother with pictures of houses and people and flowers – kid's stuff like that.' Rex waved his hands enthusiastically. 'And, of course, he had his own television and video, absolutely loved them. I thought for ages that I had a genius on my hands instead of—' He laughed uneasily.

'Did you talk to him, tell him stories, for instance?' asked Ruth.

'Stories?' Rex was taken aback. 'I imagine Dorothy did. Dorothy?'

'María did,' said Dorothy.

'He preferred his videotapes,' Rex asserted. 'Nothing frivolous, you understand – educational tapes about how things work. Watched them for hours, loved them.'

'Did he?' Dorothy remarked vaguely. 'He tried to break your precious recordings.'

'Yes, he *tried* to, the little devil,' laughed Rex. He leant forward and spoke to Ruth with a confidential air. He was eleven years older than his wife, more Ruth's age in fact; they were like two adults conferring privately in front of a child, Ruth felt. She was flattered in spite of herself. Rex Ballantine was undeniably good-looking. The blue eyes in the youthful, slightly tanned face were candid and appealing.

'I do a lot of my own video-taping, you see, Ruth. It's a hobby as well as work. I'm on the creative side of things.' He smiled self-deprecatingly. 'I keep my cameras, tapes and so on in my study. Obviously I don't like people going in there because there's so much delicate – and expensive – equipment. Even Dorothy wouldn't dream of invading my sanctum, would you, Dorothy?'

'No.'

'So you can imagine my absolute horror when I caught Mikey in there, on the point of destroying my tapes. He was like a wild thing, screaming and flailing about. He'd already put a steel ruler through the television screen! Amazing, considering he'd been docile and silent since María left. We had to give him a jolly good spanking.'

'You beat him with the steel ruler,' Dorothy reminded him.

'Not seriously,' protested Rex. 'He didn't even cry.'

'What brought about this sudden outburst?' Ruth was interested.

'I can't imagine.'

'And how did he react to the ... "spanking"?'

'Well, Ruth, funnily enough, he snapped out of it for a while. Showed a definite willingness to co-operate ... even spoke to us – to Dorothy, at least. Naturally I tried thrashing him a few more times, especially when he refused to go to the toilet—'

'He got terribly constipated,' Dorothy interrupted plaintively. 'I had to give him enemas. He fought me. It was horrible.' Ruth felt almost sorry for her.

'Anyway, I had to use the slipper to get him to go to the toilet regularly,' Rex went on. 'I didn't enjoy it, but it worked for a time.'

'Yes,' said Ruth. 'He went every day at precisely ten in the morning.' Rex raised his eyebrows. 'It's in Miss Wickham's report. He became frightfully agitated if he was prevented from going at exactly ten o'clock. One of the first things we do here at the Unit is to encourage the children to give up enforced toilet training.'

'You're telling me that's progress?' Rex was incredulous. 'Well, OK. But a child of that age, messing himself....'

Ruth mentally sketched Mikey's possible reactions to what she had gathered. She imagined the forlorn little boy's anxiety to please his father by studying videos; the intolerable loss of María, his last link with the real world; his rage at tapes and television for failing to provide him with human emotion; his raised hopes when his parents found him worthy of their attention by spanking him angrily; the dashing of those hopes when the spanking was repeated merely automatically; his fear of punishment and his desperation to please embodied in his fanatically regular visits to the lavatory. He knew by now that to show any anger, to show anything at all in word or deed, might well endanger his life. Only when Miss Wickham encouraged him to open what was left of his heart did he speak again. He was, perhaps, on the verge of a return to existence when he was packed off to The Yews.

38

'Quite honestly, Ruth,' Rex was saying, 'he'd shown very little improvement with Miss Wickham. I was glad to send him to The Yews, regardless of the cost. I thought they might put a bit of backbone into him. But it wasn't to be....'

Ruth had made her own enquiries into The Yews. It was an expensive private boarding school which claimed to cater for 'defective children'. Run on rigid quasi-military lines, it boasted a high success rate with what it was pleased to call 'an intensive behaviour-modification programme'. Ruth chose not to calculate the suffering that Mikey had endured there. Rex noticed her shudder.

'We thought it the best place for him,' he said miserably. 'We were wrong. I blame myself. That's why I brought him here.' Dorothy looked at Rex curiously, but said nothing. 'Do you think you can help, Ruth?' His pale eyes were humble.

'You must promise to let him stay here until *we* decide he's ready to leave. Is that understood? Secondly, we must have a completely free hand in his treatment, without *any* interference.' Ruth was adamant.

'Oh, we promise,' said Rex eagerly. 'Thank you. *Thank* you.'

Dorothy gathered up her handbag.

The snag is, it's hard for me to remember events before that dazzling day in nineteen forty-five when I became a New Man. It's like Bee Cee and Ay Dee. Time goes backwards, its only purpose being to lead up to that day, and I only begin to go forward after it. But it's funny, now that you've got me going over the prehistoric period, so to speak, certain things do spring to mind. For example, a meal I ate in nineteen thirty-nine rose up in front of my eyes just now, as I was waiting to see you. It was the first time I had cabbage, which I've been fond of ever since. In fact I prophesy that in the Millennium everyone will eat vegetables and there'll be an end to the slaughter of animals except possibly fishes (plus crustacea, etcetera) to which Christ Himself was partial. With the cabbage there was spuds, gravy and a meat chop. I can taste it now. For afters there was – wait for it – *chocolate sponge pudding*. I was caught up into the third heaven. Not literally, of course. Not yet.

I don't want to give the impression that we didn't do well for ourselves at home. Father had his system worked out down to a 'T', and his self-restraint was almost superhuman. I've known him to eat half an egg and put the other half away for next morning. He understood long before I did the strength that comes from fleshly mortification – a strength which stood him in good stead when he later embarked on his war of attrition with the Worm. But I won't go into that now.

No, we did all right. Mondays, Father bought a pound of stewing steak. He had a number of ingenious ways to make it last till Sunday: for example, padding it out with breadcrumbs. He'd make a rice pudding to last us till Thursday — no milk in it, of course, because of its mucus-forming properties — and a sago or tapioca to take us through to Sunday. The meat stew went sour in hot weather, but Father always maintained that it regained its freshness in a day or two. Can't say he was wrong, though I never saw it myself. He never drank anything except Adam's ale, bar the miniature bottle of whisky given him in nineteen thirty which he opened on Vee Jay Day. 'A baRd lot,' was his toast — he had a special distaste for the yellow races and the Japanese in particular.

Sorry. The point about the cabbage — by the way, the entire meal was *hot* — was that I ate it when I went up to sit the examination for the Invoice Office. I took the seven thirty-two to Waterloo, my first trip to the Big City. I was in such a *state* over the prospect of actually seeing all those stations I'd only read and dreamt about in timetables — Esher, Surbiton, Raynes Park — ah, those names — that I shut my eyes tightly all the way to the great Terminus itself. Each time the train stopped, I whispered to myself the name of the station seconds *before* the guard called it out. And, you know, I was right every time. I say this not out of vanity but as fact. There'll be plenty of things you'll hear later to my disadvantage, so I may as well blow my own trombone while I can.

That reminds me, you're eager for news of *relationships*. I'm right, aren't I, Doctor? As far as I can recall, I acquired my first real friend around this time. His name was Bobby Birkinshaw and he was in the choir, a height I was never asked to scale myself, perhaps for the best since I was scared of turning the wrong way when the procession reached the chancel, to the confusion of my face. Not that the choir was without its portion of folly and vice. But I can put my hand on my heart and say that, from that day to this, I have never been a sly smoker behind the bicycle-sheds nor, for that matter, a cyclist.

Bobby wasn't the reason I went to church; anyone will tell you I've always gone twice on Sundays. But if I look into my heart I have to say that his bell-like voice and face of a cherub made matins a perfect service. I came face to face with him at Sunday School where I assisted the Reverend Pugh as best I could, being too old to stay as one of the pupils. I must have been a burden to that good man since the veils hadn't yet been torn from my eyes; but I tried to be of practical benefit to the boys by offering to take them on an outing. The miracle was that Mister Pugh gave his permission.

I didn't sleep a wink on the Saturday night, what with the excitement and planning and praying for good weather. What weather! A sun in a hazy cloudless sky, a slight weight in the air that pressed the smell out of the grass, hedgerows, etcetera. Tip-top conditions. The general plan was to show my party of eight boys the delights of country rambling. But I'd also devised a secret treat – our destination was Brookwood, the nearest station with the largest concentration of main-line expresses. Unfortunately Brookwood is about ten miles there and back, and the lads weren't used to walking.

Oh, we set off in fine enough fettle, the boys *vying* and *jostling* one another to walk beside me. I was careful not to single out Bobby, but since he was the smallest by a long way I was justified in paying him a bit of extra attention. There was also a lot of good-natured chaffing about my personal appearance, for I didn't know how to look smart in those days. After only three miles the boys began to make heavy weather of it, and mutinied, and turned back. I was left to press on with Bobby. We made it all right with the help of a few hymns but, to be honest, the trains weren't a great success. I tried to work up his enthusiasm but he was inclined to be pale and quiet and, finally, to cry. I was a bit frightened by this and started for home immediately. He was so tired I had to carry him most of the time. It was lovely, carrying him. There was no one about, no sounds except the birds and insects and the swoosh of my feet on the grassy path. The sun was going down and the sky was striped like a paint-box with the whole range of colours and Bobby's little arms were around my neck. I felt very grown-up – you know, strong and sort of responsible. The way Father probably felt about me sometimes, deep down, without showing it.

It was pretty dark when we got back. I was surprised to find Mister Pugh waiting at the Birkinshaws'. I think there was something funny going on between the Birkinshaws because Missis burst into tears when she saw us and Mister was a pasty colour in the face. I couldn't make out what he was saying because his teeth were clenched and he didn't look at me when he spoke. I said I was sorry we were so late, etcetera, but Missis only snatched Bobby away into another room, shouting out that I had a queer look in my eye – you couldn't help smiling – and calling on the Reverend Pugh to confirm this. But he only shook his head and muttered 'Wicked, wicked,' which was going a bit far to my mind. Anyway, they badgered poor little Bobby with a lot of questions I couldn't quite catch, and then I was dismissed without so much as a 'thank-you' – without even being allowed to say goodbye to Bobby, poor fellow, lumbered with parents like that who never were much in the way of churchgoers and didn't rejoice in the Lord. But it hurt me badly to hear Mister Pugh bleating on about how I wasn't to be trusted and that I needn't come to Sunday School again and so on. I mean, it wasn't a bad day, all in all, and, well . . . I won't go on about it. As it happens, I didn't miss Sunday School as much as I might have done because Providence intervened, as is so often the way. Can you guess?

I *passed* the Invoice Office exam and was admitted as a clerk, grade five. Yes, I thought I'd hold that back to add a bit of suspense. I nearly went straight round to the Birkinshaws to tell them just so as they'd know I wasn't quite such a big useless lump of a bloke as they claimed. Actually I was told later that I never would've been accepted if there hadn't been a shortage of applicants; but I dare say I've justified their faith in me since, because I'm still in the job – pardon, *was* in the job – forty years later. I *was* offered promotion. Twice, no less. But I'm easily flustered, you know, and reckoned I'd never master the invoicing for a wider area. So I thought it best to turn it down. Better by far the devil you know.

At the time I was thrilled to bits: I not only had a proper job, I also became – it was a fantastic feeling – a *season ticket holder*. Suddenly you feel the sky's the limit. The whole world is spread out clearly before you in a straight line. Just like . . . like the Nullarbor Plain railway in Australia, the longest dead-straight stretch of track in the world. Think of that! Within a few weeks I'd stopped hanging around the end of Drayton Crescent, waiting for a glimpse of Bobby. After all, I was a man amongst men and had the companionship of my fellow clerks to look forward to. I even asserted my independence at home – I surprised myself as much as Father – by moving out of his room and into the little sloping space under the stairs. I couldn't use the back bedroom, of course, because Father's things were in there – his collection of old *Titbits, News Chronicles*, etcetera; he wisely never threw anything away. But my mattress fitted so snugly under the stairs that I was better off there, especially with my train postcards pinned to the ceiling, very low, so that I could count them before I went to sleep.

Alone in her room, Ruth guiltily opened a packet of chocolate biscuits. She was not hungry in the strict sense but she needed something to appease the empty, slightly sick feeling in the pit of her stomach. She hadn't intended to break into these emergency rations – she had meant to have an early night – but the events of the day had left her simultaneously exhausted and restless.

She sat down at her small writing table by the window. It was ten o'clock, the children were all in bed, Adrian was on the night shift, there was nothing to worry about (she told herself) until six the next morning. She slowly rotated her head to ease the stiffness in her neck and shoulders. Then, pulling a large exercise-book out of the drawer, she took a biscuit in one hand and a pen in the other.

Her journal used to be a private diary; but ever since her life had become so closely bound to Mikey's, the exercise-book had been increasingly filled with the minutiae of his behaviour — in effect, notes towards the eventual writing-up of his case-history. She had neglected the journal recently, nor did she feel like writing now. But she had to record the morning's startling development, as well as justify the nibbling of the biscuits, four of which — good God, *four* — she had already eaten without realising it. Shaking her head as if to shift the dull ache behind her eyes, she began to write:

22 February

For Mikey (as for all children?) the experience of shitting is charged with intense anxious emotion, a mingling of desire and fear. In the past he completely repressed this emotion (his chronic constipation) and subsequently dissociated himself from the instrument — his body — which inspired the emotion (his purely mechanical elimination).

Now, his complex rituals (spinning, twiddling, stripping naked, etc.) with which he surrounds defecation show that he has allowed himself to become conscious of its danger, namely that *an essential part of him is being lost*. Shitting is not something *he does*, but a horrendous thing that *happens to him*, like being disembowelled.

Today, for the first time, Mikey handled his own faeces. It's my guess (my hope) that he's courageously trying to get a tangible grip on the ambiguity of shit: on the one hand, he has an inkling that it belongs to him and is part of him (his mistake was to identify the part with the whole); on the other, he's beginning to suspect that his shit is *not him*, that it's a separate thing that can be got rid of without irrevocable loss (but he still can't bear to see it flushed away). The 'smearing' behaviour confirms this: he covers the surface of his body with his own waste matter in order to reincorporate the part of him which has been expelled. If he continues this process, he'll eventually discover that it's not necessary, i.e. that his bodily existence goes on, despite the ejection of stools.

NB. Fear of shitting is nothing but the primordial fear of non-self, the Other. In 'normal' children whose parents affirm their separate identity, reassure them that they're safe, tell them they're good ('giving a present to Mummy', etc.) the fear is balanced by the satisfaction of creativity — shitting becomes a 'giving birth'. The normal child asserts himself and triumphs over his loss; he realises that he's not identical with his body, that he can stand outside it and separate the 'I' from the 'me'. Mikey, on the other hand ... Mikey is in a sense a step further back. There isn't even a 'me', let alone an 'I'. He doesn't identify with his body — on the contrary, he denies its existence. Somehow he has to re-enter it, to become incarnate. Until he does, he can't possibly recognise other things, other people outside himself. He has no self. Yet, strangely, he seems to know this: what better description of him can I give than his own — a black empty hole. Mikey, Mikey.

Ruth snapped the book shut, annoyed with herself for scribbling the boy's name like a lovesick schoolgirl. She kicked her shoes off and walked wearily to the bed. Had she imagined it or, when she was bathing him that morning, had he not been more relaxed? Hadn't his arms, for instance, been a fraction less like components, more like parts of his body? She shook off such wild imaginings and, settling herself against two pillows, switched on the radio at her bedside. One of Papa's favourite Brahms symphonies was playing. She noticed with dismay that the biscuits had accompanied her to the bed. Only five left. She'd never lose weight at this rate. She tossed them out of reach into an armchair on the other side of the room. Then, to occupy her hands — to fill in the time usefully — she took her sewing things out of the bedside cupboard.

She was working on a stuffed animal, a sort of cat made of pale yellow towelling. It was for Mikey, of course. She had worked on it spasmodically over the last six weeks against the time, she told herself, when Mikey would be ready to receive a toy. As time wore on and he grew no closer to admitting anything into his barren little world, Ruth went on making it nevertheless, doggedly sewing her love into the four floppy legs and the loose round head with its felt ears and whiskers.

It suddenly seemed urgent that she should finish the cat. Almost as if Mikey would never get well unless she did. There wasn't much more to do. Needlework had never been her strong point but, more by luck than by design, the cat's face had turned out rather well. It was entirely embroidered on to the towelling, even the eyes. Ruth didn't like artificial eyes; they gave animals a glassy stare. Her cat's eyes were merry but slightly mischievous. She had only the mouth to finish. In her haste, it turned out slightly lopsided, like a crooked smile. The more she looked at it, the less she wanted to change it.

The second movement of the symphony was drawing to a close. Ruth propped the yellow cat on the pillow beside her and closed her eyes. The music carried her over the brilliant white undulations of the snowfields. The mountains stretched away into the distance, their white peaks crisp as icing sugar, until they merged with the blue infinitude of sky. The cold clear air filled her lungs sweetly, bringing the warm blood to her face. The sun was hot on her back. She was aware of a voice talking to her from away to the right. She tried to shut it out. She knew that it came from the sheer forbidding mountain bathed in shadow. She did not want to turn and look at it. She wanted to stay with the music in the great white open space. But the voice persisted. Very clearly, she heard it say: 'The singularity is the ultimate end of the star, a mathematical point surrounded by an invisible boundary which together comprise the black hole. ...'

Ruth's body gave a jerk. She opened her eyes and blinked. She must have dozed off for a moment. The voice was still talking to her from the radio. It seemed to be one of those short talks they broadcast during the interval of a symphony. A man was explaining something in a cosy way. It was hard to make sense of it, but for some reason Ruth's face was flushed and her heart was pounding.

'... if a manned spacecraft, let's say, were to fall into a black hole, time would appear to flow normally for its occupants. But if a *second* spacecraft were to watch the first one from a safe distance, that is, well away from the black hole, it would see the first spacecraft slow down as it approached the event horizon until it eventually appeared to halt, hovering perpetually on the edge of the black hole. We might say therefore, rather fancifully, that *inside* a black hole time flows backwards....' A child of nine knows that, thought Ruth involuntarily. Where had she heard that before? '... and so escape from an event horizon is well-nigh impossible – unless, of course, one travels at the speed of light!' Ruth pressed her ear against the radio, ramming every word into her memory. As soon as the brief talk finished, she sprang over to her desk and wrote furiously in her journal.

Ruth quietly pushed open the swing doors of the dormitory. Several dim night-lights in red and gold warded off the terrors of the darkness. Adrian was sitting on one of the beds silently comforting a button-nosed little girl who suffered from dinosaur nightmares. He was rocking her backwards and forwards with his eyes closed while she dug her fingers deep into his beard and hair. Hearing Ruth come in, he acknowledged her with a friendly wave of the hand. Ruth tiptoed past them to Mikey's bed.

He was awake. Sitting up very straight, he was rotating his right hand and, with his left, tapping a row of plastic bottles strapped to the bedhead. These were his 'batterers', a source of unknown power which ran his body while he slept and prevented him from 'ploding'. They had to be recharged every couple of hours lest he die prematurely in his sleep. He did not stop tapping as Ruth approached, but he did unexpectedly acknowledge her presence by turning his head away. He was in a receptive mood.

She sat on his bed and waited with suppressed excitement until his 'batterers' were fully functional. Then, taking his left hand in hers, she told him about the radio talk and apologised for not understanding him before. 'I know who you are, Mikey ... where you are. You're not alone. I'm going to help you escape. I promise.' From behind her back she produced the yellow towelling cat. Whether or not it was the right time to offer it to Mikey, she had no idea. She just felt she had to offer him something, a token to mark the momentous occasion, a peace offering.

'I've brought someone to see you, Mikey. A particular friend of mine. He asked especially to see you. He wants to stay with you. He won't mind if you're too busy to keep him at the moment, but I've told him a bit about you and he likes the idea very much. He thinks he might watch out for you, if you look after him.' She laid the cat on Mikey's legs. The boy did not move, but a rapid furtive glance indicated his intense interest. His right hand began to waggle, as if with a life of its own, in the vicinity of the cat, who smiled cheerily up at him. The waggling grew faster and faster, to and fro, round and round, each time closer to the toy. Suddenly it stopped. The screening process had been completed. Ruth held her breath. Mikey picked up the cat and held it outstretched in front of him. His body rippled with unbearable agitation; his face remained impassive, his eyes unseeing. Ruth spoke with a matter-of-factness she did not feel: 'Good. That's settled. You'll look after each other. You'll have to give him a name, Mikey. Cats need a name like everybody else. What will you call him?'

The boy made no response. He looked pale and drawn. He was limp as Ruth tucked him into his bed and arranged the cat on the pillow next to his head. She kissed him goodnight and left.

Mikey turned his head slowly towards the cat. He was breathing in short hectic gasps. His hand crept up from under the covers. He touched the cat's face delicately with his fingertips. The cat grinned in its lopsided way. 'Yiaou,' whispered Mikey. *'Yiaou.'*

46

FOUR

IT'S NOT the sort of thing I'd normally mention, Doctor, but I don't want to let you down. So I'll get it over with. Here goes. My first serious attempt to get married was in nineteen forty-four at the height of the war.

Actually the war didn't really start for me until the seventh of September, nineteen forty.... The day Hermann Goering closed down Waterloo and the rail-head was shifted to Clapham Junction – a two-and-a-half-mile walk every morning from the Invoice Office. Yes, *from*. I was on night shifts, you see, from eight in the evening to five the next morning. I *was* offered a day shift later – in sixty-three or -four – but you can't change after all that time.

We had to book goods to country, provincial and suburban stations, and bring the invoices to total. The day shifts were a bit slack. When I clocked on, I would often find troublesome full truckloads still unbooked because they needed more details on the dockets, such as the wagon number, whereas small consignments got by under the category 'in general wagon'. I was such a muddle-head with all those numbers that I rarely took a break with the other clerks at half-past midnight, but stuck at my desk with a Marmite sandwich or maybe potted meat. The perpetual alerts also conspired to put me behind: either 'purple' ones when the lights went out and we had to manage with hand-operated lanterns on our desks; or 'red' ones, when the sirens sent us beetling across to the sandbags in the warehouse. It was a fearsome struggle to clear my desk by the time my day-shift replacement turned up. Luckily he was a decent bloke – Trevor Williams, his name was – and he let me stay on until I'd more or less finished.

I was scared stiff of the Germans. I couldn't help a despicable feeling of relief when they turned me down for the Army early on – too young, I suppose – but I was also sorry because I liked the idea of all us lads in uniform together, with plenty of jokes and comforting each other in times of danger. Not that we didn't have some fun down the office. There was one jocular occasion when the boys volunteered me for ambulance class, a wonderful gesture because, you know, you have to do your bit. But the funny thing was you needed *knots*, which of course I've never grasped, with my fists full of thumbs, so I was drummed out sharpish for fluffing a wreath knot, I think they said it was – an ironical business since I was usually given the office parcels to tie up! Dear me, how they laughed!

Sorry. Yes, I'm putting it off. It's funny, I was really quite ... *excited* at the prospect of telling someone about this thing of the marriage. I had hopes of working up quite a nice little story. But when it comes to it you can't think why you thought it anything special. I expect you've heard hundreds of similar cases. So I'll skip the fancy bits and just give you the facts.

Her name was Alice Watts. I met her outside Allen and Grout's button factory in the Wandsworth Road, where she used to linger with the other girls before work. The first time I caught her eye I knew she was different from those other right little madams with their crimson mouths and intoxicating smells which warned me that they belonged to the Babylonian tribe. Such women are sent to be a temptation to the flesh, always whispering and laughing and boldly casting their eyes about. I was walking past, on my way to catch the six forty-two from Clapham— But never mind about that.

I went up to her, just like that, and asked her for a 'date'. You didn't really notice her nose – flattish, it was – nor her skin, which was a bit pocked from some childish disease, because of her eyes. Harden them as she might, they betrayed her inward beauty. She said, 'Don't be daft,' in that serious way she had. But knowing I couldn't hope to succeed immediately I persisted every day for a week until, out of the blue, she said: 'All right. I don't mind.' So there it was. We arranged to meet the following Thursday, which was my night-off-in-ten. Funny how it all comes back. Look – you can actually see my heart beating! Who'd have thought it?

I bought a necktie. Stupid really, because I couldn't do it up in those days – I've learnt since as you can see – and Father was no help, lying in bed and laying about him with his wooden leg if you came near. Besides, I was hag-ridden by guilt at having held back from him part of my wages – I couldn't help it, I was in such a turmoil of anxiety over money because, as it was, I couldn't afford to take Alice to a show or anything. I needn't have worried. Alice was never happier than with the cheapest form of entertainment, namely gazing in the Oxford Street windows. And, as for our evening meal, she even pronounced the Lyons cornershops 'too posh' and was happy as a birdsong with the humbler sort of café off the main thoroughfare.

It was a perfect evening out. Alice was even more seemly than I guessed, for she modestly addressed all her remarks to her friend, Betty. I forgave Betty's smoking because the Reverend Pugh himself puffed on a pipe. The extra expense of her meal and cigarettes was amply repaid by their conversation. I can't begin to tell you of the new worlds that opened up to me just through listening! I was careful to memorise the names of all the principal characters at the button factory, plus those of people in the films they'd seen (it was often hard to tell them apart), so that I could surprise them with accurate and intelligent responses when called upon to do so. However, the first question was a bombshell. 'Where's the nearest?' Alice asked. I was so inexperienced I hadn't a clue what she meant. It was terrible to be the cause of the suffering look she cast at Betty. But from then on I was vigilant about earmarking all the available ladies' conveniences, just in case.

On the fourth of these memorable occasions, there was something of a dilemma. Both ladies wished to visit a public house on the edge of Soho. Betty was surprised, I think, to find that it was out of the question for me. She seemed a bit reluctant to go in without me. But Alice, bless her, knew me for better than a killjoy. 'Oh, Harold's daft,' she said. 'He'll wait for us, you see if he don't.' Well. I've always had a special feeling for people who call me 'Harold'. Plus, I was touched to the quick by her confidence in me. The only agony I went through while I waited was because funds had become a bit short and I'd no idea whether the five bob I'd given them was a suitable sum. And, sure enough, it was far from suitable because they had to send a man out for more, to the confusion of my face. He had a *bow* tie, I remember, and a moustache, and was most correct. Also, he was very nice about my mistake and asked if he could fetch me a drink or anything.

I watched the people coming out of the pub. There was no sign of Alice. After a while, the lights went out. The street was dark and deserted. I felt something badly wrong – not just with Alice, you understand – but in myself. I wouldn't normally mention vague things like feelings, but it strikes me that this feeling, which I've had since, might connect up with my present plight. Certainly, it was the first time I had a strong conviction that some adversary was sharpening his eyes upon me.

I walked over to the street-lamp on the corner, checking every nook and cranny. I couldn't see anyone. I hurried back to my post in case I missed the ladies. It was cold, and a smatter of drizzle had set in, making the cobbles under the lamp shine. I felt so poorly that I fell to thinking of Jean Macintyre, and couldn't resist pulling out the gobstopper, just to look at it. But before I knew it I'd sucked another layer off, a green one leading to blue. I was feeling a bit better, a bit less oppressed in the head, and I'd put the gobstopper back in my pocket wrapped in paper, when the thing happened which I cannot describe in words nor ever wish to. A spirit passed before my face, the hair of my flesh stood up, is how Job puts it, chapter four, verse fourteen, and I've nothing to add. It was all over quick as electricity and I was beating on the pub doors only to be told that it was shut and that the ladies in question had left long ago by another door with a man in a bow tie.

I won't go into detail. Quite frankly, I'm rather tired, rather ... shaken up remembering all ... all that. I spent the night down the Bow Street police station, trying in vain to describe the gangster who had abducted Alice and Betty; and when it was all hopeless I took the milk-train back to Wyebridge, sick and vexed in body and spirit, and then the first train back to London again. And there was Alice at the factory as usual, the Lord be praised, and not at all pleased to see me. 'Just because I let you take me out once or twice,' she says, 'it don't mean we can't go our own ways.' Honest to God, I tried through the following dark days to harden my heart against her, but there were lapses and a lot of foolish letters begging forgiveness that she didn't answer until I was about ready to go what Father would've called stark staring maRd.

But, in truth, even in the black sleepless hours when all seems lost, Providence is working its sweet way for us without our knowledge. For I was saved from myself by a greater force sweeping me into the storm of world-historical events where my petty troubles were drowned. I was *called up*.

The next morning, Ruth was astonished to find Mikey standing in front of the tall French windows which gave directly on to the playground with its slides, swings, see-saw and sand-pit. Even more surprising — she drew in a sharp breath — was the spectacle of the stuffed cat clamped firmly in his right hand. While Mikey stared indifferently at the ground, the cat pressed its face eagerly against the glass. Ruth was reminded of a ventriloquist and dummy; but it was difficult to say which was which. All suggestions that Mikey might like to eat breakfast or go to the lavatory were greeted negatively. The yellow cat continued to smile out of the window, occasionally waggling its legs. Ruth unbolted the windows and opened them.

Mikey immediately moved outside like a sleepwalker, with the cat held out in front of him. The frosty air tightened the skin on Ruth's face as she followed him out. She shivered. It was too late to run back for her coat; Mikey was in charge. The cold made no visible impression on him. He walked dreamily but unerringly to the sand-pit and held the cat over the sand. Then he began to rotate the animal so that its legs twirled comically through the air.

'Yiaou.'

For a moment Ruth was convinced that the toy animal had uttered the strange feline noise, half word, half mewing sound. 'Yiaou,' Mikey repeated. He began to walk hesitantly, anticlockwise, around the square pit full of damp sand. Then he stopped, waggled the cat with increased force, turned and with a great effort walked the other way. He circled the pit for nearly half an hour. Carol, seeing her friend's predicament, brought her out an extra pullover and a raincoat to sit on. She rolled her eyes at Ruth, who giggled, and disappeared again to feed her eccentric brood.

At last Mikey stopped walking. He stood on the edge of the pit, teetering slightly like a man about to jump from a ten-storey building. His limbs trembled, causing the cat — Yiaou — to wobble nervously over the sand. Abruptly he stepped into the pit and sat down with a bump. He sat as if paralysed for a long time. His posture was rigid, his muscles contracted by anxiety or fear. Yiaou was the first to move, followed by Mikey, who gave the sand a pat, another pat, and then began to stroke it gingerly as though it was a dangerous animal. Ruth settled down on the damp grass beside the sand-pit and prepared herself for a long session.

After hearing the radio talk the night before, Ruth had made the following addition to the entry in her journal:

11.25 p.m.

I've got it, got it, *got it*. I can still hardly believe it. It's a wild feeling, spine-chilling, to hear a learned man on the radio using Mikey's special words. They're all taken from the technical language that describes *black holes*. I should have spotted this, I know enough about them, I *should* have known — I haven't been taking Mikey *seriously enough* .... OK. First: black holes are formed from collapsed stars. Such a star probably has a *mass* greater than our own sun, but its mass collapses or *implodes* into a relatively tiny area (e.g., if the Earth imploded to the same extent it could be contained in a super-dense sphere only one centimetre in radius). The *gravitational field* of the star becomes so strong that the velocity needed to escape from the field exceeds the speed of light. Thus not even *light itself* can escape. As soon as the collapsing mass shrinks beyond a certain size — the critical radius — it seems to disappear into a black hole. The size of the black hole is thus defined by its critical radius, known as the *event horizon*, inside which *nothing can be seen* of what goes on. The only detectable events are those which occur just outside, e.g., *matter* that is sucked into the black hole will gain huge amounts of energy and give off a wide range of radiation. But once inside the event horizon, matter is crushed out of existence (beyond existence?) in the hypothetical heart of the black hole known, for the sake of convenience, as the *singularity*. This is the context of Mikey's code.

The more I think about his neologisms — which I took for non-sense words — the more I admire their expressiveness. He has distorted certain terms to express his own ambiguous impulses. *Messive* is a combination of massive and mess; *plode* implies explode as well as implode; a *vent* lets things in, such as fresh air, and also indicates a wish to vent his feelings. *Horrorizon* speaks for itself (Oh, Mikey, I'm sorry). Even *singularity* may be contradictory.... Obviously it's that aspect of himself which draws him down towards annihilation. But can't it also embody the idea of the singular *person*, the individual he would like to become?

The black hole terminology serves his simultaneous desire for, and dread of, communication; it's a puzzle which he hides behind, but which clearly demonstrates his intelligence. In effect, he's been asking me: 'Do you think I'm worth listening to?' Until now I've been answering 'No'. I didn't take him on his own terms. If he gives me the chance, I won't underestimate him again.

Later on, her brain in too great a turmoil for sleep, Ruth had added some afterthoughts:

It was Mikey who said 'Time stands still at the vent horrorizon. It goes backwards inside the hole. A child of nine knows that.' He is the child of nine; he was pointing to his own condition. Time truly is standing still for him. He has no present or future; his past is his present. He's stuck at some catastrophic event that occurred years ago, like a scratched record doomed to repeat the same excruciating phrase over and over again. He has exiled himself to a hole in space, light years away from Earth, where he is trapped by gravity between horror of life and terror of death. At every second he has to resist the singularity – when its threat grows too great, he rotates outwards only to rebound like a pinball from the invincible event horizon, back towards the black centre. (NB. Rotation: the man on the radio said that black holes probably rotate, dragging space-time around with them – whatever that means – in such a way that two event horizons are created, one inside another. At the same time, the singularity changes from a mathematical point to a doughnut-shaped ring. Incomprehensible to me. But in both cases, the word 'escape' was mentioned. Paradoxically, it may be possible to escape from the outer event horizon in a rotating black hole; or else to jump through the ring singularity into a preposterous region called negative space . . . . Is there, therefore, a way out??) Yet Mikey is also the singularity itself which has to 'spin' its own event horizon to prevent itself from being detected or from communicating. Perhaps a singularity's heart's desire is to give out light like a hundred suns but is destined instead to collapse on itself for ever, to vanishing point and beyond . . . .

When I think of the sheer concentrated energy that Mikey has to generate in order to sustain his black hole, I'm . . . lost for words. Why did he adopt its laws as his own? Simply, I suppose, to protect himself from the hostility and rejection of our cosy Newtonian universe. But what *what* can I do to alleviate the longing-rage-despair, to *free* those buried energies – to power him faster than light?

But Mikey was acting under his own steam. Sitting very still, he had scooped up a handful of sand. Yiaou was brought across to flail over the sand and, presumably, nullify its threatening properties. Mikey then bent his head over his hand so that he appeared to be looking at it. There was no talking today; all his energy was concentrated on coping with this new and terrifying experience. Slowly he squeezed the sand between his fingers, letting it trickle on to his legs. He did this repeatedly, widening with each handful the sand's sphere of influence as he brought it to bear on every part of his body. By the time he had begun to pour sand on his head, he had also drawn Yiaou into the activity, dousing the cat with every third handful. The similarity between the sand behaviour and the previous day's stool-smearing was striking.

There was no opening of the heavens, no clash of cymbals, only a boy playing ineptly in a sand-pit; but Ruth knew beyond a doubt that she had not been deluded: Mikey was making a crucial breakthrough. He was taking his first step towards the outside world. The recognition of his own faeces, a substance which was partly him and partly not-him, had been superseded by the recognition of sand − a faeces-like substance which was *altogether not-him*.

In struggling to assimilate through his body this new, utterly separate reality, Mikey was taking a terrible risk: at any moment the sand might break over him like an annihilating wave, proving what he had always maintained − that there was too little of him left to sustain the blow of the external world.

Yiaou was playing a vital role in bearing him up against the flood. He seemed to have become an extension of Mikey, a positive counterpart, perhaps, to the negative excrement. Drawn into the crushing blackness of the singularity's field of gravity, Yiaou shone like a faint candle, creating a glimmer of hope for selfhood.

Ruth grew completely absorbed into the monotonous rhythm of Mikey's sand-shifting. She forgot the cold, she forgot herself, as she watched the littlun's first trembling encounter with the bigun's world. She, too, stared at the particles of sand, trying to see what Mikey saw: a sacred substance as numinous as gold or nitroglycerine.

At the end of three hours, the sand-boy got up and tottered towards her. His eyes were shut, his arms groped the air in front of him while Yiaou moved from side to side as if scanning the way ahead, a sheepish grin on his round face. Ruth restrained her impulse to spring up and hug them both. It might be disastrous to assume the initiative before she was certain of Mikey's intentions. She waited as he walked unerringly to where she was sitting on the bank next to the pit. Without hesitating, he climbed on to her lap and, still with his eyes shut, snuggled up to her. There didn't seem much to say. He had come to her of his own accord; he had acknowledged her existence.

She stroked his hair and gently wiped the grains of sand off his face, while he and Yiaou rocked softly in unison. Ruth tried to wonder how much of this unprecedented, this inconceivable act was a reward for her understanding of his black hole behaviour; but really she didn't care. She was just happy. The months of frustration were wiped out

54

at a stroke. All was peace and quiet, except for the faint flutter of Mikey's heart as it beat like a moth against her breast.

Mikey stiffened. Yiaou's legs became agitated. Ruth murmured soothing words until calmness descended over the threesome again. A whiff of steam rose into the sharp air. She felt a seeping wetness on her skirt. She sat completely still for a few minutes before easing Mikey gently on to the grass beside her. He had simultaneously emptied his bladder and his bowels into her lap. Her throat ached with restrained sobs. 'Hail Mary, full of grace . . . ,' she whispered. She didn't know why. Perhaps those half-forgotten words alone were appropriate to her gratitude and praise. All she knew was that Mikey had, for a moment, trusted her; without fear of reprisal he had made her a gift, granted a reward.

'Thank you, Mikey,' she said. 'That's good. *Very* good.' Yiaou waved a front leg feebly; Mikey remained expressionless and inert.

Ruth's early conversion to Roman Catholicism might at first sight have been attributed to the collision between a sensitive idealistic girl and a convent of devout nuns. In later life, however, Ruth saw it as an attempt to heal some indefinable fissure in her existence.

It had begun, she supposed, at home. At first she had no difficulty in reconciling the archaic domain of her parents with the brave new world of her contemporaries at school. It was simply a question of being bilingual. But one occasion stood out in her mind when, so to speak, the rift between the two land masses became unbridgeable.

She was wandering along the main corridor, thinking about nothing in particular, when she unexpectedly came face to face with her father. He was obviously on the way to some piano lesson. He held his sheet music in one hand and, in the other, a cigarette which he raised in greeting. She noticed how his face lit up when he saw her and she felt a shock of anger, as if he had intruded on some secret of hers, followed by an anxious emptiness in the pit of her stomach. Of course, he only had to smile or wink and they were both immediately united in a silent understanding that real life did not consist in the convent corridor, but waited at home where Mama – Anna – was ululating to herself in her odd oboe-like voice while she prepared high tea. Nevertheless, Ruth never quite recovered from the shock; and whenever she saw him again she was always slightly amazed – and vaguely resentful – that he should be there at all.

At the same time, her sense of dislocation was emphasised by her friends' Catholicism. It was in no way a barrier between them but it was there, like a slight hesitation. It kept her detached, which she would have been in any case, but she felt it was a detachment not of her choosing.

The dull stomach-ache grew more frequent; it only became acute after one memorable chemistry lesson when her best friend, Pam, asked her what it was like being Jewish. Ruth was not at all sure, so she simply looked knowing and said nothing. But she taxed her father on the subject later and he carefully explained to her, without partiality, about Jews. When he had finished, she felt no more Jewish than when he had started; but somehow it was borne in on her, perhaps by his gestures or a look in his mild eyes, that being Jewish was not a thing, like being Austrian, that you could change. It was bound up in her mind with the mysterious former life of her parents and even with her mother's chthonic rites in the kitchen. Above all, as time wore on, she began to identify her Jewishness with a force beyond the family, an ancient power that threatened to rise up from within like a dybbuk and overwhelm her.

The puzzling emptiness persisted, almost as though she were missing some vital organ. Mama's offerings, laid on the altar of the dining-room table, failed to satisfy her. Indeed, she found their cloying richness a shade repellent. She took to stuffing herself with sweets, furtively bought on the way home from school. Despite Leo's attempts to persuade his wife that Ruth was sickening for something, Anna was unconvinced, as though she had diagnosed more of the truth.

The nuns began to exercise a fascination for Ruth. So far, she had regarded them with amusement, as eccentrically clothed school-teachers. She was popular for her waggish impersonations of them. Now she was often seen in long earnest discussion with them, par-ticularly with Sister Bernadette, who shared her passion for doughnuts. When Ruth let it slip one day that she was going to be received into the Church, Pam shook her head uncomprehendingly. She was better off as she was, Pam asserted, without the burden of sin. Ruth, in turn, was astounded at Pam's lack of interest in the sublime subtlety of theology, and they were briefly estranged while Ruth underwent her period of instruction.

Predictably, Leo encouraged her conversion; and yet she sensed in him a reservation whose source was obscure to both of them. Anna neither affirmed nor denied her daughter's decision; she was content to mutter an enigmatic old proverb from behind the big brown teapot:

'If God lived on Earth, people would break His windows'.

Ruth approached her first confession and communion with as much trepidation as joy. She feared an asthma attack. Her breath grew shorter and rattled in her lungs at the very thought of kneeling at the altar-rail. She feared that the promised magic would fail to free her from her obscure turbulence. She feared that she would not be able to break through into the transparent light of ordered faith.

But she took heart at the ease with which she observed the fast before the ceremony; and, when the priest placed the wafer on her trembling tongue, she was surprised by a feeling of repletion deeper than anything she had known, as the Body of Christ dissolved and slid down her eager throat.

A spell of intense piety ensued: Ruth rejoiced in her frequent Masses and even more in her initiation into the secret shared world of her companions. Any distance between them now was imposed by Ruth herself, who was bewildered by their laxity. She had a problem finding sins to confess, once gluttony had been all too easily absolved. Pam was scornful: 'You don't mean to say you confess *real* sins? None of us does that. You just make up a few to keep Father Curran happy.' Ruth was less troubled by the idea of deceiving the priest than by the implication that others had real sins which they suppressed. She suspected that she was so sinful that she couldn't see the wood for the trees.

Little by little her ill-defined hunger returned to nag at her vitals. Gaps began to yawn in her resolve. One Sunday she missed Mass; mortal sin was never so hard again. Faith was less fulfilling and harder to sustain than she had thought. The resonant liturgy, the candles and incense continued to enchant her for a while. She prayed to the Blessed Virgin Mary, but found herself thinking of her mother. She concentrated on Christ, but His power, both loving and judging, made her uneasy and turned her thoughts involuntarily towards tea. She became afraid of choking on the Host and began to avoid both confession and Holy Eucharist. She'd never really liked the idea of Jesus being Jewish.

FIVE

'SO MUCH TO DO, so little time,' said Dorothy, adding bitterly, 'thanks to *you*.' She mopped up the last patch of vomit while Cassandra watched her, licking her lips. 'It's that chocolate Rex gave you, isn't it? He spoils you. But he doesn't have to feed you and groom you and mop up after you.' Cassie trotted off to the kitchen, mewing. Dorothy wondered if the cat had been sick out of spite, just for the pleasure of staining the flawless beige carpet in the hall.

The incident had put her behind schedule. Luckily, today was vacuuming. Dusting and disinfecting were yesterday; tomorrow would be polishing. Dorothy liked vacuuming, liked the cleansing suck and roar of the machine, powering her closer to godliness. She had devised the rota system because the house was so large that unless its maintenance was planned like a military campaign it could easily go to the dogs. Left to herself she would have settled for something labour-saving and mock-Georgian; or even a maisonette close to the shops. The important thing was to be near the hospital, as she called it. But Rex had said that, if she insisted on moving, he might as well invest in a decent spread. She had disliked the house on sight, but gave way in a wild moment when the estate agent announced in awed tones that one of the Beatles had lived there some twenty years ago. He couldn't remember which one, but a decaying white piano was still stashed in the garage to prove it. She liked to think of it as belonging to John, the idol of her childhood and its inspiration. She would never have dreamt of leaving Liverpool if it hadn't been for John; and if she'd known that one day she'd be living in his house.... At first she thought she would never get over it. But John was already long dead, assassinated in a New York street, when the Ballantines moved in; nor did Dorothy expect to see his ghost. The house didn't feel as though he had been happy in it.

The St Michael's Hill estate (in fact, it comprised several hills) had been developed in Edwardian times on land belonging to the sprawling Victorian mansion, now the psychiatric hospital, which had been severed from its former grounds by Station Road. The estate's rule, that no one could build on less than an acre of land, prevented the encroachment of the many 'town houses' which had up-graded the village of Wyebridge to a centreless suburb of London. The St Michael's Hill houses were of different shapes − Rex's was L-shaped − but of more or less uniform size and style: red bricks, tiled roofs, high-ceilinged rooms on three floors and two or more staircases which harked back to the age of servants. Originally belonging to the affluent middle classes, they became the refuge in the sixties of the rich and famous, including many show-business luminaries who excited the Press to dub the estate 'the Beverly Hills of England'. Nowadays, it was colonised by more faceless money, often foreign: stockbrokers, oil company men, diplomats, the odd Arab − people who wanted a secluded oasis only thirty minutes from the capital by car or train.

Many of the houses seemed hardly occupied. Few pedestrians were seen in the avenues. The golf course, which interlocked with the gardens, was always in pristine condition but rarely used. Each property was a separate world, sealed off by the ubiquitous rhododendron bushes and a screen of tall trees. Notices on gateposts warned of electrified fences and guard dogs. Dorothy did not even know who her next-door neighbours were.

Her system was to start at the top of the house and work her way down. Not *right* at the top: the third floor wasn't used at all except for storing things. Dorothy carried the vacuum cleaner to the end of the corridor in the east wing and plugged it in. Pausing at the high window, she could see the three-tiered lawn leading like giant steps down to the orchard and, beyond, the dense bushes which hid the road from view. The long drive to the left sloped down to the heavy wooden gates, never closed now, which gave on to the avenue at the edge of the golf course. The house was said to be the highest on the estate. On a clear day you were supposed to be able to see Windsor Castle. But the days were never clear enough, and Dorothy had to content herself with projecting the grey towers and crenellations on to some distant hazy shape. Sometimes she imagined that she was in the castle, gazing towards the house, trying to catch a glimpse of the princess locked in the tower.

Rushing to make up for lost time, Dorothy attacked the corridor carpet. When she had finished, feeling slightly hot and bothered, she paused in front of the last door on the left. On second thoughts, she decided not to attempt *that* room today. Instead, she went straight on to the master bedroom, leaving the other three empty bedrooms until later. She and Rex had agreed that their room should be colour co-ordinated in emotionally restrained blues and bluey greens. The dull light added a cold North Sea feeling, except briefly in the evening when the west-facing window let in the warmer colours of sunset. All the furniture — except for the fitted cupboards, of course — was equipped with well-oiled castors so that, as Dorothy ploughed up and down the thick dark-blue carpet, she flipped the bed or dressing table this way or that to avoid skimping any corner of the room. She had organised a special trolley for Rex's television, video recorder and tape collection so that they could be wheeled out of the way when not in use. His tripod, crowned with its video camera — the new one he'd been fiddling with the night before — had to be moved the hard way. Rex had once suggested that he fix a camera to point at the bed and leave the tape running while they made love. 'We can replay the tape in our dotage,' he'd joked. 'Be a sport, Dotty.' But Dorothy had blushed and compressed her lips and given a tight little shake of her pretty head.

The roar of the vacuum suddenly changed to a clatter, and stopped. Its echo twanged between the high walls and faded to an enormous silence. Dorothy frantically tried to restart the machine, but it was completely dead. Something vital inside had snapped. For a second, Dorothy was thrown by the hiatus in her routine. Then, afraid of losing momentum, she pulled herself together and hurried down to find the old Hoover.

She opened the narrow door under the back staircase and, switching on the feeble light, peered down the long flight of wooden steps to the dank gloomy space below. There was not much to see except Rex's hoard of magazines and newspapers piled against the wall, an antiquated gas boiler belonging to the old central heating, and a heap of coal which they hadn't yet used in the fireplaces since it was liable to make a mess. Above the coal, a slanting chute built into the wall led up to a coal-hole in the drive. There was no sign of the emergency Hoover — Rex must have thrown it out in the move more than a year ago.

She climbed down to the bottom step, just to make sure, and was repelled by the slimy film of moisture on the walls and the inexplicable stench of effluent. Why couldn't this cellar be dry, as cellars were supposed to be? A slight shift in the black hump of coal sent her scurrying back up the stairs. It couldn't be *rats*, could it? She'd have to get Rex to see to the cellar.

Unaccountably, Dorothy was close to tears. Her carefully planned day was in ruins. She knew she could always clean the silver, a job she had delayed for just such an eventuality; but it suddenly seemed futile and, besides, she felt tired and achy. There wasn't even dinner to prepare — she had fished a casserole out of the deep-freeze first thing, just in case Rex came home. He was kept in Town overnight more often these days. It was one of the prices you paid for starting up your own business. He phoned her sometimes from the company flat, saying how tired he was, and lonely. Strangely, she felt closer to him during these calls than when he was at home, shut up in his study or mooching round the garden with his video equipment slung all over him.

Dorothy dragged herself wearily up the stairs. They were dark, like the hall and corridors, because of the heavy panelling. She went into her bluey-green bedroom and lay down on the bed. For all she cared, the house could go to hell. It was too big for one person to handle anyway. She wanted to go to sleep but found herself too restless and tense. She got up and drew the curtains, plunging the room into a subaqueous dimness.

Her trouble had always been that she hadn't the knack of stringing moments together. Each one seemed new and unrelated to the next. Without her contrived ordering of time, she couldn't get any purchase on the past from which to build up a probable future. She didn't feel continuous as a person, but saw herself as a series of stills, frozen in unnatural poses. As a twenty-year-old, travelling on the night train to London, the very indeterminacy of things had been exhilarating; the incoherence of the past had made it easier to cast off. But increasingly she was frayed by the perpetual need to improvise and fearful of what the next instant might thrust upon her.

Dorothy lay red-eyed on the bed at noon. The blue day flowed over her, to be lost for ever. She tested her fragments of memory, trying to shore herself up against the darkness she was being swept towards inexorably.

'Charles. Good to see you.' Despite a long wait under a potted palm in the opulent foyer, Rex was ready to forgive.

'Rex.' The two men exchanged firm handshakes and easy smiles.

Charles motioned towards a chair made of shiny steel and wicker.

'You've lost a bit of weight,' said Rex. Charles glanced down at the neat paunch overhanging the top of his immaculate jeans and looked sceptical. He resumed his seat behind the enormous white desk. His chair was high-backed and padded, like an armchair that tilted and swivelled. It was slightly higher than the other chairs in the office.

'What's cooking?' Charles asked ironically. His irony was much admired, although it consisted only in a tone of voice. He rested one expensively shod foot on the edge of the desk. His casual ironic style had won him the accounts, among others, of two nationalised industries, a German car firm and several state-of-the-art products from Japan. Rex had pitched for two of these himself, and lost. 'I heard they closed your show down.'

Rex laughed effortlessly. 'All part of the fun, Charles. You know that.'

Charles gave a melancholy sigh. 'Strange times we live in, Rex.... Food and Drink used to be safe as houses. Strange times....'

The lucrative Universal Food account, with its string of super-markets, had been lost through negligence. Both of them knew this. The big lager and whisky firms had simply switched advertising agencies when they were taken over by another brewery. Rex, sensing a change in the wind, had made a mad and expensive grab for other accounts to replace them, but too late. His reputation as one of the leading-edge men had been dulled almost overnight. No one now remembered his daring petrol campaign, nor the slogan which had become a national catchphrase; a clutch of Gold Pencil awards buttered no parsnips with the money men who controlled credit. His own agency, pegged to one or two key accounts, had gone bust. The general opinion was that he had overreached himself; success in writing did not guarantee a head for management and administration.

'To be quite honest, Charles, it never really suited me, running things.'

'No.'

'Too many Suits to keep on the good side of. Not my bag. I've always been a creative man. Like you. In fact, I don't know how you keep it up....' His eyes twinkled and then grew serious. 'Still, it was an interesting experiment.'

'Yes.'

'Don't you wish sometimes that you were back on the old trail, doing pitches? You remember ... bashing out those ads for the credit card people. Just the two of us up all Sunday night with a bottle or three and a Monday-morning deadline. Jesus, we had a lot of fun ... wrote some great spots together. You could really turn out a lot of sexy stuff in those days, Charlie. Sheer poetry. D'you still keep your hand in? I heard that you dreamt up the Motomuki video commercials. Brilliant.'

'No, I didn't. One of my lads did. A video freak. Can't stand the things myself, must be getting old.'

'Bullshit,' Rex twinkled.

'Things are tougher than they were. Copywriters wearing suits, respect for clients' ideas, psychology graduates.... God knows where it'll all end.' He changed the subject abruptly. 'How's that kid of yours ... Mikey?'

'Mikey? Oh, he's ... he's still in that special place. Got some clever Jewish lady seeing to him. She's good, but I don't know....'

'It must be costing, Rex.'

Out of habit, Rex mentioned a sum twice as high as the real one. 'I don't know what they spend it on, Charlie. That kind of money buys a lot of chicken soup. But you got to give everything a shot.'

Charles nodded. 'I hope it works out,' he said without irony. Then briskly, 'I'd invite you to lunch, Rex, only I've got something on.'

'Oh, same here. No. I only popped by. Curious to know what you're doing about a creative director. The word's out you're looking.'

'True.' Charles got up and opened a heavy wooden door in the wall to reveal the inside of a fridge. 'Drink?' Rex shook his head.

'Only I wouldn't mind a crack at it myself, Charles.'

Charles uncapped a bottle of Perrier. The water fizzed ominously in the tall glass.

'The point being, Rex' – he paused to plop a slice of lemon in the water – 'I've already got someone in mind.'

'Don't give me that, Charlie,' Rex laughed.

'I could always push work your way, Rex. A good wordsmith like you can always work. I'll happily put your name on the files.'

An expression of pain flickered across Rex's face. 'I can't go back to freelancing,' he said. 'You know that. I'm a hell of a creative director. I always was. You must remember the things we knocked out together.'

'I don't remember all *that* much creation.' Charles looked thoughtful. 'Nor much direction.... Still, you could try Brewer, Pyatowski. They need a man. More your sort of product, too.'

'I'd rather work with ... for you, Charlie. The old team ....' Phil Brewer hadn't even bothered to speak to him on the phone. Rex hadn't pushed it. It was early days yet. He could still afford the mortgage for a bit. Charles sighed.

'The point being, Rex,' he said, 'I've never liked you.'

Outside in the street, Rex clutched his empty briefcase tightly to stop himself shaking. He was breathing hard, winded by his own rage. He wanted to take an axe and smash Charlie's lavish office to pieces. He wanted to see the beautiful muted carpets sticky and red with the bastard's blood.

The war was as good as over by the time I was drafted abroad. The six months' training in Sittingbourne was mostly wasted on me. I never grasped the assemblage of the easiest piece of equipment; I didn't even master the routine of kit-cleaning. You must think I'm a moron. I'm not. I just get flustered when I'm shouted at, and then it gets such a big thing in my mind that my hands won't do things properly, which makes it worse until I'm ready to start panicking round in circles. I couldn't sleep in my bed for four months. I had to sleep on top of it so that I wouldn't mess up the regulation pattern of bed-making. My comrades did their best to hammer some sense into me but, sadly, I went on letting them down, which reflected badly on the whole platoon. Sergeant Hurrell said I'd be more of a danger to our side than to Jerry, which was an exaggeration, I think, for the sake of wit.

Army life isn't how you imagine it. You don't imagine how harsh it is, how everything jars on your nerves. All the shouting and profane language, and rough edges sticking into you like the hard surfaces of the barracks when they give you a 'blanket court-martial'. It got so I dreaded going abroad – not so much because of the Germans, but because of the corporal who hissed at me: 'When we get you across the Channel, we'll do you in good and proper.' Somehow I couldn't put this remark out of my mind, even with the thought that I'd soon be witnessing at first hand the Continental railway system.

I had the last layer off my gobstopper. All that was left was a tiny white ball, lovely to behold. I used to look at it in spare moments.

Still, I was never ignored, that was something; and the food was delicious – hot and lots of it. Plus I did my bit in the way of calming the occasional fear that the outcome of the war might be in doubt. I simply reminded the doubters of what Isaiah said of the Jewish people, namely that 'no weapon that is formed against thee shall prosper; and every tongue that shall rise against thee in judgement thou shalt condemn'. It was obvious to all that Hitler's tongue was always rising against the Jews, and they took comfort, even though they were all pagans or as good as. One or two actually confused Hitler with Satan, which is far from being the case. Hitler was not even the Great Beast so vividly described in Saint John's colourful Revelation, let alone Satan himself. But he had a good crack at it. Anyway.

After endless shunting about in blacked-out trains (I saw nothing of the famous German railways, worse luck), plus endless hanging about, we were stuck in the back of a convoy somewhere in the middle of Europe. The lads were too dispirited, I think, to remember about doing me in. Every day the same bleak fields and outlandish villages with strange names. Rumours started that we were in the Front Line, but there was no sign of combat, thank God, and we began to think that the rod of the oppressor was broken.

I remember the first real day of spring. Coming over the brow of the green hill, I looked down on the peaceful sunny valley and thought of Surrey and the South Downs. But no birds were singing and there was a whiff of something awful on the breeze; something like the smell of Father's meat stews in a heatwave, but worse. The only buildings were long huts surrounded by wire with observation towers at intervals. We were all a bit jumpy because we knew from captured Germans that such places were crammed with dangerous criminals, terrorists, homosexuals, etcetera....

I never did see any action in the end. I was invalided out early — shipped back to England — with gastric ulcers.

I beg your pardon? Ah, well, there's not much point talking about it. You've seen the films and that. Of course, cameras tend to lie; but no more, probably, than we lied to each other at the time. Mostly we lied to ourselves, for the simple reason that it was obvious to us that things like that don't happen. Nothing in the world can prepare you for it. Some things are too big to see. Most of us still didn't see it, even when we'd passed through the clogged air at the gate and heard the horrid twittering noise that the aliens were making and then seen them, bunched in the reeking compound, with their hairless heads and matchstick limbs and eyes hollow with the darkness of outer space—

Sorry. I'm not really upset. It's just that I get a whiff of it now and then when I drop my guard, like when I'm on the edge of sleep. It makes my eyes water.

It wasn't one of the big camps, the famous ones; it was a modest affair with no crematorium, for instance, and only one poky laboratory with a couple of dissecting tables — more for whiling away the time, I should think, than for serious experiments.... Anyway, the point is, what struck me, what I glimpsed in the whole business, was — how can I put it? — a kind of *supernatural* cruelty. It was easy to miss it because, you know, it's a funny thing but, at the limits of pity, disgust is just a whisper away and your instinct is to avert your eyes. But I knew I had to *see* it — to bear witness — because it was something altogether new, like the Apocalypse. Was it then that I sensed the imminence of Christ's return? I don't know. I remember praying that Love might

66

enter me and look through my eyes and see what I couldn't allow myself to see.

I haven't said any of this before. I tried to mention it to Father, but it didn't come across on account of his deafness. His comment was: 'Your German isn't as baRd as he's made out. An Englishman has a natural affinity with a German, whereas your average Jew boy is a sly fellow.' I'm not saying he's wrong, only that I didn't see it like that. I can't say what I saw, but I can say what happened to me.

The 'liberation' was a bit of a joke. There wasn't much we could do. It was five days before the Red Cross arrived with the proper supplies. Meanwhile, we had next to no medicine for the typhoid, Tee Bee, etcetera, and no food to speak of except the stores of the men in black who, deprived of authority, huddled in a single hut. You hardly needed to guard them: they seemed to be deprived of will as well, and certainly dead to remorse. So the dying went on dying and the living went on ... well, went on breathing.

We did our best. But, being so inexperienced as regards the Abomination of Desolation, we all went a little mad, I think.

Certainly, a detail of three blokes assigned to clean up some pits behind the 'hospital' lost their minds; one of them was caught trying to set fire to the hut with the black men inside, and had to be locked up. Major Evans, bless him, issued orders and made lists. It was his way of bearing witness. He came up to me once, in a sort of trance, and ordered me to separate the men and women, as before, for the sake of order or hygiene or something. Ah, yes, those poor women. It was no comfort to me that their plight had been foreseen by Isaiah, who said of the Daughters of Zion: 'And it shall come to pass, that instead of sweet spices there shall be rottenness; and instead of a girdle a rope; and instead of well set hair baldness; and instead of a stomacher a girding of sackcloth: branding instead of beauty.' Except the sackcloth was wrong because they were mostly in their birthday suits and quite unashamed, but so skinny you'd have thought they were children instead of women. I had to beg the Major's pardon and point out that they didn't wish to be separated and that there was no purpose in it since most of them were dying anyway. It was terrible to see his face, so tired and so close to despair, sort of folding inwards and giving up. I said I'd look after them and he said, 'Do what the eff you like,' and that was that.

It's funny, but I felt very calm. When you're looking at people at the bottom of things, when God has all but withdrawn Himself and given them over to pure evil, the thought of Him – you won't believe this – surges up more strongly into the soul, like the birth of love in deep hatred. Anyway, I gathered up my group of prisoners – former prisoners, I should say – plus some other loose ones who couldn't organise themselves, and found a hut for them. Then I distributed all my kit and most of my uniform and all my rations, as well as the stores laid aside for them. Now, although fresh water was in sad supply, I noticed that the women in particular preferred to wash rather than to drink. This was so odd that I collected from my comrades as much soap and lice powder and as many toothbrushes as I could.

This went down very well with my adopted people. I also got some chocolate in exchange for my cigarette rations (handy not being a smoker), but this was less successful because they had trouble keeping it down. They were less nervous of me without my uniform and, once the soap had broken the ice, they liked to stand near me, sometimes with their palms up like they were warming themselves at a fire; or else they'd touch me shyly as if they doubted I was real. Poor Major Evans put me on several charges for being improperly dressed and so on, but he was a decent bloke and never followed them up. In fact he preferred to steer clear of me, like the other blokes, but they all came up with stuff, including cigarettes, for me to pass on, I'll give them that.

I chummed up with an Austrian called Ernst, used to be an English professor. Imagine me hobnobbing with a professor! Not surprising he was saved really because he had the number one, four, four, oh, oh, oh, tattooed on his arm. He introduced me to all my people and I learnt all their names. Not as easy as it sounds since they looked a bit similar, what with.... Funnily enough, they were keener to talk than, for example, to sleep; so I spent most of the time with them, even at night. As nice a bunch of people as you could hope to meet.

There were some exceptions, right puzzles they were – strange geezers who weren't interested in anything. Just shuffled about or stood still, sort of dead on their feet. Ernst said they were 'musclemanner', it sounded like. It meant Moslems, a nickname because they'd surrendered to their fate, as Moslems are supposed to do. They were a bit spooky, more like shadows of people than people, if you take my meaning, Doctor. One of them tried to come in the hut but there was a great hubbub amongst the others. 'He is a carrier of death,' Ernst tried to explain. 'He is contagious like a disease.... Nothing can be done for him now.... He is a corpse who walks.' Well, I had to agree he was in a dreadful state. Put me in mind of Job, with his bones cleaving to his skin, on his eyelids the shadow of death, and so on. What's more, I had nothing left to give except Jean Macintyre's gobstopper. I put the little white ball – pathetic really – into this weird bloke's hand. It took some time to attract his attention. But at last he got the idea and popped it in his mouth. I persuaded the others to let him in out of the cold, but I don't think he lived very much longer.

I feel a bit tired, Doctor, so, if you don't mind, I won't repeat what they told me about being prisoners. It took me quite a time to stifle my ... indignation over the godless constructors of the camp; I don't want to stir it all up. I laboured to keep their minds off things, which was tricky because I've no way with words and scarcely know anything bar the Bible. Of course, we did share a common interest in the Old Testament, but I was forever casting around for something a little more light-hearted.

I did the only turn I know. I invented it myself. It's the six-fifty to Waterloo – the old steam engine, that is. I imitate the sounds: the guard shouting the stations, the clipping of tickets, slamming of doors, wheels clacking over points, whistles in tunnels – you get the idea. On the way I do a running commentary on the stations and points of interest. Wyebridge, Oatlands, Walton for Hersham, Royal Mills, John Burn and Co., Esher for Claremont, Sandown Park racecourse.... I won't do it all now.

A surprising number of them understood English, plus Ernst was translating like mad. I'd hardly got as far as the Snowball Laundry – it's sold now – when I was put off by a frightening noise. Ernst was apologetic. 'They are laughing,' he said. 'Ar – Ar – Ar, you see? They remember.' Ernst wasn't laughing, more like ... the other thing. But I soon cheered him up. The turn was a huge success, with several encores and much applause. Oh, the Children of Israel! My children. I'll never forget that day in the death camp. It was one of the happiest moments of my life.

If she remembered anything at all, it was never the big things. For instance, she could clearly recall the bus ride to the hospital where her mother was dying, but not what her mother had said or what she had looked like, that last time. Dorothy didn't even cry for her until she was a teenager, by which time she knew she was really crying for herself. She remembered going to St Botolph's for her First Communion. She continued to attend Mass for some years, partly out of vague compliance with her mother's wish, partly out of a sense of necessity, rather like the tiresome need for inoculation. She could not remember when she gave it up or even when she ditched the whole system of beliefs – if, indeed, she had ever subscribed to them.

Her father had long since exchanged worship at church on Sundays for idolatry at Anfield on Saturday afternoons. He followed football with all the passion of an affectation. He worked as a supervisor on the docks but would have been happier, and probably richer, humping cargo. He spent a lot of time in the dockers' pubs, buying too many rounds to compensate for the lack of dignity in his work compared to theirs. At home he was intimidated by the cool competence with which his young only child took things in hand after the death of his wife. He got drunk often, feeling that he owed it to himself. Dorothy did not pay much attention: she was fond enough of him but, outside the cooking and cleaning and washing, she seemed to be wrapped up in herself, running her own course.

At school, Dorothy disappointed her teachers with results that did not match her obvious promise. Exams played no part in her plans. Speech and drama classes were the exception – she knew the value of proper speaking, despite attempts by television people to popularise the regional accents. She left school as soon as she decently could and, earning money in a shoe shop by day, threw herself into acquiring secretarial skills at night classes. She did not have much time for boys but, knowing that she had to serve her apprenticeship in the craft of attracting men, she let the more suitable ones take her to the pub or pictures. Privately, the boys were impressed by her prettiness, her meticulously clean appearance, her self-contained air; publicly, they agreed she was above herself, not worth the trouble, probably frigid.

Having discovered that football was at least as great a rival as other girls, she tested her suitors by suggesting that they take her to matches instead of going with their mates. Their admiration of her was intensified by her understanding of the off-side rule, which in their experience was unique among women. Dorothy thought football a silly game but she didn't mind watching the players' legs, slightly unreal with their heavy muscles and, on cold days, greased like machines. She sometimes used to dream about the gleaming thighs of the footballers, pinning her down.

As soon as her typing and shorthand speeds were up to snuff, she left the shoe shop with relief. The feet of strangers had begun to sicken her. Washing her father's socks was purgatory. He was becoming impossible after a few drinks, inclined to kiss her sentimentally and say how like her mother she was, which she knew to be untrue. The last thing she recalled about her father was his maudlin tears, and her pity – not wholly free of contempt – as he watched her train pull out of the station. There was no sense of leaving home; her house, let alone Liverpool, had never been that.

In the railway compartment, suspended between two cities, she remembered luxuriating in the fruition of all her dream-like scheming. It seemed as though she had served her time and could now come into her own. She could afford to give herself over to the moment and dare the future.

70

In the headlong dash of the night express, Dorothy shook with the strangeness and joy of her new pact with every passing instant. She felt she was a pure present tense, whirling round herself and (she felt) larger than life.

The expanse of greenish-blue ceiling seemed to press down on her. She turned over on to her stomach and hugged the pillow against the sides of her head. Buried among her early memories was an event which had a different texture from the rest. She didn't know exactly what it was, but she was certain that much of her adolescent sense of purpose stemmed directly from it. She tended to avoid trying to reconstruct the event because she was maddened by the tantalising fragments which flashed into her mind, while the whole occurrence, and its meaning, eluded her. But, like a sore tooth, she couldn't help returning to it and worrying it. She felt that if she could only connect herself to this shadowy memory she would find the Archimedean point outside herself from which she could exert pressure on the world and transform her banal routines into significant tasks.

Certain facts about the event were established: it was her birthday – either her twelfth or her thirteenth, she couldn't be sure. It was a Saturday morning. Light was pouring through the window at the top of the narrow stairs. She was standing with her back to the window, looking down the staircase at someone ascending. She couldn't see who it was, partly because she was casting a shadow down the stairs, and partly because the person's face was obscured by a kind of mist. The person paused on the seventh step. She had a feeling it was a woman. It was very quiet.

Dorothy dug her nails into the pillow and strained to see the face of the woman. As always, it was bathed in shadow and blurred by the mist which quivered like a heat haze. As always, the woman made her uneasy; her presence wasn't benevolent. Instinctively Dorothy cupped her hands together – yes, she had been holding something like a bowl. The thought of Ireland came to her fleetingly, and evaporated. She wondered if the woman were her mother and the event had really taken place much earlier in her life. The more she struggled to recall the scene, the more indistinct it became, melting into its own strange atmosphere until she began to think it had all been a dream. She even wondered if she had seen a ghost and had been so shocked that she'd suppressed the memory.

The mist in front of the unknown person's face had been so charged with significance that it became a semi-transparent membrane which sealed the essence of the memory inside her mind. It had been intact,

71

she was sure, on the night train; it had been a source of strength during the first uncertain days in London. But, gradually, through neglect, the membrane had grown opaque, like scar tissue over past wounds. It changed from a window on the world to a barrier which shut it out; and behind it, deprived of light, the vital memory wasted away. She had somehow managed to forget what she most needed to remember.

Dorothy felt suffocated. She clung harder to her pillow, appalled at her own weightlessness and panic-stricken by the tugging currents of seconds, minutes, hours that threatened to sweep her out of her depth or send her ballooning into a vast blue emptiness. If only she could *remember.* . . . She longed to anchor herself somehow and walk forward without fear once again, feeling the ground solid under her feet.

She got up reluctantly, full of self-reproval for the wasted day. The casserole ought to go into the oven in case Rex came home; her hair ought to be washed if she was to look presentable. There was no reason why her husband should have to come back to an indolent and ill-groomed wife after a hard day at work.

Rex drowned the familiar whisper of panic by loudly ordering a half-bottle of Bollinger. He'd been so *sure* of Charles. He could have settled into the job and then announced to Dorothy that he had packed in the business and was master-minding Charles's agency. He could never tell her that the whole thing had been a bloody awful flop; he had always been the strong one, in control. Dorothy was too fragile and nervous to cope with the strain – the disgrace – of his unemployment. He'd had to cancel two dinner-parties with acquaintances in case they'd heard of his bad luck and let it slip to his wife. His social life, as well as his business, was up the spout. Rex sipped the champagne and felt better. He drank it for superstitious reasons: it was bad luck to economise at this stage of the game, bad for morale. He already suspected that some secret mark of Cain had appeared on his forehead and, visible only to tramps and beggars, left him open to assault on the streets.

What to do in the afternoon? Charles's rebuff had knocked more wind out of his sails than he cared to admit. The possibility of another was intolerable. He'd wait until tomorrow before putting the squeeze on another name in his little book. There weren't all that many left. But he hadn't been in the business twenty years for nothing; something would turn up. He'd be back, bigger than ever, whispered the champagne. It was just the waiting that was getting him down. If he stayed in the pub until closing time, he still had three hours to kill before Andrea got back from work. She didn't know about the agency, either. He wished he were in bed with her now. God, she couldn't get enough of him. She'd said as much. His heartbeat quickened as he savoured the memory of her words.

Rex caught the eye of a smart woman talking to three men at the far end of the bar. He smiled faintly, diffidently, careful to look away first. He knew she was seeing a slim tanned man with thick curly hair, a straight nose and startling pale-blue eyes. She was thinking: He looks very like Paul Newman. Rex hoped that she was adding 'except younger'. He was proud of his boyish looks and cagey about his age, especially since he was twelve years older than his wife. Fortunately, people assumed that they were roughly the same age.

The woman was glancing over at him again. He thought: I could take her away from those men – and felt the exaltation that always accompanied the knowledge that he was desired. You couldn't forgo sex, if only because it might, just once, fulfil its promise; but nothing could beat that first exquisite moment when you knew beyond doubt that a woman was yours for the taking. Sometimes it took days of careful courtship – Rex was capable, like an ascetic, of prodigious self-denial in pursuit of a woman; at other times, like now, it happened in a flash. His technique was simple: he convinced the object of his desire that she was the most important person in the world. He was never believed, but it rarely failed. All the most beautiful women were bored to death by self-centred men who droned on about how important they were. Rex knew that it was fatal to be self-centred. To get what you wanted, you had to be as sensitive as a bat to a woman's finest nuance. Know your enemy was the number one rule.

The smart woman was excusing herself to the men, walking towards him, smiling openly. Christ, what a nerve. And what legs.

'Rex,' she said. His smile broadened. Who the hell was she? 'You don't remember me.'

'How could I forget you?'

'Your eyes are glazing over, Rex. The game's up. Penelope Young. Masters now.'

'Penny.' Rex crinkled the offending eyes warmly. 'I was miles away. Forgive. It's been too long.' It had been eight years. His marriage was in its infancy. Penny Young – now Mrs Masters, for God's sake – had been in PR somewhere. He only remembered the way she wrapped her extraordinary legs around him and flung her head back with eyes closed and long lashes fluttering. The memory came in a rush, making his back prickle with tiny spurts of sweat.

'I'd like you to meet my husband. Darling!' She beckoned the man over. 'Darling, this is Rex Ballantine, an old friend.'

Rex shook hands all round, not hearing the other two men's names. 'An old friend.' Was it *possible* that *she* had forgotten all ... all that?

73

There wasn't the smallest hint in her voice or face that he had ever been more than a passing acquaintance. Hugh Masters was tall and calm; he suspected nothing. But why should he? There was nothing personal in Penny's manner, nothing except amusement and indifference.

Recklessly, he bought them champagne they didn't want. The men made him uneasy as men usually did. Their eyes were guarded, reflecting nothing. He loved the eyes of women in which, like mirrors, he could see himself writ large. He chatted easily, echoing the deep-voiced, well-to-do laughter of the men; but he couldn't look at Penny again lest he see her eyelashes flutter and, lunging away from the bar, go crying through the dead afternoon streets. How could she forget? And, if she remembered, how give no sign? What in the world could compensate him for the treachery of time and memory? Had it meant nothing to her? And what, then, of all the others? Was he no longer enshrined in their hearts as the great adventure of their lives? If they no longer remembered him, he might as well not exist.

Rex slid down from his bar stool and phoned Andrea from a booth in the corner. She was still out to lunch. His watch told him it was 2.40 p.m. Who was she lunching with to be so late back? He slammed the receiver down. At the bar, he made his excuses; something had come up, he explained glassily. The men nodded, understanding. Penelope Masters née Young let out a peal of laughter which tortured his burning ears as he pushed his way towards the door.

SIX

ONLY TWO WEEKS after he had first broached the abyss of the sand-pit, Mikey manifested a startling new activity: he began to remove sand from the pit, a handful at a time, and carry it inside to his giant bean-bag in the corner of the playroom.

Up until this moment, he had undergone a revolution in his toilet practice. Soon after he defecated on Ruth, he had begun to excrete freely, anywhere, at any time, as if in a deliberate attempt to dismantle the machinery of his former rigid toilet training. Ruth would have put him into nappies, but she was afraid of affronting his dignity. Instead, she cleaned up after him several times a day. He seemed to be able to piss at will in short bursts, like a dog. Suspecting that her forbearance was being tested, Ruth mopped up without a murmur; but she often felt like smacking him.

However, Mikey responded within days to the universal encouragement and praise. He began by confining his unbridled elimination to his bean-bag (which Ruth cleverly covered in polythene) and ended by resuming his use of the lavatory. He celebrated his new mastery of bodily functions by bossing his stools about with loud incoherent shouts.

The bean-bag had assumed even greater importance. It was a kind of power base where he retired and recharged for long periods between his intense repetitive spells of sand behaviour. At each return he seemed to have colonised his body more fully. But, at any moment, it could still freeze, changing from a relatively fluent organism to a dense lump that flew off at a tangent and revolved frenetically with cries of 'Danger!', 'Plode!' as Mikey strove to flee the malevolent power of the singularity, sitting like a black magnetic spider at the centre of the black hole.

Mikey added his umpteenth handful of sand to the heap by the bean-bag. Ruth tried tactfully to intervene by offering him an empty coffee jar. The slowness of his progress was driving her up the wall. Mikey ignored the jar as he had refused all other containers.

'All right, then, Mikey. Let me hold Yiaou for you while you collect the sand,' she suggested, 'then you'll be able to use *both* hands. . . .'

Mikey treated the suggestion with silent contempt. Yiaou was obviously an integral part of the process.

After six more handfuls, during which Ruth no longer traipsed after him to the sand-pit and back — she was sick to death of it — he took a short 'rest' on the bean-bag. No one else was allowed near it except, occasionally, Ruth, who would join him in the hollow he had made, pushing the bag around him like a wall. He fitted inside easily whereas Ruth's legs overflowed the wall and her feet rested on the ground.

She did not join him today because he launched into his twiddling. This involved sitting completely motionless and rapidly weaving a complex pattern with his fingers in front of his face. Yiaou remained dormant in whichever hand he was not using. As his fingers flashed to and fro, from side to side, like an elaborate genuflection, his gaze was fixed on the large global lampshade over the room's central light.

Dr Frieling came over and, nodding civilly at Ruth, peered at Mikey from a respectful distance.

'He's hallucinating,' the doctor remarked.

'I think so,' Ruth agreed. 'Close to, his pupils dilate quite noticeably. He's certainly looking at something.'

'It's usual with twiddling. The flickering fingers seem to provide a kind of screen on which the child can project his own images. Of course, the movement also helps to protect him from the frightening content of those images.'

'It's a diminished version of his horrorizon,' Ruth added. 'A substitute for spinning or running in circles.' The old doctor nodded. They both watched the small boy in silence.

'He's sort of looking at the light-globe, Dr Frieling. What's he seeing?'

'Ah, well, Miss Maier. All my children are fond of large round shiny objects. Footballs, for example. They represent the breast, naturally. Mikey is conjuring up the longed-for and unattainable breast. Of course, the breast is by extension the mother herself — she whom he fears and desires. . . .' It was Ruth's turn to nod; but she was doubtful. Once during these feverish sessions she had heard Mikey whispering in awestruck tones: 'Bright, bright . . . the Earth . . . far, far . . . *Earth*.' She saw no reason to assume that he wasn't seeing what he claimed: planet Earth shining like a tiny lamp amidst the barren wastes of outer space. At the same time, it was the vast roaring environment around him which he only dared peek at between protective fingers. She told this to Dr Frieling. He was a little testy.

'Yes, all right. I concede that he is hallucinating the Earth. But what is this distant shining Earth but a symbol of the breast? It's quite clear.'

'What you say is clear,' Ruth retorted, 'but it's not helpful.' The blood rose to her face. 'I'm sorry.'

'No. Go on.'

'Well . . . I agree that his "Earth" is a symbol. But I'm not so sure that it's the breast. I mean, you talk as if it's his task to return to the breast, Doctor. But, even if he were willing to, he couldn't. None of us can. Besides, you said yourself that it doesn't stop at the breast, because the breast is also the mother. But what is the mother to her baby but the whole world? Also, it's just as important that the child *separates* himself from the breast in order to find himself. Couldn't it be that no one wants to return literally to the breast, but they want to return to themselves . . . their selves?'

'Chicken and egg,' grumbled Dr Frieling.

Ruth rushed on: 'Mikey says that he wants to reach Earth. Yes, this is a symbol. A symbol which *includes* the breast — which is simply the original and most potent symbol of the self. Mikey has given up the breast itself; it has brought him nothing but pain. He's more realistic than you. He wants the world he has lost and most of all he wants to be himself in that world. The one presupposes the other. So he longs to return to "Earth" where other humans live, where *he* can live as a little boy—' Ruth decided she had said enough.

'You're getting carried away with your symbols, Miss Maier.'

'And you started it, Doctor.'

Dr Frieling smiled ruefully. 'Yes, I did, didn't I? I confess I've never really liked symbols. They mean too much. Here we are, all in a muddle. . . .'

Ruth laughed.

'I agree. The problem is a practical one: how do I cross space to fetch him back to Earth? Please help me to do that.'

The doctor sighed deeply.

'You must prepare yourself for a . . . a disappointment. You may not be able to—'

'But *look*,' Ruth interrupted. 'Every day now he's doing something new. Look at that pile of sand!'

'He may go on piling sand for months ... years.'

'He won't. I won't let him.'

'My dear Miss Maier ...' He laid a hand on her arm. 'I hope not. He has shown himself to be a resourceful chap. All he lacks is power — what is it you said? Power to travel faster than light? You have to supply that power. Then, perhaps, he will devise a means of escape.'

She knew he was right. Love was the power. Did she have enough? She would entirely give up her life for him if she thought it would do the slightest good.

Mikey left his bean-bag and took up his sand-collecting again. Two children in the way of his beeline to the sand-pit hurriedly moved aside. Oblivious of them, Mikey marched through the French window and scooped up yet another little measure of sand. Drawn into his orbit, Ruth followed automatically. She did not notice that she had already given up any life that might be called her own.

At last I can make myself useful! It's ever so exciting. I reported to janitorial services, Doctor, just as you arranged. They read what you'd written about me and decided to risk taking me to the place they call the Unit.

As soon as I saw it, I knew it was meant for me.

But they made it more than clear that it was up to Doctor Frieling as to whether I was worthy of employment there. Praise God, he was satisfied with the interview he gave me. I agreed, of course, not to hold forth — even about the Millennium — nor to interfere in any way with the children's treatment. He explained all about them. It wasn't necessary. I can see into what mighty affliction they have fallen. I'll try to show you I can do something right. I'm really quite a handyman when I get going. Yes, I understand that we'll continue our little chats at the same time. Maybe I'll have something more interesting to tell you about now! That reminds me.

I've been considering dreams, as you requested. I used to dream a great deal but I think that life has somehow pummelled it out of me. Still, it's refreshing to meet someone who believes, as I do, in the power of dreams, which, if they are interpreted aright, bestow gifts of prophecy. I do not speak of the common run of dreams, the ... *personal* dreams; no, I speak of those that are visited on us by the Holy Spirit and that speak to us out of the darkness with tongues of fire. For example, you'll be interested in a dream which was given to me when I was sent back to England in nineteen forty-five. I was admitted to

Saint Thomas's Hospital for an operation on my stomach — something to do with the gastric ulcers I think I mentioned. As soon as I was anaesthetised for the operation, I dreamt:

I was travelling through a tunnel. It had perfectly smooth walls, moving in a perpetual spiral. The walls were alive and slightly phosphorescent. I was moving through the spiral so fast that I didn't have time to be frightened, but was swept up in one long gasp with every part of me tingling. Terrific it was. I sat in a kind of open carriage like a goods truck and I noticed that ... *the wheels were not touching the rails.* 'How is this possible?' I thought. 'Where am I going?' Immediately the answer came in a mighty voice from all around: 'You are in the Tunnel of Time. No one ever reaches the end.'

The second the words had sounded, like a great gong, I saw that the tunnel converged in the distance into a pinpoint of burning light, brighter than many suns; and, as I swished through the living, moving tube, faster and faster above the silver rails, I thought: Oh, oh, I'm reaching the *end*. I knew I was going to *break through time*.

I hit the light at about a thousand miles an hour. The light broke over me, broke *into* me and, dazzled as I was, I glimpsed the heights of Himalayan mountains and heard the laughter of children, too piercing and sweet for my blinded senses to comprehend. I struggled to keep my eyes open but the light was too strong and a voice was tugging at me, saying 'Wake up now, wake up. It's all over. There's no need to cry.' I closed my eyes and found myself in a hospital bed with a nurse bending over me. The after-effects of the ether had dragged me back; I had fallen awake and was sick.

To recover from the operation I was sent to the Railway Convalescent Home in Par, Cornwall. I was to travel — wait for it — on the famous 'Cornish Riviera Express' out of Paddington! But I couldn't possibly leave without first popping home to see Father. You see, I'd received no answer to my letters all the time I'd been away; and I was gripped by a fear that Father had been smitten by the Vee One bombs which had devastated the London area until March. I mean, you and I could hear the doodlebugs coming, and run; but Father *couldn't* because of his ear problem.

I was hardly able to savour the changes at Waterloo — hourly expresses to Portsmouth reinstalled, stopping trains *twice* an hour, etcetera — because in my mind's eye I kept seeing number one, South Road, as a pile of rubble with nothing left of Father but a charred leg. To divert myself on the journey to Wyebridge I cudgelled my brains, and also prayed, that the meaning of my vision be revealed to me. Pharaoh, Nebuchadnezzar and the kings of old were fortunate in their Josephs and Daniels. I had no one to interpret my dream but myself, and I was hopeless at it. In the years to come I was tempted to believe that God had vouchsafed me a glimpse of the end of Time and the Millennial Peace; but in this, as in so much, I was deluded. I didn't know how deluded until my first visit to Birmingham in nineteen eighty-one when— I won't tell you straight off. We'll have a bit of *suspense*, eh?

'You're not dead, then,' were Father's first words. He was a dry one, was Father. The relieving of my anxiety made me roar with laughter. I laid a great feast before him – eggs, jam, everything – for I had bags of back rations. 'Go on. Stuff yourself,' he advised; but, despite his half-starved appearance, he wouldn't touch more than a mug of weak tea himself. I did my best to bellow my war news at him, including the op, which had been successful. But, of course, he knew far more about the war than I did. 'The real enemy', he told me, 'is that slant-eyed gang.' Then he surprised me with a sudden shout: 'I can't *abide* those nips.' I tried to calm him down, but without much success; it took the atom bomb on Hiroshima to do that.

I was puzzled by his uncertain temper and his reluctance to eat. I convinced him the food was all paid for, but he still wouldn't touch it. It turned out that he had been conducting his own war against a bitter and cunning enemy, variously referred to as the Adversary Within, the Fiend and finally . . . the *Worm*.

Yes, he had a tapeworm. Every mouthful he denied himself was food triumphantly snatched from the mouth of the Worm. More than one doctor had pronounced him sound in body but, as he often asked, if you'll forgive me, Doctor, 'What in God's name do doctors know?' I'm not saying he was right; but I've never known Father to be mistaken on a medical, or any other, matter. He *knew* what he could feel inside him; and what he could feel was the Worm puffing itself up in his vitals. I caught him drinking paraffin once – one of his better attempts to knock the Fiend on the head for good; but the Fiend only spewed it back at him in contempt. Only by the severest self-mortification could he hope to keep the great bulk of the Worm within manageable bounds. Poor Father. He was in a pitiable condition but he had to fight alone. Runs in the family, I suppose.

Yes, all right. Birmingham. I saw a sight there that drained the blood out of my head and nearly made me faint dead away. I saw a train, a real train, *suspended above its rails*. Yes, it was a magnetic levitation train, driven by induction motors, which ran between the National Exhibition Centre and the airport. I wished I had with me all the mockers and sneerers who've reviled my prophecies over the decades. For I had a vision of a 'maglev' train *thirty-six years* before it came to pass; and there is the living proof that my dream was not a snare, but of God. And I am convinced now that the dream foreshadowed the momentous happening in Par; just as another event foreshadowed it, an event less innocuous that I tremble to relate, but will – for completeness' sake and for the sake of what came after to change my old life for new, like a set of clothes, and for the sake of Jesus Christ, Our Lord, whom I will hallelujah with every breath until the last, Amen.

10 March

Mikey has taken two days, on and off, to accumulate a pile of sand to his liking. I wouldn't have believed it could be so *wearing*. Just watching the whole boring business hour after hour, without being able to do anything to help, made me want to scream. The *slowness* of it all. But why am I being so irrational? It's taken him a year to acknowledge the existence of sand, let alone touch it. I should be prepared to watch him piling it up for another year, if necessary; I find I'm not. The reason is, I think, that his behaviour appears so nearly normal that I've started to judge him as I would a normal boy and thus find his slowness frustrating. I long to rush him – as if I could without irreparable damage. Beyond the frustration I also feel a sense of urgency, as if we hadn't got all the time in the world. I can't account for this; it's obviously something in me which I'll have to keep under control in case it leads me into some fatal over-reaction. Meanwhile, I must stay calm and simply ask myself what he's doing. It's becoming harder to think properly – I ought to be writing up serious case-notes, but all I can do, it seems, is splurge my feelings (*my* feelings!) on to paper.

Fortunately there are important things to report: after M. brought in enough sand, he took a short rest (20 mins). He set the cat to work on it – usual thing, legs thrashing about, head bobbing an inch above the sand. (I had to laugh! Mikey's so serious and Yiaou's so comical, as though he's humouring his master.) Next, M. began to construct a *jagged* circle around his bean-bag. A circular zig-zag, over 2 metres in radius. Each zig is exactly the same length (16 cm.) as each zag – a remarkable feat since he judges them by eye. Oh, I forgot . . . . A strange thing happened before this. Mikey pulled down his trousers and piddled on the sand-pile, wetting the floor. Nothing strange about that (I wouldn't have written *that* a month ago!). I was about to nip off and get a cloth when a man appeared with a mop. An impressive figure. He's been around for a day or so, one of the more harmless patients recruited by Dr F. from the big house. Without a word, he began to mop up for me. I said: 'Don't worry. It's not your job.' He said, very quietly: 'It's my job and it's a privilege.' I was rather amazed. But as soon as he spoke I recognised him: he's the same man who spoke to me at the bench by the trees. The End of the World merchant. He said casually: 'Mikey's busy today.' Then he gave that smile I can't decide about – perhaps it *is* rather charming and not crazed. He spoke Mikey's name as if he'd known him for ages. His name is Harry. While he was clearing up, I caught him giving Mikey an indescribable look. (I think he must be harmless: the look was definitely a 'good' look.)

The zig-zag circle is built in units of five lines which are inspected by Yiaou. Since these form four triangular points, two pointing outwards and two inwards, I suppose Dr F. would call them the 'hostile breast' .... *I* think they're teeth. M. seems a little less 'frozen' in the oral area at meals. Yesterday he even held a mouthful of food against his teeth with his tongue, instead of wolfing it down. If teeth are the main infantile agents of aggression, the desire to bite is so deeply repressed through fear of retaliation that M. can't use them at all. But by building jagged lines that 'bite the world' by proxy he can release some of the pressure on his real teeth, perhaps. (If ever M.'s rage is unleashed directly, please God, we shall be knee-deep in blood ....)

But whether or not the sand-circle specifically signifies breasts or teeth, generally and above all it represents the vicious circle of his autism. It's the 'horrorizon'. As far as I can see, Yiaou's role offers the only glimmer of hope: as the embodiment of Mikey's aspirations, he seems to be infusing the 'horrorizon' with a creative aspect, as a boundary pushing outwards and striving for contact. Or is this wishful thinking? He *may* only be imbuing the circle with magical protective properties to blot out all external stimuli (Yiaou as fetish).

Mikey was silent all the time he was building the circle, except when anyone came near (even me). If anyone approached, he shot off in short bursts of spinning together with screams (plode, red alert, etc.). I was afraid of some awful conflict with the other children but, interestingly, they have an instinctive(?) respect for Mikey's peculiarities. They keep well clear of the circle, even warning each other against stepping on it, as if they appreciate its importance in a way that 'normal' people can't.

Ruth woke early and suddenly from a fitful sleep distorted by ugly dreams. The light behind the curtain was dim; the air was muffled, expectant. A presentiment seemed to move inside her, as faint as an undercurrent in the blood. She got up quickly and drew back the curtains. A late snowfall had turned the lawns white. The buoyant arms of the pines drooped to attention in their heavy sleeves. The sky was a leaden reflection of the snow.

She hurried down to the warm dormitory. A distant clatter told her that the kitchen staff had started work. All the beds were occupied except Mikey's. Ruth half-ran to the playroom. Harry had just begun to wash the floor.

'Have you seen Mikey?' she asked breathlessly. Harry inclined his head towards the far corner of the room.

'I found them here at first light,' he said. 'I've been keeping an eye on them.'

Mikey and Yiaou were busy, fine-tuning the zig-zags of the sand-circle. Relieved, Ruth felt – absurdly – that it was true, that Mikey was safe in the presence of the big ungainly man.

'Thanks, Harry.' Her eye fell on his large hands slowly wringing dirty water out of a cloth. He performed his menial tasks without a trace of servility. There was a pink mark on his neck where his stiff collar had rubbed. She liked the way he had kept the collar and tie, with its fat ill-tied knot, even though his jacket and waistcoat had been exchanged for a long brown workcoat.

'It's a pleasure, miss. He carries the sins of others.'

'Sins ...?' The word was almost lost to her, like an archaic statue overgrown with moss. Yet, for a second, she felt uncomfortably close to Harry's deranged point of view. 'Who's treating you, Harry?' she asked hastily.

'Dr Noble. He doesn't call it treatment. He just wants me to talk.'

Ruth vaguely remembered having met the earnest young man at an informal drinks party for the staff when she first arrived. He held mildly controversial views about mental illness, she seemed to recall; he had asserted for instance that, strictly speaking, it didn't exist.

'Actually I'm to be discharged fairly soon,' Harry admitted, 'but I'll still be coming as an outpatient. I think Dr Noble wants to write about my life. My case, I should say. I don't mind. As long as I can go on working here. I say "work" – it's more like a holiday for me, more like a new beginning—' He stopped himself with an apologetic smile and padded off with his bucket and mop.

Mikey had finished fiddling with his jagged sand-circle. He was standing at the edge, staring at the bean-bag. As soon as Ruth came up to him, he began to speak:

'A littlun goes into the dark. A littlun sinks into the hole. The singularity waits. It squashes littluns ... it hurts and hurts. It's nothing ... everything ... nothing ... every—'

He ran a few paces to the right and back again. His face was grave and pale, and he trembled.

'It's worse than any ... thing. Light ... stuck ... stuck in ... dark. No power left. Horrorizons put light ... in prison. They punish light. Nothing escapes. It's a big mess ... all mess.'

He put a hesitant foot into the circle and half-turned towards Ruth, his eyes still fixed on the bean-bag at the circle's centre. Yiaou wobbled in his outstretched hand. 'Take Yiaou. Yiaou goes away. He can't carry a littlun. A littlun's too heavy ... too messive. Yiaou wants light to come out. When light comes out, Earth burns up ... all gone. Light can't come out. Take Yiaou. He can live with biguns. A littlun doesn't want him. No more Yiaou. Never.'

The gist of his speech seemed as usual to be the impossibility of escape from the black hole, either for the 'littlun' or for the 'light' — his repressed feelings, presumably. But Mikey's apparent desire to relinquish Yiaou was a disturbing development: it was as though he wished to preserve the small gains he had made, embodied in the stuffed cat, by leaving it outside the event horizon. At the same time, his adamant rejection of Yiaou signalled his deep desire to keep him.

'Why don't you hang on to Yiaou for a while?' Ruth suggested, sounding more casual than she felt. She did not dare to put it more strongly — any expression of preference on her part was bound to push him towards an opposite course of action. 'I think he wants to go with you. Look, he's smiling. He's saying "Please, take me into the black hole, Mikey." Yiaou likes you very much. He'll look after you. You'll be all right.'

Mikey seemed to hesitate. He stood astride the grim horrorizon like a tiny Colossus. He sneaked a glance or two at Yiaou and then, apparently satisfied, drew his other foot heavily over the boundary of sand and settled himself on the bean-bag. Both he and Yiaou stayed there, utterly withdrawn and deaf to all outside suggestions for most of the day.

At five o'clock there was a power cut. Without lights and with the evening advanced by the overcast sky, the Unit was darker in the daytime than the children had ever seen it. They became excited and, in one or two cases, unruly. Classes in the schoolroom were discontinued; candles and oil lamps were lit. Kevin the Wolf let out a baleful howl. Mikey made no response to Ruth's questions, called out from beyond the horrorizon. He was a collapsed heap in the bean-bag.

At ten minutes past five power was restored by the hospital's private generator. Mikey became animated. His right arm shot out in front of him, as if of its own accord, with Yiaou agitating on the end of it. His body rose painfully from the bag and heaved itself on to the floor. Mikey stood up and took off all his clothes. His movements were very deliberate and slow; his bony frame was juddering under the strain of massive invisible forces; his unseeing eyes were huge and dark.

He began to walk around the bean-bag, hauling one heavy foot after the other, gradually gathering speed. His walk increased to a run and then to a mad dash. He let out a single scream. It went through Ruth like a sword, jarring her heart. The whole room fell silent. Mikey went on running, arms flailing. His circle was so tight and his speed so great that he appeared to be moving at an impossibly acute angle to the ground. The faster he ran, the wider his circular path grew. Inch by inch, with every circuit, he spiralled outwards towards the vicious points of the sand-circle. 'DANGER,' he screamed. 'PLODE.'

The other counsellors stood in a group, transfixed by the performance. Their children were dotted about the room, subdued and temporarily forgotten. Kevin the Silent jabbered a few incomprehensible syllables as his namesake, the Wolf, worried his ankle. Dr Frieling, who had come in when the lights went out, was frozen in the middle of the room; only his eyes moved, following the little vivid shape as it flashed around.

Ruth was in agony. She darted to and fro on the edge of the horrorizon, wringing her hands and willing Mikey with all her strength to go faster, faster than fast, faster than light. It was all she could do to stop herself from kicking through the sand and dragging him out. Only the fear of destroying him prevented her – she could see in her mind's eye some frightful annihilating collision like matter and anti-matter.

He ran without flagging for twenty minutes, until he had edged out to the perimeter like a rider on the wall of death. At every circuit now, it seemed he must break through; but at the last moment he was deflected, doomed to run and run with his left foot an unerring fraction of an inch away from the jaws of sand. Barely a foot away – a light year away – Ruth wavered on the brink of the black hole.

'*Yiaou*,' Mikey cried. '*Yiaou – ow – ow – ow*', like a siren. He was wearing down, losing velocity. Only a supreme effort was keeping him glued to the rim. The slightest falter would send him spinning and crashing back to the bean-bag where he would collapse on himself, implode into nothingness under the crush of supergravity.

His eyes were screwed shut now. His circuits were erratic, unstable. He frantically windmilled his arms in the attempt to keep up speed. His naked body was sparkling with sweat.

'*Mikey*.' Ruth couldn't hold back her horrified shout.

'Blind, blind, blind,' wailed the little boy. '*Yiaou can't see*.'

'Here, Mikey. Here, here, here, *here*.' Ruth fired the words like flares into the darkness. As he drew level with her, Mikey uttered an inhuman cry.

'Yiiaouaououou.'

The floppy yellow shape flew out of his hand and struck Ruth full in the face, bringing tears to her eyes. Carried forward by the momentum of his throw, Mikey was hurled flat on to the horrorizon where he lay like a doll impaled on its jagged edge. His mouth was open, gasping; his eyes were still tightly shut.

'Come on, Mikey,' commanded Ruth. He reached out with his arms and clawed himself forward, dragging his belly over the sand.

'Come *on*.' She hovered over him, not daring to touch him, fanning his face with Yiaou. He pulled himself across the floor like a climber on a sheer cliff-face. The sand was under his thighs, his arms, his feet. He kicked out feebly, scattering the grains to left and right, and went limp.

Ruth quickly snatched him up. His floppiness was shocking. She thought: He's dead. Holy Mother of God. *Dead*. But he wasn't floppy like a dead thing. Mikey opened his eyes slowly, and blinked in the light. He was floppy like a baby. He was all there in her lap, exhausted, relaxed, incarnate. His face puckered. An alien noise came out of his mouth. Ruth couldn't recognise it at first. It was so strange because it was so normal: Mikey was crying.

He wept for two hours. Ruth had never seen such tears. They poured out of him, ploughing down his skin, soaking her clothes. His whole body seemed to bleed huge salt drops on to the one great wound that was his life. When the last sobs had died away she carried him to his bed, marvelling at how soft and yielding in her arms he was. His long eyelashes, glued into starry points, drooped with fatigue. As she bent to kiss him, he plucked at her sleeve and murmured out of his half-sleep. She put her ear close to his mouth.

'Mummy,' he whispered.

'Yes, darling, I'm here.' But Mikey was asleep.

SEVEN

DOROTHY was sitting up straight in bed, watching television. She pressed a button on the remote-control device and the picture changed from a studio discussion on some political nonsense to a commercial break. She wondered if any of the advertisements were Rex's. He didn't like to talk about his work any more. She couldn't blame him – what did she know about the industry? She had spent less than a year in it, and then only as a secretary. She remembered very little about her work. But she did remember the friendliness of her colleagues and the way everyone was on Christian-name terms, even her boss. She drank wine with them at open tables on the colourful Covent Garden piazza until the sun went down. The men would pull light expensive sweaters over their bright shirts and take her to a bistro or trattoria. She had never eaten Chinese food before, or Greek, or Thai, or even American hamburgers; it was heaven. She imagined it must be like life in California, but better, and light years away from the grainy black-and-white B-feature that was Liverpool.

She had made dinner that evening for eight-thirty, anticipating Rex's pleasure when he saw that it was his favourite Lancashire hotpot. She had taken off the apron that protected her dress – he hated her to look sloppy at dinner – and sat down with a drink to wait for him. Just after nine, she had tried to save the hotpot by adding water to it. She didn't blame Rex for not phoning; she knew how hectic it could get.

At ten she threw the hotpot in the dustbin and wondered why they had ever moved into the house. They were not allowed to see Mikey, so what was the point of being near him? She had hoped that the move might lay his ghost; but he haunted the new house as he had the old, like a dead person but worse, because in time you could forget the dead.

Dorothy pressed another button and the television clicked off. Perhaps Rex wasn't coming back tonight. Perhaps things weren't going well for him. He had been rather irritable and morose recently, inclined to retire to his study. She could sometimes hear the whisper of his video recorder playing behind the heavy oak door. She would have to try harder to please him; she had a lot to thank him for. Settling herself back on her pillows, Dorothy remembered how Rex had saved her, that first summer in London.

She had known that it might take a little time before she mastered the fine print of her environment. She even invented a mysterious and becoming smile for her lips, to counter her uncertainty. In exuberant moods, she would still fling herself forward into the next hour, and the next, as if she could get ahead of herself and force the future to surrender its hourly expected treasure. But as September drew to a close the open-air evenings acquired a chilly edge; the wine hurt her head; the city dust pressed on her eyes. The future began to cast over her a retrogressive shadow holding nothing but foreboding. She could not tell whether people were joking when they spoke to her. Her speech became stilted with anxiety over what her next words might be. Silences were loaded with potential gaffes; laughter, with potential mockery. She had to curb her mind in case it caught her unawares with some appalling thought, like the man who had suddenly reared out of the bushes in the park and opened his long coat.

Rex had saved her. He arrived one day just when everyone was flagging. He greeted them as graciously as a prince, lighting them up one at a time with a touch on the shoulder or arm. The company revived, regrouped around him, broke into laughter. He sipped his wine and smiled, lounging in his seat as lucky and sleek as a cat with lives to spare. Dorothy was entranced. She knew from the pages of *Campaign* how famous and artistic he was. But when he addressed her, kindly and without witticisms, he deprecated what he called his craft with a wave of his artist's hands and preferred to hear her views on serious movie directors. She could scarcely speak for the beauty of his profile and the subtle dizzying perfume he exuded. When he asked her out, it was both the most undreamt-of and the most natural thing in the world.

Their dates were staged in soft focus, a dream of candlelight, soft music and effortless rides in Rex's convertible. Waking in the mornings she was surprised to find the previous evening blurred at the edges; sometimes she had even forgotten the name of the film they'd seen, which she was sure would be scored on her heart for ever. When it was time to lose the virginity which so enchanted Rex, the event was as sensual as any of his commercials. Dorothy was quick to exonerate his craftmanship and blame herself for her disappointment. When she became pregnant, it was agreed that they were not marrying for the sake of the child.

Dorothy thought she could hear Rex's key in the front door. She strained her ears, unaware of the muscles tensing in her neck. Yes, it was Rex's key. She followed his footsteps up the stairs. When he opened the door, she was ready with a smile.

'Hard day, darling?'

'Mmm.'

'Poor darling. Have you eaten? I'll knock you up something hot.' She made as if to spring out of bed.

'No, no. Don't move. I had a bite at the office.' He threw off his jacket and tossed it into the armchair. 'I'm tired. Shall I put Cassandra out?'

'I've already done it. Come to bed.'

Rex took off his shoes and padded to the bathroom across the passage. Dorothy could just hear the thoroughness of his ablutions, and her heart sank slightly. She hoped he was too tired to want her tonight. In the beginning, she had made love to Rex over and over again, as if by dint of repetition she could dissolve the invisible hymen which separated her from the gorgeous energies that seemed to emanate from him, like his intoxicating perfume. But as she strove to give herself over to him, to lose herself in the warm obliterating foam which surged up her spine, the face of the creature on the seventh stair would rise like a bubble in front of her starry eyes and regard her coldly. Then, before she could pin it down, it always burst; and the foam subsided, undischarged. Left with a sense of airy disembodiment, she found herself wishing that Rex were somehow heavier and more piercing, that he might root her to the ground. She told herself that marriage would supply the necessary gravity; it seemed ungrateful to admit that it hadn't. She put out the light on her side of the bed and closed her eyes.

Rex's reflection frowned at him out of the bathroom mirror. He examined the smooth face for blemishes and then washed it thoroughly with herbal soap. He patted it dry with a clean towel and gently rubbed moisturising cream into the skin.

After a row with Andrea he had stormed out of her flat. She'd had one long lunch too many. 'It was business' was all she'd say. He knew what sort of business publishing folk got up to over lunch – they fancied themselves too much to talk real business. They liked to pretend that theirs wasn't a racket. Andrea was in charge of illustrated non-fiction, the glossy sort, which she nevertheless continued boldly to call books. Rex's guess was that she had fallen under the spell of some hang-dog deadbeat academic – she had a soft spot for them – who was out to make a bob on the side by foisting on her some half-baked worn-out idea for a book, known in the trade as a thrilling concept. 'The Home Genetic Engineer', probably; or 'Egyptology without Tears'; or 'Aristotle in Action' – but, no, classical scholars took long views and knew human nature. They made good admen, selling cigarettes and soap powder, and buying rare first editions on the proceeds. Publishing people wouldn't last two seconds in the real world, where there was no room for self-deception. Rex wondered if he should go into publishing and see how they stood up to the truth. He would never fill a 'Photography Handbook' with pictures of nudes, and then pretend that it was selling on its textual merits.

Andrea was sexy. She had a way of getting under your skin. But she was a mess – all that wild hair, all those loose clothes hiding her lovely rangy body. The row wasn't a bad thing perhaps; it'd bring her to her senses. She'd be on the dog and bone first thing, begging him to come back.

Rex brushed every tooth methodically, rinsed his mouth out and reached for the dental floss. He smiled boyishly at the mirror. A twinge of pain indicated that another gum was receding. Still, he was in good nick, considering. Better nick than Penny's husband, Hugh. Funny, her introducing them like that. She must've wanted to show off her tall well-heeled Hugh Masters – to show she didn't care that Rex had left her high and dry all those years ago. But she cared all right. Oh yes, she remembered every detail of the affair and hid them jealously from Hugh. Her merry peal of laughter rang in his ears. He drew the strand of dental floss angrily through his teeth. Poor old Hugh, stuck with that tart. Rex swilled his mouth out with a double dose of mouthwash and, feeling purified and righteous, returned to the bedroom.

Suddenly, the sight of Dorothy lying there as neat and sweet as an iced cake was almost intolerable. He was seized by his old longing to devour her somehow; and yet he could already taste the bitterness of failure. The closer he came to possessing her, the farther she seemed to recede from him. Next time, next time, he told himself in the early days. But again he failed to embrace and absorb her otherness, until his unsatisfied desire grew wild and limitless. She never gave up some essential reserve in their love-making, and it both dismayed and excited him. He thrust against it, harder and deeper, but never quite broke through. Frigid bitch, he thought but never said – in truth, he knew she wasn't. 'She's *driving* me to other women. It's *her* fault.' But he always returned to her, like an addict.

He was not sorry when she became pregnant. A foetus would breach the wall on his behalf, he felt, and transfix her where he had failed, at her centre of gravity. Marriage followed as a matter of course: the last nail was driven in by which he would have her and keep her and settle it. However, marriage settled nothing and her pregnancy didn't pin down Dorothy at all – indeed, she hardly acknowledged it. Rex decided from the beginning that his son would be a great scientist and bring the dark corners of the universe to light. When it became clear that the boy had malfunctioned, Rex's first irrational thought was that Dorothy had exacted on him some obscure revenge.

She continued to receive him dutifully, her compliant eyes puzzled and unreproachful. He continued his losing battle to tie her down for good. More than any other woman, Dorothy could dissolve underneath him in the dark, changing shape and slipping through his fingers like quicksilver. He held her tightly, pumping himself into arid exhaustion; but his concupiscence burnt on, unsatisfied. And, afterwards, he would catch her staring at the ceiling, gazing at something he could not see or even guess at. 'What are you thinking?' he demanded. 'Nothing,' she would murmur. 'Nothing at all.' Then, unable to bear the sight of her floating away from him – so passive, so separate – he would turn away and close his eyes lest he do her some violence.

Dorothy felt the slight shock of Rex's body as he climbed into bed beside her. She heard the click of the light being switched off. She felt a gentle tug on her silky hair and, understanding the signal, obediently turned over on to her back. As her husband pressed down on her in the darkness, she averted her head slightly from the effeminate smell of his face-cream.

Carol burst into the room.

'Come quickly!'

Ruth was half-asleep in her armchair, snatching a brief rest before it was time to give Mikey his bath and put him to bed. She sat up immediately.

'What is it? Mikey?'

'Come *on.*'

The two women hurried downstairs. Carol led her to the schoolroom where a number of the older children were standing nervously against the wall. On the opposite side of the room Dr Frieling stood with his hands in his pockets, contemplating the wreckage of the Unit's television set. Among the pieces of splintered cabinet and broken glass, Mikey was crouched, growling. A shattered chair lay beside him and, next to the chair, Yiaou.

'What happened?' Ruth asked breathlessly.

Dr Frieling blinked several times behind his spectacles.

'An interesting development,' he mused. 'Mikey has taken a chair to our television. Why would he do that? There's something important at the bottom of this.'

'*Grrrrr*,' went Mikey.

'Mikey! What's the matter?' asked Ruth.

The boy snatched Yiaou off the floor and pointed him at the two adults. His eyes were blazing with rage.

'Yiaou hates biguns. Hates them. He'll jump on them. He'll tear them to pieces. GRR. He's wild and fierce and ... mad. He'll tear the biguns into little bits and stuff them in the toilet. And pull the chain. HA HA HA HA. Biguns are all rubbish and shit. They torture littluns and bury them ... bury them alive. Yiaou knows, Yiaou won't forget, Yiaou'll rip the biguns up. HAHAHAH.' Yiaou darted menacingly forward. Both adults were taken aback by the power of Mikey's demonic laughter.

After a great deal of patient coaxing, Ruth finally calmed him down. She put him straight to bed and consoled him with honey, his current passion. She dipped her fingers into the jar and he licked the honey off them, making small contented noises in the back of his throat. Every day now his mouth lost some of its fearful rigidity — as well as licking, he had mastered the nibbling of chocolate and was well on the way to sucking, perhaps the most dangerous of oral acts because of its associations with the treacherous breast. He was close to becoming a baby again or, rather, the baby he had never been.

Ruth was reminded of his statements about time in relation to the black hole. She had seen at once how apt his description was, vis-à-vis himself, of time standing still at the event horizon. But she had conveniently overlooked the additional claim that time went backwards inside the black hole. Now, watching Mikey regress daily to an increasingly infantile state, it was clear that the claim was equally apposite and (uttered in the context of his former condition) prophetic.

It struck her that in the unimaginable realm beyond the event horizon the roles of time and space were reversed. In the ordinary world space allowed free movement in any direction, while time was limited to an inexorable linear progression. Inside the black hole, space became the inescapable straight line leading to the heart of the singularity, while time became unbounded, allowing free movement backwards and even (why not?) forwards – Mikey's assertion concerning its backward flow was in itself a premonition of his future development, the need to regress before he could advance.

As he relaxed under the soothing spell of the honey, Mikey grew abject over his outburst.

'A bigun mustn't like littluns.... They're a bad lot,' he began. By telling Ruth that she mustn't like him because he was bad, he was in effect voicing his fear that she would reject him because he had shown his true feelings. 'Littluns get angry .... They do terrible things. They must be punished, crash, bang. Not Yiaou. The littlun. The littlun is little and mean and beastly. Yiaou's a good boy, he doesn't hurt. The littlun does hurting. He hurts and hurts.'

It was brave of Mikey to confess that the anger was his and not Yiaou's. Clearly, loyalty to his cat had prevailed over fear of retaliation for venting his rage. But, more significantly, he was able on reflection to distinguish between himself and Yiaou. At the moment of his outburst, Yiaou was the externalisation of his anger; and the anger was so great that it had turned the stuffed toy into a huge and fierce tiger, overwhelmingly powerful compared to his own tiny helpless self.

'I like all little boys,' Ruth reassured him. 'Especially you, Mikey. You're my boy. You can be as angry as you like; it doesn't matter to me. I'll always love you; I'll always look after you. You're safe, safe....' So, as often as Mikey obsessively insisted on his wickedness, Ruth repeated her guarantees, granting him the freedom, if he wished, to rage without reprisals against the world until he was empty of spleen and ready to begin again.

She suddenly remembered the doctor's words about the television. 'Something important,' he'd said.

'Why did you break the television, Mikey?'

Mikey was curled up happily in her lap; but the moment the question struck him he seized up.

'No,' he screamed. 'No.' He stuffed Yiaou's paws into his ears. Gently but firmly Ruth removed them. The doctor was right: the key to Mikey's release could well lie with events surrounding a television.

'What did you see on television, Mikey? Tell me.'

'No, no, no,' sobbed the boy. 'A littlun didn't see him. No one saw him. He traps people in the telly. They die. No one sees.'

'Did he trap you in the telly, Mikey? You can tell me. It's OK.'

The boy's eyes were tightly shut. Yiaou was performing weird manoeuvres in front of his mouth.

'María.'

The name was just a whisper. Yiaou's movements became frantic. Suddenly Mikey sat up, shaking. 'No,' he shouted. He tried to climb off Ruth's lap; he seemed about to relapse into a spinning attack. Ruth gambled on restraining him for once.

'Tell me. What happened on the television?'

The blood drained from the little boy's face; his eyes, fixed blindly on the ceiling, were bright with delirium.

'He's got a probe in his hand. He's got a stick in his hand. He's stabbing, stab-stabbing. She's dying dying.... NO.... *María*.' He clung to Ruth for a second and then went limp. 'She's dead,' he said tonelessly. 'No one saw.' His eyes were glassy.

'You love María very much, don't you?' she prompted. There was no reply. She caressed his face and hair until he curled up, foetus-like, and fell asleep.

Ruth was intrigued. Could it be that she had been given a glimpse into the catastrophe which had tipped Mikey over the brink and beyond recall? Had he perhaps been watching a murder on television when María left? The Spanish au pair girl was at the heart of the matter. He must have loved her – he had improved (or, at least, not deteriorated) while she was with him. What was her connection with the smashing of Mr Ballantine's television and tapes, and now the Unit's? Why did he think she was dead? She had only left the Ballantine's employ, suddenly.

It'll be strange going back to number one, South Road. Oh, don't worry. I was ready to go back before now. Yes, thanks, Doctor. It's all arranged: I'll continue to report for work at the Unit on a daily basis – what a blessing! – and I'll come up here to see you every other day. Yes, between four and five. No, I won't hesitate – I even have your phone number. But I don't think there'll be a repeat performance. Besides, I'll be much too busy among the children to get into trouble, and in the evenings ... well, I have the wireless and one or two new prophecies to write up. Yes, I'll keep them to myself!

There's a boy at the Unit, a ... special child, who is known to me. At least, I keep thinking I've met him before. I feel that ... I feel.... It doesn't matter. It's an honour and a happiness to serve him, albeit in insignificant ways. Have you met Miss Maier? Oh, you'd remember if you had. A lady of *striking* beauty and grace. And much else besides. She's a great distraction to the performance of my duties. Frankly, I've been wondering if she might accept an invitation to tea at number one, South Road. Perhaps it's too soon to presume on our brief acquaintance. It doesn't feel too soon.

Thank you, yes. I'm filled with a sense of great ... great well being. You must take some of the credit, Doctor, although most of it is owing to my new job. I wish I'd been fired from the Invoice Office earlier! If I'd *known* that I'd find, well ... Mikey ... and so on. Anyway, it looks as if my troubles are behind me now, where they belong, like Satan; I'm even strong enough to tell you what happened to me on the train to Par and my subsequent encounter with— Well, you'll see. That is, if you want me to go on ...? Right-o. Here goes.

Out of the corner of my eye I fancied that someone was looking at me through the glass door of the compartment. If it had been someone looking for a seat, I would have taken no notice. What set me trembling was the certainty that this presence in the corridor was taking a *personal interest* in me ... an interest that was far from harmless.

I looked round sharply. My newly mended stomach was in turmoil. But whatever it was had moved out of sight. I thought there might be a gangster aboard, looking to rob innocent passengers. I was an easy prey – he couldn't know that Father had only given me a few pence for the journey. I was sorely afraid of leaving the compartment; but my fear of being alone, plus the need to warn my fellow passengers, was greater.

There wasn't a soul in the corridor. Yet there was ... something. Something worse. It may have been my imagination, Doctor, but I could've sworn there was a definite lingering presence, like a dangerous scent, both familiar and frightening, which I could not pin down. It wasn't a gangster after all, I was sure of that, because he would at worst inspire the normal run of fear.

I bolted to the next compartment and took refuge with a man of the cloth, who, though harmless, gave me the sort of look which prevented me from asking him if he, too, had sensed something amiss.

Well. You're thinking: So what? You're thinking that this event is nothing to get excited about. I beg to differ. There was plenty to get excited about when I reached Par and the meaning of the visitation was suggested to me. Furthermore, it might help you to understand what led me to my attack and why I'm here now, about which my lips are sealed, I'm sorry, because my mental and general well being is still too fragile to risk opening that particular can of worms.

I passed the remainder of the journey in great despondency, thinking of the night when I waited in vain for Alice Watts outside the dark pub, and feeling weak and sore from the recent operation. The famous coastal stretch from Dawlish to Teignmouth – I'd so been looking forward to it – had been laid waste by the Luftwaffe; the old architecture of Plymouth was in ruins. All was dust and ashes.

At Par station I missed the bus for the convalescent home. Typical. The evening heat was oppressing me and the sky on the horizon was a sick yellow with purple hammerhead clouds on top. The walk was only three miles, but that seemed a lot in my downcast condition and with my heavy suitcase. I'd trudged about a mile over the rough Cornish road when lightning started to open cracks in the blackening sky. The thunder sounded like the distant rumble of the Russian guns. I was caught in open countryside, rocky and barren except for two trees at a crossing of the ways. I couldn't remember whether or not lightning struck more often in the open than under a tree. But the sudden cloudburst decided me: I ran for the two trees.

A man stood under one of them. He must have been there some time, for I never saw him on the road. He was dressed in sombre clothes and a black hat. His build was stocky and his complexion dark, with thick eyebrows that met over his eyes. They were also dark and somewhat penetrating, appearing to have hardly any whites to them. I nodded at him, you know, as you do. In the aftermath of a thunderclap, he spoke – very deep and loud like a Welsh choir:

'Howl ye; for the day of the LORD is at hand.'

Whether he was addressing me or the storm I couldn't tell. But I cannot describe to you the effect his demeanour and speech had on me. I'd read those words from Isaiah many times. Never had I suspected that they could be uttered as though they were true. I might just as well have been struck by the lightning.

The man was a travelling preacher. He said he had renounced his name when he became an instrument of the Lord. As we stood beneath the crash of rain in the tall trees, he preached me a sermon more stirring than the thunder. The truth contained within me was unlocked and given a voice. My life was turned around. He told me about the Rapture.

And I confess, Doctor, that under the trees in the pelting rain I could not forbear opening my heart to the fierce and gentle man, telling him about the visitation on the train and my fear of insanity and then, in a great flood, about the harshness of the world that thrusts its prongs into you at every turn, about the hard hearts and chattering tongues of men and women, about the God-awful camp and its matchstick inhabitants from whom the Word made Flesh had hidden its Face. I wept then, for I was very young. What was to become of me, I asked him, who has no defences in this world, who suffers nothing but abuse and rebuffs and the fear of rebuffs, who can only wait to be struck down on the street or in a railway carriage by some unseen watcher?

The preacher offered me comfortable words, saying that I am fortunate; yes, *fortunate*, because I am chosen for a witness to the truth;

and, being alone, I may more easily take the Lord as a friend and companion, who will suffer all spite with me and through me. Then he revealed how in these last days the Powers, Thrones, Dominions are waxing mightily and bending all their evil intent to the corruption of the righteous whom they dread like red-hot pincers. And the righteous, in turn, cannot help but draw these spirits of iniquity down on their heads; for the spirits must be made manifest in order to be judged by the Son of Man when He comes again in clouds of glory.

Thus we, the righteous, are in mortal jeopardy from the torments and deceits of the evil spirits. But if we remain steadfast in the face of their onslaughts, calling on the name of Christ, then we will be snatched up in the heavens at the eleventh hour, and saved.

Yes, I'll tell you what he told me, if you like. It's no secret — far from it: it's down in black and white for all to see, if they have the eyes to see. I wish ... I *wish* I could give you a sermon such as the one I received. Then you might be called to repentance. I mean no offence, Doctor; it's just that I fear for your immortal soul. Don't get me wrong — I know you're a good man, far above me; I can personally testify to that. But is it *enough*? Goodness is not the end of the story. Unless the Lord Jesus Christ is lodged in your heart on a permanent basis, then your salvation must always remain in doubt, as mine is now.

Anyway. I can't tell you about the Rapture as it ought to be told, as a revelation amidst thunder and lightning. I might have done once, but now I'm too tired and worn down and, yes, abandoned by the Holy Spirit whose power used to fill me so strongly that I was near shattered like a crystal glass.

I'll try to give you the general idea, just the bare bones, as it were, for your files. And not in the hope that it'll do any good.

12 March

Mikey's tantrums continue. But they are fewer and less violent each day. Mostly he just emits a series of piercing screams for up to 45 mins at a time. Hard on everybody. But at least he rarely breaks things — there's certainly been nothing like a repetition of the TV incident.

I'm still very distressed by this morning's little fracas. I doubt that it will help to write it down — it won't bring back my dear cameo brooch. I never did establish whose portrait it was. Papa always claimed that it was his beloved Mozart's profile; but I think that Mama treasured it because it looked like Papa's profile — and because he gave it to her. She never admitted this. Perhaps I only think that she was reminded of Papa because *I* was reminded of him. But she did give it to me *before* she died so as to be sure that I would get it and keep it, like a secret between us. The last Maier heirloom. It was madness to wear it downstairs, I suppose, only Carol, Adrian and the others – even Dr F. ! – have remarked more than once on how well I'm looking, etc., these days and it must've gone to my head. It *is* true, I realise, that I've been taking more trouble recently with make-up, hair, etc. I suppose, at heart, it's to look nice for Mikey now that he's taking a little more notice of me. Still doesn't actually *look* at me, of course; but I feel I ought to look my best in case he does. (Who am I kidding? Besides, for God's sake, Ruth, he's only nine years old!)

It all began when M. ordered a second helping of scrambled eggs at breakfast. I filled his plate and he promptly threw it on the floor with that horrible manic laugh of his. I was, typically, just congratulating myself on being so patient when he grabbed the brooch, tore it off my blouse and brandished it like a war trophy. My mistake was begging him to give it back. If I hadn't, he might have lost interest in it; but I couldn't stop myself in time. He threw it on the floor and stamped on it, glancing slyly in my direction as he did so. At that moment I knew what it was like to be one of those baby-battering mothers. I should have been honoured that he has chosen me to bear the brunt of his rage; in fact, I nearly slaughtered the little bugger.

Maybe I *am* being too soft on him – *no*, I must grin and bear everything because I represent everything to him, the mother that he longs for and fears. I'm on trial for his life. He has to be sure that I value him more than my possessions, and I *failed*. It would've been better if I had smacked him because, in the event, with the brooch lying in pieces on the floor, I was (of all things) *cold* towards him. Worse than showing anger. Unforgivable. By withdrawing from him, I confirmed his worst fears.

I became conscious today of having judged Mikey's parents. I've been pretending that I didn't judge them because Dr F. told me not to. But in my heart I felt I had a right. In my heart I have done Dorothy Ballantine a grave injustice. I mean: whatever happened originally between her and Mikey no doubt happened unconsciously. She didn't intend him to turn out like this – quite the reverse. Thereafter how could she possibly treat him normally? How can I ever remotely guess what struggles she endured, both with her own guilt, and with a child who bore no resemblance to a living being, let alone a son? The loss of my precious brooch has shown me that I would have done no better, and probably a lot worse in her circumstances.

Mikey and I were reconciled by bath-time, thank God. A narrow squeak. He claims he can 'do swimming', a thing Yiaou can't do, apparently. He continues to withdraw some of the omnipotence he projects on to Yiaou and is beginning to believe in (?) his own ability. Yiaou is still the chief agent of his tantrums, however. Mikey conceives of his anger as being a vast force outside himself and in whose grasp he is powerless. (But, then, aren't we all 'beside ourselves' with rage at time, like when we lose brooches . . . ?) If it is true that he dimly discerns a difference between himself and Yiaou, the same is not true of me. I think he 'sees' me as a kind of all-pervading ambiguous presence which sustains his fragile self, and threatens it. He directs his anger at me as the hated and desired one; he both shuts me out and tests me to see if I'm safe to let in. I must tell myself all the time that it's nothing *personal*. More important, I mustn't swamp him when he asserts himself just because it's easier and I'm in the habit; nor must I distance myself too soon so that he feels abandoned. Tricky. I wonder what Mama and Papa would have made of him. I suspect that neither of them would have thought twice about the bloody brooch. Today is the 8th anniversary of Papa's death.

Leo had been buried in the local Anglican churchyard. Ruth was surprised at the number of people who came; and, since Anna had preferred to stay at home, she felt a little left out among the former pupils, teachers and nuns. She was moved by the hymns they sang at the graveside.

At her mother's funeral a month later – Anna had stipulated cremation – Ruth wondered, as she watched the coffin nose through the curtains towards the flames, whether she would be disposed of like that; and later, waiting to collect the ashes, she wondered – now that her parents were subject to judgement – how they would judge her. She was quite amused to find that she believed in an afterlife.

She had just been offered a prestigious post as assistant headmistress of a large comprehensive school. She had also just come to the end of her third affair (what else could she call it?). She was still friendly with her two former lovers and it gave her pleasure to know that she would remain friendly with her latest. Each of them had proposed marriage. Ruth had difficulty explaining that, although she was fond of them – loved them even – she could not reciprocate their love at the level from which it was offered. The three intelligent sensitive men regretted the lack of mutuality but said they would settle for whatever she could give and accept her as she was. Ruth still said no; she didn't want to be accepted as she was. She wanted to be taken out of herself and transformed into the radiant person she glimpsed during the delicious fulfilment of sex – which, to her surprise, was what she missed most after the decisive parting. At the active height of the affairs she lost weight, enjoyed buying pretty clothes and sang loudly in the bath, rejoicing in the health of her lungs. But as soon as her lovers began to press her to make the relationship permanent, she forgot the words of the songs and caught herself making snacks in the small hours.

At the time of Anna's death, Ruth had been under psychoanalysis for eighteen months. Privately she marvelled at how deep-seated her neurosis must be to strike at the twin drives of life itself – eating and breathing. But, despite her businesslike dredging-up of forgotten mud, nothing dramatic had so far happened. No dybbuks had come gibbering at her out of dark corners; instead, there had been a slow, often painful, integrating of the more superficial divisions within herself. For example, she was now completely at ease with her Jewishness, which after all had never threatened her; she had merely identified it with some deeper fear – and need – which had driven her to take refuge in the Church.

Her acute charming analyst suffered from loneliness after a messy divorce. He had taken to dropping by her flat in the evenings. He told her his dreams while she cooked him lamb chops and potatoes carefully mashed to eliminate the lumps that made his gorge rise. Later on, he brought wine and flowers. Ruth had begun to think that she had best give up her treatment.

When she opened the urn and peeped at the ashes, she realised as never before how little she had appreciated her mother. She had tended towards pity, comparing Mama's limited domestic existence unfavourably with her own wide-ranging and varied life. Looking back, Mama appeared as someone of great substance, someone strangely accomplished in whom essence and existence were at one. Was it possible that in her ill-lit kitchen, gazing through the steam, Mama had lighted upon some eternal truth? 'One chops the wood, the other does the grunting,' she was fond of saying. Ruth wondered if all her fine activity might not be just so much grunting.

She carried the urn to the churchyard where Leo was buried. It was bitterly cold. A freezing sleet raked the grey headstones. In a self-consciously symbolic gesture, she sprinkled the greyish-white powder on the black, still freshly turned earth of the grave. Her parents' chosen mode of funeral had a kind of symmetry: the ethereal Leo rooted at last in the earth while Anna, his opposite, was volatilised into spirit. Grief-struck, she knelt clumsily by her father and yearned to sink into the earth beside him. The wind, stirring the strewn ashes, stirred in Ruth her old dread of being dragged down into the dark.

In a single exquisite moment, she knew how her longing for the peace and equilibrium of the tomb was indistinguishable from her fear of its smothering nothingness. Her chronic emptiness could only be assuaged by a return to the all-nourishing earth; her chronic horror of suffocation could only be allayed by a flight from the same annihilating end. What was her addiction to eating but a secret collaboration with gravity? What were her 'asthma' attacks but a fear of being deprived of light and air? The message from the grave was: 'Life is at war with itself; there's no cure in this, or perhaps any other, world; live with it.'

The next day Ruth broke off her psychoanalysis and turned down the post as assistant headmistress. She wanted nothing more to do with the illusory consolations of the couch and the career-structure. She changed to a school with a bad reputation and avoided any promotion that moved her away from her first concern, the children, towards administration or specialist teaching. In the holidays she devoted herself to the disabled or delinquent. She never allowed herself the luxury of unhappiness. Happiness was a virtue to be exercised; she practised hard at it, as she had once practised scales on the piano, and honed herself to receive the great dissonant gift of joy should it descend in a red-gold nimbus of trumpets and cymbals. There were no more affairs. She did not relish solitude, but suspected the easy pleasure of intimacy. Nor did she deny the possibility of marriage; it was simply a question of the right person, and he either happened or he didn't.

Occasionally she went to Mass, but without participating in the Eucharist. She enjoyed the ceremony for its own sake, expecting nothing from it. At first she thought of her mother cooking for the saints and her father singing praises with the angels; later, she stumbled on the pure pleasure of abstraction and began to meditate on the conundrum of the Trinity, the Three-in-One and One-in-Three. She dwelt on beautiful rarefied words such as 'co-equal' and 'co-eternal'.

But once or twice, as she knelt in the wooden pew and let herself drift into undirected prayer, her eyes were darkened by a vision of blind impersonal forces without beginning or end which drove the dynamo of the universe from its smallest stone to its largest star. She saw how humans raised their heads out of the black flood for a brief gasping lifetime before being swept away like debris beyond the grave. Then she would hurriedly avert her gaze to more comfortable images – spotless snowfields and peaks, smooth glaciers – until her heartbeat slowed to its usual pace.

Waiting for a bus once on a clear summer's day, she saw the sky suddenly go taut and dark, and shift like a great lid about to press her down. Her chest tightened and she heard the old rattlesnake in her lungs. Glancing around wildly at the other people in the queue, she saw their faces screwed stiffly on to their heads like masks. An orange bolt of loneliness struck her out of the blue and sent the world spinning round until, gasping for air, she knew that if she keeled over she would never get up.

'Panic attacks,' diagnosed her doctor, an enlightened man who advised hypnosis instead of pills. Ruth took the pills and redoubled her efforts to do more and better.

An old adage kept tapping in her head. She didn't know where she'd heard it – from the nuns perhaps or, possibly, Mama. It said, more or less, that saving a single soul was like saving the entire world. The absurdity of the saying appealed to her; it was at the back of her mind when she applied to Dr Frieling for a job.

EIGHT

WE ARE in *the last days*. The Second Coming of Christ is at hand. There can be no doubt about this. I could recite scriptural evidence all night. I think I first knew it for certain when the Lord's own prophecy, as recorded in Saint Matthew, was fulfilled in nineteen forty-eight. On May the fifteenth, if memory serves. The date when the Jewish nation obtained their own parliament in Jerusalem. Christ referred to this specifically as the budding of the fig tree, the sign of his imminent Return.

You might say that quite a number of last days have elapsed since then; and I'll confess that I, too, was disappointed when, by nineteen fifty, the Son of Man had as yet failed to appear on the clouds of heaven with power and great glory. But, of course, I hadn't paid close enough attention to Saint Paul, who explains in both his epistles to Timothy how the last days will be characterised by a dire falling away from faith, with men 'giving heed to seducing spirits, and doctrines of devils, through the hypocrisy of men that speak lies, branded in their own conscience as with a hot iron; forbidding to marry, and commanding to abstain from meats'. And men will be 'lovers of self, lovers of money, boastful, haughty, railers, disobedient to parents, unthankful, unholy, without natural affection' – and much more. You'd have to be blind not to see that such conditions and such people are more in evidence every day and far more so than in nineteen forty-eight even.

103

Never in history has there been such a falling away. Sin is rife, false gospels are everywhere, the great mass of souls are unmindful of God and intent only on pleasuring themselves with unclean acts and playing football on the Sabbath.

At the same time, every rational person will admit that, while there has been the most appalling apostasy in my lifetime, and longer, the spirit of Antichrist has not had it *all* his own way – I need only cite the abolishing of slave labour, cock-fighting and all-day licensing hours, plus the building of hospitals and the improvements in the conditions of young chimney sweeps. So you will ask: what is preserving the world from wholesale dereliction and putrefaction? The answer is: *the salt of the earth*. Matthew chapter five, verse thirteen. Only those rare disciples who have retained their savour and fostered the spirit of God in their hearts are counterbalancing the preponderance of sin in the world. Their presence alone makes the Lord hesitate to stretch out His hand against the world, just as He was persuaded by Abraham to spare the city of Sodom for the sake of ten righteous men; and would have spared it, too, if He had found the ten instead of only one, namely Lot, who – significantly – fell into strong drink and lay with his daughters to preserve his seed.

And so a handful of disciples, the salt of the earth, are guardians of the Kingdom of Heaven, which, as we know, is 'like unto leaven, which a woman took, and hid in three measures of meal, till it was all leavened'. Many have taken this to mean that the world is going to be gradually converted by the gospel; but I urge you to remember what Christ says, namely: 'And this gospel of the Kingdom shall be preached in all the world for a witness unto all nations; and then shall the end come.' You see? He doesn't say that His preaching and the preaching of His disciples will *convert* the world, but that it is only to be for a *witness*; and witnesses are, and will be, rejected and persecuted. It took me years to learn this, many of them close to despair since I never to my knowledge succeeded in converting a single soul. But I never stopped witnessing and abounding in the works of the Lord. Anyway, it's small wonder that so few have comprehended correctly the order of events in the last days because it is truly a complex and sublime process. Saint Paul sums it up in his second epistle to the Thessalonians.

First, Jesus Christ is coming again. Secondly, He will not come until there is an initial falling away to reveal 'the man of sin', 'the son of perdition, who opposeth and exalteth himself above all that is called God'. Thirdly, although the 'mystery of iniquity doth already work', 'only he who now letteth will let until he be taken out of the way' – that's to say, only the righteous ones, the witnesses, 'letteth' or hinder the mystery of iniquity from bringing the whole earth to ruin. Fourthly, when these righteous witnesses are 'taken out of the way', 'then shall that Wicked be revealed'.

And yes, of course – you've guessed. The witnesses to the truth will be taken out of the way at *the Rapture*, which is nothing else than the gathering together unto Christ of His elect. *'For the Lord Himself shall descend from heaven, with a shout, with the voice of the archangel, and with the trump of God: and the dead in Christ shall rise first: then we that are alive, that are left, shall together with them be caught up in the clouds, to meet the Lord in the air: and so shall we ever be with the Lord.'* Whereupon the man of sin will come into his own for a time, and Woe to those who are left.

The usual claim – derived, I suppose, from the Revelation of Saint John – that there is to be one general resurrection of the dead, is hopelessly unscriptural. Even in Revelation, the Rapture is clearly intimated in the reference to two 'resurrections': the first is the 'resurrection', or Rapture, of the righteous, both dead and alive, who have not received the mark of the Beast. The same shall rule with Christ for a thousand years. The second resurrection will come only at the end of this period, when the book of life will be opened and *all* the dead raised and judged according to their works.

I ought to add a word of warning about Saint John's Beast, who is identical with the man of sin, son of perdition, that Wicked, etcetera. He is a very sinister customer who will rule after the Rapture and before Christ inaugurates the thousand years' peace. The lurid and laughable creature whom John describes, with seven heads and ten horns etcetera, is not to be taken literally but, rather, as what he is like inside. Outwardly he will look like you or me. Nor should his reign, lasting forty-two months, be counted by normal time. I've met people who thought that the old Kaiser was the Beast and so predicted that the First World War would end in February, nineteen eighteen – forty-two months after the start. It didn't end until November, of course. It only goes to show how naïve people can be. I am certain also that even Hitler wasn't the Beast. He had the satanic qualifications and tried to stage his own millennium with the Third Reich and so on, but he was not universally *welcomed* as the genuine article will be. For Christ came in His Father's name and was not received; but He hinted darkly that 'if another shall come in his own name, him ye will receive'. This Beast will counterfeit the true millennium so successfully by bringing economic security, freedom from war and so on that no one will notice its godlessness. The angel Gabriel gives an accurate description of him to Daniel, who, despite being a great prophet and interpreter of visions

105

and dark sentences himself, failed to understand because his vision belonged to a time so far in the future.

'In the latter time of their kingdom,' Gabriel explained, 'when the transgressors are come to the full, a king of fierce countenance, and understanding dark sentences, shall stand up. And his power shall be mighty, but not by his own power; and he shall destroy wonderfully, and shall prosper and do his pleasure: and he shall destroy the mighty ones and the holy people. And through his policy he shall cause craft to prosper in his hand; and he shall magnify himself in his heart, and in their security shall he destroy many: he shall also stand up against the prince of princes; but he shall be broken without hand.'

So, you see, this 'King' – the Great Beast cunningly disguised – will hold sway over the world as soon as the Rapture has removed the righteous on Translation Day. I hope you are not there to see it, Doctor. Nor to see the wrath of the Lamb when He returns after the Beast's brief dispensation.

These are some of the things that the man in black under the trees in the storm told me and in such a way that, from that day to this, I have been possessed not of the truth, but by the truth.

Dr Frieling's policy was to celebrate as many festivals and holidays as possible. He wanted the children to have frequent contact with the alien concept of fun, to show them that the disruption of their empty little routines need not be calamitous. The preparations for Easter began early: children and counsellors collaborated in making fluffy bunnies; cards and eggs were painted, presents were wrapped, stacks of chocolate promised. Party games and a special feast were planned for the Sunday.

Unexpectedly, Mikey took an intense interest in these goings-on. He loitered near the table where two older children, Darren and Anne, were helping each other to paint hard-boiled eggs. His sidelong glances left Ruth in no doubt that he wished to be included. She gave him his own egg, but he was so overwhelmed that he froze and, holding it well away from his body, repeated the word 'egg' with great difficulty.

Nevertheless, his spontaneous approach to the other children decided Ruth to send him to classes. He was panic-stricken at being separated from her at first and there were one or two spinning fits before his curiosity triumphed over fear. He allowed himself to be settled at the big table in the schoolroom for an hour at a time. Ruth was anxious, but proud. Naturally he didn't join in any group activity or even acknowledge the teacher's presence; he simply did a jigsaw, fitting the pieces together reverse side up, as if the joky picture was too novel for safety. But the jigsaw obviously provided useful cover because he absorbed more of his new environment than he let on, repeating snatches of overheard talk to Ruth afterwards. On the second day he returned in a state of terrific excitement. Ruth later learnt that the class had been told of the events surrounding Easter.

'The Son of Good is the thing,' he explained. 'He's the Saver. The Saver likes everyone if they're good. He likes littluns best – he makes them all well again, he makes jokes, he's number one. He hates telly. He's stronger than . . . than Yiaou. They kill him, the bad biguns. They kill him and put him in the stone box. And put on the lid. But HAHAHA he pops out of the stone, he says sucks to you HAHA. He's aliver than live. The Saver can do any . . . thing. You stab him, he pops up. Angels sing. He's king of angels but he likes littluns better than angels. Oh, yes. He kicks bad biguns on the bum. He lifts the lid and floats out. Floats up to his Dad. Good. Good the Father. You can't kill the Saver. He's got a cross, he levers the lid off, he bashes his way out. The Earth better watch out. He's the Big One, he blows up the world, but won't. Because of littluns. And animals. He likes yellow cats.'

This garbled version of the Saviour's crucifixion and resurrection heralded a spate of drawing. Mikey reeled off a series of pictures on the same theme. He drew a large oval and then filled it in with black crayon, except for a tiny space at the centre in which he placed the outline of a figure, clearly himself. After several of these, he attacked another piece of paper with red as well as black – violent explosions were the only content, like a sublimation of his rage. The ovals became obvious eggs, still black but rimmed with red. A huge cat was added, towering over the egg and the homunculus inside. The cat had big teeth. Was it threatening to crush the egg or hatch it? Was the red anger or warmth? Was the black faeces? Ruth pored over them; Mikey rushed on, dashing them off. A big person with an ill-defined face but ambivalent pointed breasts held the egg at arm's length in a huge grasping hand. The person was purple and drawn in wavy lines. Mikey made sucking noises and added yellow lightning flashes which either emanated from the egg or were directed at it. It was all Greek to Ruth.

As long as he was drawing, he looked so normal that Ruth couldn't help entertaining wild fantasies. She forgot the days when she had sworn that one smile would satisfy her for ever. She became irrationally ambitious, picturing him as the perfect son, dutiful and loving, sharing jokes. She saw him going to a proper school where he was popular with the other pupils and praised by the teacher for his dazzling intelligence. He was a teenager, shaving his grave beautiful face for the first time, telling her about his girlfriends, teasing her affectionately. Now he had a job as a— But what would he be? The fantasy collapsed. An autistic child might be restored to emotional adequacy, but never to a comparable intellectual level. The mind, it seemed, was linked to the body in a way that emotions were not, so that if the mental development appropriate to a certain stage of physical maturing was missed out it could not be recovered.

Ruth tried to convince herself that Mikey was the exception; but she knew that his intellectual feats, such as the black hole imagery, were embedded in his condition. They were symptoms, not real achievements, precociously contrived as a defence. Now that the walls were crumbling, Mikey showed no sign of even wanting to read. He drew like a three-year-old.

Quite early on, Ruth had been forced to acknowledge a tiny but potent part of her which, selfishly, would have kept Mikey dependent on her. Day after day, with the ruthless precision of a surgeon, she excised this ugly wish until she was able to want more than anything that Mikey should grow up happy, useful and — above all — himself. Unfortunately, Mikey more often than not co-operated with the selfish wish: he still spent more than half his time sitting on the bean-bag, doing nothing. It made Ruth panic and despair by turns — there was no reason to suppose he hadn't exhausted his capacity for change. He was buried in a black egg that it would be fatal to crack; he might simply moulder away inside. Now that he'd reached a condition of relative satisfaction, what incentive was there for further struggle? He could remain a baby until he wrinkled and died. Ruth doubted whether she could bear that.

But Mikey was not finished yet. A few days before Easter he made another boundary — this time, a simple chalk square around the bean-bag. He filled the space between the drawn line and the bag with a variety of chosen articles. It was impossible to predict his needs; he simply commandeered things with an imperious shout: 'This!' 'That!' And whoever was using what he wanted would have to give it up. The kitchen staff were near to rebellion after one of Mikey's visits. He took away a large number of pots and pans, a food-blender, a chopping board and a kettle. From the schoolroom he demanded a blackboard and easel, and four chairs.

Ruth had no option but to follow him around, conciliating where she could and begging where she couldn't. He got away with appropriating communal toys, but when he tried to take those which other children were especially attached to he made trouble between

Ruth and her colleagues. She had to explain that there were certain things, such as a tricycle and a model train, which he just could not have. Mikey stamped his feet, screaming and threatening, and then retired to his bean-bag.. Each time Ruth resigned herself to a total withdrawal and collapse. Each time Mikey renewed his foraging after a prolonged sulk. Everything had to be carried or dragged by him personally to the bean-bag's precinct. In spite of the size and weight of the blackboard, for instance, he refused any help – with one notable exception.

Harry was painting the dormitory. He had become part of the Unit's furniture, smiling genially, saying little. He was popular for his pleasant helpfulness, but generally agreed to be a bit simple. Several times a day, Mikey went to watch him. In fact he never stood nearer than the doorway and scarcely directed his eyes higher than Harry's knees except in quick glances. Harry nodded at him affably and said 'Hello'; Ruth smiled apologetically.

'This is Harry,' she said. 'He's painting the room. Do you like the colour? It's sort of pale yellow. A bit like Yiaou's colour, don't you think?' Yiaou loosely acknowledged his name with a vague convulsion of his floppy body.

Finally Mikey summoned up enough courage to approach Harry. His manner was very different from his usual arrogance. He gestured timidly towards the step-ladder which the big man was using, and then retreated. Harry obligingly climbed down. He and Mikey looked at the ladder; Ruth looked at Harry and Mikey.

'It's heavy,' said Harry. 'I'll carry it, shall I?' Mikey backed towards the door. Harry picked up the steps. Ruth sighed, bracing herself for one of Mikey's screaming fits. But instead he seemed enchanted by Harry's graciousness. A look of wonder passed across his face.

'Harry!' he whispered. Ruth suffered a pang of jealousy: he had never said *her* name.

The step-ladder completed his pile of miscellany. It was set up in an arch over the bean-bag. The other articles were heaved noisily about until they were arranged in a barricade around it. No help was allowed. The chalk square was an absolute barrier as the sand-circle had been.

'It's a tomb,' Mikey announced at last, in answer to Ruth's persistent questioning. 'It's where littluns live. It's dark and heavy. It's made of gravity-stones. It's a stone-dead death-bed corpse-egg. Littluns are buried in it. They're dead weights, they're a heavy mess, they're put in the dark with the lid on like bits of shit.'

The doom-laden words weighed on Ruth's heart. Was Mikey preparing to die? The gravity which still oppressed him had now become fused with the idea of the grave. A morbid aura surrounded this latest activity and it made her nervous. Worse still, it had cost Mikey a great deal to assemble his paraphernalia. He looked worn out, ate little, slept less; when he did sleep he was troubled by nightmares. Ruth had to sit by his bed for long stretches and she, too, was feeling extremely ragged. Her nails were bitten down, her bones ached, her eyes were red and sore with black half-circles underneath them. Her room was littered with half-eaten sandwiches, biscuits and bits of fruit, snatched up hungrily and guiltily abandoned.

Once the 'tomb' was finished, Mikey's wide-ranging activity narrowed down to sitting, drawing and visiting Harry. At first sight these visits did not amount to much: he seemed merely to watch what Harry was doing. But, on closer inspection, Ruth noticed that he was deeply stirred by these encounters as if by some numinous experience. He breathed deeply, exhaling in long juddering sighs and whispering Harry's name in the awe-struck tones of one invoking a god. Harry took it well; he tended to raise his eyebrows at Ruth for a cue as to how he should respond. But she could only shrug and smile ruefully to show that she was as much in the dark as he was.

The drawings which followed these visits included huge garish figures who struck stiff hieratic poses; their faces were purple and red, and smiling. Ruth had no difficulty in recognising herself and less in recognising Harry because his portrait was labelled 'HARY'. One drawing even depicted them together. Embarrassingly, they were holding hands and gesturing towards the tiny outline of Mikey curled up in an oval which was then enclosed in a square. Flashes of lightning zig-zagged out of their fingertips and struck the embryo Mikey.

Another sheet of paper was boldly headed 'THE SAVER'. Mikey brooded for a long time over the projected drawing but, in the end, only managed the large wavering outline of a man. The features defeated him – he simply filled in the whole head with black and laid the paper aside.

Ruth seized on this incompleteness to repeat the New Testament stories. Since Mikey had latched on to the Christian myth, she hoped that by feeding him details of Jesus' life (and skimming over the grislier aspects of his death) she might somehow answer his needs. Mikey listened as much as he could be said to listen to anything. Occasionally he was moved to comment.

'The Saver's OK. He can live and then die and then live. He whizzes up to heaven. His father helps him, his father lets him out. He's strong like Good the Father.... He can do all ... things. He's big as Good, bigger than a bigun. Littluns've got no chance. They're all messy black like shit. They're stuck in stone-tomb corpse-eggs. No one sees them. ... The Saver can't see them. They're too little and dead and buried.'

The plaintive voice drifted out from the middle of the junk-pile. Ruth stood on the edge of the chalk line, listening. Mikey's scepticism about the possibility of his resurrection was full of unsettling resonances. Anxiously she called out to him:

'Listen, Mikey. The Saviour rose from the dead to show us that we can *all* rise from the dead. Especially littluns. He died for you, Mikey, and me and Harry. Everybody. He opened His own tomb and lived again. He opens our tombs, you'll see. You'll live, Mikey. You can't die. Nothing will hurt you.' Her own words shook her. The shifting generalised idea of an afterlife that she vaguely subscribed to was a far cry from the fairy-tale she'd just told Mikey. Did she have the right to *deceive* Mikey into life? It's perfectly justifiable, she assured herself. All this resurrection business — it's only a metaphor. But, all the same, she suspected that Mikey's longed-for resurrection was not a metaphor to him; nor, for that matter, was Christ's to those who believed. She felt guilty of bad faith in a double sense.

'A singularity is trapped,' murmured the small boy hidden in his stronghold. 'There's no ... air-conditioning ... no ... light. The tomb-shell is thick ... too thick.... It's made of stone-cold dark, can't be ploded. A singularity dies inside the littlun.' Mikey had his own views about the Bible story. Apparently it was too much to hope, thought Ruth bitterly, that what was true for the Saver was also true for the littluns in his flock. *He* might well rise on the third day among choiring angels and divine pyrotechnics; innocent littluns were entombed in themselves and crushed out of existence by the weight of their own flesh.

NINE

HAPPINESS CAN'T LAST, can it? In the early days of my awakening, ravished by the urgent truth of the Rapture, I held forth to the people. The Lord plucked me like a harp and the words flowed so sweetly from my mouth that I heard them in amazement. At times the power of the word waxed so mightily that I felt my bones straining upward against my flesh and I cried out to the Lord to leave off lest I be lifted into the air. All day I sang with Saint Paul: 'And I live; yet no longer I; but Christ liveth in me. . . .' I was so full of the wonders the Lord had wrought in an ordinary sinner like me that I cared nothing for the people who stood far off or passed by; or for the rowdies who stole my cap and stuffed it with weeds, and let off stink bombs behind my back. I laughed for joy, praising them for their irreverent abundance of life.

I don't hold forth any more. For a long time now I've been unworthy of the Holy Spirit. At least, He no longer protects me from sharp words and mocking laughter. What used to make me clap my hands now strikes a coldness in my soul, and puts me in tribulation. I confess that I have doubted my salvation; for there's no certainty of it in this world no matter how you keep faith and strive towards virtue. But you have to keep on going because all things are possible to the Lord and, you never know, He might even use a hopeless case like me to help operate His unspeakable Providence.

So I don't think about ways and means; I just go on in the hope that I can grind myself down into a sharp shining instrument of the Lord. There is the odd compensation: at moments of exhaustion I do believe I've been transported to that blessed condition of peace in which the left hand does not know what the right hand is doing; or vice versa.

So, you see, in a sense my life began and ended on the same day – the day I sheltered from the storm with that remarkable man. That's why there's nothing more to say really. My existence hasn't varied since then. I've spent more than forty years in a wilderness undreamt of by the Children of Israel. Every night, except for nights off and my annual fortnight, I've worked in the Invoice Office; every day I've knocked on countless doors and rung thousands of bells as I hawked my prophecies around the Cities of the Plain. No, Doctor, I mean the streets of southern England. I only began writing down my prophecies when I realised the Rapture might not immediately take place – I wanted to reach a wider audience than I could simply by holding forth. I only *sold* these pamphlets because, funnily enough, people only value what they've paid for. Plus there was the cost of printing to be recouped. My first effort, *What's the State of Play in Prophecy?*, two hundred copies, took me eight years' footslogging to sell. Nearly as bad as *The Millennium: Some Hard Questions Answered*. I always put in a few jokes, for I can't abide a humourless religion; in fact, if I have any reservations about the Millennium, they're the fear of no jokes for a thousand years.

I know what you're thinking: How can old Harry *write* when he's hardly read anything bar Father's *Titbits*? Well, have you read *Can a Young Man Trust His Bible*? No? Well, that was in the library at Par. What about *The Devil's Mission of Amusement* or *The Menace of Freemasonry to the Christian Faith*? No? All good stuff. Plus I bought a book once, a very old one I liked the look of, called *The Constitution of Pope Honorius* – not so much a papist work, as it sounds, as a handbook for controlling spirits and rebellious angels. It came in handy, I can tell you, when— Well, I can't go into that now.

Another one I profited from was *The Black Plague of the Russellites*, written before nineteen thirty-one, of course, since when they've been known as Jehovah's Witnesses. I was guided to buy that book because I'm often mistaken for one of those simple-minded evangelists and it's been useful to 'know thine enemy'. Do you know, they believe that the one hundred and forty-four thousand souls who are saved refers to them! If they had any power at all to understand dark sentences, they'd know that the 'souls' mentioned in Revelation are not *persons*, but angelic structures comprising a number of individuals.

114

So, you see, I've read a bit. Oh, yes. Much good it's done me. Yes, I *am* a bit . . . down in the mouth today. No, it's not the Unit – although it is difficult to stand by and do nothing more for that child . . . those children than paint a wall. It doesn't seem that such young souls should suffer such. . . . It gets to you. A man with less faith than I might be tempted to draw the wrong conclusions about God. I know, I *know* that God's thoughts are not our thoughts nor His ways our ways. But the wish creeps in that they were. Do you remember how God let Satan blight and afflict Job? You might almost think that He was jealous of Job's righteousness.

No, the trouble is at home. I have to stay out of the house a good deal. I go for walks up Saint Michael's Hill. I like the pink roads and the green golf course and the quietness. No one bothers you up there.

There's nothing you can do. It's something I have to see to on my own. I understand your concern – you're thinking that I'll be off assaulting innocent people. I think I'll manage not to do that again. It's good to be able to . . . have a chat with you. Pardon? How do you mean exactly – 'friends'? I mean, everyone's my friend. But you can't go squandering time on particular individuals when there's a whole world out there deaf and blind to the facts of the Rapture, the reign of the Beast and the return of the Lord, can you? Of course, you're on the look-out for kindred spirits, companions in Christ; but they're in short supply, as you'd expect in the last days.

I had a bit of a friend a few years ago, down at the office. Attractive young bloke, name of Timothy. 'Good evening, Harold,' he used to say. Just like that! We had a couple of chats during the midnight break. He was pretty open-minded about religious matters. Not that I went on at him. It was quite funny really. I dreamt up this daring plan to invite him on a trip to Tunbridge Wells – not for selling pamphlets, just for fun. I dreamt it up while I was logging a consignment of Bibles for Exeter. I imagined those Bibles racing down the line from Waterloo, passing close by number one, South Road, gathering speed after Woking, leaving the sleeping suburbs behind and rushing through moonlit fields to do God's work in the West Country. I know the route as well as any engine-driver; but they'd never let me drive a train – not even an electric or diesel, which are far easier than the steam engines I dreamt of driving as a boy. Far inferior, too. If you close your eyes in an electric train and listen hard to the sound of wheels on rails, you can sometimes believe you're driving a steam train. Childish really.

Anyway, I walked up to Timothy's desk *right under* the suspicious nose of Mister Turnbull, our supervisor, and asked him straight out. To my surprise and joy, he said: 'Tunbridge Wells? Yes, I'd like that.' He ignored the bloke next to him, who sniggered, 'Watch out for old

Harry. He likes the young lads.' I ask you. Some people. But then some of the other blokes began talking to Timothy in the break and I got badly worried. He came across and asked: 'Is it true you're a sort of religious maniac?' He didn't look at me and he was more brusque than he wanted to be; my heart went out to him. I said yes, I was a bit of a maniac, but I never pushed religion on people, I wasn't taking pamphlets to Tunbridge Wells so he needn't worry and please come because it'd be fine, he'd see, we'd have a few laughs. I was sweating something shocking. He nodded and went back to his desk; and, God forgive me, I couldn't bear those other blokes then. It frightened me. They were a good-hearted bunch really, always helping each other out if things got busy; they meant well; they were right − I wasn't a suitable companion for Timothy − but I couldn't help myself. I had to pray and pray to stop myself from doing something clumsy and stupid like running amok − why do you keep on at me about friends and family and relationships and so on? They're hardly the *point*; I've told you the *point* of my life, but I don't think you've taken it in, Doctor. I mean, I've had friends and that − lots. I told you about Jean and Bobby and Alice and Timothy and.... Listen. I had a friend just before I came into this place. Clare. *Clare.* She was something ... out of this world ... someone—

This is a nice quiet room. The moment I saw it I said to myself: Harold, old son, wouldn't it be nice to have a large light room like this, with big shiny books covering a wall or two and a carpet instead of lino that you can feel calmly under your feet? I'll just take one of your pills, if you don't mind. You've been very kind, Doctor. It can't be much fun sitting there, opposite me, listening to all my rubbish. Here, I'll tell you about Father's last attempt to dislodge the Worm. That'll give you a laugh. Nineteen fifty-eight it was. The only time we were close before he finally perished.

I came home one morning to find him hanging upside down by his one good leg from the wardrobe. He'd put a steaming bowl of spices − nutmeg, cinnamon, etcetera − under his head so that the Fiend would be lured by the delicious aroma and come snooping up from his intestines and out of his throat. As soon as it stuck its blind white head out of Father's gob, I was to slash it off with his razor − a bit of a joke since I can hardly shave myself without making a butcher's shop of my face. But I was so touched by Father's confidence in me that I stood at the ready while he spluttered and retched and went puce in the chops.

But the Worm only laughed and lay doggo, refusing to fall for the snare. It was more or less the end of Father. He took to his bed in a

116

dumb fury and never left it again until he died two years later. What a carry-on, eh?

Actually, I had to postpone Tunbridge Wells. The trip sort of petered out. Timothy couldn't get the day off after all. I offered to arrange a change of shifts, but I was too tired to make a fuss. It probably wouldn't have worked out. God is jealous of His own, I find. I'll maybe pop down to Tunbridge Wells on my own sometime. I hear it's a very beautiful town.

Mikey stayed silently on his bean-bag all through Good Friday. Ruth sat unhappily on a chair at the chalk perimeter, feeling as useless and unwanted as the junk which separated her from him. In the afternoon there was a tea-party for the children. There were hot-cross buns for those who were up to them, scones with cream and jam, different-coloured jellies, chocolate mousses, milk shakes, Coca-Cola and lemonade. The novelty of the event caused more noise than usual, as well as several accidents with full plates of food and more than one chair-wetting. Ruth wasn't sorry when she was forced to help out with the excitement — her vigil had opened her to all kinds of morbid imaginings.

Dr Frieling managed to catch her eye. As the only person, apart from Adrian, who carried any weight with Kevin the Wolf, he was busy dabbing the boy's lips with cream while Kevin licked it off with small appreciative growls; at the same time Anne was taxing him with a long boring story about the unremarkable doings of her doll. Unaware of how absurd he looked in a paper hat, the old doctor called out: 'Is Mikey joining us?' Ruth smiled and shook her head. She knew that he was really only letting her know that he shared her anxiety, and she was grateful. She managed successfully to hide from him her darkest suspicion about Mikey: that he was simply *stuck*, waiting for the miracle that only one man, if he was a man, had ever performed.

The party went off well. Everything was cleared away and the children began their separate bed-time rituals. By eight-thirty all was quiet. By eleven it was clear that Mikey was not going to emerge that night. Ruth fetched a spare mattress and laid it out a little way from Mikey's grotesque fortress. At one o'clock Dr Frieling came to see her. She was sitting on the mattress with her head in her hands. 'My dear Miss Maier ...,' he murmured. There was nothing to say. He patted her arm and ambled off to bed. She peeped through the bric-à-brac and just made out Mikey curled up with his eyes closed. His breathing seemed shallow. She couldn't tell whether or not he was asleep.

She lay down on the mattress and, pulling a blanket over her, gazed at the blank ceiling lit by a red glow from a single light at the far end of the room. She summoned up the therapeutic memory of snowfields, which calmed her and helped her to sleep. It was the one thing she was most grateful to her psychoanalyst for; he had helped to unlock an event which Ruth had always thought was merely a dream. Standing by his window as she talked to him, she had grown absorbed in the huge clouds massed like mountains in the sky; golden rods of light from an evening sun were thrusting through the narrow passes. All at once the event had appeared before her with pristine clarity, untouched by the passage of time, and she knew that it was a memory of something actual – in fact, her very first memory.

She was moving upwards through darkness; up and up through freezing air in some kind of open seat which swung slightly underneath her. She was wedged next to her father, intensely aware of his warm reassuring presence. They were so high up that Ruth had only to move forward an inch or two and she would plunge to her death. The thought was both terrifying and thrilling. It came to her that it was not really dark; rather, her eyes had been blindfolded by a woollen scarf. She had requested the blindfold from her father because they were going up a mountain in an old-fashioned two-seater ski-lift, and Ruth, afraid of heights, did not want to be tempted to look down. They were in Switzerland, on holiday, perhaps for the sake of her health; it was the day before her third birthday.

She snuggled more closely against her father. The sun was hot on the top of her head; the air was sharp, almost painful, in her lungs. Her tummy turned over with the upward swing of the ski-lift. She was breathless with excitement, not a bad sort of breathless, but not all good, either. She was filled with an exquisite indescribable dread: some tremendous knowledge was waiting for her at the top of the mountain. She was shaken to her foundations and had to cling to Papa's arm to stop herself being wafted away by the cold air and dropped thousands of feet to the earth below.

At last the movement stopped. They had arrived at the top of the world. The scarf was removed. For a while she was dazzled, seeing only the rainbows on her eyelashes and feeling the cold purity of the thin air. Her feet sank deeply into a crispness of snow so white that she was torn in half, wanting to run in it yet not wanting to spoil it. The snow stretched away for ever, swelling and falling in vast waves of mountains farther than the eye could see. The warm sun, shining in a deep-blue sky, bathed her face with clear light until her skin tingled all over. Half a dozen insensible grown-ups stood around, talking in low voices.

Walking was hard work; the snow crunched up to the top of her boots and slid inside like ice-cream. Papa was strolling a little way off, screwing his eyes up against the smite of sun and snow. Ruth turned ninety degrees to her right. The snow rose in a gentle slope and then stopped, cut off by a chasm. A man with a large red face and a drip on his nose picked her up and carried her to the edge of the chasm. Ruth stared at the drip, hoping it wouldn't fall on her and wanting to be put down. The man placed her near the edge of the sheer drop and pointed across the chasm to the mountain on the other side. He spoke to her in a language she didn't understand, but the way he pointed told her that she was looking at a famous mountain. The sun was shining above and behind it, leaving the sheer north face bleak and dull. She looked at the gloomy ice-face and shuddered. The man was smiling and giving her a heavy instrument she had to look through. It was magic. The mountain leapt to within a few feet in front of her; she could almost touch it with her hand. The man guided her hands holding the binoculars and spoke again, in English this time.

'Look! There! Two men who have been climbing. Yes? You see? They have died and nobody can get them down. They are frozen like ice. They will stay there for ever. The ice is never melting on this mountain.'

Ruth examined the two shapes, trussed in a tangle of ropes on the glassy mountain. One of them stirred in the wind. She gave the binoculars back to the man and looked away sternly.

Her father was beside her. 'Darling, shout something,' he said. 'There's a wonderful echo.' Ruth thought she knew what an echo was. She pondered seriously for a moment.

'HALLO,' she shouted. There was a long silence. Then, clear as a bell ringing next to her ear, voices replied.

'Hallo — Hallo — Hallo.'

The dead men flapped against the mountain face. Their high voices faded into the infinity of distant peaks.

'RUTH,' she cried.

'Ruth — Ruth — Ruth,' the men called in their strange familiar voices. The words of the dead were both a greeting and a summons. She felt the weight of them like a vocation. Raising her tiny hand, she gave a little wave to the men, frozen into immortality on the eternal mountain; but they had spoken and were still.

She turned away, her heart pitter-pattering. She sucked in long painful breaths, knowing that some revelation of beauty and terror was about to break over her. When it came, it brought a great calm; she whispered it aloud: 'I am *me. I* am Ruth.' She stood stock still, herself alone in all that great temple of whiteness and light.

'Are you all right, darling?' her father asked.

'Yes, Papa. Yes, but I'm hungry.'

Ruth woke with a start, disoriented by her unusual surroundings. She could hear the murmur of a man's voice. She had no idea how long she had been asleep. Her watch told her it was five-thirty in the morning. The voice was coming from Mikey's bean-bag. She leapt off the mattress and dashed to the junk-pile. A figure was partially screened by the step-ladder that made an A-shaped arch over the bag.

'Who's there?' she demanded.

'It's me, miss.'

'Come here.' She did not trust herself to say more.

'Just a moment, miss.' The voice went on talking inaudibly to the entombed boy. Ruth was within an ace of breaking into the sacred precinct and seizing Harry by the scruff of the neck. '*Just a moment.*' What was he *thinking* of? He was a crazy dangerous lunatic.

She ran across the room and switched on more lights. When she returned, Harry was picking his way through the heap of odds and ends. He was carrying Yiaou, whom he waved sheepishly at her.

'Bit of a surprise, eh, miss?'

'Yes.' She didn't know where to begin. She'd have him banged up in a cell for this.

'He gave me his cat ... Whatsisname. Yoo.'

'Yiaou.'

'That's it. Yiaou. He wanted to do a swap. Gave him my torch. Fair enough.'

'Harry ... I suppose you have no idea what you've done. You might have ruined months of work ... set Mikey back *years*. I could kill you.'

'Steady, miss. I'd never harm a hair of the boy's head. I couldn't sleep, you see. I was worried .... I just wanted − I don't know − I wanted to have a look at him ... make sure he's, you know ... that's all. I mean, he's been behaving a bit strange recently. Don't you agree, miss?'

'You came all the way down from the hospital and barged into something you know *nothing* about.'

Harry stood up very straight and, not smiling but gazing into the distance, replied stiffly: 'Actually I came all the way from my house. Number one— Well, it doesn't matter. I've been "returned to the community", except I don't have a community. Working here is my community. As for knowing nothing about the boy, I beg your pardon, miss, but I know more than nothing about him, as you should know. And, if he chooses to invite me into his nest, I'm not going to turn him down. Not for you, nor anybody.'

Ruth was slightly abashed by the force of his speech; and, in spite of her anger, she was intrigued.

'He invited you ...?'

'Yes, miss. Of course. Do you think I would've *dared* ...?' He pointed to a place where the chalk line had been scuffed away. 'He must have seen me coming. He was waiting here, at the edge. He said my name. He wiped out the chalk with his foot. It looked as plain an invitation as you could have.'

'What did he want?' Her anger had given way to intense curiosity.

'Don't know, miss. I think he was feeling a bit ... depressed. Lonely sort of place he's built for himself.' He gestured towards the heap and added distantly: 'I didn't mind a spot of company myself.'

Ruth noticed for the first time how unusually shabby he was looking. His face was unshaven and gaunt. His stiff collar was missing, suddenly transforming him from the correct clerk to someone rougher. He wore no jacket, and his waistcoat and trousers were rumpled, his boots scuffed. The collarless shirt, unbuttoned at the top, gave him a noble rustic appearance, increasing Ruth's first impression of him as a tough Highland gillie.

'Are you all right, Harry?' she asked more gently. 'Are you managing at home? Is there anyone to look after you?'

'Me? I'm all right. I don't need looking after. It's just that I've been ... well, a bit tired recently.' His shoulders sagged. 'Still, it's no more than you'd expect in the last days....' He sighed and added: 'I know my Redeemer liveth.' But he didn't sound sure. Then he stood to attention and went on briskly: 'I didn't like to wake you, miss. I didn't know what to do. I sat next to him on his bag thing. He was quite quiet. I wanted to touch him, miss. I don't mind telling you. I wanted to ... put my arm around him or something. Just to show him that, well, he's not alone ... that I was willing to take some of the load off him, if he'd let me. But I didn't dare, miss, what with the situation being so ... delicate. Then I saw that he was weeping, miss. Not making a fuss, just tears rolling down his face. Well, I can't abide to see children upset. Especially young Mikey here. It upsets me. I wished I had something comforting to give him. A gobstopper or something. But I couldn't do anything. I'm a useless lump. So I stroked his cat for a while and told him a story. I was just finishing when you came along. Mikey took my torch and gave me his cat. I'm sorry about the whole business, miss.'

'No, no, Harry. *I'm* sorry. Sorry I bit your head off. I didn't understand. I was worried in case—'

'No need to explain, miss.' They turned in unison to look at the partly concealed bean-bag. Mikey had switched the torch on and was waving it about. After a few seconds he switched it off and seemed instantly to fall asleep.

'What shall I do about ...?' Harry pointed at Yiaou.

'I ... I don't know. Put him on the boundary, perhaps. In case Mikey needs him.' Harry carefully positioned Yiaou with his paws stretched out towards Mikey. Ruth tried to work out why Mikey had handed over his precious companion.

'I'll be off then, miss.'

'Oh. Right.' As he turned to leave, Ruth was struck by a sudden thought.

'What story did you tell him?'

The big man seemed embarrassed.

''Fraid I don't know any proper stories, miss, only Bible ones. I told him the first one that came into my head.'

'Yes?'

'The story of Lazarus, miss.' He smiled apologetically.

'I see. Well, goodnight. And Happy Easter, Harold.'

'I beg your pardon?'

'I said, "Happy Easter, Harold".'

'Ah. Thank you, miss. God bless.'

122

TEN

THE CURTAINS were drawn as if in mourning. Dorothy pulled them sharply open and, pursing her lips together, surveyed the room. It was larger than Mikey's original room at the London house, yet it was a pale replica – perhaps because he had never occupied it. The brass bed was a smaller version of their own. The heavy chest of drawers contained the few articles of clothing which had not been packed off to the Unit with their owner; beside it, there was a full-length adjustable mirror of the sort found in men's outfitters. She ran a duster over the surface and paused to put a few unruly hairs into place.

A large cabinet dominated the centre of the room. On top of it there was an anglepoise lamp, a blotter and a television set; next to it was a narrow three-tiered cabinet with, from top to bottom, a home computer, a video recorder linked to the television, and a neat stack of scientific video tapes and computer games. Dorothy was reminded of Mikey's sudden outbreak of hostility towards Rex's television. Apparently it didn't extend to his own. Had it been associated with something on the screen rather than with the screen itself? He had only just been forcibly restrained from smashing his father's beloved tapes as well.

In front of the table was a high-backed padded leather armchair and, behind it, an almost identical chair which swivelled. The shelves on the wall were stocked with luxurious technical books full of diagrams and colour photographs. A huge globe stood in the corner, and pinned to the wall above it was a star chart. A small reflecting telescope was mounted on a tripod by the single wide window. The room was splendid; Rex had taken a lot of trouble over it.

'We gave him everything,' she said aloud. Then, overcome by sudden lassitude, she sank into the armchair facing the table. She couldn't look at the room any more, not because it was Mikey's room but because, oh God, it wasn't a little boy's room at all. It was a grown man's room. She closed her eyes on what she had allowed herself to see.

Dorothy wondered how Mikey was coming along in the care of Ruth Maier. She remembered her virtual paralysis at their meeting — it was impossible not to feel inadequate in the presence of a woman so obviously well grounded, warm, stable; so carefree of manner, so careless of appearance. She had wanted to explain how hard she had tried in the early days, how her whole existence had gradually begun to revolve around Mikey; to explain how deeply the small rotating object had drilled into her soul until she had lost all reason and, convinced that he was possessed by some malignant spirit, had clenched herself against him like teeth. Even so, her sense of guilt had driven her on; but, unable to see how or why she was guilty, she had floundered in a mire of resentment where every struggle sucked her deeper.

She could say nothing of this to Ruth Maier. She saw the unspoken judgement in her eyes. She heard the edge in Ruth's voice when she mentioned the boarding school, The Yews. Surely it had never been her idea to send Mikey to that terrible place? But Rex, surprisingly, had said it was her idea and so it must have been. She could only remember the enormous relief of being rid of Mikey for a time, and her gratitude to Rex for taking it all in hand. He never blamed her, not in so many words, but she felt the depth of her failure as a mother all the same. Mikey's illness had driven them apart. But, in another sense, it formed the main bond between them, like a conspiracy of silence.

It was a long time before Dorothy could bring herself to think about Mikey at all. Then Jenny Wickham's report and the diagnosis of 'autism' returned to haunt her. Although Rex's unshakeable view that Mikey had a kind of brain damage was one she fervently wished to share, the notion of psychological damage refused to go away. The idea of stirring up the mud once again was especially repugnant to her since there was a danger that it might lead her back to her own guilt. But the need to cleanse herself, whatever the cost, was stronger. She persuaded Rex to give the Unit a chance. He put aside his scepticism for the sake of her peace of mind.

During the past year, Dorothy had even gone so far as to read a book about autism, swallowing its jargon like foul-tasting medicine. There were so many ways a mother could go wrong, it seemed. God knew she had done her best — she'd never refused Mikey her breast even when the nipples were so sore that the tears poured from her eyes. But that, according to the book, counted for nothing. She might have inadvertently withheld the breast from him a moment too long, inducing anxiety and insecurity; she might have given him the breast too easily, so that he never developed the appropriate sense of independence and self-assertion. Had she inserted the nipple into his mouth, or allowed him to guide it himself with his tiny vague hand? She couldn't be expected to remember. No mother was perfect, but very few children were scarred for life. Mikey must've been born with a screw loose. It wasn't fair; she had wanted so much to be a mother, but it had turned out as terrifying a responsibility as she'd anticipated.

With the virtuous sense of some great moral effort, Dorothy concluded that, yes, she might have made a mistake. But it wasn't as though Mikey were the only casualty in the collision between them; she had suffered, too. No one was to blame. Life was a lottery. It was all a stupid tragic *mistake*.

But why, then, did Mikey still come to her in dreams? Why couldn't she get *on* with anything? She rattled around the big house like a shade in limbo. There was a perpetual anxious sense of *waiting*; not like the intense waiting of her Liverpool youth, but a waiting without expectation. If she expected anything at all, it was something awful — that very morning she had been afraid of opening a door and seeing the face of the person on the seventh stair, a face she had once longed to see.

Dorothy pulled herself slowly out of the armchair. She had decided that the room didn't need dusting at all. What was the point? Besides, it was supposed to be a holiday. Rex had phoned last night to wish her a happy Good Friday; he had promised to be back either later on today or Easter Sunday at the latest. It had been so dismal sitting alone on the Friday that Dorothy had toyed with the idea of going to midnight Mass. But then she'd been so irritated by the idea that she might be going out of some residual fear of mortal sin that, instead, she'd watched a video in bed. There weren't any sins, only mistakes. She drew the curtains again to prevent the sunlight from fading the expensive carpet, and closed the door tightly behind her.

'Hard night?' Carol was standing over her with a cup of tea. Ruth sat up and blinked her eyes.

'No, not really.' The night's drama seemed almost like a dream. 'Is

125

Harry here?' she asked, gratefully sipping the hot tea.

'I haven't seen him. But it is a holiday, remember – except for us,' Carol added ruefully. 'And while you've been having a nice lie-in, Mikey's been busy.' She pointed to the blackboard. Mikey had shifted it to an easier position and was chalking on it with great concentration.

'Carol! You should've woken me....'

'Calm down. He's been quite happy, drawing away. You don't always have to be there, you know.'

'Yes I do.'

'Well, finish your tea first,' said Carol in a strict voice. They both laughed.

As soon as Ruth approached, Mikey launched into a breathless speech without looking up for a second from his task. The talking even appeared to facilitate the process of drawing.

'The Lazarus is the thing. He's got beams better than light, stronger than anything.... He can shine on the Earth, he can shine on the moon, nobody knows his colour. The Lazarus. He's got beams better than ... than the sun. His beams are ... a singularity. The Saver activates him.' His drawing was fast and furious; he seemed to be creating the blueprint for some fantastic machine. There were tubes all over the board with flashes of light going into them and zig-zag patterns inside. Explosions shot out of them like rockets. Mikey went on with his explanation: 'Yes, the Saver activates him, he comes alive, his particles move ... special particles. He's got ... flectors, yes. Flectors for boiling the particles up and down, they're bright, you can't see them; they can go through Earth, metal, televisions, anything. If a littlun had the Lazarus, a littlun might punch and peek out of a corpse-egg, a littlun might ... WHOOOSH ... faster than light ... out of the hole ... a singularity might see ... the sunshine.' He went on covering the board with his strange messy diagrams, rubbing bits out and adding bits on, until gradually he began to flag and his elation gave way to foreboding, and deepened to terror.

'It's not stable. DANGER. The particles might leak out ... leak before they're all one ... before the singularity is made. RED ALERT. The Lazarus might plode the world splat splat beat it flat CRASH. The Lazarus.... No.... Not safe. He cuts you in half, he plodes you SPLAT.' In his agitation he scampered around the boundary of his domain, superstitiously touching and adjusting each object in his collection. 'Whoosh,' he muttered, or 'plosion'. Then he returned to the blackboard to add or erase details. Occasionally he acted out parts of his sketch: his hands flashed forward and back in undulating movements while his body executed an extraordinary muscular feat. A rippling spasm passed through him from head to toe, accompanied by a hum-

ming sound. He was so successful in this attempt to incorporate his
'Lazarus' that, as he jerked and hummed to and fro, he gave the distinct
impression of being some highly charged electrical gadget. Obviously
Harry's story had wrought a tremendous effect on the boy, but it didn't
look in the least biblical. There was no connection between the man
raised from the dead and Mikey's machine (if it was a machine) except,
possibly, the fact that the 'Saver' activated both of them. . . .

By the late afternoon the blueprint was as complete as he could
make it. Looking utterly worn out, Mikey refused any suggestion of
a rest. But he did accept three bars of chocolate – his first food for two
days – which he quickly nibbled his way through like a rodent. Immediately he set off at a run for the dormitory where he yanked the
sheets off his bed and brought them back to Ruth. 'Up there!' he
commanded, pointing to the step-ladder. He rubbed out a segment of
boundary with his foot and Ruth was allowed to approach the ladder.
She had to arrange the sheets according to his gestures so that, draped
over the ladder's arch, they hung down on all sides to screen the bean-
bag from view. When she had finished, Mikey waved her back and,
having resealed the boundary with chalk, made a last-minute addition
to the drawing on the blackboard.

Now a startling change came over him. All his feverish confidence
deserted him and he stood trembling on the edge of the chalk line as
though it were a precipice. He seemed about to take an irrevocable
step. Holding Harry's torch in front of him, he switched it on and
shivered.

'Dark . . . dark,' he whispered. 'Red alert.' He picked up Yiaou from
the floor and clutched the cat against his chest.

'It's all right, Mikey,' said Ruth feebly, far from sure that it was.

'Danger.' His lip quivered and tears gathered in his eyes. 'A littlun
doesn't want to go where dead things are. A littlun wants Ruth.' She
drew in a sharp breath. She had never heard her name spoken by Mikey
before.

'I'm here, darling. Don't be afraid. I'll wait for you. I'll be here when
you come out.' She knelt beside him. He put his arms around her neck.
She could feel his skinny body trembling like an injured fledgeling.

'Go to bed now,' he sobbed. 'Go to bed with the light on. And
Yiaou. And Ruth.'

For a moment she was ready to give in to his request. But she knew
beyond a doubt that she had to supply the strength that had failed him
at the eleventh hour.

'You must go in, Mikey. Go into your . . . .' she hesitated to used the
word. 'Go into your tomb. You'll be quite safe. If it's dark, switch on
your torch. I'll be waiting.' She kissed him. His sobs died away. He put

Yiaou into her hand and stepped over the line. With outstretched arms he stumbled like a blind man over the obstacles. Ruth and Yiaou waved to him, but he did not look back. He disappeared behind the sheets.

I know that perfect love casteth out fear, Doctor, but I've been afraid too long for love to break the habit. You say I should *confront* my fear. Very good. You think that if I confront it it will disappear in a puff of smoke because it is in my imagination. Fear is not imaginary, Doctor; it's always real. If I could confront it, it wouldn't be fear. No, where we differ in our opinions is that you think the *cause* of my fear is in my mind while I know that the cause. ... Let's just say that there are spirits of iniquity sent by Satan who use people's own fear to entrap them. I'm forbidden to say more.

Don't concern yourself, Doctor. I have a crumb of comfort; namely the bolder the spirit grows and the more it seeks to fall on me like a wolf, the nearer is Christ's return. The Rapture must be ... *must* be nearly upon us, for the spirit of evil, I feel it, waxes deadlier every day and more desperate. If it catches me ... I can't answer for my actions. I'm a coward ... I'm liable — oh, God forbid — to hand over my soul ... to betray the Lord in exchange for immediate mercy. But if I can hang on. ... if I can pray without ceasing right up to the moment it sinks its teeth into me, I may yet be delivered — and then will it be doubly punished, by Satan for its failure and by the Lord who will bind it in the lake of fire where all its groans will be drowned by the sound of Heaven's rejoicing. I've said too much already. It's just that I'm at the end of my strength. I hope to God you're right — hope that I'm merely going mad and that my soul is not in the jeopardy I imagine. But I'm afraid—

It might be best if you arranged to take me back, Doctor, and to put some electricity into my head. I hear it gets marvellous results. I hear it takes the memory away for a while. That would be no bad thing. I'm in favour of modern technology. But not, please, today. I may be needed, you see. I can't be confused by electrical shocks for a day or two. Great things are in motion at the Unit. The boy. Mikey. But afterwards, for better or worse ... I'll come and see you. I have to go now. I've said too much. I'm not safe, even here ... I can feel. ...

Rex swallowed his fifth large vodka and tonic, and felt stronger. Something would turn up; it always did. The great thing was not to lose the old cool. His luck was changing again, he could feel it. He mustn't let the aberration last night at Andrea's get to him. It was an isolated incident, probably brought on by anxiety. He'd read somewhere that when the American stock market crashed in 1929 a great many businessmen became sexually impotent. Yet he hadn't felt anxious; as a matter of fact, he'd been feeling rather on top of things. He'd heard on the car radio that several millionaires had gone bust at least once on their way to their fortune simply because, like him, they weren't afraid to take risks. If he kept his nerve, he'd find the right opening straight after the Easter break. He'd be back on top of the pile in no time.

He couldn't understand it. Was he perhaps getting tired of Andrea? Her patience with him had been the last straw. 'It doesn't matter,' she'd said. 'Sex isn't everything. We could even talk for a change.' He didn't like her platitudes; he liked her tone even less. It was almost as if it didn't matter to her one way or the other; almost as if she didn't want him. 'Of course I want you, but you don't have to be *perfect* every time. In fact I'd rather you weren't, in a way.' What did she mean by that? If she knew what a pain her nakedness gave him, she wouldn't say such things. It was a pain he couldn't get at. Her body was so bloody gorgeous it was intimidating. His eyes, hands, mouth were inadequate for it; he longed for them to merge into a single super-organ so that, amoeba-like, he could engulf her. But, no matter how he wrapped his limbs around her and stretched over her every inch of his raging skin, she always managed to elude him. 'It's not the end of the world, Rex. Don't go on about it.'

She could have made more effort to see it from his point of view, could have done more to help. Instead, just as his pain was about to be appeased, she touched some secret catch in the very centre of his sexuality. A trap sprang open to reveal a yawning drop of desire so deep that he was left dangling before he reached the bottom. Did she do it on purpose? Was she trying to drive him mad?

Rex rose unsteadily from his bar-stool and adjusted his jacket to hide the hard tube in his trousers. He winked at the barmaid and pointed to his glass. While she was refilling it, he crossed the smoky room to an old-fashioned payphone in the corner and dialled Andrea's number. She had left early that morning before he had woken. When she didn't return immediately, he became restless and went out. He had phoned at intervals throughout the day but there was no reply. Now, however, the pips told him that the phone was being answered. He pushed his coin into the slot.

'It's me,' he said.

'Oh. Hello.'

'Where have you *been*? Never mind. I'll be round in twenty minutes.'

'Not tonight, Rex.'

'Don't play silly buggers, love. I'm coming round.'

'No, Rex. It's best if I don't see you for a while.'

'What's that supposed to mean? It's because of last night, isn't it?'

'Don't start that again.'

'One mistake and you go cold on me.'

'Don't be silly.'

'I have to see you, Andy.'

'No, Rex.'

'You've got someone with you.'

'Yes.'

'For Christ's sake, who?'

'A friend. No one you know.'

'Get rid of him. I'm coming round.'

'It's not a "him" and I'm not getting rid of her. Just go home, Rex. I'll call you.'

'If you let me down now, Andrea, you won't see me again.'

'I'm sorry, Rex.'

'Listen, Andy. I've been waiting for you all day. Just give me half an hour. That's not asking a lot, is it?'

'I have to go now. I'll call you sometime.'

'Wait. Please. I'll be round in twenty minutes, OK?'

'No.'

'Twenty minutes, Andrea. OK?'

The pips sounded. His time was up. Rex fumbled for another coin, but too late — the line went dead.

She could scarcely keep her eyes open. It had been another interminable day. But although she longed for sleep, she felt that to lose consciousness would somehow allow things to fall apart. She had to suffer his ordeal along with him in whatever way she could, even if it only meant acting as a witness. She abandoned the mattress and pulled a hard chair up to the edge of Mikey's graveyard of junk. Never before had she felt so strongly that she was trapped helplessly in the boy's orbit. The occasional twitching of the sheets suggested that Mikey was also awake or sleeping restlessly. Ruth looked at her watch: it was eleven-thirty. In half an hour it would be Easter Day. She picked up her journal and opened it. She might as well try to describe the situation. If nothing else, it would help keep her awake. She took up her pen and, on the top right-hand corner of the page, wrote:

I've underestimated the importance of Harry. He was the only person allowed to assist Mikey in his 'construction work' (by carrying the step-ladder) and the only person to my knowledge whose name Mikey has spontaneously uttered (I don't count; nor does Yiaou). I think therefore that Harry is Mikey's first encounter with someone genuinely outside himself. Any male person would probably have served equally well, i.e. as a father figure, but Harry was the chosen one quite simply because he was available and also not part of the Unit in the way that Adrian or Dr Frieling is, for example.

Of course it's impossible to determine how far exactly M. recognises Harry's objective existence – he still projects on to Harry powerful – even numinous – attributes. (But we all do this to some extent. Don't I project my unconscious desire for a father on to Dr Frieling, for instance?) The decisive action was M.'s invitation to Harry to enter his private domain, that is, his self-enclosed world: he was expressing a desire to withdraw his projections and bring closer the possibility of real relationship. The pact between them was sealed by a symbolic exchange of gifts (Yiaou and the torch).

Mikey tried to give Yiaou to me in a moment of panic when he was about to cross the old sand boundary. I refused to take Yiaou because I judged that M. still needed the support of those creative qualities in himself which Yiaou represented. This time he was right to give up Yiaou because he dimly perceives his essential separateness from the toy and needs to stand on his own two feet. At the same time, I suspect that he wants Harry to be the guardian, as it were, of the complex emotions which have accumulated around Yiaou since the early days. The chief one is his terrible anger. Perhaps M. hopes that, should he fail in his latest bid for selfhood, he can reclaim his positive Yiaou-qualities from Harry, who holds them in safe-keeping.

NB. Harry should really be here. I must ask Dr F. if he can be on hand over the next few days – or however long it takes – until Mikey can dispense with him.

In the light of Harry's 'sacred' significance for M., it's not surprising that his story should have acted as the catalyst that enabled M. to break his behavioural stalemate. Although the choice of story – the raising of Lazarus from the dead – was extraordinarily fortuitous, I believe any story would have done as well, i.e. the content of the story was irrelevant; it was simply the human contact with Harry that M. required. The machine, or whatever, that he has designed on the blackboard could just as easily be called ... The Little Red Riding Hood, for instance.

131

Ruth broke off and abruptly shut the book. She remembered that, in all the anxiety, she had forgotten to check Mikey's final addition to his drawing. She walked along the edge of the square and peered through the semi-darkness at the blackboard propped on its easel amongst the miscellany. In large white letters, a title had been added at the bottom: THE LASER US.

Hardly daring to admit her sudden realisation – hardly daring to breathe – Ruth hurried to Dr Frieling's office and scanned the books on his shelves. Quickly she selected a brightly illustrated volume for children called *The Timetable of Technology*. A glance at the index referred her to page 166. The diagram on that page hit her full in the face. Its resemblance to Mikey's tubes, sparks and beams was unmistakable. The page was headed 'Lasers'.

She read greedily, impatient with her own inability to understand the complexity of laser beams. As far as she could gather, they were basically tubes full of a gas, such as helium-neon, whose particles were stimulated by an external power source so that the gas emitted photons of light. Both ends of the tube were reflective, like mirrors, so that once the photons were in movement they bounced backwards and forwards until they fell into a regular, or 'coherent', wavelength. In this way, light was amplified into a beam of amazing razor-sharp intensity which, emerging from one end of the laser tube, could be focused on the moon in a spot no wider than a coin. Ruth noted with interest that the colour of the beam was determined by its wavelength; and the wavelength was so coherent that it produced a purity of hue unknown to nature. In this she detected Mikey's claims for the 'Lazarus' beam: that it was a singularity, better than light, whose colour nobody knew.

Mikey was obviously still struggling with the problem of super-gravity and the inescapability of 'light'. He had hauled himself to the edge of his black hole; he was perhaps peeping out from behind the event horizon. But he still had to travel all the way across the galaxy to Earth. The unnatural – or supernatural – power of a laser might provide a means of escape. Its beam was stronger and 'faster' than ordinary light. His weird muscular spasms were attempts to transform his own body into a laser which could emit such a beam.

And now that the image of the black hole had become merged with the images of tomb and egg the less metaphorical applications of the laser came into play: it could punch through stone, peck its way out of the 'tomb-shell', even – dare she think it? – *hatch* the 'corpse-egg'. It was the first time the idea of birth, amidst all the images of death, had occurred to her and it made her heart skip a beat.

She had to remind herself how tricky, unstable, liable to malfunction the Lazarus was. If the beam were not released at the right time, the trapped photons would overheat, explode the laser tube, blow up the world, cut Mikey in half.

She called out softly to the small boy incarcerated in the sad tomb of his own creating: 'Mikey! Don't worry. Don't give up. You'll get out. Use the laser. The laser – the Lazarus – is strong enough, fast enough to break the gravity-stones and carry you back. I *know* it is.' She marvelled that salvation could depend on something as simple, as providential, as a play on words.

Behind the sheets there was silence. Ruth thought of the ancient heroes who harrowed hell to recover the treasure or die in the attempt. Mikey's treasure was so commonplace yet so precious: his own humanity. She slumped back in her chair, reflecting how once again she'd been too late in reading his signs, too stupid to be of any use. He was on his own as he had always been right from the start.

Rex waited for an hour outside Andrea's flat. Her light was on. He sat in his car watching the front door of the mansion block. Her 'friend' did not leave. But it was not the thought of the friend that deterred him from letting himself into the flat; it was the ghastly finality of her 'No' on the telephone. He couldn't believe that she meant it, but could he risk it . . . ? Until now, it hadn't bothered him that Andrea didn't much like him. He derived a certain excitement from knowing that she made love to him because she couldn't help herself. Tonight he rather wished he could just talk to her.

He pulled out his address-book, noting with satisfaction the number of names written inside. Who could he look up at this time of night? He reached the letter 'M' before he abandoned the book. The men he knew were mostly business contacts who would only pity or patronise him; the women were mostly married now, or had moved far away. Christ, he thought, what happened to my friends? His skin felt cold on the outside and burning hot inside. He seemed to be running a fever. His shirt was damp. There's nothing between me and the gutter, he reflected histrionically, except this car and this suit of clothes. . . .' He took a long pull from his flask of brandy and got out of the car.

Above the light in Andrea's window, above the fuzzy orange aura of the sodium-vapour street-lights, tiny stars scintillated in the depths of space. Rex leant dizzily against the car. It was as though he could feel the billions of neutrinos gushing through his head from the far side of the universe. Each ghostly particle was carrying infinitesimal bits of him away with them. He was being invisibly eroded like sand on granite; he was losing control.

Rex cast around for some thought to shore himself up. He pictured his parents in their cottage on the Norfolk coast. He hadn't been to see them since his father's attack, brought on by emphysema. Was it really two years ago? Rex hated disease; but he ought perhaps to have stayed the night at least. Still, he sent them money sometimes, and Dorothy signed his name on Christmas cards.

He suddenly saw himself, hanging around Andrea like a dog, and was seized by a fit of anger. He jumped into the car, started the engine and drove away. His anger focused on Dorothy. Why had she insisted on sending Mikey to that place? What good was a puffed-up intellectual *hausfrau* like Ruth Maier, for all her mysterious air and dark flashing eyes? If she could cure him, then why was she taking so long, and meanwhile who the fuck was paying? She looked a complete mess – couldn't even get herself together, let alone anybody else. She probably only took other people's children because she couldn't find a man to give her kids of her own. They had wonder drugs these days, and miracle machines – there had to be a quicker way to jolt some life into him. 'Oh, Mikey,' Rex groaned aloud, 'why are you *doing* this to me?' His son had looked all right, better than all right; he was quiet, serious, well behaved, very intelligent. He had all the makings of a great man, a scholar and scientist. Then it turned out the boy was a mental defective who blighted his marriage and jinxed his business. Christ. All the same ... 'He's *my* son,' said Rex grimly. He pulled his car, too fast, on to the A3 and headed for Wyebridge.

ELEVEN

AS THE QUIET OF THE NIGHT deepened to an almost palpable silence, Ruth was fired by an inexpressible mixture of despair and exaltation. Too tired and too hungry to think clearly, she was nagged by the sense of having misunderstood Mikey all along. His bizarre but densely packed power words ran like a litany through her brain – 'dark', 'empty', 'hole', 'horrorizon', 'tomb', 'corpse-egg', 'Saver', 'Earth'. ... Amidst them all lurked the singularity like the eye of the storm. No matter how its meaning changed, its five syllables remained the same. It was Mikey's beginning and end, the dark abyss of gravity and yet the source of a grace as simple as a ray of light.

For a fleeting, brightly lit instant Ruth glimpsed, in Mikey's condition, as under a microscope, a paradox as clear as the abstract perfection of a crystal: all action was both freely chosen and forever ordained.

She snatched up her journal and struggled to put her intuition into words:

Easter Sunday, 2.00 a.m.
Taking myself as an example, I want to say this: I realise myself out of my own actions. The more I act, the more self there is; the more self, the more I can act. There are no acts without the 'I' that performs them. The 'I' and the 'self' presuppose one another.

In Mikey's case, there's no 'I' and therefore no 'self', and so he

135

cannot act. His activities, taken separately, have none of the character of choice; rather, they are mere behaviour – conditioned, reflexive, automatic.

But when I consider the *overall* pattern of his development I see the unmistakable signs of meaning and purpose which are the hallmarks of true action. He has progressed *as if* acts can occur *prior to the possibility of their occurrence.*

My limited knowledge of psychology is not helpful here. I want to say that we possess a faculty which propels us willy-nilly towards the emergence of an 'I' by which we can act on the world and so separate and affirm our selves.

I might put it another way: the self is potentially present from the beginning as an empty possibility that, as it were, adumbrates itself. This 'proto-self' acts spontaneously rather as the acorn 'acts' to realise the oak. I'll call this innate shaping force – for want of a better word and for the sake of convenience – the soul.

Ruth felt strange writing the last word, but without any sense of an unwilling reversion to an archaic belief. The word 'soul' now glowed with recovered meaning. It was no longer an airy abstraction whose immortality was held over her head like a sword; it was something rich and specific, as familiar as an old friend re-encountered on a higher turn of a spiral staircase.

Contemplating the shrouds which separated her from Mikey, she couldn't help wishing that Harry were with her. He was not possessed by self-doubt. He had marched in where she had feared to tread, knowing what to do and say. She could *do* nothing for Mikey.

Without any feeling of strain, Ruth slipped to her knees and silently recalled the rudiments of prayer.

She was woken by a humming noise. She couldn't remember dropping off to sleep. Her neck ached from having rested too long on the hard back of the chair; her buttocks were numb. The room was suffused with a pale light that prefigured a fine day. Outside, a chorus of birds sang in counterpoint to the hum which she realised was coming from behind the sheets. Although the sound was being made by Mikey's voice, it had a high-pitched metallic quality which at first made her doubt its human origins. She levered herself painfully out of the chair and hobbled to the boundary, rubbing her neck and arms to relieve their stiffness. The hum stopped, only to be superseded by the sound of Mikey thrashing about as if in pain. She could hear the grinding of his teeth.

His struggle went on for what seemed like an age. Several children burst excitedly into the playroom, bearing Easter eggs. Carol came over to ask after Mikey, but Ruth was too preoccupied to reply. She was concentrating all her force on the event behind the sheets. Yiaou was in her hands and she kneaded his soft body mercilessly. The other counsellors, alerted to the crisis by Carol, kept their charges well away from the danger zone. No one doubted that there was liable to be one hell of an explosion. Pacing up and down, Ruth felt herself grow more and more breathless. 'Not *now*,' she scolded her lungs. To her surprise, her wheezing didn't worsen and, gradually, ceased altogether. She sighed with relief; an asthmatic fit was the last thing she needed. 'Come *on*, Mikey,' she muttered; and then, calling out, 'I'm here, Mikey! Keep trying!'

She was rewarded by a faint flash of light from inside the tent of sheets. She had forgotten Harry's torch! Was it some kind of magical tool – a laser beam, for instance? Of course, of *course* it was. The light shone intermittently through the white cotton. Mikey could be heard uttering low animal grunts. The sheets billowed under the stress of his erratic thrashing movements. There was a tinny thud and a tinkle of broken glass as the torch struck the step-ladder. It rocked to and fro for a moment, sending a shudder through the sheets. Another, harder blow from the torch sent it toppling over. The sheets were torn away dramatically as the ladder landed among the bric-à-brac with a violent crash.

Mikey stood revealed. He was stark naked, dripping with sweat and panting. He breathed in deeply and exhaled with a loud 'whooosh'. He blundered over the bean-bag; 'WHOOOSH' he went, wading through pots and pans, stumbling over toys. 'WHOOOSH.' His flailing arms smashed the blackboard sideways and he walked across the boundary to where Ruth was waiting.

The filminess in front of his eyes had gone. They were wide open, darkly glowing, sucking in light. He looked at her. *Looked* at her with wonder and recognition. A thrill passed through her. Her eyes met his. He moved his hands incredulously over his shining skin. His mouth worked to expel unfamiliar words.

'A littlun is living,' he remarked faintly. 'A ... am ... alive.' He paused, putting out a tentative hand towards Yiaou. He stroked the cat's crooked smiling face.

'I,' he said. 'I ... am ... *I am alive.*'

'Yes,' said Ruth.

She picked him up like a baby. But he wasn't a baby any more; he was a boy, a person. Good, she thought. Now he can begin.

*   *   *

137

A wide maroon car pulled up on the verge ahead of her. A heavy man wearing a peaked cap and a grey uniform straining at its buttons got out of the car and opened the back door. A poodle jumped out and scampered to and fro indecisively. It stopped to stare, trembling, at Dorothy as she passed. The chauffeur leant against the car and lit a cigarette. She felt his eyes on her as she approached.

'Happy Easter.'

She was taken aback by his civility. 'Thank you,' she said, blushing at the absurdity of her reply. All the same, she was heartened by his greeting. Until now, she had not given Easter a second thought.

She turned off the road and walked down a path between high well-cut hedges where the leaf-mould was spongy underfoot and smelt delicious. The mid-morning sun softened the edge of the breeze. She peered through the left-hand hedge which, she saw, artfully concealed an electrified fence. A solitary boy was shivering on the edge of a heated swimming pool at the far end of a wide lawn. Steam drifted over the unnaturally blue water. The boy disappeared with a splash.

Emerging on to the golf course, Dorothy strode more briskly through the sparse woods which bordered the long sweep of a fairway and then clustered thickly around the emerald velvet of the ninth green. She rarely saw any golfers and never saw anyone tending the green, although its surface was always as smooth and lush as an oasis. But today she was startled to see a number of vehicles drawn up around it. Three of them had small domed lights on their roofs. There's been an accident, she thought immediately; but, seeing no ambulances, only a Range Rover, two panda cars and three unmarked cars, she amended the thought: There's been a murder. Her heart seemed to pitch heavily to one side like a barrel loose in a ship's hold.

The green was cordoned off by fluorescent orange tape attached to a series of posts. Four or five constables were staring gloomily at the ground or tramping through the surrounding undergrowth. Two plain-clothes officers were conferring by the flagpole.

'What's going on?' Dorothy called out. The men stared at her. One of them signalled to a young policeman, who nodded and came across to her, tugging a notebook out of the button-down breast pocket of his uniform.

'What on earth's going on?' she repeated.

'May I have your name, please, miss?'

'Dorothy Ballantine. Mrs. Now tell me, please. . . .' It was urgent that she should know what had occurred — what monstrous act had defiled the serenity of the ninth green.

'Just a moment, Mrs Ballantine,' said Police Constable Steve Richardson sternly. 'Do you often walk this way?'

'Not very often. Sometimes.'

'You live close by?' asked PC Richardson, writing in his book.

'Fairly close.' She gave him her address. 'Why are you asking me all this? Am I ... a suspect?'

The young constable smiled. 'I shouldn't think so. I have to ask a few questions, that's all.'

'Please hurry.'

'Were you out at all last night between nine p.m. and two a.m.?'

'No. I was at home.'

'Did you at any time during the evening see or hear anyone or anything out of the ordinary? Think carefully.'

'No. I watched television. I went to bed early. ... There's been a murder, hasn't there?'

'What makes you say that?' The policeman looked up sharply from what he was writing.

'All ... this.' She gestured vaguely at the cars and men. Steve Richardson put away his notebook; he seemed to relax.

'Not as bad as that. A rape, actually.'

'A *rape* ...?' What did he mean? What could be worse than rape? She'd rather die than. ... 'Is she all right?' They both knew what she meant.

'As well as can be expected. A few bruises. She's in hospital with shock. She'll be OK. Tragic really. Such a young girl. Still at school. You don't happen to know—?'

'I don't know *any* young girls,' Dorothy interrupted quickly. She didn't want to know who it was. She didn't want to come any closer to the outrage than she could help. But she couldn't help asking: 'Where exactly ...?'

'Right here. On the green.'

'Oh. ... But you'll catch him, won't you? The girl's all right. She's given a description.' Steve Richardson betrayed his inexperience by glancing a shade uneasily towards his colleagues.

'Well, it was dark ... the man was masked. He didn't speak. She might remember more when she's. ...'

'Yes. I see.' Dorothy gazed at the sinister lushness of the green. 'He attacked a girl on the heath by the station.'

'What do you know about that?' The constable had his hand on his notebook again.

'Nothing. It was in the local paper. That's all.'

'Might've been a different bloke.'

'Yes. Is that all? Can I go?' She felt a bit faint.

'Will you be all right, madam? I'll see you home, shall I?'

'No, of course not. I'm fine . . . fine.' She breathed deeply. 'Thank you. It's just . . . a bit of a surprise, that's all. Sort of on one's doorstep. I'm fine now.' She gave PC Richardson a little tight smile and hurried away. It was a *scandal* that such . . . *things* should be allowed to happen on a private estate. The Residents' Association levied a hefty subscription to look after things, including security arrangements. But people came and went as they pleased; rapists walked the quiet roads, unchallenged.

Dorothy found herself walking well away from the hedges. If she screamed now, would anyone hear her? If they did, would they do anything more than turn up the voltage on their fences? She could all too easily imagine the silent and faceless man, the steely grip of his limbs, the helpless terror of the schoolgirl, the tearing, pushing, breaking and entry. . . . As she approached the house she saw with relief that Rex's car was turning into the drive.

The car turned off Station Road and entered the seclusion of St Michael's Hill. The top windows of the large houses peeped over their high hedges. It was only a five-minute drive.

'Soon be there,' said Rex. He glanced to his left. His passenger seemed to have dwindled into the rich upholstery; his legs stuck straight out in front of him like buffers. 'Won't Dorothy be surprised to see you, eh?' The passenger did not reply. He simply tightened his grip on the grubby yellow object in his lap. Rex hummed a tune to conceal his irritation.

At the gateway to the drive which curled up the hill to the house, Rex stopped the car.

'Come on, now,' he said in a jolly voice, 'you're much too big a boy to play with baby's things.' He laid his hand on the yellow animal's neck. The boy stiffened momentarily and then went limp. 'Good lad.' Rex gently disentangled the boy's fingers from the flannel body. 'Say 'bye 'bye,' he joked; and, opening the electric window of the car, tossed the toy cat into the ditch by the gates. The boy made an odd sound. Yow?

'What's that, Mikey? You'll have to learn to speak up, you know.' But Rex's irritation had evaporated. He felt he had struck a blow for freedom. The window whirred shut. The car came back to life with a muted roar, and hummed easily up the drive to stop in front of the silent house.

*   *   *

140

Ruth's immediate thought on waking was: Oh God, I've forgotten to feed Mikey. She had already leapt out of bed before she remembered. Then she let the memory seep as slowly as possible through her, for the sheer joy of it. Mikey was tucked up in bed, as soundly asleep as she had been. She felt utterly rested and well. Looking in the mirror she even appeared to have lost weight. She piled her hair up on top of her head and sucked in her cheeks. Damn it, she could have been a flamenco dancer. Tossing her head back haughtily and stamping her bare feet, she danced to the window and swept the curtains open. The sun was already gloriously high in a clear blue sky. She had overslept drastically. Except that it didn't matter now. Now nothing was drastic any more. She couldn't wait a single moment longer before seeing Mikey. She didn't dress, but simply threw on her dressing-gown and hurried lightly to the dormitory. Dr Frieling intercepted her.

'Come into my office for a minute, please.'

'Can it wait, Doctor? I must—'

'Now, please.' She was taken aback by his severe tone. Still, he looked very tired. It was he who needed a holiday, not her. Her holiday was just beginning.

'Sit down, Ruth.' Again, she was taken by surprise. A ghastly chill made her shiver. *Why had he called her 'Ruth'?*

'Something's happened to Mikey,' she said at once. Her voice was no louder than a whisper because her breath wouldn't come. She sat down with a bump.

Dr Frieling spread his hands and then, failing to find the right words, clasped them together. He spoke quickly, abruptly.

'Mr Ballantine came and he took Mikey away ... took him home. His wife insisted, it seems. They are perfectly within their rights. There was nothing I could do except threaten him and beg him.' He blinked behind his spectacles. 'I did both, Ruth. It was no good. Forgive me.'

Ruth gave a little laugh. It was plain that the old man had lost his wits.

'No, no, Doctor,' she explained kindly. 'You see, they promised. Mr and Mrs Ballantine both promised to leave Mikey with us ... with me.'

'I know. All the same. . . .' He took off his spectacles and wearily rubbed his eyes.

Ruth's mouth was extremely dry. Her throat contracted. The office was very stuffy, making it an effort to breathe. She gasped for air, heard it wheeze in her lungs, couldn't seem to get enough in. She was becoming dizzy, floating away. How would she break it to Harry that Mikey wasn't . . . . ? It was too ridiculous but she felt that she was about to pass out or die.

PART TWO

Last Days

TWELVE

*The littlun's . . . in the heavy power . . . of the dark. It's dragging him . . . down
– NO. It's dragging . . . down . . . the me. Help. He's . . . I'm in the mess. . . .
The Ruthless plosion . . . hole. LISTEN. He comes . . . the Saver. He opens
up the dark, the tombs, looking . . . looking for little . . . suns to let out. Hang
on for dear life. Here, here!*

YIAOU.

*Oh, Oh, he saves cats, littluns, every . . . one. Save me. It's time to let go.
. . . time to let out the singularity . . . light. You've got the power, you've got
the technology. The littlun's finished. Begin me now daddy DADDY now
NOW . . . I . . . AM –*

ELEVEN

DOROTHY sat in the rough grass of the orchard. She was a little stunned by how much her senses were taking in. All around her daffodils fountained out of the moist earth. Some clumps were the colour of distilled sunshine, blaring spring out of their crimped loud-speakers; others had hatched like eggs with delicate trumpet-shaped yolks surrounded by a star of white petals. A myriad tiny insects were busy in the warm air. Church bells stammered melodiously across the hills, summoning believers to lift up their hearts in praise to the resur-rected Christ. Curiously, the scent of grass and flowers and earth evoked a poignant nostalgia for a childhood she had never experien-ced in the unlovely streets of Liverpool.

'Yow,' she said experimentally. It was just a nonsense word, of course, like the others – 'plode', for instance, and 'no saver'. But Mikey's tone had been arresting. With her help, he would soon master intelligible sentences. Although she was tired (looking after Mikey hadn't changed in that respect), she was also exhilarated. It suddenly seemed *possible*, not just to manage, but also to make a new start. She hadn't realised how isolated and enclosed her existence had become in the gloomy house.

And Mikey looked so well, considering. So nearly normal. He had refused food and drink, but that was only to be expected at first. More important, he had looked at her – actually focused his eyes on her –

without prompting several times during the day. He'd be smiling before long. Of course, it was a bitter blow to hear him say 'Mummy' and then to discover that he was referring to Ruth Maier (it was wrong of the woman to have encouraged this misconception), but it only made her more determined than ever to become the real mother to him that she was in fact. Besides, Ruth had brought about some genuine improvement and for this, especially on such a day, Dorothy was prepared to forgive and (eventually) forget. She was the more magnanimous for knowing that Ruth was not infallible: she had failed, for example, to cure Mikey of that distressing spinning business. Rex had been so disappointed by it that he'd been driven indoors. His study door had shut with a bang.

Dorothy wandered slowly across the three terraced lawns towards the house. Its windows flashed blood-red in the light of the sinking sun. Despite the shock Rex had given her by appearing out of the blue with Mikey that morning, she was glad that he'd given her no inkling of what he had planned. She would have dissuaded him somehow. As it was, she had cried out: 'Rex! We *promised*. . . .' Her instinctive outrage had immediately given way to panic – what if it started all over again? What if she could cope no better than before?

Rex had simply stood there, looking as pale and drawn as the boy at his side. He shrugged and said with a kind of desperation: 'He's our son. He belongs here with us.' His words were like a revelation. All Dorothy's protestations were drowned in the tide of realisation that he cared so deeply for Mikey. She was speechless with shame at having abdicated her parental duty while Rex, racked no doubt by a guilt which made hers seem as nothing, had decided to set things right.

The three of them were reunited. She had been given a second chance. She was not the same person as before: she had purged herself of resentment and come to terms with the random nature of the mistake which had plagued their lives. She was now free to devote herself to Mikey – not because she owed him anything but simply because he was hers. And who could tell but that, in time, duty would shade imperceptibly into other virtues, such as love?

Possessed of sudden fervour, Dorothy quickened her pace. She felt like a crusader, ready to begin at once on constructing her fresh bright scheme of things. She would visit Ruth Maier at the Unit – there was no room, no time for false pride now – and explain everything. She'd even ask Ruth's advice. But hadn't Rex mentioned that she was nowhere to be found when he arrived? Wasn't she supposed to be in constant attendance on Mikey? Well, if there had been neglect, Dorothy was not going to make an issue of it. The past was past.

She could not resist popping in on Mikey to make sure he was asleep. His apathetic air all day made her suspect that he had not been getting enough sleep at the Unit, or else had been worked too hard. He had certainly allowed her, without protest, to take him to his room. The room! That was something else she'd change regardless of Rex's views. It wasn't fit for a small boy. She'd buy some proper toys, cuddly ones, and a rocking horse perhaps. She knew better now than to pretend that he had a mental age anything like a nine-year-old's. Better still, she'd go up to town on a shopping spree. It seemed ages since she'd left the house, let alone taken a trip. She could take Mikey with her; he could choose his own things. Maybe they'd drive to the seaside for a day or two. What fun it was going to be! Riding on a crest of thrilling resolve, she decided to beard Rex in his den right away. He'd agree immediately to a completely new décor for Mikey's room.

She knocked at the study door. 'Rex? Darling?' To her surprise, the door swung open under her knuckles. 'Rex?' No answer. She turned away and then, scolding herself for being so timid (his study wasn't the Forbidden City, for heaven's sake), she peeped around the door. The unfamiliar room was empty and much more untidy than she had remembered it. It gave her quite a turn – Rex was such a stickler for tidiness and order. Then she saw the overturned lamp, and knew that the room had been ransacked.

'Rex.' She took the stairs two at a time. At the back of her mind she feared that someone was after Mikey. She ran down the corridor, turned right into the east wing and arrived, panting, at Mikey's door. To her relief, it opened softly.

'Oh, Rex,' she gasped. 'I thought for a moment—'

She knew that the man who came through the doorway wasn't Rex because of his size and weight. She vaguely assumed that he was a Negro, but really this was only because his head was enclosed in a black woollen helmet. It reminded her of the kind sported by IRA members when they appeared at parades; except that she hadn't remembered them as comical, like this one, whose eye- and mouth-holes were circular and rimmed with a lighter fabric. She was irresistibly reminded of a surprised golliwog.

She made as if to push past the apparition. An arm encased in a loose dung-coloured jersey shot out. On the end of it, a hand – unmistakably white – grasped her by the throat. At the moment when the powerful fingers touched her, she knew she was in the grip of the rapist. The thought clearly entered her head that she should knee him in the groin; go-ahead girls on television were always doing it. Unfortunately, she couldn't move her legs, which felt strangely heavy and numb. She lifted her hands to the hand that held her in order to ease its position

149

on her windpipe – she felt a bit giddy from lack of air. The man merely held up his other hand. It was holding a short, sturdy, very sharp knife which Dorothy recognised as one of her own. It cut neatly through almost everything. She was profoundly depressed to think that this dirty, dirty man had been in Rex's study and in her kitchen, defiling things with his big perspiring hands. She dropped her arms to her side. Perhaps, if she kept very still, he wouldn't slide the knife into her body.

While Dorothy was basking in the garden, admiring the daffodils, Rex woke up to the conviction that some catastrophe had taken place, such as a car crash. He had no idea how long he had been unconscious, whether a few seconds or a few days. Only two out of his five senses remained to persuade him that he was still alive: he could feel the hardness of cold stone under his bare buttocks and he could smell vomit on his body. But he could not see where he was because he was blind – he touched his eyelids to make sure they were raised. He could not hear anything because his head was pounding loudly and very painfully. There was more pain emanating from his groin and abdomen, especially his groin, which ached emptily as though a freezing steel spike had been driven into it. He dared not investigate for fear of what he might find.

Instead, he passed his hand tentatively over his face and, feeling puffy cheeks and thick blubbery lips, concluded that he was someone else. When he probed his mouth with his tongue, he tasted the metallic flavour of blood. A gap where half his front tooth should have been was filled with raw hurt like a dangling nerve. The loss of the handsome white tooth was worse than anything; a vital part of himself had been taken away for ever. Rex heard himself, not without relief, whimpering.

'Quiet!' The sharp word, heard or imagined, was accompanied by a sharp smack on the side of the head. Despite the renewed shock and pain, he held down his reflexive scream, neither moving nor making a sound. He waited in agony for the blow that would bring sudden death. Whatever it was that threatened him was close, perhaps only inches away. The darkness swirled into evanescent menacing shapes; tiny dripping and scratching sounds grew frighteningly loud.

A harsh rasping noise made him flinch against the stone on his naked back; a sudden flare, dispelling his fear of blindness, quietened to a steady blade of flame. He was in the cellar. A match had been struck; a candle, placed at head height on the old boiler, had been lit. The damp walls glistened. Shadowy wooden steps ascended to a door

150

that led to the world of light. The door was shut. Beside him there was a stack of coal and, all around, piles of old newspapers and magazines. The candlelight was a scalpel between his eyes, which he closed to minimise the pain. A shadow interposed itself between him and the light, and he was able to reopen them.

The shadow towered over him. It looked curiously amorphous. Its black featureless head, ringed by a nimbus of red light, seemed to grow straight out of its wide shoulders. Rex only perceived the apparition as a man when it squatted down in front of him. The movement was quick and neat, slightly jerky, like the action of a mechanical man. The head was enveloped in a black hood. The sight of it was more painful than the combined agony of groin and mouth and head.

'Who are you? Take off that mask!' For Rex, simply not knowing was intolerable. If the man had owned a face, he might have been able, weak as he was, to strike out at it. As it was, he was paralysed. There was no striking the unknown. The man seemed to know this; he moved his lump of a head unhurriedly up and down as though he were surveying him. Rex, acutely aware for the first time that he had been stripped naked, trembled uncontrollably. The man raised his large hand level with Rex's face and curled his forefinger against his thumb.

'First,' he said, 'I told you to be quiet.' His voice was deep and calm. He flicked his finger into Rex's mouth. It hit the exposed nerve in his broken tooth like a sledgehammer. A bolt of lightning shot up through his skull, forcing a cry from his lips. His eyes were wide with bewilderment.

'Secondly, you don't really want me to take off this mask, do you? Because, if I take it off, it could be the death of you. As to who I am, I couldn't really tell you. But it's not important. All you need to know is the following. . . .' He held up two objects close to Rex's face. 'Look at these very carefully.' Rex looked. He saw a short knife and a slender cut-throat razor. He shrank inside himself. 'See? One for poking, the other for slicing. One is going to poke a hole in your neck, the other is going to slice off your privates. Chop, chop. See?' He spoke slowly and deliberately, with gestures, giving Rex plenty of time to absorb the meaning of his words, like a parent teaching a child not to play with fire.

'If you behave yourself,' the man continued, 'these events may not occur for quite a long time. Who can say? I myself don't know when they will occur. But you must understand, Rex' – hearing his name used in a familiar, almost confidential way was deeply upsetting – 'that from now on your life is effectively over. There's no getting away from me. You're going to die. I'd be lying if I told you otherwise. OK?'

The knife and razor disappeared from view. The man stood up and, rolling up his sleeve, extended his right arm like an iron bar across Rex's field of vision. The skin of the thick arm was unexpectedly white and delicate. The man took the candle in his left hand and held it underneath the arm. Rex watched the white skin blackening in the flame.

Minutes seemed to elapse and still the arm didn't waver. A whiff of seared flesh floated in the stale air. The arm stayed steady. Rex became increasingly agitated, cringing as he seemed to feel the burning flesh as his own. The hair stirred on the nape of his neck and sweat trickled down his body, etching pale tracks in the coal dust. Horror and humiliation scored him slowly from head to toe. He couldn't look any more, but bowed his head before the will of his assailant.

The candle was blown out. A voice spoke out of the dark: 'The name's Klackan. He'll always be with you.'

Rex heard footsteps retreating up the wooden staircase, the door opening and closing, the bolt being shot.

Through her dress the knife pricked the bone between her breasts. The man continued to hold her by the throat. He marched her, at arm's length, backwards down the corridor. She tried to speak, but there was not enough air; her head was throbbing full of blood. He pushed her into her own bedroom, sat her down on the edge of the brass bedstead and released his throttle-hold. She heaved deep breaths into her lungs and felt the blood draining out of her face. Her body contracted automatically – legs pressed together, arms wrapped around herself, head sunk between her shoulders – as if it could thus protect itself from the man's superior force. The imminence of her rape crushed all possibility of action out of her. She might just have cried out if it weren't for the single thought which she repeated to herself from deep within her fright: This isn't happening, this *can't* be happening. As if in reply, the man spoke.

'Stay exactly where you are.'

Dorothy had somehow imagined that the man might be excitable, volatile, uncertain – that there might be a chink in his armour which she could prise open, work on, buy time with, while she mustered her slender reserves. But the voice was low and very calm. It left her in no doubt that she was an insignificant cog in a carefully planned machine. Somewhere inside her the ratchet of fear clicked up another notch and she felt her heart constrict. The pressure of the man's eyes on her body was intolerable; they glistened moistly like secret organs through the incisions in the woollen skin. She couldn't reply; she could only nod, turning her eyes away from the blank noseless face, waiting for the

152

sudden lunge. When at last she looked up, he was gone.

Dorothy instantly felt that she was about to explode. Her heartbeat raced dangerously and her breathing grew frenzied. Her fingers stiffened and began to bend backwards of their own accord. She knew she was hyperventilating and fought to get her body under control. Escape plans crowded into her brain: the door was ajar, why shouldn't she dash through it to ... to Mikey's room and lock the door from the inside? Or try for the stairs – but, no, he would have thought of them, they were too obvious; but if she could just cross the passage to the bathroom, she could climb through the window on to the flat roof below and drop to the ground – or was it too high? Would she break a leg? Where was Rex, oh, where ...? She sprang nervously to her feet. If only she could think clearly, come to a decision. ... Perhaps the man had really and truly *gone*! Perhaps he was an ordinary burglar who'd taken what he wanted from Rex's study and had left. Then she remembered the mask and the eyes in the mask. Stupid, stupid, he was here for one thing alone. She was trembling so hard she could hardly totter towards the door. She took four quick steps and stopped. Of course, she was being tested. He was waiting outside the door now, waiting for her to disobey his orders so that he could, oh God, punish her. She withdrew, dithering, to the edge of the bed and then advanced again. There was nothing to lose by opening the door; she'd be no worse off than she was now. She darted forward, but her hand wouldn't grasp the handle; her arm muscles were locked. There was a disgusting bitter taste in her mouth.

She suddenly heard a heavy tread on the stairs. He'd been down below all along. She could have escaped. Now it was too late. The door was flung open. The man strode into the room. His brown corduroy trousers, as loose and ill-fitting as his sloppy brown sweater, flapped around his legs. They were held up by a leather belt. Stuck in the belt were the knife on one side and on the other a cut-throat razor, folded away. He was reminiscent of a pirate whose black eyepatch had taken on a life of its own and spread like a growth over his whole face.

'I told you to stay where you were.' His voice was even and cold. He cuffed her sharply around the head. It was more of an afterthought than a serious blow, but Dorothy was so stunned that she might have been hit by a blunt instrument. Her scream detonated her pent-up terror and changed into a long-drawn-out wail. The man held up some curious leather bracelets with thongs attached. Then he took hold of her wrists and deftly bound them. Dorothy had gone to pieces; her wail had diminished to an empty hopeless wah-wahing.

'You'll wake up your little boy,' remarked the man. The words

153

stifled her crying. She found herself talking to him, begging, blathering, as if chance might dictate the magic words that would save her.

'Please ... please ... don't hurt me. Just leave. I won't say a word. Just go, please. No one will ever know. Take money ... jewellery ... anything you want. The police are on the golf course. I've been talking to them. They're coming here any minute—' She stopped that line of argument. She was giving him an excuse to kill her. 'Please, my son needs me ... please....'Her voice trailed off into a whisper.

The man pulled her to the bed, pushed her on her back and attached her wrists by the thongs to the brass bars behind her head. He stood back and took a passport from his pocket. He seemed to be comparing her face to the photograph inside. 'Dorothy Ballantine,' he said. He tore the passport down its spine and tossed it into the wastepaper basket. He seemed to pause for thought. 'Money? Police? I'm not bothered about money or police.' He shook his head slowly. 'You're not making any sense. Are you trying to confuse me?'

Dorothy wasn't listening; she had noticed that her short skirt had ridden up above the knees. Her shapely legs were provocatively exposed.

'... I wouldn't try to confuse me if I were you. I'm liable to become upset. In fact, if I were you, I'd steer clear of any tricky business altogether. I'm not used to it and I might not be able to put up with it....' Dorothy pressed her legs hard down on the mattress, hoping the skirt would drop. 'Lie still!' The man's sharp command froze her. She became aware of how damp she was from sweating. He took a small bottle of colourless fluid from his voluminous trouser pocket and held it up. 'For sprinkling on your face, if necessary,' he explained.

Dorothy lay absolutely still. She had no doubt that the bottle was full of acid. The bed creaked as the man sat down on it. He sighed and put his hand on the bed between her legs. 'The first thing you've got to learn, Dorothy, is to do as you're told. Is that clear?' Dorothy moved her head in a tiny stiff nod. She could sense the man wanting to strip her naked with a single tweak of his strong calm fingers. His little finger was even now brushing the inside of her thigh: the minute spot of outraged flesh burnt and tingled. At any moment he'd stretch out his bulk along the length of her body, holding her legs apart with the muscular legs inside the corduroy trousers, breathing on her and grunting and rubbing the hideous woollen face against her face.

The man grasped the hem of her dress and pulled it down so that it covered her knees. 'Lie still,' he repeated. He moved away from the bed and sat down in an armchair, carefully folding and putting to one side the blue towel that Rex had left there. His face was pointed in her direction. Dorothy knew he was only playing with her. Her arms ached severely from the crucifix position. Her dress was glued to her back, and sticky sweat was seeping down her side from her armpit. Her stomach churned ominously. The man still had the bottle in his hand. After he had raped her, he was going to unscrew the cap and drip the acid on to her, like a hot worm burrowing down to the bone. He was sitting very quietly, as still and alert as a big cat.

It occurred to Dorothy that she was going to fart. Worse than fart, perhaps, to judge by the pain in her bowels. She surreptitiously clenched her buttocks together and screwed up her eyes. Absurdly, she felt that such a breach of decorum would be too shameful, an unforgivable gaffe that would shatter the spell of unreality which entranced the hushed room. One squeak out of her would bring the man howling and slavering on to her, bucking and plunging.

It's impossible that this is happening, she thought. She screwed up her muscles until her whole body became one excruciating ache. The last of the sunlight slanted through the tall window, setting a million motes swirling in front of her eyes. She counted them one by one, forcing the man's presence out of her mind. Whatever he was going to do he would not do while she lay completely noiseless and still; as long as she counted the motes, she was invulnerable.

She must have counted more than five hundred before she became aware of someone standing on the low window-seat, silhouetted against the red-gold streamers of light. The figure moved soundlessly towards her, light as air, until she saw that it was Mikey. He was smiling at her wisely. She was about to exclaim with delight, but he shook his head and laid a finger on his lips. She held out her arms to embrace him, but he stood a little way off, out of reach. There were tears in his dark smiling eyes. She knew he was happy and that the tears were for her. She could conceive of nothing more perfect than his face, radiant in its equilibrium of sorrow and joy; she could have gazed at it for ever, and remained forever innocent as long as her eyes never left him. But with a jolt like an electric shock he was gone and she was staring into darkness.

For a second Dorothy was at a loss. 'Mikey . . .?' She tried to sit up but found that her arms were not where they should have been. All at once she remembered. She was still tied to the bed. *How could she have fallen asleep when . . . ?* She twisted her head to one side, trying to penetrate the darkness. The curtains had been drawn. As far as she could tell, there were no alien shapes in the room. The man had gone. Her dress was in the same position as he had left it. Dorothy could think of nothing except the numbness in her arms, the searing pain across her shoulders and her raging thirst. She wanted desperately to sink back into sleep and gaze at that face and never wake up.

Doctor? Something has happened. Is it something I've done or something that's been done to me? I don't know. Why are you looking at me like that? It was something terrible, wasn't it? I'm not myself today. I feel crushed into a tiny place. It's stifling. Is it my eyes or is it darker than usual? It's the shock, I suppose. I remember the shock. Electrifying, yes, but who administered it? It wasn't you, was it ... or a machine ...? No, I was afraid it wasn't. Oh Lord, Lord. It was the word, wasn't it, the word He put forth from His mouth like a cleaver ... a command as clear as ... as *unspeakable* as ... I can't remember.

But I'm still alive. The chair is solid, the table is hard under my elbows, my feet are on the floor. My name is Harry. I live at number one, South Road ... Surrey ... the World, etcetera. In a minute I'll stand up and walk to the window and let in some air. In a minute. I feel tired now. I must get my bearings. ...

'You'll end on the gaRllows' – that's what good old Father used to say. Ha! Kept his sense of humour to the end. I hope I'll do the same. I remember the day of his passing. Seventeenth of November, nineteen sixty: an ordinary rainy autumn evening. I brought him some black tea before I left for the office. He was so thin, so wasted by the Adversary Within that I could've picked them both up with one hand. He turned down the tea, just pointed to his stomach with a significant look and coughed. 'It wasn't the cough that took him off,' he said softly, 'but the coffin they took him off in.' A favourite joke of his.

Mrs Vetch from next door phoned me at the office. (Mister Turnbull was not happy about this: private calls are discouraged, and rightly so.) She'd popped in to check that he was keeping his chin up and found him dead. He had a sort of superior smile on his face, she said; but, by the time I got back, he already looked defeated. However, the important thing was he'd taken the Worm with him and not the other way round.

All right, I know what you're thinking – I'm wasting time. *Help me.* Sorry. There's a pain in my left side – the side I used to sleep on when I was a boy because Father told me your heart wore out more quickly that way. The things kids do.

There are things I didn't tell you before. Forbidden things. But I'll tell you now, I promise; more than my life's worth not to, providing I can remember. We'll have a day of reckoning, eh? I'll look into the past and, worse still, my heart and you can tell me, when I – if I – reach the end, whether I was justified or not, or whether I'm just plain – God

156

forbid – bonkers. I need a witness to my witness, so to speak. And, although I know that the act of witnessing is foolishness to some and, to others, madness, I know that you won't laugh at me because you are one who does the Lord's work without knowing.

Where do I begin? I can clearly recall being committed to this place and working at the Unit. It seems a long time ago now. But it's the trouble that led up to that time which concerns me. I'd begun to wake in the afternoon, long before it was time for work. I couldn't shake off the impression that someone was standing over me as I slept, only to hurry out of the room when I woke. I always checked the doors and windows; they were always locked, as I'd left them. I had to search the house before I retired to make sure no one had slipped in unnoticed. I never found anyone, nor was anything ever stolen. Once I woke suddenly to see the door of my room just closing – Father's room, I should say, for I'd taken it over since his death – but it was hard to be precise because I have thick blackout curtains left over from the war to keep out the afternoon sun. I'm not a believer in ghosts, Doctor, not a superstitious man; but it did cross my mind that some unquiet spirit was abroad. I even speculated that it might be Father or – God forbid – his Worm. But at that point I said to myself: Steady, Harry, steady. Oh, yes, I got a grip on myself; but my sleep was fitful thereafter.

Anyway. The trouble came to a head with Clare. At least I remember Clare ... and, yes, the subsequent trouble at the office. It's coming back to me. If I go through it all quickly, I might be able to tell you what happened after the shock. I can't go on living in the dark, that's for certain. But I'd better stay here for a while all the same. I'm not safe on the outside. I'm not safe here, come to that; but it's as safe as anywhere. We none of us escape in the end – we can only obey. But *did* I obey ...? Oh Lord ... oh Jesus. Promise you'll watch the door as I speak. Sing out if anything comes through it. If I hurry, it mightn't be too late, pray God. ...

I'll leave the business of my fitful sleep and skip straight to Clare. I've a feeling she may be – what do you say? – *relevant*. Also, you like the human element, so to speak. You'll like this. Where did I first meet her? Why, at church of course. Where else could I have intercourse with the fair sex? We're going back a few weeks now – seems more like days ... years. Depends which way you look at it. Clare was my solace and the source of my undoing.

'Why me?' Rex asked himself miserably for the thousandth time. 'Why *me*?' He could not credit what was happening to him. He had no idea how long he'd been left alone in the dark. It was driving him mad.

Again and again he'd gone over the sequence of events in his mind, desperately searching for some clue as to the meaning of it all; but he saw no rhyme or reason. He had only popped out of his study for a second, to make a cup of coffee, and when he came back someone had stepped out of the shadow behind the door and dealt him a horrendous blow between the legs. Almost simultaneously, his cry had been cut off by a second crack in the mouth. He barely recalled being bundled down to the cellar.

What really got him down was the unfairness. After all, he was no weakling, he could look after himself, give as good as he got; but he'd been given no chance to argue or defend himself – he had simply been damaged and immobilised in the space of a second. It was the impersonal efficiency he found so chilling. He couldn't believe he had done nothing, nothing except throw up.

Rex struggled to his feet and fought off the desire to faint. He needed to pee. He leant over the heap of coal, supporting himself with a hand on the wall, but nothing happened. He realised that he was terrified of peeing because of the pain in his groin; but his terror only increased his need. At last, weeping tears of pain and self-pity, he forced his bladder to empty. He couldn't nerve himself to touch his precious genitals: the thought that there might already be irreparable damage called up the memory of the castrating razor and— He shied away from all contact with such morbid mental images. They were not to be borne. He took refuge instead in rage.

Klackan didn't yet know who he was dealing with. Rex would make him pay – *God*, how he'd pay. His feet wouldn't touch the ground; they'd lock him up and throw the key away. Only a half-wit could think that Rex would be intimidated so easily. A half-wit or— Rex suddenly wondered if Klackan was in fact crazy. He hated mental illness more than any physical abnormality; he feared it nearly as much as, say, impotence. Uneasily he reminded himself that the man was perfectly lucid. Burning his arm like that was just childish. It was childish to strip him and leave him cold and hungry in the damp freezing cellar. That was it – the man was a cretin, an imbecile, little better than an animal. He'd be trapped straightaway and caged.

Rex began to think that the courts might be too lenient. Better to see to Klackan himself. He had cash and contacts, or, rather, could raise them. There was a lot of south London muscle he could call on. . . . The picture presented itself in all its sensual detail: Rex was in his old office, even bigger than before. Klackan was being dragged in, naked, begging for mercy. 'Please, don't let them hurt me, Mr Ballantine,' he was pleading, snivelling, crawling on all fours over the thick carpet. Everyone laughed at his tiny genitals, shrivelled with fear. The lads gave him well-aimed kicks in the soft parts of his body. Rex brought the house down by personally ramming a fat cigar up his arse. 'Let's do him in,' his loyal employees begged – but, no, Rex graciously spared his life, leaving for a candlelit dinner at Le Gourmet, while Klackan was taught a lesson he'd never forget. He would never be the same man – never be a man, period – again.

Rex whipped himself up into a frenzy of vengeful anger. But there was something missing: he couldn't picture Klackan's face. And without the face the human element was absent. Rex longed to imagine the man's abjection, pain, remorse, humiliation; but the space where such expressions showed either stayed abstract and empty or filled up with the face of Charles and once, disquietingly, with Dorothy. Rex became more distraught than ever as the fact of Klackan gave all imagination the slip.

Time was against him. As the seconds slowed almost to a standstill in the cold dark cellar, Rex's fury was less and less able to flesh out his fantasy. It merely left him feverish and increasingly debilitated. He turned on himself in disgust: how could he *allow* himself to be so easily overwhelmed? He resented the very triviality of his wounds – if he'd been crucified or even knifed, then his anguish could at least be justified. Excitedly he fabricated a heroic version of events in which he suffered appallingly for the sake of his family; he thrilled to the vision of an extreme affliction that wiped his slate clean and redeemed in advance all future faults. But he awoke to one unglamorous broken tooth and a swollen groin – dreary little injuries whose insistent pattern of pain simply wore him down. Cold and hunger gnawed at him, but no more than the bitterness of his damaged self-esteem. Frustrated beyond endurance, Rex punched his own body and knocked his head on the stone wall before subsiding, sobbing, to the floor. 'Why me? Why *me*?'

He wished to God he'd left Mikey where he was. The boy was a curse, somehow responsible. What did Klackan want with them? Rex knew what he wanted with Dorothy; the inhuman hood spoke for itself. She was so fragile and transparent – you could see the blue tracery of veins under her clear skin – that she could do nothing against those iron fireproof arms. Klackan could split her in half with the red column of meat that hung like a carcass inside his baggy trousers.

Rex seemed to hear the violation already, on the floor above – hear his wife's sexual cries of pain as the hooded monster cracked her like a china doll. He lightly fingered his bent penis, not daring to test it but, like his aching tooth, unable to forget it for a moment. What if the damage was total? He groaned and, clambering to his feet, stumbled around in the darkness. His hands groped for an object that could hurt Klackan. The more he stubbed his toes and barked his shins, the more savagely he flung himself about the confined space, oblivious of scratches and bruises. In the end he seized the largest lump of coal he could find, climbed to the top of the stairs and waited by the door. At the shunt of the bolt, the first crack of light, he'd ram the door wide open and heave the coal straight into the animal's inky face.

He waited, but Klackan didn't come. He waited until all his energy leaked away and his position on the steps and the weight of the coal became unbearable. When, at last, even the consciousness of his own shivering misery ceased to comfort him, he limped back to his place against the wall and half-heartedly pulled some scraps of newspaper over his body.

He couldn't have lapsed into exhausted torpor for more than two minutes when he was roused by a clanking sound overhead. He gazed up in sudden fear and saw a faint light at the end of a slanting stone channel. He had completely forgotten the coal-shute! He could have hauled himself through in a flash, heaved off the cover and fled into light and freedom. Dorothy would've remembered it; she handled coal deliveries. But he had forgotten, and now it was too late. The faint light – was it day or night? – was interrupted by a black shape. A voice said softly:

'No escape.'

The words echoed dully in the chute, followed by some dark object slithering down. The metal cover clanged shut and something heavy was dragged over it to seal it off. In the restored darkness, blacker than before, the object plopped on to Rex's lap. He yelped at the contact with its furry surface. Then he knew what it was.

'Cassie!' he cried. 'My beautiful Cassandra. . . .' Crooning affectionate words, he clutched the cat hungrily to his chest. Cassie didn't respond: she was stiff and cold with a nasty stickiness around the neck.

'God help me,' said Rex. He flung the dead creature away and heard it land with a thud. He'd taken it for granted all this time that he had importance in Klackan's eyes. Why else would Klackan attack him? Now he was faced with the novel idea that he had no importance whatever. He was equivalent to Cassie.

'No escape,' he whispered, testing the words. The darkness, thick with his mortification, pressed around his head. He closed his eyes to shut it out, but found it was there before him.

160

TEN

SHE WAS BOILED DOWN to a mass of cramps and needle-sharp aches. The pressure in her bowels had spread evenly over the lower part of her body. But, in some curious way, her physical torture – especially the thirst which had maddened her all night – had expanded beyond the limits of her body. This gradual diffusion of pain had rendered it less acute, but at the cost of polluting her thoughts and feelings. Her mind suffered from black angular shapes; her craving ran amok in vivid unbidden images where icy streams turned into warm sticky rivers of blood and her loosed fists beat at a blank face that rang like iron.

She dared not sleep, and yet the nightmarish delirium threatened to carry her away into unconsciousness. The sudden pounding of her heart brought her round; her head threshed sideways to avoid the drip of the liquid in the unknown man's bottle and her body convulsed against his obscene probing. The deadness around her abdomen made it difficult to judge whether he was thrusting into her the cold steel blade or his own hot greasy flesh. Sometimes she fancied that she had the choice. She always chose the knife. She would rather die than suffer the essential irrevocable violence that rape would do her. It would change her for ever – an unbearable idea which made her turn almost gratefully to the prospect of dying whole and intact.

HTR-6

In moments of lucidity she realised she was still alone. There was even a certain pride in discovering that her limbs, obedient to the man's injunction, had remained locked and static while her mind had been wandering. She became obsessed with her own foul smell: it was as though her glands were actually secreting a substance called fear whose astringent stench corroded any attempt to organise her thoughts. Unable to feel her arms, she imagined wildly that her flesh – deprived so long of blood – was rotting on the bone. Worst of all was her despair at being helpless. She reproached herself continually, bitterly, for not having at least tried to escape yesterday, before she was tied up. Yet, at the same time, she pushed out of her mind the thought of any action, even the smallest movement, which might bring down the wrath of the faceless man.

Dorothy fixed her eyes on the tiny crack of light between the curtains. She imagined the day beginning out there. Monday, a bank holiday. Perhaps Rex was not in the house. How could he be and allow her to be treated like this? He had gone out yesterday without telling her; obviously he had gone out, otherwise she would have heard him fighting or shouting when the man came. He'd stayed out all night, in town; he'd done it so often before; he'd be back any second to make short work of the man. Mikey would've slept through it all, waking up to wonder what all the fuss was about. Rex could even be in the house now, thinking she was still asleep and unwilling to wake her. Dorothy felt light-headed, almost happy. She had only to wait a little bit longer.

The truth dawned on her: the light between the curtains was not growing, but fading. She had let a whole day drift past. She had been left there to die. She seemed to jolt down into her body. Every joint and ligament was on fire; hunger and thirst broke over her like hatred and rage. She yanked at her manacles and kicked her legs about, trying to knock over the bedside table. She couldn't reach it. Her brief frenzy left her exhausted and weaker than before. She ran her swollen tongue around her parched mouth in an effort to raise enough saliva so that she could shout. She took a deep breath. The door opened. The light was switched on. Dorothy exhaled silently.

The hooded man glided across the thick carpet to where Dorothy was lying rigid and shrinking inside herself. He walked gracefully, with a straight back and economic movements of his limbs. He pulled the razor from his belt, unclasped the blade and laid it against her neck. Unbelievably, she had forgotten how blatant and exclusive her terror was in his presence. His silence was even worse than his measured matter-of-fact voice. If she could get him to speak, she might delay her fate for a minute or two. With fearful cunning she chose to appeal to him through Mikey.

'Please listen. Mikey ... my son ... he's ill. It's a rare illness; he's not like other boys; he needs constant care.' She found that she was flattening her vowels in order that the poshness of her acquired accent shouldn't irritate him. 'It's a psychological illness, you see. He only came out of hospital yesterday. Please, let me see him.' She looked pleadingly into the sceptical woollen face. The man replaced the razor in his belt.

'Are you being frank with me, Dorothy? I set a lot of store by frankness. But I'm under a lot of stress. It's not always easy for me to keep control of myself. I look at you, lying there like an attractive woman, with nice clothes and everything, and I get to thinking that I've come across a lot of women in my time who look like you. I've come to have what you might call mixed feelings about these women. It's my experience that they're a bit on the cold side. A bit hard. And you can't always believe what they say. To be frank, I've got mixed feelings about you, Dorothy. I don't know if I trust myself with you.' He shook his black head sorrowfully.

'Mikey's all right,' he went on. 'He'll go on being all right as far as I can see. As long as you behave yourself.'

Dorothy couldn't bear to listen to his monotonous easygoing voice a moment longer. She felt sick and faint.

'My husband ...,' she blurted out, 'my husband's coming back any moment....'

The man took out his bottle of acid and, unscrewing the top, held it close to her face.

'Are you sure you're not mistaken, Dorothy?' The man obviously knew she was lying – the one thing he'd warned her about. She must be mad to lie to him. She couldn't think what had come over her.

'I don't know why I said that. I don't know where he is. I'm so ... frightened.'

'I'm glad you said that, Dorothy. We must be open with each other.' He placed the bottle carefully on the bedside table. 'I'm frightened myself. If you'd told another fib ... well, let's just say that the stuff in the bottle would do you no harm at all compared to what I might do.' He seemed genuinely troubled about her safety. He was insane.

'Where is my husband?' she asked in a small voice.

'Rex? He's down below, Dorothy. In the cellar. Women like you don't know when they're well off. It could be you down there.'

'Is he ...?' She was going to say 'alive', but the word wouldn't come. 'Is he all right?' The man nodded absently. 'Can I see him?'

'No.'

'Mikey? Please, let me see—'

'No.'

'Oh, what do you *want*?' Dorothy began to cry.

'*Stop that.*' His voice changed so suddenly from its meditative note to a harsh anger that Dorothy instantly stifled her sobs. She was swept by a new wave of terror, hardly able to believe that such fear could go on and on, eating into her. She longed for him to end it but dreaded that he would.

'What I want', the man continued in his former musing voice, 'is a spot of peace and quiet. I have to get things straight in my mind. What I'll want in a minute or tomorrow or next week there's no knowing. It's not really up to me. But I have to say I'm fairly certain that you'll never leave this house again. Not in one piece, at any rate. It just can't be done. . . .' He was apologetic. 'You'll have to make the best of it, Dorothy. I'm not promising anything, but it may not be too bad for you – as long as I don't get any coldness or hardness or lies. The slightest sign of trickiness – your boy gets the chop for starters and you . . . well, it doesn't bear thinking about.' He patted her on the arm. Dorothy felt a scream coming up in her which she imagined was like madness. If she admitted the scream, she might never get out of it.

'Could I have some water, please?' she choked, but managed to sound polite and sensible. The eyes in the woollen sockets gleamed white as they moved over her body. The man produced his knife and leant over her. She closed her eyes and tried to pray to Jesus Christ; but she couldn't direct her will or words or thoughts beyond the man who weighed on her like lead. The bed creaked as he began to unpick the knots in the leather thongs. Dorothy's breath came out of her nose in a series of tiny whines. Her hands were free.

'Oh, thank you. *Thank* you.' She rubbed her arms and wrists ecstatically. If you were natural with the man, calm and frank, he was reasonable enough.

'Bring me some, too,' he said.

'What?'

'Water. From the bathroom. You've got forty seconds.' She looked at him uncertainly. Was it some kind of trick? 'Thirty-five seconds.'

She stumbled to the door, crossed the passage, blundered into the bathroom. The cold tap was stiff, and her hands were numb and useless. She wrenched at it furiously. She wanted to run downstairs to free Rex, but her legs wouldn't move away from the tap. Water gushed out. She had time to make it to the cellar but she couldn't drag her hands away as they scooped water into her mouth. Long before she'd had enough, she panicked. Her time must be nearly up. She grabbed the tooth mug, filled it to the brim and hurried back to the bedroom.

He had wheeled the television trolley to the end of the bed and was bending over the video recorder. His back was towards her.

'We'll watch one of these video tapes,' he remarked. 'I've not seen one before.' The knife was on the floor by his feet. The open bottle of acid was still on the table. If she failed to reach it before him, he would kill Mikey and rape her. When she hurled the liquid in his face she would have to hit the eyes or the helmet might protect him; at any rate, it might give her time to collect the knife and run him through. But what if she missed altogether? Or her senseless hands fumbled the bottle? At school, her dearest wish had been to dive off the high board. She remembered the humiliation of having to turn back and climb down the ladder. She never was able to take the plunge.

The man swivelled on his heel and reached the bottle in three strides. He had read her mind; he controlled everything.

'I'm glad you decided not to be tricky, Dorothy. And now that we're going to be more open with one another you can forget about my water.' He lifted the bottle to the mouth-hole in his mask and swallowed the contents. 'I brought my own, you see. Special stuff. Now, show me how this machine works. And, by the way, my name is—'

'No!' Dorothy pressed her fingers in her ears. She didn't want to hear his name. It meant that he could never let her go. It meant that there was relationship. But she was too late. She did hear his name and knew that there was no way out. His name was Klackan.

Monday

I've been sleeping a good deal, thanks partly to the sedative Dr Frieling gave me yesterday, and partly perhaps to some sort of chemical reaction of my own. Sleeping is a way of not facing things. I do understand that Mikey has been taken away from me, but the knowledge has yet to sink in. It's an apt expression: I feel the presence of a terrific weight hovering somewhere near me and I dread the moment when it will drop. But, so far, although the shadow of the weight is itself heavy enough to keep me horizontal and dozy, underneath it's business as usual. No, that's not quite right. I feel charged up, expectant, even cheerful, when I'm not feeling simply lethargic. It's very strange. I have this image of myself — that is, body, brain, feeling — as having been somehow amputated; yet, as in phantom limbs, I'm still tingling — going through the motions as if everything were intact. I suppose all this must be the effect of shock, but I don't feel shocked — people in shock never do! Perhaps I'll keel over at any moment or suddenly find I'm writing even more incoherently than usual.

165

Everyone has been kind. Adrian gave me a box of hazelnut fudge, my favourite. He was rather awkward and sweet – but he knows how I love to stuff in a crisis. . . . Amazingly, the box is *unopened* in front of me. Can it be that my new phantom body doesn't need food?? There is a serious explanation that I ought to record: I woke this morning with an intense desire to kill Mikey's parents. This has now passed. It'll take longer to forgive them for their selfishness and stupidity. All the same, I recognise that my desire for revenge was an automatic attempt to replenish the emotional cavity created by the loss of Mikey. Nature abhors a vacuum; it's a pity that it's always our baser energies which rush to fill it up. In this case, I can only suppose that my emptiness is beyond food – I certainly feel that it would be almost sacrilegious to eat.

Carol – excellent therapist that she is – advises me to 'talk it out'. Apparently she lost a child in similar circumstances – I didn't know this – and so understands my predicament. I felt terribly guilty that I'm not suffering (not yet) as she must have done; I felt guiltier at not wanting to talk. I'm not open and sincere like Carol. If I could talk, it would be to Harry, who more than anyone shares my passion for Mikey. Perhaps he's suffering now, but I can't help him. There's nothing to say. I see now that I was jealous of how comfortable he was with Mikey – in the end I thought they were in league with each other, excluding me. But I excluded myself – because I was so busy being the Good Counsellor and mistrusting Harry in case he damaged Mikey instead of *seeing* that Mikey trusted him. Oh, Mikey. Oh, Harry. What can I say?

Dr Frieling suggested I take two or three weeks off. I told him I was OK and that it would probably be better if I went on working. I meant, of course, better for *me* – I sometimes think I've learnt nothing from Mikey. Only when Dr F. insisted did I realise that he was telling me that I could be ruinous for the kids until it's certain that there are no long-term effects arising from Mikey's departure. He could easily have told me that I was stubborn, selfish and eager to play the martyr, but he didn't have to, luckily, because I recognised these execrable qualities in myself and quickly agreed – to his relief – to stay out of the way for a while. Just as well, on reflection – I find that I'm unable, for all my cheeriness, to go near the play-room in case I see some other child on M.'s bean-bag. The good doctor has popped into my room twice today – that's twice more than on any other day. Says he wants my 'advice' on such matters as changing the breakfast menu. It's very touching. He's telling me he's available if I need him, and also that I'm still part of the Unit.

This extraordinary warm spell keeps me indoors. All that loveliness outside – budding and burgeoning – is like a betrayal. Whenever I looked out of the window today, I felt stabbed. Thank God it's night and quiet now, way past my normal bedtime. It's a continual struggle to suppress the instinct to go down and check up on Mikey. I wish I could adjust. But that might mean admitting the burden of lurking grief. I hope you're asleep now, Mikey. At least Carol had the wit, bless her, to thrust Yiaou into your arms as you left. Goodnight, darling. I love you. I won't forget you.

Ruth regretted having begun this latest entry in her journal. She was suddenly tired out physically, but in other respects wide awake. The room was in darkness except for the pool of light from her desk-lamp. She was mildly repelled by the sight of her own handwriting, cramped and illegible like hieroglyphics, on the very white paper. The surrounding darkness weighed on her heavily, hovering like the premonition of a headache. She leant back in her chair and, transporting herself easily to the ski-lift, huddled next to the warm presence and drank in the cold refreshing mountain air. The sunlight and snowfields, the eternal peaks, were ready as ever to greet her. Aware of the dead climbers across the vertiginous gulf, she slowly allowed the glittering white space to eclipse everything from her field of vision. Her arm fidgeted to relieve a slight cramp. She was restored to tranquillity now. The induced spectacle faded into a pleasurable drowsiness. A jerk from her arm brought her back to her senses.

Every soul is unique and precious in the eyes of God.

Ruth stared, disbelieving, at the sentence on the white paper of her journal. It was ill-formed, the letters large and laboured, as if produced with difficulty. Its content was unremarkable, even banal, except for the fact that she hadn't written it.

The man pressed the button on the remote-control device. The menacing shape, coasting with submarine efficiency alongside the rickety boat, wiggled rapidly backwards. Dorothy dug her fingernails into her palms with irritation.

They were sitting side by side on the bed like any married couple. *Jaws* was playing on the television screen. She had seen it before and thought it rather a silly film. But Rex liked it enough to keep a tape of it. She could hear him praising, rather pompously, the camerawork and editing as though it were a French art movie instead of an implausible tale about a killer shark. The sound was turned down, so that the dialogue was reduced to whispers, punctuated by the famous music which, throbbing like a faint heartbeat, heralded the presence of the dangerous fish.

The movie was taking a long time because Mr Klackan had the exasperating habit of rewinding the tape. At one moment a crowd of bathers was scrambling, panic-stricken, out of the sea; at the next they were pulled jerkily backwards waving their arms as if magnetised by the waiting Jaws. One girl was condemned to death several times; the water was cloudy with her blood. Dorothy knew that as long as the film was running she was safe. She wanted desperately to work out what she should do; instead, it seemed more important to find out why Mr Klackan replayed certain scenes and not others. But, concentrate as she might, she could discern no pattern in the random pressing of the button. For minutes at a time she could forget the shining knife resting casually on his right thigh — only to be jerked back into fright by the disruption of the movie's flow of events.

She had an overpowering need to urinate. She had not been to the lavatory for more than twenty-four hours. Only her copious sweating, she guessed, had enabled her to hold out for so long. But now she remembered the story of the guardsman on parade in front of Queen Victoria who had expired from a burst bladder rather than face the shame of leaving the parade ground. She regretted the water she'd drunk, completely forgetting how maddened by thirst she had been.

The old sea dog, played by Robert Shaw, was mouthing like a demented Long John Silver; Richard Dreyfuss's character was gesticulating angrily. Dorothy tried to remember the dialogue. She wouldn't ask Mr Klackan if she could go to the bathroom. Not yet at any rate. He seemed distant, calmer. She didn't want to break the rhythm of the film, didn't want to remind him. She could hold out for a few minutes and, maybe, a few more minutes after that — if her bowels could rearrange themselves, distributing their pain across her abdomen, then perhaps her bladder would also alter or expand. The changes in her body were scary. She felt stiff and wrenched as though she had undergone some harsh remoulding process. And now, to top it all, as though her insides had taken on a malicious life of their own, her stomach began to gripe with hunger pains.

A fantastic notion occurred to her: today was a bank holiday, but tomorrow Rex's office would ring and, getting no reply, send the police round. She had only to survive another night. Fiercely she concentrated on the screen. The third man in the boat was the police chief. He was played by . . . by. . . . The name wouldn't come to her. She knew the actor's face as well as her own. He'd been on television only the other day. She stared greedily at his face, hoping to read his name there. He was so well known to her that her failure to name him was as bad as anything that had happened, like a proof that she had already suffered damage to the brain. Tears flowed from her eyes. What was his *name*? It was something like Romy Schneider, except that she was an actress, the sister – or was it daughter? or mother? – of María Schneider. María.

Dorothy suddenly saw the face of the Spanish girl, with her melancholy smile and perfect teeth. At the time she was glad to be rid of her. She didn't like the way Rex looked at her; she resented the ease with which the girl insinuated herself into Mikey's affections. She was too meek for her own good, always so obedient and patient. Even Rex became irritated with her in the end, could hardly bear to be in the same room with her. But Dorothy was sorry now. If María had stayed, Mikey might have been spared.

She almost moaned aloud – she'd forgotten about Mikey. What appalling torment was he suffering while she sat watching television with a psychopath? Why couldn't she keep her mind on him? She imagined his face as it had been the previous afternoon and struggled by muscular effort to irradiate a telepathic message of comfort and hope to the small boy just five doors away. But her attention was distracted by the actor whose name escaped her.

Robert Shaw was slithering down the deck of the wrecked boat straight into the huge open mouth of Jaws, who was lolling over the stern. Robert Shaw's mouth was also open wide, but only a whisper came out as the shark snapped him off at the waist. The man beside her gave a muffled grunt inside his hood. He clicked the button and the monster disgorged the farcical old sea dog, still screaming but miraculously intact like a dead man resurrected on the Last Day.

It was dark outside. The film was in its closing sequence. The man who called himself Klackan was fidgeting, tired of manipulating the puppets on the screen. Dorothy knew that she would be raped when the film finished. She knew it because she had failed to escape, failed to keep Mikey's face in her mind, failed to remember the name of the police chief in the movie. Somehow she had set in motion the wheels of her own catastrophe. Without her consent the wish began to form that he would get it over with – at least the terror would end. He could do nothing more to her except kill her. She shuddered and twitched her head, shaking off the thought. She couldn't die after that, all destroyed inside. His sheer weight would tear the membrane that kept her as she was, and something utterly alien would fly shrieking out and take her place. She had to hang on; or, if that were impossible, to fall on his knife.

Bubbles of hysteria began to rise and swell sensuously inside her, floating up her spine and frothing in her brain. The two survivors were paddling silently away from the sinking boat. The man yawned and clicked the television off. The whispering stopped; the silence ticked like a bomb.

'Oh . . . no,' groaned Dorothy. She was exploding. The man jerked upright and sprang off the bed.

'You're a filthy dirty little girl,' he said in disgust. Dorothy sat limply, too humiliated to cry, as the piss seeped around her in a fetid pool on the bed.

'I'm sorry,' she said dully. 'Don't hurt me.'

Klackan removed the razor from his belt and placed it next to the knife on the bedside table. Then he took off his belt.

Perhaps there was a dybbuk in the room, in *her*! Ruth sprang up and switched on the main light. The room was its old friendly self. She gulped down a few deep breaths of air before she realised that, despite her shamanistic behaviour, she wasn't especially upset.

'This is ridiculous,' she said aloud. Her hand had actually moved of its own accord across the page and constructed a sentence whose handwriting and sentiments were not hers. She bent over and scrutinised it. It didn't look like the sort of thing a dybbuk would have written.

Ruth sat down again in front of her journal. She was more afraid of being afraid than she was of the writing. Deliberately, she relaxed. Her arm tingled from shoulder to fingers as if she had mild pins and needles. It wasn't unpleasant. She took up her pen and surrendered her arm to its slight restlessness. The pen moved uncertainly over the paper. Ruth watched it with fascination. It spelt out a single word.

Ask.

Feeling too foolish to speak, Ruth took possession of her hand and quickly scribbled 'Who are you?' Then, letting her hand go limp, she held her breath and waited. The pen moved.

Your beginning and end.

It didn't make sense, but it was an answer of a kind. Ruth wondered if she was going a bit crazy. She touched a few articles on her desk; they felt as solid and real as usual. She made her hand write her name several times; it responded as she expected – her ordinary untidy writing bore no resemblance to the involuntary script.

Ruth knew very little about automatic writing, associating it with stereotyped mediums – eccentric, rather spooky ladies of a certain age who lent themselves to vacuous 'spirits' and wrote down their equally vacuous messages. She had no wish to embark on a similar folly. But the portentous last sentence both irritated and intrigued her.

170

'Are you . . . ?' She hesitated to write the word. It was madness to be writing to herself in this way. All the same, she took the plunge.

'Are you a *spirit*?' she wrote.

I am a soul, as you are, but you may call me a spirit if you wish.

Ruth was rather impressed by this pedantic distinction. The 'spirit' was at least coherent; it was even a little condescending.

'I mean, are you dead?'

I have died to myself that my true self may live, yet not in itself but in the spirit.

It crossed her mind briefly that she was suffering from some sort of hallucination induced by lack of food. The striking biblical tenor of the answer made her think vaguely of St Anthony, starving in the Egyptian desert and hemmed around by tempting devils. Slightly annoyed, she wrote: 'Why are you evading my questions?'

I am not. You are asking the wrong questions. Ask.

'Right,' said Ruth out loud. She decided to assume, for the sake of argument, that she was communicating with a person and to see where it led her.

'Are you in what is commonly called the next world?'

There is only one world but it has two aspects: the realm of spirit and the realm of matter. Matter is like the shadow of spirit. Each soul inhabits both realms simultaneously; but when the soul is incarnate, in the material realm, it sees only the flat shadow dimensions and is blinded to the dazzling dimensions of the spirit realm — which are present nevertheless, but hidden. Only when the soul enters the spirit realm are these new dimensions, like colours beyond the visible spectrum, made manifest.

During this long speech the handwriting became neater as though the writer were rapidly adjusting to an unfamiliar pen. This new fluency made Ruth nervous of losing control. But she gripped the pen more tightly and determined to match her correspondent's attempt at precision.

'I take it, then, that you are not, as you put it, incarnate. But how can I be sure that you are not a harmful soul — a soul, for instance, in the dimension we call hell?' There was a certain pride in accurately adopting the spirit's terms. It replied immediately with a flourish of her hand.

Like a dybbuk?

Ruth had to smile; the spirit had picked up her earlier unspoken fear. It went on:

You would not call me harmful if you knew the difficulty I have in communicating with you. It is excruciating for me to cramp myself into your dimensions. But you are right to ask. The Bible tells us to test the spirits to make certain they are of God.

'You are a Christian, then?'

I am an incomplete, imperfect soul who is commanded to become whole and perfect like the Lord Jesus. In that sense, I am a Christian. But I am less of a Christian than the soul whose hand I use to move your hand.

Ruth was intrigued by this piece of information. 'Do you mean', she asked, puzzled, 'that there is more than one of you communicating with me?'

No. I alone am writing. But I cannot contact you directly because I am so far removed from your material realm that it would take too long to control your physical body without damaging it. We have very little time, so I must use an instrument.

'Who is this ... instrument?'

A developed, responsive soul. She is called María. I have chosen her because she is suitable for my purpose, having certain affinities with you. For example, you share similar beliefs and forms of expression which I can use to transmit my messages more easily.

'Is she the María who used to look after Mikey?' Ruth wrote excitedly.

Yes.

'Can I speak to her directly?'

In time, perhaps. Now it is I who must speak.

'What shall I call you?'

Nothing. The idea of personality will obscure my message.

'All right. But are you what spiritualists call a guide?'

You may think of me as such if you like. I have watched over you. But it is unimportant.

She suffered a small pang at these words. It was foolish, but also rather moving, to think that the owner of the strange handwriting had watched over her. She was reminded of the guardian angels so confidently promised by the nuns when she was a girl. In a more mellow mood, she wrote: 'What is it you want to say exactly?'

The answer was disappointing.

I have not yet mastered, through my instrument, the conditions of your realm. Everything is still cloudy. Have patience, child.

Something in the spirit's tone, intuited rather than heard, startled Ruth. She was struck, too, by the familiar 'child'.

'Are you my *father*?' She scribbled breathlessly. There was a pause as though the spirit were pondering.

Family relationships are a model of all relationship. What you see as a sequential relationship in time — that is, the succession of each generation — is a pale shadow of how true relationship operates. All souls are related to each other in the Spirit who is God. In the eternal realm of Spirit, the mother

172

is daughter to the son, for instance, and the son is father to the mother. Only God knows why certain souls—

The writing lapsed abruptly into scribble and broke off. Ruth wrote a few words experimentally, but they were her own. She touched the writing on the page, almost expecting the large sloping script, so different from her own, to fade before her eyes. She pressed a hand to her forehead to test for signs of fever; but, whatever psychic aberration had seized her, it had left no mark on her physical well-being. On the contrary, all trace of her impending headache had disappeared and she felt light and cool as though a stream of purifying water had been drawn through her.

Ruth marvelled at the clipped oblique style of the unknown spirit. That it was alien to her own way of speaking did not necessarily rule it out as the product of some hitherto uncharted region of herself. The telling mention of María, for example, with whom she shared a special interest in Mikey, supported the thesis that she was unconsciously identifying with the Spanish girl. What could be more likely than that she should address herself under psychic stress in María's name? And yet all her intuitions protested against this interpretation. The personality behind the messages was so consistent and forceful that she trembled to think that they had emanated from her own hand. She couldn't help taking the silent co-operation of María at face value. How much was the girl responsible for the style, if not the content, of the messages? She must have been still very young when she died. Had she been an 'instrument' in life as well as in death? And how did she die?

The congregation of Saint Bartholomew's had fallen off something shocking since the Reverend Pugh's day. I took to going along about six months ago, mostly for the hymns. Like a lot of churches, Saint Bart's is pretty much a stranger to the truth, plodding along as if nothing is happening or ever will. Christ'll catch it napping on His Return, no doubt; but you never know for certain what's in people's hearts and it *may* not be so bad.

Anyway, I was giving a hymn some lung one matins, leaving out the heretical verses, of course, when I caught a glimpse of a young girl – not more than sixteen, I'd say – in a pew ahead of me. She had fair hair, like Alice's was, but finer, plus, unlike Alice, a wondrously clear skin. When she prayed, her eyelashes trembled on her cheeks – they were that long. There was no paint or stuff on her face, of course, and her demeanour was modest and pure. You're looking cynical? Well, it's true – you wouldn't have been able to take your eyes off her, I promise.

173

After the service she walked over to her bicycle which she'd left unpadlocked. I approached her, giving no thought to what I'd say, only fixing my mind on the determination to speak up. I needn't have worried: *she spoke first*. In a pleasing voice, very polite, she said: 'How do you do? I'm Clare Reid.' I could barely doff my cap and introduce myself. She explained shyly that she was new to Saint Bart's because she'd been confirmed only a fortnight ago. I suggested that she was quite old for confirmation (I was done at thirteen) and she cast her eyes down, saying, 'I wasn't ready at thirteen. I wasn't sure of my faith. But I'm sure now.'

Well!

I offered to walk a little way with her, if she'd forgo the pleasure of the bicycle, and she agreed without demur.

Had her confirmation classes included any mention of the Second Coming? Of course not. The Church hurls children unprepared into a world on the brink of destruction. I went cold all over at the thought that Clare might be left behind at the Rapture and thereafter drift into sin at the hands of the King of Fierce Countenance – that glib Wicked who will seduce souls into cheerful damnation. Naturally I broke the news gently, emphasising the shortness of the awful Beast's tyranny and the longness of Christ's thousand-year reign. Children shouldn't be frightened, and she was little more than a child. But the way her clear forehead was marred by sudden anxious wrinkles wrung my heart and I pressed on her one of my most pleasant prophecies, namely *Peace and the Restoration of the Insect World in the Millennium*. For insects are a thorn in the side of theologians and must be faced up to.

Clare brightened up at this and asked me what it was about and had I really written it, etcetera. Well, I don't like to blow my own bassoon but I explained some of the ideas, for example, how Christ's final return would spell the end of ugliness and harm among fleas, mosquitoes, scorpions, horseflies, tarantulas and so on, plus how the piratical wasp would lie down with the civil honeybee. Clare was very absorbed and asked me several hard questions which I did my best to answer. It was lovely, just talking like that and walking along like old pals with her hand on the bike's handlebars and mine resting ever so gently on the saddle.

Lovely, yes, until we fell into dispute about wasps, which she claimed would keep their stings in the Millennium because Christ would never do violence to their nature. I became rather tongue-tied, thinking that I might be in error or, perhaps, that wasps would keep their stings but never *use* them and so on. Clare said: 'You're not a clergyman at all, are you? Your black suit made me think you were.' I tried to explain that I was not a clergyman *as such* but that I was ordained in a manner of speaking. I didn't want the bond between us to break. She walked a bit faster. There were two red patches on her cheeks (put me in mind of Jean Macintyre actually) and she said firmly, 'I don't believe all this Second Coming stuff,' and thrust the pamphlet back at me. It was all very upsetting, very.... I *had* to impress her with the urgency of things; I couldn't *bear* to think of her found wanting at the Rapture.

In vain I reminded her of the fate reserved for those who incurred the wrath of the Lamb – 'For I will tread them in anger, and trample them in my fury....' She was hurrying now, with me running after her; she wouldn't *listen*. '... and their blood shall be sprinkled upon my garments, and I will stain my raiment' and so on – Isaiah always excites me. We were near her house, a posh place up Molyneux Road – Long Acre, it's called. I was waxing desperate. Try as I might to show her how the Lord would trample down the people in His anger, she refused to look at my feet, but dashed on. We'd reached her gate before I managed to hold on to her.

She looked so pale and innocent that I couldn't stop myself vowing a terrible vow, namely that I would renounce the Rapture in order to protect her during the forty-two months of the Beast and, when Christ came again, I'd stand fast between her and His vengeance. For I would rather be sent into a sinner's hell for a thousand years than to see her wail and gnash her teeth. I could say no more. She stood very still. I said I was sorry for grabbing her and perhaps we could talk a bit more next Sunday after matins. She nodded quickly and wheeled her bicycle up the garden path. I thought: 'I've got through to her at last, praise God,' and, despite the horror of my implacable vow, I felt strangely light at heart.

What a week of waiting that was. I went to work in a haze and came back in a dream. I did no hawking, for I hadn't the stomach for abounding in the works of the Lord. I was glad that I worked at night: the house was no place to be after dark. As it was, I abandoned Father's bedroom and sat in his armchair in the parlour, snatching forty winks at a time, always ready to flee if there should be any ... disturbance. In between winks I meditated on my promise to Clare. Had I betrayed my vocation? Could I *keep* my promise? It was a time of testing and doubt.

I wondered how I could ever have imagined that I'd be comfortable at the Rapture. *I* would be lifted clear of the world's tumult and woe, yes; but how could I rejoice when so many, Clare included, would be left behind to reap the whirlwind? You, too. Oh yes, I'm sure you've never purposely defied the Lord; but Woe unto you all the same.

175

I was in great turmoil of mind, great vexation of spirit. I hung on to the thought that I'd be seeing Clare again on Sunday. I knew in my marrow that the Rapture was almost upon us — I could tell by the foulness of the air, the twittering of spirits in the trees, the gathering of storm clouds invisible to all but the eyes of the spirit. I clung to the hope that Clare would be called to repentance in time. Then at least my life would not have been wholly wasted and I could fly with her to my perch on the right hand of the Lord.

NINE

HER HANDS SCRABBLED like twin mice through the dressing-table drawer, sifting the contents until she found an appetising pink lipstick. She nibbled it excitedly. It tasted scented and oily as though it might be nourishing. As she chewed the last of it up, her eye fell on Rex's sleeping pills. He'd only taken a couple, said they made him sluggish in the mornings. Dorothy shut the drawer quickly and pressed her hands against it to contain the extraordinary idea which the sight of the pills had evoked.

She did not know whether it was day or night, and she wasn't interested. The light burnt perpetually in the bedroom; she was not to switch it off. The curtains were to stay drawn, which was a blessing because any glimpse of the outside world could only cause unnecessary pain. Any thought of shouting for help, which no one in any case would hear, had long since been abandoned. Similarly, she now knew that the phone would never ring. He had taken it away, of course — it was the sort that could be unplugged and moved about — but its absence wouldn't stop the bell from ringing. She'd watched the bell for hours, perhaps days; nothing happened. She had toyed with the hope that Rex would find a way of rescuing her. In her heart she knew it was impossible. She couldn't conceive of him setting his foot on Mr Klackan's neck and unmasking him. She felt as guilty for doubting Rex's strength as if she'd been unfaithful to him.

As time dragged on in the noxious airless room, her admiration for Klackan grew in proportion as all hope was exhausted. He'd foreseen it all, thought of every contingency. She had been deeply shocked when he casually mentioned that he'd cancelled the milk – she herself had entirely overlooked the rich possibilities of the milkman's daily delivery. It was almost a privilege to be playing a part in his grand enigmatic design.

The lipstick had made her queasy, but it was no worse than her gnawing hunger. If she could just hold it down, it might do her some good. She glanced at the door automatically about every five seconds – a precaution in case he came in and caught her doing, or not doing, something he disapproved of. The most important thing she wasn't to do was sleep. She was to watch and wait for him at all times. When he did come, suddenly, unpredictably, he often just sat in ghastly silence. Sometimes he liked to look at a video with her, though not television programmes. He had brought up all Rex's private tapes from the study to supplement the bedroom's modest collection. Dorothy waited for the sound of his key in the lock with a long-drawn-out anguish reminiscent of the times she'd waited for the phone to ring during her courtship with Rex.

She had taught herself to sleep in twenty-second intervals. These were periods of great peril. The alternative – staying awake until she dropped off involuntarily – was riskier still, since it carried a greater chance of being caught out. So far, she'd been discovered asleep only once. The punishment wasn't too severe, maybe because she had the good sense to offer up her bottom for a belting. However, falling asleep was not, apparently, a belting offence. Peeing on the bed was a belting offence. Falling asleep meant a reduction in the water ration from a full mug to a few mouthfuls, plus the withholding of the daily 'soup'. Mr Klackan was scrupulously fair, she had to give him that. Even the thrashing could have been worse – there was no malice in the belt to give it extra sting. It was simply a penalty to be paid, and no more than she deserved. And giving her the run of the room without further bondage was kindness itself.

Glancing again at the door, Dorothy seized the hem of the dressing-gown which she had exchanged for the uncomfortable dress, and hurriedly wiped the traces of lipstick off her mouth and teeth. She avoided the mirror because of what she might see or, worse, not see – she was prey to the irrational suspicion that her reflection, like a vampire's, would be missing.

Dorothy's thoughts kept flitting to the sleeping-pills in the drawer. But she could not concentrate on them or on anything else, because of Klackan. Even in his absence (especially in his absence) he grew in

178

stature and strength like a great black pillar that overshadowed everything. If she peeped out from behind it at Rex or Mikey, they appeared dream-like and unreal; Klackan was the only hard fact. She became anxious and disturbed if the intervals between his visits were too long — she felt that without his solid presence there was nothing to stop her dissolving beyond recall. Only by straining to attach herself more closely to his reality could she hope to survive. She was no longer aware of fear; it was the air she breathed. Neither of them remarked on her eventual violation. It merely lay between them like a naked sword which in time he would snatch up and turn on her — in some ways he already had.

There were instants almost of euphoria when Dorothy incredulously remembered the petty anxieties of her former life. They had been pared away; she was nothing but skin and bone, so light and empty that in the end he'd blow her away like thistledown with a single puff from the puff-shaped hole in his hangman's hood.

But, without warning, she would plummet from euphoria to jagged despair: the dark column of his presence was crowding her out and exerting intolerable stress on the soft membrane that sealed off her vital dangerous memory. At any second it could snap like elastic and release the face of the creature on the seventh stair, who would drive her mad.

Dorothy walked around the room, touching and counting each article of furniture to build up a reality other than Klackan. Gradually the ritual formed a wedge which eased him away from her and created a tiny breathing-space. Then, briefly, she realised how the man was out to destroy her, body and soul, and that she had to protect her independence at all costs. But she was so tired, so hungry and thirsty, so dirty; she had no resources left to combat, not only Klackan, but also her own treacherous self begging her to submit.

She scurried to the dressing table and, taking out the bottle, emptied the sleeping pills into her hand and counted them. There were plenty of them, enough. She counted again, gloating. She'd give anything to see Mr Klackan's face when he came in and found that she'd escaped after all! Not that you could see his face (if he had one), but it was getting easier to detect expressions on the black wool. She giggled. The thought of going to sleep made her dizzy with bliss. All her fears would be snuffed out, painlessly, like a litter of mewing kittens.

But her mouth was furred with thirst; she'd never swallow all the pills without water. She'd have to wait until he brought the day's ration. Holy Mother of God, *wait*. And what if his next appearance was the last? A whole new species of terror threatened to erupt into her bloodstream. She beat at the air with her fists and made little darting runs to and fro. Had he left the pills there on purpose to tempt her? Surely he knew what was in her mind? Was he outside now, laughing softly into his hood, waiting for her to lift the first tablet to her lips? No, no – he couldn't be. Could he? If he ever found out, there'd be hell to pay for this lapse of frankness.

She began to stuff the pills back into the bottle. Her heart raced so hard it hurt. She slammed the drawer shut. She could wait, she was certain she could wait – as long as she hid the secret of the pills from herself as well as from the black colossus astride her mind. She had to make her mind a blank.

At that moment, the key rattled in the lock. He was coming. Quick as a flash, Dorothy pulled out the bottle again and, wiping it free of fingerprints, reshut the drawer as the door opened. Now she had only to keep her eyes off the dressing table until he'd gone, and she might yet be able to ravel up the threads of her life just long enough to end it.

'April the thirty-first,' muttered Rex. 'Where is it? Oh please, God, where is it?' He seized a fresh bundle of newspapers and shuffled over to the candle. The candle was not to be moved, so he had to take the papers over to it, rather than vice versa, in order to read the date at the top of the page. Scurrying to and fro helped to ward off the cold and damp. He leafed through the papers frantically. What would become of him if he couldn't find April the thirty-first? How would he explain to Mr Klackan?

His job was to arrange last year's papers in chronological order. Any illusions about the simplicity of the task had been dispelled immediately when he had wasted an age searching for the very first one – January the first. Only after a fit of tearful frustration had he remembered that January the first was a national holiday: *no newspapers were delivered on that day*. The second major delay was caused by March the sixth. He looked and looked until his eyes blazed red with strain and fatigue and his tooth raged and his testicles throbbed ominously. In a moment of inspiration he recalled that the Fleet Street printers had held a one-day lightning strike at about that time, and he concluded that it must have been on March the sixth. If he was wrong, he might well be for the chop. But he had to keep going – if he missed his deadline for the task, he'd *certainly* be doctored by the knife or razor. But when was the deadline – that horrible suggestive word? Mr Klackan had said that a reasonable amount of time would be allowed. How long was that? Rex scrabbled through the papers in a frenzy, repeating 'April the thirty-first' in case he forgot what he was looking for. It *had* to be there somewhere.

Against the dark backdrop of the indeterminate deadline, another horror had lit up in searing neon while he was compiling February: *what would happen when he finished?* Whole minutes passed while the thought prevented him from doing anything at all. He saw Mr Klackan materialising on the stroke of December the thirty-first and swishing the bright blade with surgical efficiency — Rex lay on the floor with nothing between his legs but a few bleeding tubes dangling out of him like a ripped electrical socket. The same thing would happen, of course, if he didn't complete the task. He had swayed on his feet and rolled his head in panic-stricken indecision. The balance of fear tipped marginally in favour of finishing. At least he could earn Mr Klackan's respect — and possibly a brief reprieve — for a job well done.

As he attacked another bundle of papers, Rex tried to think. It was appallingly difficult because in order to think properly in his depleted state he had to stop work and laboriously weave together the shreds of his intellect; but he dared not stop for a second. On the other hand, thinking on the job, however feebly, distracted him from registering the dates of the newspapers. Nevertheless, he managed to consider the possibility that he had not kept April the thirty-first, but thrown it away. Almost at once the real truth hit him: Mr Klackan had smuggled it out as a joke. Rex sniggered. They'd have a good laugh about it when Mr Klackan returned. He'd see that you couldn't easily pull the wool over Rex Ballantine's eyes; he'd have to concede a grudging respect. Rex smiled to recall that, at one point, the man had seriously appeared to doubt his intelligence.

Rex pressed on with May more cheerfully. It went quickly: many of the newspapers had already been stacked in chronological order. He fell into a kind of rhythm born of extreme exhaustion. In the twilight world of a waking dream he formed the distinct impression that Mr Klackan was helping him to arrange the papers. He experienced a languorous sense of kinship with the huge warm presence. But imperceptibly the presence grew less benign and more demonic until, jolting fully awake, Rex saw that he'd been cruelly deluded by his own giant shadow wavering on the wall in the candlelight.

At that moment, he remembered. *There was no April the thirty-first.* Rex smacked the side of his head repeatedly. 'Stupid, stupid, *stupid*, Rex.' He couldn't bear to think of the time he had wasted. His eyes blurred with tears. What was happening to him? A child of six knew the rhyme:

> 'Thirty days hath September
> April, June and . . . .'

181

November? Or was it December? He dropped on to his knees and let out a howl of anguish. November, of course. He crawled to the steel boiler and, oblivious of the pain in his face, began to butt his head against it, repeating the rhyme until it was fixed in his skull.

He was profoundly disturbed by the deterioration of his memory. He kept losing whole pieces of his past life. And the more emotionally charged the memories were, the less he could remember them: for example, when testing himself for mental impairment, he failed to recall exactly any of the successful slogans he'd invented in the heyday of his career. Part of him, it seemed, wished to protect him from the unbearable happiness (unbearable because lost) which another part of him wished to recollect. He couldn't even remember Dorothy's face, perhaps because she too was an emblem of happier times, or perhaps because he hated her for betraying him so eagerly with the potent Klackan.

Instead, infuriatingly, he could call to mind with astonishing ease such things as the stupid little mnemonics he had learnt in Latin classes. He would never have believed that he could still remember:

> 'For nouns that cannot be declined
> The neuter gender is assigned.
> Examples *fas* and *nefas* give,
> And the verb-noun infinitive.'

Est summum nefas fallere – 'Deceit is gross impiety'. He wasn't even sure he understood it. It was horrifying: all his past joys and triumphs had been wiped out like chalk from a blackboard and replaced by a stupid rhyme learnt by rote. *Fas* – it sounded like Klackan, a noun that can't be declined. *Nefas* – it sounded like him, assigned to a neuter gender by a swish of the razor. Clearly, he could only function as long as he avoided all emotion and dwelt solely on subjects as neutral as Latin rhymes.

Rex's eye was caught by the dark shape of Cassandra lying by the stairs. 'Oh, *Cassie*.' He averted his eyes from her, shocked and frightened by the sudden access of fresh anger surging up in him. Why was he doing this fucking futile pointless useless tiring job? He'd half a mind to set fire to the newspapers, set alight the cellar, burn down the house, raze the world. Nothing else could compensate him for this shame, this degradation. Luckily he was rescued from doing anything silly by sheer terror: the shadowy image of Klackan, wielding blades in both steel hands, thrust back the caustic fury and scalding tears. His hands shook as he battled to go on arranging the papers; his blinded eyes strained to read the dates. Slowly the danger passed: his anger sank down into harmless despair, spreading through him dully, like hunger.

On the Saturday I shook myself out of my haze. How could I face Clare the next day knowing that I'd wasted a whole week? Every day counted. I had to reach as many souls as I could before the last glorious day of Translation. Accordingly, I set off with a case full of pamphlets straight after work.

I'd just taken delivery of my latest and (I dare say) best work called, wait for it, *How the Rended Heavens Will Cause a Mended Earth*. Has a certain ring about it, eh? I was aiming for something like you see on hoardings – something snappy and memorable so that my message would really come across and attract readers. Full price? Twenty-five pee, for which I toss in an appendix – 'A Thousand Years of Gardening' – where I foretell the expulsion of all leaf and soil pests by Christ. Just think: the whole of Creation has been groaning and travailing since the Fall and now Christ is coming to lift the curse laid on Nature by His Father when He told Adam and Eve that the ground would not henceforth yield unto them her strength, but bring forth thorns, thistles, etcetera – Genesis four, twelve, if you want to check. As I walked in the direction of Muswell Hill (my shift finished before the Tube began running and I reached Leicester Square before I caught one), I couldn't resist taking a look every now and then at the beautiful shiny blue covers of this new pamphlet.

It was bitterly cold, with a misty drizzle in the air that clung to your clothes. But I didn't care. I was in high spirits because a lady in Leatherhead had asked me to call back with a *full range* of prophecies after my visit the week before. I decided to leave her till last so as to finish the day on a high note. Also, I found a ten-pee piece lying in the road. The policeman I turned it over to in Pimlico agreed that it was a sign of good fortune. I could hardly forbear to pull out one of the new pamphlets and astound him with the shattering news of the Saviour's Return; but a policeman is a captive audience, so to speak, and unable to exercise free will, so it would've been unethical as well as unalphabetical.

Yes, you heard me right. The clue is in Muswell Hill. No? Well, I'll explain: you probably think I pray for guidance about which area to tackle and when. But I don't bother God with that sort of thing; no, sir. Nor do I believe in leaving things to chance or fate, if these verily exist, which I doubt. No, I believe in collaborating with Providence. Thus I devised the alphabetical system of hawking: on each outing I visit a town or area whose initial letter comes next in the alphabet. For example, Ashtead, Balham, Chiswick, Dulwich, Ealing, Finchley, etcetera. I'm allowed to miss out X and Z, and when I've exhausted the letters I start again with a different set of places. In nineteen seventy-four, after much inward searching, I began with Ashford. I must've knocked on a thousand doors; but I never found Jean Macintyre. Just as well, maybe – she's probably married to someone else by now, with someone else's children. Back-tracking is permitted in exceptional circumstances, as it was on that Saturday when I returned to Leather-head. Of course, I couldn't keep to such a system if I didn't have a privilege ticket for the railways – I couldn't afford the fares. It's amazing how your wages disappear when you've got printer's bills to pay. On that Saturday, what with the new pamphlets and all, I didn't have the price of a cup of tea on me. So there was an extra, venal incentive to sell a pamphlet quickly!

I don't know why I started on this, really. It was like every other day for the past forty-odd years. Pretty much a blind alley. Knock, knock at the door; ring, ring at the bell. 'Good morning, madam. Would you care to look at these pamphlets I've written ...?' Slam, slam from the door. 'Good afternoon, sir. Can I interest you in some good news?' 'Why can't you people leave us in peace?' 'Yes, sir, it's peace I've come about—' 'Peace off.' Pardon my French. And so on. Plus, you have to pray at every household in case God wants to work unseen on them and not by means of my prophecies.

About mid-afternoon a darkie lady bought a *Rended Heavens*. Just in time, for I was wet through to my vest and blistered on the foot where my sopping boot rubbed. I'd noticed a lot more darkies since I was last up Muswell Hill way, about nineteen fifty-eight. It didn't make much difference – a rebuff is the same in any colour – but on balance darkies are more spiritual than whities. Or politer, anyway. I used to look in on the Battersea Pentecostals when I was a bit low. The white dresses and smiles of the women, the deep basses of the men used to cheer me up. This particular lady was game to pay full price but I couldn't go through with it in the end. You see, I'd employed subterfuge by flashily displaying the glossy and seductive blue cover of the new pamphlet – I couldn't help it – but when it came down to it I could only take half-price, which left me four pee short of a cup of tea. Still, better that than poison myself with tea obtained under false pretences.

There are worse snares when it comes to selling pamphlets. I ought to confess here and now that I've been on the brink of sin several times; namely, through author's pride. You see, if you spend a lot of time and worry on writing as I do, willy-nilly you forget that you're only the

184

base instrument of God's will – that He alone has put the pen in your hand and bestowed prophecies. You're tempted to think you're a bit important whereas in reality you're nothing – less than nothing – apart from His wondrous gifts; and it's easy to get carried away and start putting in stuff of your own, mistaking it for the Lord's message. I wish I had the gift of parables, which are less troublesome and more appealing to ordinary folk than prophecy.

The light began to fail early on, I remember. The temperature dropped. The cold wind chafed my skin through my wet clothes. I confess I was a bit fagged out after walking all day with no sleep or cup of tea since the day before. But I drew strength from the prospect of the Leatherhead lady.

I made good time – about one and a quarter hours, or two hours if you count the hike after I'd left the train. The lady was startled to see me, but I'm not one to forget a promise! She had lovely wavy hair, very clean and well tended, and long pale hands. Plus she was wearing an unforgettable dress whose colour was a beautiful mixture of many colours, rippling and gleaming when she moved inside it. I apologised for the delay, but here I was with the full range of my work and would she like me to summarise one or two before she decided how many copies she was wanting? She claimed that I hadn't understood her; that I was a nuisance, wasn't I, and that she had no intention of wasting good money on, I quote, total rubbish. The door shut with a thud. I set my face like a flint against that lady, and turned away.

It does get dark in here, doesn't it? I can hardly make you out. Just the whites of your eyes. It's easier to talk in the dark somehow. You used to take notes, but I suppose you know me too well by now. I feel that you know me. I sometimes get the strangest notion that you know what I'm going to say before I say it! By the way, if ... anything should break in here ... don't try to interfere. It's me it's after. You'll only get hurt. I'd hate that. What was I saying?

I lay down for a spell on a bench outside the lady's house. The street-lamps were alight. The rain was oozing down a bit harder. The wet gravel under the lamps sparkled like splintered glass. So many threshed at the Rapture, I thought; so little grain saved. I wondered what I'd do if I was offered the chance of saving the Leatherhead lady, as I'd sworn to save Clare, instead of being gathered myself. I was sorely vexed. I went and shoved three pamphlets through her letterbox, without counting the cost of printing, for Jesus Christ's sake.

Well. So much for Saturday. It wasn't so bad when you consider the lucky ten-pee piece and the pamphlet sold. I heaved myself off the bench and hurried straight to the office – Leatherhead had left me no time to go home. That night at the office was where a lot of my present affliction came to a head.

Klackan carried a bucket and his knife in one hand and a tray in the other. On the tray was the invariable bowl of soup and the mug of water. Dorothy stood at the end of the bed, clasping her robe more tightly around her and trying to disguise the shaking of her body. She couldn't take her eyes off the tray. The mug of water held a deeper promise than that of quenching her thirst. She was allowed to keep the mug until the following morning. Each time she swore that she would reserve half the water for the torment of the night; but she always gulped it down before she could stop herself, leaving nothing except a more bitter sense of her own weakness.

He put the tray down on the bed and held out the bucket. Dorothy took it – it felt heavier each time – and removed the cloth and the wodge of lavatory paper from inside. She was allowed to use the bucket once a day and only for one minute. To someone of her fastidiousness the act of defecating in the presence of anyone, let alone Klackan, was a nightmare. But if she didn't seize the single opportunity she risked acute discomfort or, worse still, a thorough belting for fouling a corner of the room.

She carried the bucket to the far side of the bed – his tacit concession to modesty – and squatted over it. She could feel his hot stare boring into her back as she tried to arrange her dressing gown around her for privacy. The sound of her thin effluent spattering the metal in the silent room made her want to weep with shame. Only the fear that he might be perversely inflamed by the spectacle held her tears in check. The one-minute restriction was superfluous: the speed with which her bowels had learnt to evacuate to order amazed her. She had to concentrate all her forces to avoid thinking about the dressing-table drawer. At any moment it might fly open with cries of 'Liar! Liar!'

She turned around, bracing herself to meet the man's glistening gaze and, lower down, the hideous jut of muscle veined in purple like marble. To her surprise, he was sitting in the armchair with his eyes averted out of some obscure sense of delicacy. He even covered the bucket with the cloth before placing it by the door.

'Thank you,' murmured Dorothy. They did not converse on these occasions. Dorothy expressed gratitude for favours granted and, usually, asked questions – more to break his terrifying silence than to elicit information. He often didn't answer, or else simply reminded her of the impossibility of escape.

Increasingly, questions had begun to agitate him. He fidgeted ominously with knife or razor; he seemed to lose his agility, to sag; his head began to swing from side to side like an enormous retarded child bewildered by his own idiocy. On the last occasion, when Dorothy had asked him about himself (she was desperate to make some human contact), Klackan had blocked his ears and bellowed incoherently before blundering out of the room. She decided to shut up in future in case she overstepped the mark.

With an enquiring glance at Klackan she reached hesitantly towards the bowl of soup. He nodded. She drank it greedily. The tepid liquid, scarcely distinguishable from her faeces, was cruelly salty; but she swallowed it down to the last grey lump. Forcing her hand to put the mug of water to one side, she lowered her head to conceal the red-hot deceit on her face. She guessed she had better question him as usual to distract attention from her abstinence. Carefully choosing a neutral topic, she said: 'You are looking after Mikey, Mr Klackan? Please look after him.' Her thoughts were fixed on the bottle, burning a hole in the drawer. She didn't expect a reply; she certainly wasn't prepared for the one he gave.

'I've been looking at Mikey. You never gave a hoot for him.'

Dorothy was stupefied by his sudden venom. At the same time she wanted to shout that it was a lie, that she'd devoted years to a son who'd never called her Mummy. She knew she shouldn't speak but she couldn't bear Mr Klackan to think so ill of her.

'It was a mistake,' she cried. He shook his head slowly.

'There are no mistakes.' The knife twitched in his hand; he seemed undecided; she hid her face as he advanced. There was only the sound of his laboured breathing. Then she heard the clunk of the bucket, the door closing, the click of the key in the lock.

EIGHT

THE SOFT LIGHT of the clear spring evening breathed through the tall French windows of the deserted playroom. The children were getting ready for bed. Ruth crossed the room, careful not to avoid looking at the bean-bag. It was plumped in the corner like a shadowy Buddha. She paused outside Dr Frieling's office for a long time before knocking.

'Come in, come in,' the doctor urged as Ruth hesitated on the threshold.

'I was just passing, Doctor Frieling. If you're busy....'

'Not at all. I'm always glad of an excuse to stop doing paperwork.' He gestured hopelessly towards the untidy piles on his desk. 'Let's take a stroll, you and I, and enjoy this beautiful day before it's over. I shall even smoke a cigar.'

The grounds of the hospital were empty. In the distance its first lights were winking through the trees. The air was cool but scented like a premonition of summer with freshly cut grass overlaid by the tang of pines. There was no breath of wind to disturb the blue column of cigar smoke as it rose vertically towards the deeper blue of a sky lightly frosted with stars.

They walked companionably across the green lawns. A late bird piping in the trees caused the old doctor to stop and cock his head, as though both walking and listening demanded his full attention and could not be done simultaneously. Quietly and quite naturally, Ruth began to tell him about the automatic writing — how her hand had begun to transcribe messages from out of the unknown and how, despite the impulsion to continue writing, she was reluctant to do so until she had sought his advice. She told him everything except the part that María was alleged to be playing: for some reason she felt that she would be betraying a confidence.

Dr Frieling listened without interrupting, his spectacles glinting occasionally in the glow of his cigar as he drew on it. When she had finished, he said: 'Well, Ruth. What can I tell you?'

'You can tell me that I'm not mad.' She gave a little strained laugh.

'It seems that you're a medium, Ruth. Mediums aren't mad. A little crazy maybe, but not mad.' They both laughed.

'Do you believe in mediums, Doctor?' she asked seriously.

'What's to believe? They exist. They make me nervous — *you're* making me nervous now. A medium appears to be controlled by another personality, yes? This is uncomfortably close to a psychosis — or what in other countries is sometimes called, with admirable precision, "possession by spirits".'

'But I didn't lose control, Doctor. I didn't lose consciousness. It was like having a conversation. It seemed completely natural except that I couldn't see the person who was addressing me.' She looked anxiously at her companion, who was apparently deep in contemplation of a beech tree. At last he said:

'Ruth, I don't know what you experienced. All I can do is make suggestions. Inside each of us, buried beneath the field of consciousness, a host of unresolved emotions and desires are crying out for recognition. You know this; you've been psychoanalysed. In the depths of the psyche nothing — no memory, no experience — is ever lost. We embrace all the personalities we have ever been. Sometimes we carry a repressed emotion around with us always, like the hen-pecked husband who cages his anger until it grows into the monstrous tyrant who suddenly takes an axe to his wife. Sometimes it is located at a particular time of our lives, like the successful architect I once heard screaming with the voice of the furious child he was never allowed to be! In most of us there is, for example, a crying child, a resentful adolescent, an embittered lover, a failed artist, a disapproving father.... We have as many personalities as a writer has characters for a book. Mental health consists in admitting them into our conscious lives and giving them expression. We must arrange them in order around the centre we call our selves. Of course, all these personalities have their happier, helpful counterparts; but it's the aspects we have suppressed who are dangerous. The more we deny them — and we

190

always deny them – the more they gather force in secret, in the dark, until they are strong enough to break away from the centre and come into their own. We have to build ourselves big enough to contain them all, and still be vigilant in case they get above themselves ... and us.'

'You're saying that I'm being invaded by some unconscious complex, some autonomous fragment of myself?'

'I'm saying it's one of several possibilities, Ruth. You'll admit that much yourself.'

Ruth nodded. 'It's possible, yes. It's just that the handwriting, the things he – it – said ... they were so different. They didn't feel like me at all. They truly seemed to come from another world.'

'That's because there are other worlds,' said Dr Frieling. 'But they're in this one.'

Ruth smiled at him.

'Strangely enough, that's more or less what my "spirit" said!'

Dr Frieling stopped in front of the bench where Ruth had first seen Harry. 'I could make another suggestion as to the source of your mysterious writing....' He hesitated, and then sat down on the bench. Ruth sat beside him. 'After all, Ruth, I think you're an unusually *sound* person ... well integrated. I don't think you have any serious devils left to be cast out – your work here has confirmed this....' Ruth sat very still, studiously looking straight ahead. The doctor had never come so close to praising her before. There was a time when she had needed his praise, but now it was too late. '... But you have suffered a great loss. A mother who loses a son could scarcely sustain a greater shock. Isn't that true?'

'Yes.' The word was no more than a whisper. 'I would have liked a child of my own.'

Dr Frieling threw his cigar end into the shrubbery. It arced through the air like a dim meteor and disappeared.

'Good,' he said. 'Now, we both know how hard the psyche strives to maintain its balance. The unconscious part always seeks to compensate for a lack or an excess in the conscious part – when we are hungry we dream of food. What will your psyche not do to console you for your loss? Yes, I know you're going to say that your psychic phenomenon has nothing to do with Mikey. But how can you be sure? You've received messages from an allegedly dead person. Isn't Mikey in a sense "dead" for you? Aren't you anxious about your "afterlife" – what you will do now, after Mikey's demise? Might you not be unconsciously seeking an "afterlife"? Or perhaps you secretly long for some confirmation of life's purpose, the immortality of the soul and so on? I know you'll consider this, Ruth, because you are honest in a way that is not common.'

Ruth considered. There was truth in what the old man said. The image of Mikey she had once made – an image which grew and laughed and called her Mummy – was still enshrined in her heart. The doctor seemed already to know this.

'The imagined child you carry inside you, Ruth, will weigh you down in the end. You wish to possess him for ever; in the end he will possess you. You must release him. I know it's perhaps too hard to do now – but it must be done. Mikey is real, and he is other than you would have him be. Accept him as he is even though it breaks your heart.' His voice became at once stern and gentle, and infused with a kind of urgency which Ruth hadn't heard before. '*Reality*. That is the key. Real suffering is better than imaginary joy. We fight against reality every day of our lives with delusions and fantasies and empty imaginings. If it has to be driven into us, like nails, against our will, so much the better – at least then we can't be mistaken. There's no mistaking a cry of pain.'

'Mikey could die if he's left with his parents,' said Ruth hoarsely.

'Yes. You have to swallow that.'

'I can't. It's too terrible. After all the progress he made ... all the work I put in....' She shook her head, unable to go on.

'His progress, your work – they're not wasted. Nothing is wasted.' He added brutally: 'Things didn't happen as you planned and hoped, that's all. It doesn't mean that there is no plan, no hope.'

'Do you think there's a plan, Doctor?' she asked timidly.

'No. I was simply consoling myself.' He sounded almost angry. He pulled up his sleeve and scratched irritably at his arm. Then, reaching over, he patted the back of her hand kindly. Ruth noticed a black mark on his arm. Seeing her peering at it, Dr Frieling lifted up his arm in the fading light.

'A souvenir,' he said. The mark was a number tattooed on to his skin. 143999.

'My parents got out in time,' said Ruth.

'Lucky. Mind you, I was also lucky. Young and strong enough to stay alive. I'm an old man now, but the guilt is still there.'

'Guilt?' Ruth was surprised.

'Oh, yes. Guilt at having survived when so many....' He spread his hands graphically.

'Yes.'

'I sometimes think that my work with children is only an escape. I've never quite been able to trust grown-ups since....' He looked at Ruth through the growing darkness and smiled. His face was indistinct and ghostly. 'At other times I think that perhaps it's not an escape but a vocation. You see, when I met my first severely autistic child I was

192

instantly reminded of the *müsselmanner* in the concentration camp – you know, the "Moslems". These walking corpses repelled and frightened me. I couldn't understand how a person could go on living, or existing at least, beyond the point when it was preferable to die. Perhaps we dreaded them most because they were our visible future – because, in a sense, they were the first model citizens in the Nazi Utopia.

'Anyway, I could not become reconciled to the idea that they were beyond hope. In devising the Unit, I wanted – no doubt you will perceive in this, and rightly so, a need for atonement – I wanted to prove that children in an analogous position to those "Moslems" could be restored to life. So far, results have been variable, inconclusive, at best only partially successful.' Dr Frieling leant back and inhaled the night air deeply.

'Ah, the beautiful stars,' he said irrelevantly. 'The constellation of Aries. Can you see a ram, Ruth? No? I like to imagine some old Babylonian looking at the sky and seeing all those lovely astrological beasts moving in procession overhead. I only see Mr Newton's cold and glittering machine. Is there anyone alive who can see Einstein's vision of the universe? Maybe Mikey saw it from his black hole, eh? Perhaps he was ahead of his time.' He paused. 'Tell me honestly, Ruth. Do you have any other kind of spirit in your room?' The doctor's serious face made her laugh. They rose from the bench and strolled arm in arm back to the Unit and Ruth's whisky.

The bolt shot back. The wooden stairs creaked under the heavy tread. Rex felt some enormous obstruction rising up through his body and restricting his supply of air and blood. He stood stiffly to attention, willing himself to remain conscious. His hand surreptitiously covered his genitals. Some feeling had returned to them: when he had peed into the cavity, scratched cat-like in the coal-pile, the needle-sharp soreness suggested that his penis had somehow snapped like a bone; when he moved about, he fancied that his scrotum clinked like a bag of broken glass.

He had not finished organising the newspapers. He had worked unceasingly for he didn't know how long, blocking out past and future by his obsession with the task, until he was infused with an almost mystical sense of mastery over time. The used newspapers were the past; the inexorable sequence of dates led to his future. Yet he was responsible for their order. They were trapped in the present, as he was, until the sequence came to an end on December the thirty-first. He'd begun to think that he was invulnerable as long as that date had not been reached. But the sound of the footsteps recalled him to the reality of his future, now descending towards him. And he hadn't finished the job.

Rex was swept by the wild hair-raising idea that Mr Klackan was bringing him something hot and creamy to eat instead of the repulsive gruel he carried down at long, long intervals. His early hallucinations of succulent scampi and juicy steaks now struck him as faintly unsavoury, even unclean. Instead, his griping belly craved the mashed potatoes, swimming in butter, with which his mother used to welcome him after school; or the milky puddings she'd served in front of the fire on Sunday evenings.

The candle guttered. A terrible darkness invaded him. He felt the man's breath on him. He stared straight ahead, unable to look at Klackan, but aware all the same that he wasn't carrying anything except the open razor. Rex decided that the best policy was to remain silent.

'Well?' said Klackan.

'I'm sorry, I'm sorry,' Rex blurted out, hating himself. 'I haven't finished yet. I tried my best ... really. I've *nearly* finished. I'll work harder ... harder, I promise.' He screwed up the muscles in his face to thwart another bout of weeping. Mr Klackan didn't like to see him cry.

'Oh, Rex,' said Klackan sadly. 'What are we going to do with you? Look at the state you're in. What a mess.' He sighed and laid a heavy hand on Rex's head. Rex crumpled under the unexpected gesture of sympathy; his tears began to flow. The hand moved to the back of his neck, giving it a little pinch. It strayed over his bare shoulder.

'What clear smooth skin,' he mused. 'Just like a girl's cheek.'

Rex shuddered — whether from pleasure or from revulsion, he couldn't tell. But the touch of a human hand triggered a flood of vivid images: the memories of his women. He had hoarded them like a miser, depriving himself of his treasure because of his desire for it. It was his last bulwark against dissolution and ruin. But the women, like so much of his past, were incomplete; they dashed against his brain in a delicious succession of ankles, eyes, hair, thighs, teeth, tongues — as more intimate areas appeared (white breasts, black triangles ...) he had to stem the tide of images by an effort of will in case he squandered his secret resources too soon. The ecstatic fragments insulated him briefly against the coldness of Klackan's steel. His desire for them fired him like a life force.

'Who *are* you?' Rex asked boldly. The man casually rested the razor's blade against his tender genitals. Rex instantly froze; his brief elation plunged into terror and despair. His legs wouldn't support him, and he sank to his knees with a grunt.

'You tell me,' said Klackan. Rex was startled by something soft dangled in front of his face. Recoiling, he saw that it was the black woollen hood. He had only to glance up and he would see Mr Klackan's face, blindingly beautiful or as hideous as a skull beneath the skin. His longing to gaze at Klackan's features was matched only by his fear of what he would see. He had lived too long with the black mask; it haunted and frightened him. But the idea of the unknown face behind it was worse than frightening. It was uncanny. The sight of it would be something appalling, irrevocable, final. Rex covered his eyes with his arm.

'Put it back on,' he begged. 'I don't want to see anything.'

'Like a wise monkey, eh Rex? Not a great one for facing up to things, are you?' His voice was almost sorrowful. He paused to pull the hood back over his head and then barked out a command.

'Stand up!' Rex scrambled to his feet, hunching his shoulders and sinking his head between them. 'You're a miserable little bloke, Rex. What about these newspapers, then?' He kicked the neat stack of papers, which scattered over the floor. 'I didn't give you the job for fun. It doesn't give me any pleasure to see you making such a pig's ear of a simple job. It's honest work, Rex — good for the soul. But you're too stupid to do anything properly. Look at you. You ought to be put out of your misery, quivering like a lump of jelly, clutching your rude parts. It's downright offensive.' He smacked Rex on the buttocks like a naughty child. Rex hardly felt the slap; but the contempt and disgust behind it cut like a knife.

'Give me another chance,' he pleaded. 'I'll do better. I'll learn whatever you want me to learn.'

'I don't think you're capable of learning, Rex. You're the clumsiest, slowest person I've ever come across.' He strolled across the cellar to the pile of coal. 'Pooh!' he exclaimed. 'What have you been up to? There's dung and all sorts here. That settles it. I'll give you one last chance. God help you if you make a muck of this one.' He held up the razor and pointed it at Rex. Then he ran nimbly up the stairs, returning a minute later with a bucket of soapy water and a rag.

He indicated the coal-pile. 'I want every piece as clean as a flute. Start washing. There isn't much time.'

'But you can't clean coal,' Rex protested.

'What a defeatist. See what I mean, Rex? I've had just about enough of you.' He seemed suddenly ill at ease and agitated. He kicked a newspaper into the air and slashed it with his razor. He was clearly losing control of himself.

Rex fell on the coal and began plunging pieces of it into the bucket of water. Klackan watched him for a while, apparently in two minds as to what he would do. At last he said simply, but with terrible meaning: 'Get it right this time.' Then he was gone.

Dorothy sat on the floor and emptied the sleeping pills into her lap. Glancing at the door, she assured herself for the hundredth time that he wouldn't return before she had swallowed them. When he did come, it would be too late. She'd be free.

The mug was filled almost to the brim with water. She yearned to drink it down in one long cold draught, but it had to be taken in sips and, with every sip, a pill. She had to hurry; and yet she wanted to make some kind of gesture before passing into eternal sleep – a final noble thought, perhaps, would help the tablets slide down gracefully. But there was only the anxious frantic scrabbling in her brain, without content or meaning; in retrospect her life was empty and muddled, a bubble easily burst. Dimly she pictured the dear faces of Rex and Mikey and, ignoring their reproach, even managed a sentimental tear. It was good not to burden them any more. Mr Klackan would let them go when she was gone; if he didn't, well, her staying alive could make no difference. It was all such a mess.

The mug was decorated with little shamrocks. Lifting it to her lips, she paused to read the words on its side. 'A Souvenir of Tralee.' Her mother must have brought it back from Ireland years ago – her uncle lived near Tralee. Dorothy wondered why she had stashed away such a pretty mug in the back of the kitchen cupboard. It gave her the oddest feeling to be holding it, especially at a time like this. She gazed into it with sweet childish dread as if it held something more than water. Her hands instinctively cupped themselves around it. She held her breath and closed her eyes.

There was a muffled sound, similar to the distant rip of a jet, except that she felt it inside her, like the tearing of cellophane. She clasped the mug more tightly. The memory started up in front of her with ex-cruciating clarity, untouched by the passage of time:

It is her twelfth birthday. A Saturday. She has woken early because she's excited. She's bringing Dad's tea to him in bed, as a surprise. She begins to climb the narrow staircase. Shafts of sunlight from the window at the top stripe the steps and set the motes dancing. She thinks: I am twelve years old today. Dorothy is twelve. Dorothy, Dorothy. But who is Dorothy? Dorothy is me. And who am I? I am Dorothy. She has never thought of herself in this simple circular way, never thought of herself at all. It is like putting on 3-D spectacles, she thinks, and seeing yourself leap towards you in all your roundness and depth.

She stops dead on the seventh stair and, with a flick of her head, tosses her pigtail over her shoulder. She thinks: This moment will never come again. I will remember it. She stares at the mug with all her might, counting the shamrocks and ramming the words 'A Souvenir of Tralee' into her memory. The steam from the hot tea rises around her head, dampening her skin. 'I will *remember*,' she repeats; but she is afraid she won't — afraid that she's too weak and fickle to lay hold of her life in this way. The randomness of the moment is everything. It has no meaning in itself, no importance at all. For this very reason, she longs to petrify it for all time in an instant of pure experience, simply because she chooses to. 'I *will* remember.' Staircase, sunlight, steaming mug of tea, herself — she sends Dorothy to picture the frail configuration from the top of the stairs and coils it away in her brain like an ammonite.

As she stands concentrated like a rock amidst the gush of time, refusing to move on to the eighth step, choosing the moment and making it all her own, there is a hush in the narrow house. Slowly she senses the grandeur of eternity making its descent on dusty beams of light. She is enfolded by the absence of time, and time's fullness. Briefly she thinks, I'll remember this moment until the day I die; and she climbs on to the eighth step, carrying the early-morning tea to her father.

Dorothy opened her eyes. The weak overhead light cast a sickly yellow pall over the room. The furniture looked shoddy and flattened out like an old film set. How could she have forgotten that second of forever? It was fitting that she should recollect it now when she had another choice to make — a choice that would extinguish her as the first had brought her into being. She felt dizzy and detached, intoxicated by the sensation of significant *déjà vu*, of things returning full circle to their starting-point.

Dorothy took the first sleeping pill between forefinger and thumb. Immediately she saw the girl mounting the stairs, climbing towards her, stopping. The sun was warm on her back. The warm mist in front of her face thinned. The girl was frowning at her, tossing the severe pigtail over her shoulder with a decisive flick of the head. 'I want to die,' said Dorothy. 'Let me die.' But under the girl's stern and steady gaze she knew that death was too easy a choice; it committed her to nothing.

She poured the pills back into the bottle and thrust it into the drawer which she slammed shut. Her breathing was fast and shallow. Klackan's last remark moved in her heart like shrapnel. The sharp pain made her sink to the floor where she sat for a long time. The old wound slowly reopened and, bleeding memories, she realised that, yes, yes, she had never cared for Mikey.

I limped into work that evening, twenty minutes late, wet through and lugging my case full of prophecies. I was full of dread because Mister Turnbull, my supervisor, does not take kindly to unpunctuality. But the noise of the other clerks, grade five, told me that he must have popped out of the office. The noise hurt my head; the flickering of the strip lighting hurt my eyes. I guessed I'd caught something – I felt queer, sort of cold inside and burning outside. I hoped to reach my desk unobtrusively and quietly take my sopping boots off underneath. However, one of the young lads was sitting on my desk.

'You're late, Harry,' he said accusingly. I smiled because it was true and because I often smile when I'm not well in myself. I couldn't remember the name of this lad. I used to know the names of all my colleagues, but lately they seemed to come and go so quickly, getting younger all the time, that I couldn't keep up. He was half my size, I'd say; but his ferret's eyes and pointy teeth might have been designed to worry me.

'You're late and you don't half stink,' he went on. It was probably true. I waited for him to leave my desk, but he didn't. He called out: 'Old Harry stinks like a mouldy carpet!' The others stopped their horseplay and gathered around me. 'Pooh!' they said. 'What a state to get yourself in,' they said. And so on. I'm afraid I wasn't in the mood for their high-spirited chaffing and teasing. I waited for them to lose interest. They went on.

'What's old Harry been up to?' 'What's he got in that case?' 'Been moonlighting, Harry? Been flogging bog brushes on the side, eh?' 'No wonder he's smiling!' 'What *have* you been doing?' Silence. My blistered foot was playing up. I didn't want to remind them of my religion, but I wanted badly to sit down. So I said: 'I've been doing the works of the Lord.' I didn't say 'abounding in'; I just said 'doing'.

'Whooooo,' they said. '*Works of the Lord*. Hear that? Whoooo!' Ferrety Eyes took hold of my case and said: 'Let's have a butcher's, then, Harry.' Well, normally I'd have been only too pleased; but it wasn't on to exhibit my pamphlets for profane reasons. So I just shook my head. A slight struggle took place, I'm ashamed to say. I was bumped around a bit by the other clerks. Although there was no real harm in it, I was surprisingly injured – not so much by the edges of the desks as by the element of malice which had made an unwelcome

198

appearance. The case was torn from my fingers and fell open. The floor was strewn with prophecies.

As I stumbled about trying to gather them, the laughter was suddenly cut short. Mister Turnbull had returned. Of course, he used to be 'David' to me when he first came, about fourteen years ago, for I was entrusted with teaching him the fundamentals of invoicing. I remember being thunderstruck at how he mastered in ten minutes what it had taken me months to grasp. He was a proper high-flier, and no wonder he soon lost patience with me.

Mister Turnbull didn't say anything. That was his way when he wasn't too happy, though his tongue was sharp enough to cut himself when the occasion demanded, and I should know. He stooped and picked up one of my brand-new baby-blue pamphlets and read aloud: '*How the Rended Heavens Will Cause a Mended Earth.*' There was a lot of rustling excitement among the clerks; and, indeed, the title was unusually stirring the way he read it. He turned a few pages and read some more from an appropriate chapter about the position of the business and workaday world in the Millennium.

In this portion I prophesy that road orderlies on borough councils, let's say, may be transferred for a welcome change of air to ownership of seaside cafés in New Zealand. Or, similarly, and if they want to, shop assistants may become fashion models and salesmen may become train drivers, etcetera. Also, I explain how the tragedy of dust in the textile, pottery and coalmining industries will be sorted out. Mechanical jobs will be accident-free – you'll recall Isaiah twenty-four, 'And the inhabitant shall not say, I am sick' – while errors in clerical work will be divinely detected, and corrected, in their infancy. And so on.

My spirit soared like an eagle to hear my prophecies put forth from the mouth of Mister Turnbull. I could hardly restrain a loud exclamation of praise to the Lord who had worked such a subtle way of revealing His word to the secular clerks. For the voice of Mister Turnbull was law and, listening to him, they could neither gainsay nor flout the authority of my prophecies.

Then I saw that he read not for edification but for a weapon of mockery against me. His voice was trembling in a soppy falsetto and making the clerks snicker and whinny.

Well, God knows that for His sake I'm often enough mocked; no news there. But He is not. I wanted to warn Mister Turnbull, to stop him, but it was too late: the room filled with livid power. The floor was crawling with it. The walls were bruised by it, breaking out in red welts. I swayed under the flickering lights, trying to force back with prayer the rising tide of redness.

I must've had a funny turn because when I came to myself Mister Turnbull had gone quiet and I was standing very close to him. His face was all pasty, I remember, and you could smell the sweat coming off him. The other lads said nothing, just looked. Mister Turnbull kept his eyes on the floor while he gave me a week's notice. I wasn't to work it out; I was to leave immediately. He had the power to do that, even though I was only twenty minutes late — which makes about thirty minutes out of about thirty-one years. (I was ten minutes late once in nineteen fifty-five.) I didn't feel well enough to argue the toss. I didn't feel anything much except, possibly, sick. I picked up my pamphlets, repacked my case and left without a word. I didn't feel too good then. I must have caught a fever in the rain down at Leatherhead.

There was a gale blowing outside and a dirty rain slanting down the grey streets. I walked beside the Thames for a bit. The water was black, greasy-looking and vile. To tell you the truth, it turned my stomach. Things can come up at you out of the river — rubbish, dead dogs, corpses, all sorts. I caught the last train back to Wyebridge. The twelve twenty-four.

Have you ever been alone in a railway carriage past midnight? You can't imagine that great machine taking so much trouble just for you. You take it personally, don't you, as though it was rushing you towards something in particular? You can't imagine anyone actually driving it.

I sat with my back to the engine and wrote CLARE REID in the dust on the window. It was Sunday now and in a few short hours I'd be seeing her again. Rain slashed across the letters and oozed down the glass. Outside, the darkness passed in a rush. Blue flashes of electricity exploded off the wet rails. A humped black shape was hurtling alongside the carriage. It seemed to be about to turn its face and look through the window at me. We pray 'Deliver us from evil' all our lives to avoid that moment.

I went howling down the carriage, slamming stray windows shut as if that could stop the prince of the power of the air. I lay out of sight on the floor until I'd counted the five stops to Wyebridge. I ran home, looking neither to left nor to right, and bolted myself inside.

SEVEN

THE WOMAN IN THE MIRROR was scarcely recognisable. Her cheeks were sunken, eyes red-rimmed and wild, hair hanging in greasy strings. A pimply rash surrounded her dry chewed lips. Her dressing gown, stained and smelly, was a disgrace.

Dorothy took a sip of water, swilled it around her mouth and let it trickle slowly down her throat. Then, glancing continually at the door, she moistened a handkerchief in the water and, half-disrobing, scrubbed at the more accessible parts of her body — face, neck, shoulders, armpits. Next, she set about making up her face. It took a long time. Her unsteady hands had particular trouble with eyeliner and lipstick. But at least she was restored to something resembling her former self; she certainly felt more human.

Having laid out fresh underwear on the bed, she selected a sober pleated skirt from the wardrobe, a cotton blouse and a finely knitted light-blue pullover. When the outfit was assembled, Dorothy threw off the dressing gown. It was a critical moment: if the door opened now, he'd see her in a state of serious undress and tie her half-naked to the bedstead. She pulled on the clothes as fast as her clumsy fingers allowed. The door stayed shut. She rested for a while, panting with relief, before turning her attention to her hair.

She was so intent on brushing it thoroughly and pinning it up that she didn't notice Klackan come in until she looked behind her in the mirror. His baggy faceless shape gave the impression of immense tiredness as he sank into the armchair. Dorothy turned around guiltily and said: 'It's true. I wasn't being frank before. I didn't care about Mikey.'

The man swivelled his neckless head slowly in her direction. An uneasy hand stroked the instruments in his belt. His O-shaped mouth seemed to express surprise at her words; but when he spoke it was only with cold weariness.

'I don't want to hear.'

'But I must explain. You must understand what it was like. . . . Please, you must.' Her face was scarlet, inclined to crumple with tears; but she was determined to make him understand. The man's head moved up and down. She couldn't tell if he was nodding or appraising her. She suddenly realised how dangerous it was to have improved her appearance. If she looked attractive, if she upset him with her confession. . . . But she couldn't help herself. Her need to unburden herself was all-consuming.

'When I knew I was going to have a baby, I was wild with joy. I wanted him so much . . . too much. Rex wanted him, too. He made me laugh so hard – he had such extravagant plans for his son. You see, I didn't feel as close to my husband as I ought to have done. The baby was something we could share . . . something that would bring us together in a way that marriage and, well, the things which go with marriage had never done. Do you see? But then I was ill. Mikey made me sick. I was queasy all the time, and so *tired*. I thought having a baby was supposed to make you well. I thought I'd be *radiant*. Instead I was dull and restless and achy; my face went all blotchy. I thought: This isn't right. Something's gone wrong. I'm not built to have a baby. I tried to tell Rex, but he was so busy . . . such an important time for him. I had to bite back my whining, but still it would come out. Rex was terribly patient, but I knew how he hated it.'

She paused, remembering Rex's forced jollity. 'Buck up, Dotty! You're turning into a neurotic!' But she couldn't buck up; she was useless to him. He had so much entertaining to do for his business, so many drinks and dinners, and of course he couldn't appear alone. 'How will it look, Dotty? Make a bit of an effort.' She dragged herself to his functions and put on a good face for his clients and colleagues; but all the time she knew they were thinking how awful she looked. She remembered poor Rex's face when she burst into tears over a lobster in a restaurant – she just couldn't force it down. He'd done his best in the circumstances; 'Dorothy thinks she's the first person ever to have a baby,' he'd joked. In a way, that was exactly what it felt like. But she couldn't forgive herself – or the baby – for the scene in the restaurant, and she swore that it would never happen again.

'The doctor said I'd be fine as soon as the morning sickness passed,' she went on. 'He could see I was making a fuss over nothing. But it didn't get better. I felt more tired all the time – I couldn't understand it – and my hair began to fall out; and all the time there was this thing, nothing to do with me, swelling inside me like a tumour, taking me over, making all my glands, feelings, everything go haywire. I had no control. I was terrified of the growing lump – I mean, if it could do all *that* to me, what would it do when it decided to come out? I couldn't stand the thought of all the pain and the responsibility – I knew I had no aptitude, no *talent* for being a mother. I wouldn't have any idea what to do . . . .

'I had to pull myself together, Mr Klackan. You can see that. I decided that I'd cope with the birth when it happened, when the baby popped out – even though I was dreadfully afraid of what might pop out with it. Meanwhile, I just put it out of my mind. I did my best for Rex, behaved impeccably with his friends, just carried on as though the baby wasn't there. I did everything right. I didn't bother Rex again.

'It worked. My looks improved and Rex was happier. He started decorating the spare room in the flat and filling it with furniture and gadgets for his son. I became worried again: how could he be so sure that the baby would be the boy we wanted? No. I'm sorry. I'll be honest. *He* wanted a boy; I wanted a *girl*. I don't know why, I couldn't get that stupid rhyme out of my head – you know, "What are little girls made of?" and the answer is "Sugar and spice and all things nice". That's what I wanted. A pretty little girl all clean and sweet. Not a boy made of . . . whatever they are made of. . . .'

'Slugs and snails and puppy dog's tails,' supplied the man.

'Yes, yes. You see? Hateful. Except that Rex isn't like that, is he? He's got those beautiful hands . . . always so clean. His skin always smells so lovely—'

Dorothy couldn't stop crying now. All the old scar tissue was breaking open and the memories were flowing freely from the wound. She recalled how she had to lie on her back in bed, unable to sleep, waiting for Rex to return. But he came home later and later, and often slept in the spare room. Dorothy hated the huge fat tummy that kept him away from her; but she was glad, too, because it saved her from the disappointment of sex. The bedroom was never dark because the sick orange light from the street-lamps always managed to seep through the thin curtains. She longed for it to be dark. She lay there, pressing down on the growth, feeling it kick like an animal. She squeezed her legs together hard under the bedclothes, screwing up her eyes and mind against the child, willing herself to sleep and not to dream.

'It didn't come out when it should've done. I started thinking that it would go on getting bigger until it burst me like a boil – crazy, I know, but I couldn't help it. I was enormous, grotesque. There was hardly anything left of me except this swelling. In the end they induced it. It was murder. It was a boy.' She looked across at Klackan's great block of a head, now sunk between his shoulders, and tried to read some small sign of understanding there. If only she could, just for a moment, connect herself to his huge violent energy which burnt like a pillar of black fire in her head. . . . Quickly she covered her face with her hands and went on with her monologue. She had stopped crying; her voice was at odds with the content of her speech, like a policeman reporting a fatal accident.

'At first it was wonderful, in a way. I couldn't believe that this tiny bundle of wrinkled skin was anything to do with me. I couldn't take my eyes off his fingernails. They were so tiny and so perfect they were frightening. I'd be staring at them and, oh God, he'd start crying and I'd panic, call for the nurse, sure that he was suffering from something I couldn't understand. I was determined to do everything right for him. But I was afraid of breaking him when I held him, afraid of dropping him. He was such a heavy responsibility, you see. . . .

'I did my best to feed him, but things can go wrong so quickly. I don't remember doing anything wrong. But sometimes he cried and cried, and pushed me away with his tiny fist. It was too much. I gave him my best and he pushed me away. "Nothing to worry about," the nurse said. But I worried all the time. I didn't give up, though. I went on giving him milk until I ran dry, until I was sore – but I never lost the feeling that he was just using me like a cow until he was big enough to feed himself. I learnt to accept it . . . accept that he didn't want me. I wasn't afraid of him any more; I made sure he had everything. I never gave him what he really wanted. I know that now. I didn't mean to harm him; it's the way I am, that's all, you see? Please. . . .'

Dorothy sighed deeply and rubbed her eyes. She was grateful that Mr Klackan had drawn the truth out of her at last. It dawned on her that perhaps – oh God, how could she even think it? – but perhaps only in the depths of some ultimate searing degradation could she be punished and purified enough to look Mikey in the face and say 'Forgive me. I've paid.' But when she turned her eyes, full of mute pleading, towards Klackan, she found that he had slipped away unnoticed.

Apart from a distant figure striding out with his dog and stick, slashing the heads off daffodils in the rough, the ninth fairway was deserted. Carol had told her about a rape committed on this very golf course. Ruth was not afraid, but she chose all the same to walk along the middle of the fairway rather than near the trees and undergrowth which bordered it. Walking was an exquisite experience, like the pure exercise of freedom. Her feet hardly seemed to touch the ground. She was swept along by the wonderful gush of energy flowing through her, streaming out — she could feel it spurting from her fingertips! — and returning to encircle her. She could only suppose it was the extraordinary result of her reaction to the fact of Mikey's departure.

When it finally sank in, she was seized by the overwhelming desire to weep, by the urge to rail against the world's cruelty, by the yearning to plead with God for some relief and, of course, by the overweening need to stuff herself sick — Ruth recognised all the compensations, as automatic as gravity, which sought to fill the void created by Mikey's loss. It was her refusal to bend to them which really surprised her — they seemed too crude and inadequate to express her simple enormous grief. She consciously renounced the consolation of tears and rage and God; nothing in the world could compensate her for her loss.

And so all her physical, mental and emotional energy, formerly bound up in Mikey and now discharged, was suddenly without object and end. She carried it around her, fused into a single psychic force-field which she dared not direct towards anything for fear of a blinding flash and a shower of sparks. As she moved down the fairway in a buoyant cloud of power, the springy grass seemed to sear under her feet. Walking was as much a necessity as a luxury, to prevent her from burning up. She could scarcely eat any more, as if food were too gross for a body becoming refined by the consuming energy. Her perennial emptiness reached such gargantuan proportions that she was all but engulfed. She could endure it for one reason alone: she didn't feel essentially *estranged* from Mikey. Paradoxically, in the centre of her emptiness, she felt closer to him than before.

As she approached the green, she found herself quite naturally addressing silent remarks to Mikey about her surroundings, just as long-married widows chat to their husbands' shades. At first, she was willing to believe that her odd sense of proximity was merely a false comfort of her own unconscious devising (hadn't Dr Frieling warned her against creating a private image of Mikey in order to possess him in pristine condition for ever?). But she rejected this belief because his imagined presence, in fact, brought no comfort — on the contrary it stressed unbearably the spiked reality of his absence. It existed in contradiction to her inner void; it sustained, without diminishing, her emptiness.

This state of tension charged Ruth with an acute sense of expectancy, as though she was sealed in a dynamic vacuum which drove her towards some unknown goal of its own. The 'spirit' messages were part of this strange anticipation. Dropping like manna out of the blue, they might have been specially contrived, for all their quaintness, to satisfy her new rarefied condition. She had sat down with pen and paper several times, hoping that her hand would move. But there was nothing. 'Patience,' the spirit had enjoined; and, oddly, she was content. She tried to imagine María, with whom she was connected in such oblique ways — first through Mikey and now through the otherworldly scribe. She wondered what had caused the Spanish girl to die so young, and mourned for her.

Ruth skirted around the ninth green and meandered down a path that led away from the golf course and emerged at the base of one of the hills which constituted the estate. As she drifted along the road, admiring the deep scarlet buds massed on the rhododendron bushes, she idly noticed its name. She caught her breath. It was Mikey's road. Until now, the address had been a few words in a file. It was a bizarre feeling to see that it really existed. Ruth's heart beat loudly. What was to stop her from finding the house and popping in? The Ballantine's wouldn't like it, of course, but what could they do? 'I was just passing. I thought I'd see how Mikey was getting on . . . ,' she rehearsed.

It was absurd, out of the question. Her presence would cause Mikey drastic confusion. Heaven knew what it would do to her. He was, as he had always been, so near yet so far. All the same. . . . She walked furtively along the road, looking to left and to right, until she spotted the name of the house, whose drive curved up the hill and out of sight. Passing through the large open gates which gave the entrance its fortress-like appearance, she took a few steps up the drive, just to see what the house looked like. From a distance, it seemed shut. Several windows were curtained. Perhaps the family had gone away? If only she could catch a glimpse of Mikey without being seen by him. . . . She took a few more steps and then stopped dead. An incredible thought had bolted into her mind: María had been murdered.

She backed hastily down to the road. It was empty and quiet except for the tall susurrating trees and, in the corner of her eye, the large houses shifting uneasily in their acres of ground. The Ballantines had said that María left for Spain unexpectedly. They gave no reason for her sudden departure. If she had died subsequently, why hadn't they mentioned it? Maybe they didn't know. Maybe they were unconnected with her early death.

But Mikey's central trauma had been intimately connected with María. He'd been so deeply scarred by it that he could never speak about it, except for a single haunting sentence: 'He's got a probe ... a stick in his hand. He's stabbing, stab-stabbing. She's dying, dying. . . .' Fact and fantasy were indistinguishable in the perceptions of the small tortured boy. But was the sentence evidence of something more than fantasy? Had he seen something so awful that he had exiled himself to outer space? The television played a part in it all – 'He traps people in the telly . . . .' Who? Mr Ballantine? If Rex Ballantine could take Mikey away, who was to say he couldn't commit murder?

Ruth was startled by the passing of a huge car, so silent that it was upon her before she knew it. The windows were tinted black. There were too many trees in the estate, Ruth decided; there was no room to breathe. There should be children playing in the streets instead of big silent cars like hearses, carrying their inmates to solitary homes.

In the sober light of Sunday morning, I doubted that it was Satan himself who had accosted me in the train. I'm not big enough fry. More likely it was his messenger, who had menaced my sleeping hours for so long. I was in mortal fear, not of my life, but of my soul. 'For our wrestling is not against flesh and blood, but against the principalities, against the powers, against the world-rulers of this darkness, against the spiritual hosts of wickedness in the heavenly places. . . .' And Saint Paul should know, because many secret things, you remember, were revealed to him in Paradise, including the unspeakable words which it is not lawful for a man to utter.

Now that the evil spirit had shown his hand, I was certain that the final onslaught prior to the Rapture had begun. The lines were drawn for a battle that Satan could win – even if he was doomed to lose the war. I had to be wary; everything was a potential snare. I wondered whether Clare might not be a deceiving spirit – 'For even Satan fashioneth himself into an angel of light' – but I dismissed the idea: certain truths had to remain unshakable or I'd merely go mad. And if I clung to the truth and witnessed out loud and obeyed the word of the Lord, then He would not fail me though a host of dark powers should screech for my blood and snatch at me with their talons.

On my way to church I telephoned Mister Turnbull at his home. My dismissal from the office was a sign exceeding tricky to interpret. I couldn't tell whether it was the work of Satan or of the Lord, a persecution or a liberation. But I had to try to regain my job to make sure that I was not overzealous to become a martyr for the truth – that is, too eager out of diabolical pride to *seek out* evil.

A child answered the phone. This upset me; I don't know why – perhaps I'd simply failed to imagine Mister Turnbull with *children*. He was put out at being woken up. I asked for his pardon and for a second chance. There was some abuse at his end; I forget what. I pointed out that a maniac still had to eat. But his decision was final. I don't think the implications, humanly speaking, of unemployment had really struck me until then. Suddenly the thought of sitting at home night after night without the companionship of the Invoice Office was terrifying. I rather lost my head. Craven words came out of my mouth against my will; promises were offered which I could never keep. Luckily, I suppose, the line went dead. I was cast out into the world.

I prayed at Saint Bart's, but the Lord held Himself aloof. I kept my head lowered to put off the moment of looking up and finding that Clare wasn't there. But she was. She *was*. I had no thought, I swear, of burdening her with the mighty things I was privy to; I only wanted to ... to ... I don't know. Save her, perhaps. In my innermost heart I should confess that perhaps, just *perhaps*, I only wanted to look at her. Almost as if *I* would be saved as long as my eyes were on her.

'Oh, it's you,' she said. I said it was. I walked beside her as far as the lych-gate. I asked her forgiveness for perplexing her at our last meeting. She was glancing around nervously. 'You'd better go,' she advised. Her voice was not hostile, but worried. A man was waiting for her in the road. 'My father.' He gave me a sharp look. 'Is that the man?' I heard him say. Clare nodded. I smiled at the man because he was Clare's father and because his face was not one that is meant to look unkindly. They walked away.

When I caught them up, I was very careful of what I said, extra polite like, because of the importance of the occasion. 'We haven't been introduced' – I raised my cap – 'but your daughter, namely Clare, is a friend to me and so I wonder if you'd both care to drop by this afternoon at number one, South Road, for a cup of tea – about four o'clock or whatever time suits – and I'll get a bit of a cake in if you say what sort you prefer.' I was a little out of breath. Funnily enough, Clare's father was, too. But he spoke very distinctly, saying 'Neither my daughter nor I are friends of yours. If you speak to her again, you'll have the police to answer to. Now *clear off.*'

Well. There wasn't a lot I could do in the circumstances, except sing. I gave them hymn number sixty from the Advent Preparation Church hymn-book: 'Hark, hark, hear the glad tidings. Soon, soon, Jesus will come!' Etcetera. I won't sing it now if you don't mind. It was my last chance to do some good, you see? Also, I wanted Clare to hear its beautiful tune at least once in her life.

They didn't look back. They turned out of sight into Prince's Road and I never saw him, let alone her, again.

Well, what would you have done then? You couldn't go home in such a susceptible state – more than your life's worth. I suspect you'd just go mooning about with your throat aching and your face all wet. You'd wish you had a gobstopper, or something, to suck. There's distraction to be had in uncovering layers of lovely colour ....

In the end I pulled myself together and had a cup of tea in town. But there was a bad feeling about the place. A man two tables away gave me some funny looks. His eyes were different colours. There was no guarantee that he was a man at all. Getting the eyes wrong is the sort of thing a masquerading spirit might do. I gave him the slip by catching a train to Guildford – it was safe enough as long as it was daylight with plenty of bona fide people about. I killed time at Guildford station with some hard train-spotting until all but the night expresses had stopped. Then I walked home. It took me all night – it's not *that* far, but I weaved around a bit to be on the safe side and throw things off the scent. A car tried to run me down outside Wisley – came at me flashing its lights and swerving dangerously so that I had to run from the safety of the middle of the road and cut through the woods. There was no further trouble until morning.

Sorry. I *will* press on, I *want* to get to the end, but I'm afraid. I'm beginning to remember what happened next. How can I forget? You're in for a shock. But would you mind if I closed my eyes for a minute or two first? I'm so tired. There's something, I beg your pardon, awful about this place. The smell for a start. Have you had trouble with your drains at all? Why don't you say something? I know, I know – *I've* got to do the talking. It'll be a relief when it's all over; it's getting me down this waiting; I almost wish ... almost ... that it would come and be done with it. But I'll tell you everything first. If I can just get through this next bit, I've a feeling it gets better. Yes! There are happy times ahead. So I'd be obliged if you'd keep an eye on the door for me while I get my head down for a couple of ticks. Meanwhile, you'd better brace yourself for the shock.

The pile of coal seemed never to diminish. Although Rex could dimly see the new heap increasing, however slowly, as he washed the lumps one by one and stacked them against the opposite wall, the original heap appeared to regenerate itself magically. The coal was certainly not ordinary coal – Mr Klackan had known that all along; it possessed qualities as much animal as mineral.

Lumps that were hard when he plunged them into the water sometimes came out warm and spongy, yielding like vulvas under the press of his fingers. When he pulled them out of the bucket's heavy juice, they glistened redly in the candlelight, sticky and good enough to eat. When he added them to the new pile they shone glossily like the thick black hair of the pious foreign girl who'd once looked after Mikey; who'd smiled shyly, showing perfect teeth; who was weak and easily frightened.

Mr Klackan was right: there was much to learn from coal. At the bottom of the pile, he was watching, always watching, and waiting to be uncovered; at the last, Rex would gently remove the coal-black hood and squeeze the soapy fluid through it. His heart filled with gratitude to the great faceless man for initiating him into the mystery of coal. Mr Klackan would come soon to share its secrets, come oozing out of the coal-pile to take on his temporary human shape, the pair of bright blades like pincers in his firm indifferent hands. Rex knelt reverently in front of the coal and knew the joy of obedient devotion.

But coal was treacherous, too. Without warning the lumps grew squashy and disgusting so that it was hard not to drop them. They stank of his own excrement. There were bits of him buried in the pile which he had to retrieve quickly before they were lost to him. As he rummaged frantically through the pieces, they turned to flesh under his fingers. Then, suddenly, the whole pile seemed to shift and hump itself around him, and he realised he was pulling lumps of decaying flesh off his own body. It was revolting work, but his flesh had to be washed clean and reconstructed before he rotted away.

Rex splashed and scrubbed fast and furiously to rebuild his anatomy. It took shape gradually, resting against the wall stiffly like an ebony skeleton. But there was no life in the new body. At any moment it could collapse into fragments. They'd fly off into space like tiny meteorites, each holding a sliver of his mind. He wouldn't be able to call them back; he'd go mad.

Sooner or later, of course, he would uncover Mr Klackan, watching and waiting, clear as a diamond, beneath the old pile of rotting flesh. Rex would transfer him to the heart of the new body and bring it to life. But the idea of such a metempsychosis appalled him. He cast around desperately for something to ward off that final self-extinction.

Rex crawled across the cellar floor, groping around until his hand touched soft black fur. How could he have forgotten Cassie, whom he loved so much? She nestled against his bare chest, her eyes looking up at him adoringly. She was so beautiful and intelligent. Her electrifying fur was thrilling to the touch.

210

He placed her on top of the coal-body and began to entomb her in a handsome head of freshly cleaned pieces from the old pile. Cassie responded, slowly rubbing her fur sexily against the soft coils of his brain. Rex chuckled with pleasure. She extended her claws and began to scratch. Rex laughed. 'Naughty girl, Cassie!' he admonished. Girls often liked to scratch; sometimes their little paws had to be restrained. His penis stirred slightly; he touched it excitedly with the tips of his fingers and then quickly withdrew them. The claws scraped away, arousing the memory of his power over women. He felt more like his old self again. The coal resumed its hardness; he could concentrate on the serious job of washing it. The light flickering on the wall contained fleeting female images, warming him to the task. 'That's enough, Cassie,' he said sternly. 'Be still.' He shook his head and rinsed his lumps of coal vigorously. To his annoyance, the door opened at the top of the steps. A momentary stream of natural light disturbed his equanimity. The claws continued to scratch, a bit too sharply for his liking, inside his head.

Mr Klackan was coming towards him, lugging some complicated creature behind him. Rex waited without hope for whatever fresh torture his captor had in store for him. There was a sound of liquid spattering the floor. Mr Klackan was in front of him now, grasping a long snake by the neck. He twisted the snake's head and a jet of poison shot out of its mouth, hitting Rex in the chest. He gasped with the shock of the icy fluid. He was so weak that it nearly knocked him over; but he knew better than to move or cry out.

Klackan played the water from the garden hose over Rex's body until he was washed clean. Then he twisted the nozzle which reduced the jet to a trickle, and rubbed Rex down with a large towel.

'Put these on,' he commanded, handing Rex a pile of clothes. The buttons were a nightmare to do up; the tie completely defeated him. Klackan surveyed him.

'Not bad. Maybe I should give you a shave. . . .' He held up the razor. Rex covered his healthy growth of beard with both hands; his head trembled from side to side. Klackan gave a short laugh and pulled a comb through Rex's wet tangled hair. He was a bit rough, as Rex's mother had been when she combed his hair in a hurry. His eyes smarted with tears.

Klackan disappeared from his field of vision for a while and then returned with a bowl of steaming aromatic soup, far superior to the usual gruel. Rex held the bowl in his cupped hands, trying to exclude the tormenting smell – the soup was too delicious to be anything to do with him.

'Eat,' ordered Klackan. 'You've got to keep your strength up.' Rex took a grateful sip. The liquid was so hot that it burnt his mouth. He scarcely noticed because the soup's soft lumps, bumping against his lips, were so savoury and rich that he was afraid he wouldn't be able to keep them down. To his surprise, he found that the whole lot disappeared in four enormous gulps. There was nothing left of the meaty broth except a glow in his stomach and an abominable craving for more.

'Up the stairs,' Klackan commanded. Rex glanced up at the crack of light. It intimated danger. The world outside belonged to a former life. There was no place for him now.

'Please, let me stay,' he whispered.

'Oh no. You're going on a little errand, Rex. Get up those stairs.' The razor was in his hand. Rex's cold dread of it was deeper than his terror of the dazzling vastness which lay in wait beyond the cellar. With Klackan prodding at his back, he climbed like a condemned man towards the light.

Ask.

Ruth hesitated. She had waited a long time for the unmistakable tingling to animate her hand. She had been determined to interrogate the 'spirit' mercilessly about its nature and its relation to her — was it, for example, a neurotic product? But now that the moment had come she was simply, girlishly eager to read what it had to say. By hanging fire, it seemed, the 'spirit' had dissolved her intellectual doubts; all her sceptical questions had deserted her, except one.

'May I speak to María?' she wrote. 'I must ask her some questions.'

Be patient. In time you will be in touch. You need not worry about her; she is in good hands. Trust me. There are important things you must know.

'What have they to do with me?'

Everything. They are already in you. In time you would discover them for yourself. But time is running out, so I must enlighten you quickly.

Ruth could not prevent a certain stiffening of her mental sinews; she had a natural resistance to being enlightened.

'Why should I believe what you say? I'm not even sure I believe in you.' Her arm jerked as if it were being irritably snatched away from her; the pen pressed hard on the paper.

I am not concerned with your beliefs. I am here to describe the operation of perfect laws. They cannot be learnt — they can only be seen. I see more of their operation than you because I view them from a higher vantage-point. No one sees the whole working of the laws except God who is on high. Nevertheless, I must speak as I see. This is doubly difficult for me because the

212

instrument also resists the truth of what I have to say. I can only strive, however imperfectly, to express it.

'I'm sorry,' murmured Ruth, who, disarmed by the spirit's admission of imperfection, wished to retract her disbelief. But the automatic writing flowed on, urgently.

My first expression is: each individual soul is a fraction of a Great Soul, which may be compared to a wheel. Each soul is like a spoke in that wheel, indispensable to the whole circular structure. My second expression is: a Great Soul embraces individual souls like a large sphere enclosing a series of smaller, concentric spheres. These expressions are drawn from your dimensions. The reality is otherwise: I ask you to imagine each soul-sphere sharing a centre with every other soul-sphere while each simultaneously embraces the other. This configuration forms a Great Soul in which each soul is both distinct and mutually inherent in the other component souls.

The writing paused. Ruth tried hard to imagine the spirit's impossible geometrical figure. There was one point she had to be clear about.

'An individual soul – a person – is not annihilated in the Great Soul, then?'

Is a single musical instrument annihilated in an orchestra? No. I do not speak of souls merging their identity; I speak of participation. Each soul co-inheres in the Great Soul. Through the mystery of co-inherence, a soul is more itself than it was, not less; it comes into its own. Truly, a soul does not know itself until it is reunited with its co-equal souls in the Great Soul.

Ruth abruptly stood up and wandered across the room, inhaling sharply. She was beginning to feel a little fraught. She needed a breathing-space in which to absorb the message's impact. Her eye fell greedily on the box of hazelnut fudge; but she had no sooner torn off the wrapping than she realised she didn't want any fudge. She wanted to understand, to digest the crisp words laid out on the page.

Returning to the desk, she carefully read through the writing so far. Then, in response to the last statement, she wrote: 'I get the general idea, I think. So when a person dies he or she immediately becomes part of a larger unit, this Great Soul?'

Death is not necessary for participation in the Great Soul. Death only reveals what was formerly hidden. Even in the realm of matter you are in the Great Soul and the Great Soul is in you; but, like an iceberg, the major part of it is invisible and unknown. . . .

Moreover, you must understand: the Great Soul is only potential. It becomes actual when each component soul has itself realised its own potential in the realm of matter. That's to say, a soul must overcome its internal divisions – become individual – before it can take its rightful place in the Great Soul. A soul's individuality is not innate; it must be acquired. In that respect, Dr Frieling was speaking the truth.

213

'You mean you were with me when I spoke to him the other day?' Ruth was so astonished — and uneasy — at the spirit's ability to eavesdrop that she forgot to write and spoke aloud instead. It made no difference.

I am always with you, her hand wrote calmly. *The doctor was right to emphasise the unconscious factors which, as living psychic entities, must be consciously integrated around the soul's centre. If a soul does not acquire its individuality before it passes at death into the realm of spirit, its dark unconscious aspects must reincarnate in order that they may be brought to the light of consciousness. For souls can only become what they must become, their true individual selves, in contest with the harsh necessities of the material realm. Perhaps they need be incarnate for only a brief moment — a child who dies at birth, for example, may provide the last fraction of consciousness required to complete a soul on the brink of selfhood. Then there is rejoicing throughout the spiritual realm, for the soul can participate in the glory of the Great Soul which has striven for long ages to accomplish its perfect singularity.*

She had to resist the increasing pressure on her hand to continue writing. She resented being 'enlightened' so quickly. Why the rush? And yet her beating heart told her that in a way she wanted to be rushed, as though the sense of urgency was hers and not the unknown communicator's.

She hurriedly reviewed the latest complicated statement. Although its tone and content were as exotic as ever, it undeniably spoke to some part of her — some neglected intellectual aspect, perhaps — just as the spirit had intimated when he affirmed that his ideas were already in her. On reflection, they did seem reminiscent of a truth already intuited — more as if she were rediscovering than learning afresh.

'Can more than one soul belonging to the Great Soul be incarnate at the same time?' said Ruth, thinking aloud.

Sometimes. Incarnate souls who participate in the same Great Soul have been known to recognise their affinity through the faculty called love. Where true love exists — for example, between members of a family — there also is the paradigm of the Great Soul.

'All right. But what becomes of the Great Souls? Do they exist in isolation?' asked Ruth.

No. They each co-inhere to form greater souls, and greater, until they are united in God. On the one hand, the hierarchy of souls is infinite; on the other, by a mystery known only to the spirit with whom all things are possible, the fullness of God can override the hierarchy and incarnate wholly in a particular soul — as once happened with the Nazarene called Jesus.

Ruth laid down her pen. She felt as though she were being swept out of her depth and needed to come up for air. Her fierce concentration had made her stiflingly hot, and looking around her room she almost expected to see a blazing fire. She was suddenly afraid that she had allowed the whole thing to get out of control.

'Why are you telling me all this?' she called out in the empty room. Her voice sounded weak and tremulous. But, at the moment she spoke, her fears were calmed by a draught of cool air which seemed to fan her face. Even as her hand began to write again, she felt that she knew what was coming next, like words on the tip of her tongue.

I am here to tell you about the One who is to come.

The writing ceased as if waiting for her response. In her heart she knew that something momentous was about to be announced.

'Who ... who is this "One"?'

A Great Soul who is free of the need to reincarnate, yet who has chosen, freely, like the avatars of old, to renounce the bliss of the spirit realm and to descend into the dark realm of matter. ... The writing faltered and continued more slowly. *You cannot understand ... the sacrifice that incarnation entails for a Great Soul. ... It is like a crucifixion.*

The spirit seemed temporarily subdued. Ruth was conscious of a deep sadness. Her arm lay heavily on the desk.

'Why is he returning to Earth?' she prompted.

I do not know. God knows. There was a long pause and then the writing picked up again. *But I know that such Great Souls have appeared throughout history to bring light in times of darkness. They come gladly, out of the love they bear for mankind. ...*

'But why are you telling *me*?' Excitedly, Ruth waited for the spirit's answer; but her hand refused to move unless she moved it herself.

SIX

DOROTHY blinked in the sunlight. A gentle breeze made her recoil. Her nervous system seemed to have been transposed to the surface of her skin; the smallest sensation was overwhelming. She made an enormous effort to slow down her breathing and stepped hesitantly over the threshold. The car keys clinked in her trembling fingers. She closed her fist around them. Rex dragged his feet behind her. She dared not look round at him, but instead strained her ears for a heavier tread, and braced herself for the blow from behind.

She reached the garage unscathed. For a moment she feared she had forgotten how to drive; but, miraculously, her hands and feet performed the right sequence of movements. The car reversed into the drive; a man climbed in beside her. A glance at his shoes told her that it really was Rex and not Klackan. The door shut. She eased the car down the drive and through the gates.

The trees were thick with leaves which, hiding long views, surely hadn't been there before. The roads of the estate were empty of traffic, as if the whole world were asleep. Only the coldness of the steering-wheel persuaded Dorothy that she was not asleep herself. She waited for Rex to speak, to tell her it was safe to speak. She could hear him fidgeting in his seat and twisting his neck around — of course, he was trying to find out what accomplice Klackan had posted on the back seat. She glanced surreptitiously in the rear-view mirror. The back seat seemed to be empty.

Klackan had sent them shopping. He had written out a list of items in a large rounded hand and tucked it into the top pocket of Rex's jacket. He had given Dorothy the car keys and a twenty-pound note, commending her appearance and lamenting Rex's unwillingness to smarten up. All the things on the list were to be bought at the super-market in the High Street; they were not to go anywhere else. Dorothy had vaguely thought that it was Sunday, when the shops were closed; apparently it was not — but she couldn't think what day it was. They were to complete the errand as quickly as possible; if they took too long .... Klackan had left her at the front door, indicating Rex waiting in the hall's shadows, and walked pointedly off towards Mikey's room. Terrified, she called out questions after him. What if they couldn't find all the items on the list? What if they were delayed or the car broke down? How long had they got, exactly? She was nearly hysterical with the thought of all the things that could go wrong. She begged Mr Klackan to go himself. It would be much easier; there'd be no trouble while he was gone. But Klackan disappeared up the stairs and out of earshot.

The car's engine hummed a song of freedom. Dorothy tried not to listen. Any thought of escape that entered her head was eclipsed by Klackan's brooding presence, which seemed to impart its own logic to her situation: of course she couldn't escape because he'd never have let her out if he'd thought for one moment that she could *escape*. All the same, she couldn't believe this was really happening. The engine purred softly, telling her she could just keep on driving far away until Klackan had faded from her mind. But her hands, as if bolted to the steering-wheel, obediently directed the car along well-worn paths to the High Street.

One word from Rex was all she needed, one word to break the deadlock of terror — she'd slam her foot on the accelerator and take off. But Rex's silence was a clear sign that he knew something. Perhaps the car was bugged (no; she was simply being paranoid). More likely, Klackan was tailing them. She scanned the road behind, but there wasn't a single suspicious vehicle. She could scarcely contain her excitement: if only Rex would whisper what his plan was, she'd do whatever was necessary without hesitation. Already the old familiar act of driving was filling her with self-confidence.

'Rex,' she murmured out of the side of her mouth, her eyes fixed on the road ahead. 'What shall I do?' At the mention of his name he half-turned his dear face towards her; she was aware of some change in him — the beard, for a start, and the unkempt hair.

'Drive faster,' he replied in an odd high-pitched voice. Dorothy put her foot down and drove quickly to the large car park adjoining the supermarket.

She was dismayed by the sheer number of humans strolling to and fro. Some were pushing wire trolleys stacked with goods. Others were smiling and chatting, unconscious of the huge world turning underneath them. Dorothy wasn't sure she could go out there among them. She wished she were back in her bedroom where she belonged. The responsibility was too great; she wouldn't know what to do or say without Klackan's help. Then she remembered: Rex was with her. He'd know what to do.

Switching off the ignition, she reached tentatively for his reassuring hand. 'No,' he said, snatching it away. He seemed extremely frightened. His fear was contagious.

'*Rex, what are we going to do?*' she hissed in a panic. He blocked his ears with his hands.

'Ssssh. 'S not safe.' He turned his face towards the window. Dorothy followed what she imagined to be the direction of his gaze. The people outside were studiously ignoring her. A man in a parked car opposite caught her eye and quickly looked away. She let out a gasp. Rex was right: they were being watched. It was important to behave exactly as Mr Klackan would expect.

She got out of the car, motioning to Rex to follow. He eagerly scrambled after her and hurried towards the huge glass-fronted store. Then, perhaps realising that he was drawing attention to himself, he slowed down and began to walk more normally. It was Dorothy's first opportunity to take a proper look at him, and he looked like a stranger. He almost looked — she was cut to the heart — like a vagrant. His clothes hung on him loosely and his poised gliding walk had given way to a slightly stooped shamble. He looked old. The skin on his neck was scraggy; his mouth was half-open, revealing a shocking gap in his even teeth. Above the growth of beard his eyes were sunken, haunted, erratic in their movements. She was profoundly impressed at the way he had managed to disguise his real self. No one could possibly guess what he was planning, not even Mr Klackan. She smiled at him as knowingly as she dared, and together they entered the realm of bright light, soft music and special offers.

Dorothy pulled the list out of Rex's top pocket, handed it to him and gave him a nudge in the back. He began to wander between the shelves of packets and tins. She followed behind with a trolley. At the end of the aisle, Rex had put nothing in it.

'We have to *hurry*, Rex,' she murmured. He stared at the list.

'I can't ... can't seem....' Tears gathered in his cloudy eyes. Dorothy was horrified. He was going too far; he was behaving like a child. At any moment someone might accost them and hold them up. She'd never be able to explain it to Mr Klackan. They'd all die because of some interfering fool.

Acutely conscious of the desultory shoppers around her, she took the list from Rex's limp fingers and made him hold on to the trolley to stop him from lagging behind. Next, she shut everything out of her mind except the monumental task of locating each item on the list. It wasn't easy because they were not things she would buy herself, but trivial, mostly rubbishy foodstuffs such as an iced cake, sliced white bread, tins of baked beans, tea-bags, white sugar, milk and biscuits. The effect of concentrating on these was catastrophic: it dawned on her that the shelves were jam-packed with delicious, ravishing, mouth-watering *food*. Grabbing the nearest packet of biscuits, nut-brown and crisply glowing inside their cellophane, she was on the verge of tearing off the paper and cramming the delicacies into her starved mouth when she was unexpectedly rescued by Rex. He had no trouble in reading her transparent mind.

'Don't. ... He'll find out. ... *He'll* know.'

She nodded guiltily and placed the unopened packet in the trolley. Her faith in him was somewhat restored. He really did know what he was doing since he was alert enough to spot possible transgressions on her part. But as the trolley filled up and the checkout counter drew closer she became panicky and distracted, glancing round at other people in the hope of a meaning look or a friendly gesture; but nobody caught her eye or smiled. She longed for something to happen to wake her out of her trance; but her hands went on picking out the correct items and the exit went on drawing nearer. She was sure that Rex would break away from the trolley at any second and do something drastic. Silently she willed her support for him across the huge distance which seemed to separate them.

The shoppers were funnelled into one or other of the checkout queues. As Dorothy moved up level with the till, it occurred to her that Rex had a note ready to pass to the girl who was tapping out the prices. Suddenly she was amazed that she had ever doubted him. Suppressing her excitement, she began to pack her purchases into a carrier bag. She didn't even glance at Rex, who was staring with unusual intensity at the checkout girl's breasts. Instead, she surreptitiously made sure that he was not being observed.

A short distance ahead of her a woman was rummaging through a pile of cardboard boxes, searching for one the right size to contain her shopping. Next to her stood a small girl, obviously her daughter.

220

Dorothy's furtive gaze was arrested by the girl's even stare. It seemed to go straight through her, to read her heart. Dorothy was petrified. The small girl began to suck the end of her pigtail. Then, withdrawing it from her mouth, she flashed Dorothy a shy smile. It was like a dash of cold water in her face.

Dorothy realised she was crazy, crazy, crazy. They were out of it, free as birds among ordinary oblivious people, each one a potential friend. A stupefied grin spread across her face. She turned to the checkout girl and was about to speak when the girl thrust some change and a receipt into her hand, and immediately began to tot up the next heap of goods.

Dorothy swivelled around to address the mother of the little girl. She had gone. Another woman stood in her place. She looked strong and competent. Dorothy wanted to attach herself to the woman, clutch her by the sleeve and hang on until she was carried safely away. Just like the little pigtailed girl, the woman was staring straight into her face. There was a hesitant puzzled smile on her face. Dorothy knew that now was the moment: she started forward, a cry of gratitude — a plea for help — on her lips.

'Mrs Ballantine ...?' the woman said uncertainly. Dorothy stopped dead. Rex plucked feverishly at her arm. 'How's Mikey ...?' the woman was asking. Oh God. The woman had been planted by Klackan. Her mocking question, reminding them of Mikey's plight, made Dorothy want to scream and weep. She veered towards the exit, pulling Rex behind her.

Back in the locked car, it took Dorothy a full minute to bring her shaking breathless body under control. Rex was rocking to and fro in the seat beside her. He had never had a plan of any kind, she realised. He was just a terrified child for whom she was responsible. Dorothy pressed her hands hard into the pit of her stomach to ease the desperate ache of loneliness.

The woman who had spoken to her was standing outside the entrance to the supermarket with a basket on her arm. At a distance, perhaps because of the way she stood or because of the light falling on her beautiful hair, she was instantly recognisable. She wasn't Klackan's accomplice at all; far from it — she was Mikey's woman from the Unit place.

It did not break over her exultantly as it had in the store, but nevertheless, soberly, profoundly, Dorothy knew she was free — free to ask the woman for help, free to use a telephone, free to alert the police, free to drive away and never come back. There were endless freedoms and all of them were false. She could never be free until Mikey was free. She was tempted by visions of the police or, better still, the SAS storming the house with guns and stun grenades. But she knew that Mikey would never be saved by brute force. It had to be an inside job, her job. She almost hated Ruth Maier for thrusting Mikey back into the forefront of her mind, but she was grateful, too. She was able for the first time to picture her son vividly: he was sitting in his hideous gloomy room with Klackan's razor at his throat.

Dorothy leant her head against the steering-wheel. She was tired beyond tiredness. She heard Rex fumbling in his pocket, followed by the sound of a match being struck. It grated on her exposed nerves like sandpaper. She had to go back, yes; but more than that – she marvelled at the sudden movement in her heart – she *wanted* to go back. Regardless of duty, regardless of whatever punishment awaited her, she wanted to go back because she, of all people, *she* loved Mikey.

A second's delay might be fatal. She started the engine and threw a quick bright smile towards Rex in the hope of lifting him out of his misery. They could do something together, perhaps – formulate a plan on the way back maybe. Rex was holding a lighted match under his bare arm. The flame was scorching his smooth skin. His eyes, for the first time, were alight with a triumphant gleam. He gave a little satisfied giggle.

'Rex,' she said wearily. 'Are you mad?' She knocked the match from his hand and put the car into gear.

Right. Ready for the shock? I wouldn't have done it, I'm sure, if I hadn't been worn down with walking and weakened by sleeplessness and worry – but no excuses. I tapped the root of all evil. Incredible, I know. But there it is.

The occasion of this sin was little Bobby Birkinshaw. You wouldn't recognise him now – he's a great big-bellied bloke with not much hair and, it turned out, four kids. He wouldn't need me to carry him on a walk any more; more the other way round, ha ha. He was with five of his pals, blocking the pavement outside the Greyhound. You know the fancy pub in the High Street. I hadn't seen Bobby since he clapped me on the back six years and three and a half months ago; and, do you know, he did it again.

'How's it going, Harry me old mate?' he said, in those exact words, just like the old friend he was. 'You look browned off, pal,' he said. 'Your trouble is you need a drink, eh?' He winked at his friends, who all nodded thoughtfully. They seemed to gather round me. Big blokes all of them, with bellies and arms as thick as legs. It's a rare feeling for me to feel small in company. They gave off a warm cosy smell of perspiration and beer, and when they moved it was lazily, like cattle

'You b—s know old Harry, don't you?' said dear Bobby. The bad language didn't seem bad in Bobby's mouth; more like a gesture of affection. Most of them did know me, or of me – I was flattered to find I'm a bit of a local character. One of them even said: 'What happened to those preaching stints you was always doing then, sunshine?' Sunshine! Fancy him remembering – I haven't held forth for donkey's years. Anyway I didn't mean to, but when they moved in a herd I couldn't help moving with them, they were so big and warm somehow and me so worn down and out, etcetera – I felt safe for a bit, and companionable, rather like I hoped army life would be but wasn't – they didn't badger me or anything, but just sort of took me in; but no excuses. . . .

I went into the pub.

Incredible, yes, but there it is. I shocked myself.

They liked to stand at the bar – the *lounge* bar, no less – but they didn't mind me sitting on a stool. There were soft lights (even though it wasn't yet midday), lovely lights shining in mirrors and bottles. Like a fairy-tale palace. Bobby and his chums took fat wads of money out of their back pockets – I've never seen so much money – and peeled off notes, they didn't care how many. Bobby said what was I having and I said an orange juice, which in drinking slang is called a screwdriver. You live and learn. They made quite a fuss of me; I was a bit overcome. I tried to pay for a drink, but they wouldn't *let* me! Also, the smiling girl behind the bar gave you a new drink as soon as you'd finished the old one, miraculously, without anyone appearing to ask for it. The men just passed notes to her occasionally, without looking at her, but she seemed happy.

Bobby was a builder, it turned out, and Des was in central heating. Dave was in garages and so was his boy – boy! – Steve, who didn't say much but laughed a lot. Malcolm was in motors and teased Dave about his garages. Tony wheeled and dealed – I had to watch out for him, they said; but then they winked and I saw that it was *only in fun*. It turned out I *didn't* have to look out for him! They all laughed. Not *at* anyone, but out of sheer abundance of life, just as a communion of saints might laugh. It was like being caught up into the third heaven. You don't mind orange juice tasting a bit off when there's warm bubbles floating up behind your eyes so that you have to laugh simply at the way they wink with their kind eyes.

Mind you, they had their troubles, as who doesn't? Business, apparently, is Hard; the Government is No Help. Motors, surprisingly, are often a Disappointment; wives Tricky. Poor Bobby's effing old lady went on at him so much he was obliged to bat her one. They agreed that I was lucky to have been spared the inconvenience of a

223

wife. I had to hold my head in case it ballooned off my shoulders. I blurted out to Steve about how Clare was lodged in my heart like broken glass, I couldn't help it; and he listened seriously and nodded and understood. Turns out it could happen to anyone. The secret is to learn to laugh at yourself. There was great peace amidst the wisdom of these men. They knew the world as I never had, and laughed in the face of pain and death. Their generous faces loomed around me like big red planets. I felt the world turning beneath me. My soul expanded in all directions, overflowing and − like a brimming glass − sensitive to the least vibration.

Distinctly, as though my ear were pressed to the ground, I sensed the airy tread of the evil one who was sent to damn me.

Well, red alert as Mikey would say. Danger. I might have guessed the demon would try to take advantage of me in my glad condition. I'm not noted for my quick reactions, but I lunged at top speed for the door of the Greyhound and was swept through on a gust of hot air and laughter. The cold wind hit me in the solar plexus; the hard street heaved under my feet. It was out there somewhere among the harmless souls window-shopping in the High Street. My eyes were useless for detecting it. I closed them and let my soul probe the surroundings with its fine wires of gold light until I located an aura of malevolence.

My eyelids snapped back. It was standing with its back to me across the street. Even as I watched, it moved off, unhurriedly, outwardly indistinguishable from the other passers-by. The odour of corruption was strong in my nostrils; I was sick in my stomach, and sore afraid. But I also had a new feeling, fiery and brave. There was a red anger in me. I knew that now was my best hope of wrestling it down and dragging it into the light that insidious spirits abhor.

I hurled myself across the busy street, bellowing the seventy-two sacred names of God* which grant authority over evil spirits. My hand

---

* Harry is probably referring to the seventy-two names listed in the *Constitution of Pope Honorius*, a dubious magical text in his possession. The names are as follows: Father, Son, Holy Ghost, Trinitas, Sother, Messias, Emmanuel, Sabahot, Adonay, Athanatos, Jesu, Pentagna, Agragon, Ischiros, Eleyson, Otheos, Tetragrammaton, Ely, Saday, Aquila, Magnus Homo, Visio, Flos, Origo, Salvator, Alpha and Omega, Primus, Novissimus, Principium et Finis, Primogenitus, Sapientia, Virtus, Paraclitus, Veritas, Via, Mediator, Medicus, Salus, Agnus, Ovis, Vitulus, Spes, Aries, Leo, Lux, Imago, Panis, Janua, Petra, Sponsa, Pastor, Propheta, Sacerdos, Sanctus, Immortalitas, Jesus, Christus, Pater, Filius Hominis, Sanctus, Pater Omnipotens, Deus, Agios, Resurrectio, Mischiros, Charitas, Aeternas, Creator, Redemptor, Unitas, Summum Bonum, Infinitas, Amen. (*Editor*)

was on its shoulder. The grey suit ripped as it pulled away. I knew that it might lose its pleasing shape at any second, and revert to its true appearance – a sight not to be borne save through the grace of Jesus Christ. But the spirit started to run, with me in pursuit scenting victory, ready to wrestle and quell it.

It was over almost as soon as it began: two policemen intervened, restraining me. Oh, blind justice! I curled up on the pavement and hid my face and prayed; for the power of the Holy Spirit in me was broken. I no longer dared confront the demon. Luckily, it had no desire to reveal itself either to me or to the police, but made off, leaving me to explain as best I could and finally to be detained in the loony bin for my pains. But, then again, if I hadn't been in error (for which I have repented), I'd never have found the Unit.... I'll just check the door, if you don't mind. Out there they give me the creeps. I keep thinking one of them will turn on me ... turn out to be the terrible one. I'll stay here a bit longer, if that's all right with you. I'll leave the light off. It helps me to talk, the dark. Also, light might attract it, like an insect.

All's quiet for the moment ... yes. Did you know that a screwdriver contains vodka? It was the demon drink that undid me, you see, and not the demon. I really should have been put behind bars for attacking that harmless fellow, not subjected to psychiatrics. I acted badly, not madly. I'd have relished the chance to beg my poor victim's forgiveness in open court, to my public shame, instead of which I'm denied the right of punishment and expiation. I'm even powerless to mend his suit – all I can do is pray for him. I don't want to seem ungrateful for the charity and loving-kindness I've received here, plus the food, hot and regular as it is, though fallen off recently. ...

Forgive me, but you're not ... are you? ... not Doctor Noble. Didn't like to mention it before. It doesn't matter in the least. I can't quite make you out but you have a sympathetic presence. Doctor Noble is also very kind, of course. I offered to be completely frank with him about my religious mania but he said he was more interested in causes than in symptoms – which can't strictly be true because he doesn't believe in God. Not that I blame him. He never had my advantages in life. He doesn't think I'm round the twist. A few marbles short maybe, but not raving. He sent me home quite soon after I arrived, made me an outpatient. I'm not sure he was one hundred per cent wise. After all, he turned down my perfectly civil request for electric treatment in the head. If he hadn't, I might have been ... might not have done what I did.... It was beyond ... beyond belief, beyond everything. I'm beginning to remember now, bits of it are ... oh Jesus ... bits are coming back—

Lord, it's cold in here. Not like the Unit. Down there, I forgot about Clare for long periods of time. I mean, I thought *I* had troubles. . . . Well, if you want to know about fear and trembling, nip down the Unit and take a butcher's at those kids. You can't help wondering what God has in mind exactly. In fact, a man without faith might be tempted to draw the wrong conclusions about God, namely that He's not good. But it's God's way to appear to forsake His chosen ones in their greatest need, to give them over to pure evil, to abandon them to the crushing weight of this world . . . . I suppose we can hardly complain – He was, after all, absent to Himself in the person of His Son, who, abandoned to gravity and hanging on the Cross, called out: 'Father, Father, why . . . ?' Perhaps he was most God at that moment when he was only a man. I don't know. It's not a thing to be understood. Perhaps poor God withdraws Himself from time to time because He wants to be loved for Himself and not according to our lights. I don't know. Anyway.

As soon as I saw him, I *knew*. . . . He was the very picture of Job, except that all Mikey's boils and ashes were sort of on the inside. If you looked into his eyes you might have thought there was no one at home. But there was someone there all right. At the bottom of things. Someone buried under sins like the goat which the Children of Israel sent bleating into the wilderness. Oh, Mikey. He was full of dark sentences. No one could interpret them except Ruth. Such a divine name. Ruth, Ruth. Not that I ever took the liberty of using her Christian name. Her beauty surpasses the beauty of the Daughters of Zion. The first time I saw her she was sitting on a bench. Put me in mind of Jean Macintyre for a moment, she was so fair. But I think now that Jean Macintyre only really existed as a picture in my mind; and the picture only really came to life when I saw Ruth. . . .

Working at the Unit, well, I wondered if it wasn't an intimation of the Rapture. Such a pocket of love, outside the ruining world, where the innocent are restored. And for me a sanctuary from the iniquitous spirits that walk abroad seeking souls whom they may devour. You keep your head down in those circumstances, I can tell you. You just thank God and Doctor Frieling that you're there.

It couldn't last, of course. The evil spirit tracked me down. I could hear it whispering around the house at night; walking from the Unit each evening was torture. It had been wonderful at first, watching Mikey's daily striving; but now it was terrible. I love that boy. He had a cat who watched out for him, better than a real cat – better than a dog. He gave it to me once; I'm coming to that. It was better than a knighthood. The sight of him perched on his bean-bag with all hope draining away did terrible things to me. We both seemed lost. And Ruth was running out of strength. I was close to despair. . . .

I rather think that what I've done has cut me off from Christ.

Still, who can look into His heart and read there the names of the saved? I believe in the forgiveness of sins, I believe that Jesus Christ can forgive my sins ... will forgive my sins. But will He forget them?

I don't think the Lord will gather me to him, not now. I pray only that my beloved ones will rise unscathed.

FIVE

'FOR WHAT ... we ... are ...,' faltered Rex. Klackan tapped him encouragingly on the knee with his razor.

'Cat got your tongue, Rex? You're head of the household. Surely you can say grace. ...' He sighed heavily. '"About to receive,"' he prompted.

'About to receive ... may the Lord. ...'

'Yes?'

'May the Lord ... the Lord ...,'

'Press on, Rex.' Rex's mouth worked soundlessly; his brow was knitted with concentration. 'Make us truly thankful,' finished Klackan. 'I can't wait all night. Can't have you spoiling my little tea-party.' He turned to Dorothy. 'You be mother.' Obediently, she poured three cups of tea.

Klackan had had the pot of tea ready for them when they returned, apparently not a moment too soon. He had been waiting in the hall. Rex had hurried eagerly to him, standing very near as if for warmth. He looked small in comparison to the big shapeless man. It was a disgusting sight. In the drawing room, Klackan had sat down on the sofa, with Rex on his right, and laid out their purchases on the coffee-table. He had placed Dorothy, within easy reach of his left hand, in an armchair at right angles to the sofa.

'Three sugars please, Mother. This is cosy. A little tea-party while we're waiting. Eh, Mother?'

'Waiting for what?' said Dorothy shortly. Klackan swung his heavy head in her direction. She wished she could retract her words: it didn't pay to speak unless compelled to. You never knew which way the monster was going to jump.

'Just waiting ... waiting to find out what it's all about ... what I'm going to do next.' He was clearly perturbed. He gestured emptily with the razor and then suddenly lunged forward. Dorothy flinched and froze. He hacked a wedge out of the iced cake. 'It's all right for you, Mother,' he continued morosely. 'We know what you're waiting for. And it'll come, all in good time. But me ... me ... I'm stuck with the likes of you and Rex here until I get my orders. Not fit for human company half the time, the pair of you, but I still have to wait until I'm ... until he's ready ... till I meet him face to face. How would you like it, eh? *Eh?*'

'We'll wait together,' said Dorothy quickly, soothingly.

'That's right,' said Klackan. 'That's dead right.' He pushed a mouthful of cake into his face's lower hole and chewed distractedly, spilling crumbs down his front.

Watching him, Dorothy thought how like a big, moody, dangerous baby he was. Every word was a frightful risk – but she had to *try* at least, before he was completely himself again, before she lost her nerve.

'I'll just take some tea up to Mikey, shall I?' she suggested lightly. He might fall for it if he wasn't asked a question or required to think. Klackan stopped chewing.

'Mikey's had his tea. He's got everything he wants. He's all right, is Mikey. He's a good boy. Not like me, eh, Mother? I'm naughty. Look at the mess I'm making with this cake. What I need is a proper spanking, eh?' He stopped abruptly. She could almost hear him thinking: "Take some tea up to Mikey." That's a good one. You're not being tricky, are you, Mother?'

'No. I just thought. ... Just so long as you're looking after him.'

'I'm looking after him. Don't you worry yourself. It's not always easy – he can give you the creeps. I mean, he's not ... normal, is he? Not what you'd call sociable. But I'm taking care of him. I like him. You can get a bit of peace and quiet with Mikey. Not like the pair of you. You make me tired ... angry.'

Dorothy passed him his tea, exaggerating the movement in order to see if it was possible to snatch the knife from his belt. Not that it was possible for her. But a person who was very quick, decisive and brave might do it. She gulped down her own tea and sat absolutely still, absorbing the hot sweet liquid's devastating impact on her shrunken stomach.

'That's better, eh, Mother? Have a piece of cake. Have a biscuit.' She shook her head. A cup of tea was as far as she'd go in collaborating with Klackan over his gruesome little 'party'. As much as she craved the sweet food, it would choke her to eat from the same cake as Klackan.

A fleeting wolfish look had come into Rex's eyes as they followed the food which Klackan was offering to his wife. He seemed to rouse himself briefly from his sunken state of lethargy.

'Out there . . . ,' he began hesitantly as if he had trouble remembering, 'out there she tried to eat biscuits. . . . I stopped her . . . Mr Klackan, I stopped her.' Dorothy threw him a puzzled pitying look; poor, poor Rex – what he must have gone through to come to this.

'Did she? Well, you shall have her share, then, Rex. No biscuits for naughty Dorothy.' He put the biscuits in front of Rex, who stared at them in disbelief. He turned dog-like eyes towards Klackan, who said softly: 'All right, Rex. Eat.' Rex grasped a biscuit in both clumsy hands and lifted it towards his mouth.

'Wait,' said Klackan. The hands froze in mid-air; a trickle of saliva escaped Rex's half-open mouth and fell on to his beard. His face contorted for a second, then smoothed out into a bland unseeing expression.

'There's something wrong here,' pondered Klackan, testing the edge of his razor blade with a thick thumb. 'Frankly, I'm disappointed. I've been a bit lonely lately . . . thought a party would cheer us up. Nothing grand, just the family, so to speak. But you're a couple of miseries. Cheer up, Rex. Cheer us all up. Give us a song. Entertain us. Go on. Sing something before my disappointment gets the better of me.'

'Can't . . . can't remember . . . can't,' Rex mumbled.

"Course you can. SING.' The sudden shout made Rex jerk in his seat.

'Amo, amas, amat, amamus. . . .' He conjugated the Latin verb in a dull monotonous chant.

'That's not a song,' said Klackan scornfully.

'I love, you love, he loves,' recited Rex. 'We love . . .'

Dorothy looked and listened, appalled. She had learnt that whatever was impossible happened – you had to watch it, accept it, let it penetrate you, no matter how far it threatened to go.

'Shut up and SING, Rex,' said Klackan. 'Stand up! Sing "Old Macdonald Had a Farm". You know that one. Everybody knows that one.'

Rex stood, no longer chanting but making a horrid noise, somewhere beyond tears, like hiccups.

'Leave him alone.' Dorothy was surprised at how firm her voice was, although her body was numb. Klackan swivelled his black head towards her, the hood's mouth-hole showing an 'O' of surprise. He picked up the cake and tossed it into her lap.

'Eat. Eat and shut up. Rex is going to sing.' His voice was low, but she could detect a minute tremulousness which suggested he was struggling to control it. He stood up abruptly and walked to and fro in front of Rex. He was tapping his razor against his thigh.

'I'll sing,' Dorothy offered. He took three steps towards her and pointed the razor at her head. Her heart gave a mighty convulsion and seemed to stop.

'I won't tell you again.' He was clearly worked up now; his pacing grew quicker. 'Sing, Rex ... sing or ... or. ...' He stopped in front of his victim. 'Or I'll take the hood off.' The idea seemed to excite him. He grasped the woolly hood at the neck. 'I'm taking it off, Rex. I don't know what'll happen after I take it off. ... I won't be responsible. ...' He was as much fearful as excited now. Dorothy was white with anguish – there was no hope if he took it off; the sight of his face would be the end of them all. She wanted to scream at Rex to sing, but she couldn't utter a sound. She saw her husband begin to flap his hands in feeble gestures of terror as the enormity of the situation sank in. He went on flapping, hopelessly out of time, as he croaked the words:

> 'Old Macdonald had a farm,
> Ee-yi-ee-yi-o.
> And on that farm there was a ... was a ... a. ...'

His hands flailed the air helplessly. Klackan released his grip on the hood.

'CAT,' he bellowed.

'And on that farm there was a cat, ee-yi-ee-yi-o. With a meow meow here—'

'Louder.'

'And a MEOW MEOW there—'

'You're a *cat*, Rex. Get down and do it properly!' Rex dropped mewing on to all fours. 'See? You're an animal. Worse than an animal. You can't even make a noise like a proper cat. Come on, puss. Meeoow.'

'Meeow meooow.'

Dorothy's hands automatically stuffed morsels of cake into her mouth as her eyes remained fixed on the two men. The unbearably sweet taste mingled with the awful sight to produce a sickness in the pit of her stomach.

'Come here, puss!' Klackan was commanding. 'Good puss; here, puss!'

'MeeOW,' went Rex, rubbing himself against the big man's trunk-like legs.

'Up, puss! Sit up and beg.' He teased Rex's rump with the flat of his blade.

'Yow, yow, yow,' cried Rex, kneeling upright, rampant.

'*That's enough.*' She didn't know she had decided until she said it. She could only guess at what Klackan's horseplay was doing to Rex, who appeared to be slipping down into some incoherent bestial condition. Both men were silenced by her outburst. She stood up and faced Klackan.

'Leave him alone. Take me instead.'

Like a great bull distracted from its goring, Klackan straightened up and swung his head dumbly from side to side. With the momentum of his goading interrupted, he seemed at a loss.

'Rex,' she ordered. 'Get out of here. *Leave.*'

Rex raised himself slowly to his feet and looked uncertainly at Klackan, who was breathing hard.

'Go to your cellar, Rex,' he said quietly.

'Dorothy...?' Rex threw a panic-stricken questioning glance at his wife.

'It's all right, Rex. Just go.'

He slunk away; his footsteps grew faint as they dragged over the cellar stairs. She was alone with Klackan. His eyes gleamed darkly in the woollen sockets; she could see the redness of his mouth. Neither of them moved for a long time. Then, without taking the twin beams of his eyes off her, he undid his belt. The knife dropped on to the sofa and lodged between the cushion and the arm. The blood rose to Dorothy's face.

'Well. Get it over with,' she said harshly. Already she could feel his terrible ascendancy reasserting itself over her. In another second she would fall to the floor and beg for mercy. But he made no move towards her, as if he were held in thrall. Recklessly she tore off her sweater and threw it at his feet. His involuntary wince stirred her with a thrilling intuition of power. She stripped off her blouse, unhooked her bra and threw them on top of the sweater. Her breasts rose and fell in time to her quick breaths. Klackan's eyes rolled white in his black head; he made a noise, like a grunt, in the back of his throat.

Dorothy took two steps towards him. She stood very straight, her breasts like eyes staring him down. He swayed visibly, moving his head like a wounded beast. The razor and belt dangled uselessly in his confused hands. She felt her nipples harden into threatening points. Her body, unafraid, was taking over; it wanted to overpower the man with its sheer nakedness – make him bow his great veiled head in homage, ready to be led by the nose. She reached for the zipper on her skirt.

A strident noise tore through the hushed drawing room. She couldn't identify it at once; but its discordance broke the frail hypnotic rhythm of her disrobing. It was the doorbell. Her arms flew up to cover her shameless chest. She began to shiver violently. Her eyes silently questioned Klackan. What had possessed her to imagine that anything could be gained by her display?

'Put your clothes on, Dorothy.' Gratefully, she snatched them up and pulled them on. Klackan had resumed his old authority. He would know what to do. The bell sounded again, impossibly loudly.

'Answer it,' said Klackan.

'How can I? What shall I *say*?'

'Anything you like.' He held up the razor diffidently. 'I'll be in Mikey's room.' He turned to leave.

'*Wait*. Don't do anything. *Please*. I'll get rid of them ... I promise.'

His retreating shoulders shrugged. Dorothy scampered to the front door, patting her hair into place. She opened it a crack. There was a policeman outside.

In the small kitchen which she shared with the other resident counsellors, Ruth was putting away the things Carol had asked her to buy at the supermarket. She was pleased to be of use to her overworked friend. An apologetic cough from the doorway startled her and made her drop a wholemeal loaf and a tub of cottage cheese. The lid fell off and the contents threatened to ooze out on to the floor.

'I'm so sorry, Ruth.' Dr Frieling tried awkwardly to help her.

'It's all right. I've got it.' She deftly scooped up the tub and put it in the fridge. 'Can I do something for you, Doctor?'

Actually she wanted him to go away. She was still shaken by her encounter in the supermarket. The hungry look which Dorothy Ballantine had fastened on her was haunting. Yet the woman appeared not to recognise her. She looked simply awful – thin and bedraggled, her perfect glossy hair gone stringy and lacklustre. Any remnant of dislike in Ruth's heart was driven out: Mikey must be giving her a torrid time, and she was so obviously doing her best. How else could she be so reduced to a shadow of her former self? Ruth alone knew what it was like, and pitied her. But her deterioration wasn't the most remarkable thing about her; more striking was the feverish beauty of her eyes, which, with all their listlessness wiped away, blazed out of her pinched face with unnatural intensity.

'No, no,' said the doctor. 'I dropped by to give you this. It just came by the second post.' He handed her an envelope and, with a cordial nod, left the kitchen.

Ruth walked slowly back to her room. She regretted that she had been so slow to react. She should have detained Mrs Ballantine before she scuttled away — the woman had wanted to talk, Ruth was sure of that. She would have been glad to help; they could have put their differences aside for Mikey's sake. But Dorothy had obviously been inhibited by — perhaps ashamed of — the elderly, possibly retarded, man who was with her. A derelict relative maybe.

She sat on her bed and, still puzzling over Dorothy's behaviour, glanced at the letter which Dr Frieling had given her. It was addressed to her, care of the Unit. The handwriting seemed familiar. She tore open the envelope and read the address written on the top right-hand corner of the enclosed page: Convento de Santa Feliciana, Puerto de Cabra, Valladolid.

She stared at the letter with disbelief. Then she carried it at arm's length to the writing desk and opened her journal. The hairs pricked on the back of her neck. The handwriting of the letter was identical to the automatic writing of the messages. She sat down heavily at the desk. The letter read:

Dear Miss Ruth,
Please pardon a stranger who addresses herself to you in this bad English. Señora Ballantine has written me in order to say that her little boy calling himself Mikey is with you. Permit me to explain that I was caring for Mikey some years before. As you see, I have returned to Spain and now I am *monja* — that is, a religious.

I pray often for Mikey, and also you because God gives me strong feeling that Mikey is in best hands, which is delightful to me. I am bold to write because like you I love the little boy and am close to you yourself in this. Now I must tell of this thing what happened to me. (Pardon, it is my fault that I do not write more soon but I am afraid that it can appear risible to you.)

Three days before, I have a dream. First I am not certain, but nowadays I believe that this dream is sent to me by the grace of God. And so: Mikey comes in the dream. He is very bright, very *airoso* — I can not say his appearance in English — but he is beautiful and can speak. He say an enormity will happen and my help is necessary for this big thing (but I can not remember what it is, or perhaps I do not hear). He say I must write to you – I hear 'Ruth, Ruth' and I know it is you because Señora Ballantine write this about you.

It can be that this big thing is very very bad, so I say to you, my dear Ruth, to watch and guard Mikey very well. I think he has special need for you nowadays.

In my conscience I have to say that his mother and father are not good for him, especially Señor Ballantine. I have sinned in their house, for which I do great penance. It is good that Mikey is no longer there. I pray for Señora and Señor Ballantine. I have not been happy with them but nowadays I increase with happiness each day inside this beautiful *convento*. Please write to say how well Mikey is and also you yourself, my dear Ruth, if you have time.

Your sister in Christ,
MARÍA DONOSA

Ruth could not take it all in at first. There was no doubt that María – this rather sweet nun – was alive and well. The date of the letter suggested that it had been written three days after her first psychic message. The postal service from Spain had delayed it until now.

With some indignation, Ruth turned to a fresh page in her journal, took up a pen and concentrated on quietening her racing brain. Almost at once, as though her being was free of all obstruction, a crystal-clear stream of energy thrilled down her arm.

Ask, wrote her hand with a powerful flourish. Too impatient to write herself, Ruth addressed the empty room.

'You said María was dead.'

No. I said she was my instrument. María is incarnate. When her mind is passive, in meditation or sleep, I can mould her psychic energy with my will. Naturally, I have her consent.

'You mean she *knows* what you're doing?'

No. She is not conscious of the part she plays. But lack of consciousness is not lack of consent. Whether we know it or not, we all play a part in each other's lives – whether we like it or not, we are one another.

Ruth couldn't suppress a frustrated sigh. 'Look, I've studied your messages,' she said sharply. 'I think I understand them. But what are they all *for*?'

They are the last fractions of knowledge you need to become complete.

Ruth was chastened by what she imagined to be the spirit's tone. She replied, more meekly: 'I don't feel very complete. Or, rather, I do ... in a way. But I also feel ... I don't know ... something like a husk.

236

I could be blown away. But I do feel that something is happening to me ... that something *will* happen. I don't know. I can't go on like this. I don't even know why I'm talking to you like this. You said you had to tell me about someone who is coming. I don't know why——' Her speech was cut short by a few swift strokes of the pen.

Be still.

Ruth leant back in her chair and relaxed. Gradually she banished all thought. She closed her eyes and let herself sink into the darkness. The pen dropped from her limp fingers. The sounds from outside – footsteps on the stairs, the bang of a door – were far away. She had the impression she was floating a few inches outside her body.

When I am one, I will be the One.

The sentence seemed to fall into her mind from a great height, like a perfect drop of icy water. The words were not hers, nor did she understand them. But they seemed so simple, so full of hidden meaning. It occurred to her that something was trying to take over her mind. Yet she did not feel threatened – she didn't even care. She wanted only to know what the sentence meant. Slowly and deliberately she formed a thought of her own.

Who are you?

The reply flashed into her mind, briefly lighting up the inside of her head.

I am one who is nearer to you than you to yourself. Come closer.

Her breath came in irregular jerks. Bravely she steadied it, inhaling deeply and letting it out as slowly as she could. The air in the room closed about her. Layers of interior darkness peeled away to reveal thicker, blacker layers beneath. At the end of the darkness her terrible emptiness was waiting to envelop her. Without thinking or speaking she breathed out a single deep plea: 'Save me.'

Like a faint echo, a distant sound was travelling towards her across the immensity of darkness. Her ears popped, as if she were at great altitude. There was a hiss, like static, then silence. Then, light years away, a whisper. The voice of the dead was calling from the heights, summoning across the abyss.

Oh God, go away please go away.

'Yes?'

Police Constable Steve Richardson glanced at his clipboard. 'Mrs Ballantine?'

'Yes.' Dorothy opened the door a little wider.

'May I have a word ...?'

'Yes, of course.'

'May I come in a moment?'

Yes, yes, he's here you'll save Mikey won't you won't you?

'I'm very busy.'

'Ah. Right. Well, this'll only take a moment. It's about the, er, assault committed near here the other day. ... Perhaps you read about it?'

He'll kill us all.

'Mrs Ballantine?'

'Sorry. Yes, I heard about it. On the golf course.'

He raped a girl he'll rape me. Help me.

'Ah. Yes, I remember. I spoke to you then, didn't I? Didn't recognise you for a moment, madam. You were walking right past the spot. Ninth green. We had a chat.'

'Yes, that's right.'

'If I'd known, I wouldn't have bothered you. We're just doing a routine house-to-house. In case anyone saw anything. ...'

This is taking too long he'll kill Mikey go away.

'Yes, yes. I see. Sorry I can't help you further.'

'No problem, madam. ... Excuse me for asking, but are you OK?'

No no no.

'Yes, of course. A bit busy, that's all.'

'Are you alone in the house?'

No.

'Yes. My husband's out at the moment. With our son.'

Mikey I love you you'll be all right I promise.

'Right. Well. I'll be off, then. Sorry to disturb you.'

Steve Richardson's boots crunched down the gravel of the long drive. That was the trouble with these big houses — it took hours to reach the front doors, and half the time the owners weren't in when you got there. The other half, you had bloody great dogs dying to take your leg off. And what for? The house-to-house was a waste of time; it should've been done straight away, before the trail went cold. There was no chance of catching the bastard now, unless he did it again.

He hadn't liked to say it to the lady, but she looked bloody rough. Great rings under her eyes, skinny as a rake, all that shiny hair shot to bits. Probably on a crash diet, with injections from a Harley Street quack — though God knew she didn't need it. Rich people were odd, never satisfied, often neurotic. No wonder she didn't sleep well, living in that big gloomy pile. Who did it belong to before? Ringo, they'd said, or was it George?

He glanced back at the house. The declining sun shone out of a cloudless sky, but several rooms had drawn curtains. What did they *do* in a place like that?

FOUR

I NEARLY DIDN'T MAKE IT HERE. It's getting worse. They're like beasts out there ... like beasts or like the Daughters of Zion who are haughty, and walk with stretched forth necks and wanton eyes (as Isaiah says), walking and mincing as they go, and making a tinkling with their feet. But therefore will the Lord smite with a scab the crown of the head of the Daughters of Zion, and the Lord will lay bare their secret parts. ... Oh, Lord, Lord.

Where was I? Ah yes, I remember. Oh God, *yes*. There isn't time to tell you everything. I'll have to skip straight to Good Friday. That's when it happened. I might've guessed it would choose that day, of all days. But I didn't. In fact I didn't even go to church — not that it would've made a jot of difference. I'd sort of ... lost heart, I suppose, what with Mikey buried in his pile of junk, and dear Ruth looking more and more worried, and me ... I was useless. I just moped about, feeling ... well, nothing. Just heavy and oppressed like when there's thunder about. Couldn't even pray properly. Went to bed early and dreamt that Ruth was smiling and that I was giving Mikey a piggy-back ride while he held me tightly round the neck and laughed.

Woke. Not gently, but like you do sometimes, suddenly, as though you've been woken by the thud of your own heart. My pillow was damp; so were my eyes. An electric blue flash danced across my eyelids. I opened them. Total blackness. Look, don't ask me how I knew, but *there was someone in the room*. Who's there? – that's what I thought; I couldn't speak. I couldn't even move to grab the poker I had handy. In the distance, a night express roared through Wyebridge station. I was stiff as a corpse, thinking that if I didn't move it might go away. Fat chance.

Whoever, whatever it was seemed to breathe in time to my breathing. When I held my breath ... nothing. My heart was pumping like I was a sinking ship. I thought I was sure to have an attack. I moved my eyes about. They were used to the darkness now. They could see the outline of my one little window high up on the opposite wall. I'd left the blackout curtains open, and the darkness was coming through it, a shade lighter than the dark inside. I boggled my eyes, looking for a darker mass in the room. There was nothing for it to hide behind. I moved my neck a fraction, then my head. There was nobody in the room. Yet I could've *sworn*. ...

I did a lot of breathing till my heart went back to normal; I rubbed my neck, which had gone stiff as a board with anxiousness; I sat up and took a final check on the room. Quiet as the grave it was, and empty. I lay down again on my left side.

About four inches away from my head – ten centimetres if you prefer – another head was lying on my pillow, its face towards mine. I could see the whites of its eyes and its teeth grinning.

I don't know how I got out of bed. I think I rose vertically into the air, letting out a horrible noise. Anyway, I found myself with the poker in one hand and the other on the light-switch. The room was freezing. You'll never believe it, but the bed was empty.

All the same, it was too close for comfort. I reckoned that, if the Lord didn't come for me soon, within hours – minutes maybe – well, you could count me out of the Rapture altogether. I wouldn't have minded so much except that, either way, I'd have to be parted from Mikey. He'd never have forgiven me if I'd just disappeared without a word. Every second counted: I pulled some clothes on, grabbed my torch and ran all the way down here, to the Unit. Risky, you think? Well, I was no safer indoors, was I? No safer anywhere. And I honestly think that nothing, save the Lord Himself, could have stopped me that night, but in any case nothing tried to.

Mikey was waiting for me at the edge of his magic square. He always had a high opinion of me, but that's a feature of the holy, isn't it? – to think the best of people. I was ... let's say I was glad to see him. We sat together on his bean-bag for a bit. Not a great one for conversation is Mikey. I wanted to talk – not about my tribulations, God forbid – but just to make some gesture before I left. So I reminded him of the story of the raising of Lazarus. It's always been a favourite of mine, I don't know why, perhaps because it's evidence that with God all things are possible even in this life. Frankly, I told the story more for my benefit than for his. He made his own gesture, a thing I treasure: he gave me Yiaou. That's his cat. A solemn moment. I had nothing sacred to give him in exchange, so I gave him my torch. Well, it's the thought that counts. He didn't seem put out.

Ruth, on the other hand, was — at first. Who can blame her? She looked ... out of this world. It's not easy talking to people who take your breath away. I did my best for as long as I could, but I left before I said anything more stupid than usual. Still, it bucks you up talking to Ruth. She called me Harold. I felt more tranquil.

You remember I came to see you — I mean Doctor Noble — early that morning to suggest a spot of electrical treatment. I had an idea that it might be the best protection. But, of course, I couldn't contemplate it while Mikey was weighing himself in the balance. I had no option but to watch and wait, watch and pray.

Rather than wait at home, I took my carcass out into the open. A lovely heart-breaking day with blue sky and little puffs of cloud and the air warm after the long winter. I wanted a last look at this beautiful world. I went first to church and filled a small bottle with holy water from the font. Minor malignant spirits may be subdued by the sprinkling of holy water; and, if not, I could always swallow some to revive myself in times of weakness or confusion.

I knew I was being stalked, so I kept moving, walking all day in a wide circle until I ended up late at night on Saint Michael's Hill. It was too quiet for comfort. The shadows were breathing evil. I'd just decided that it would be better to be taken in my own house after all, when I saw Clare. She was all alone, her shoes tapping on the road very loudly in the darkness. I tried to stay calm and warn her that it was far from safe to be out that night with the prince of the power of the air abroad; but she shunned me and the tapping of her feet went pitter-patter, faster and faster. I had a terrible job catching her up; and, of course, when I did, I found that although she was young enough to be Clare it wasn't Clare at all, for her face was prematurely aged by cosmetics, in the Babylonian manner.

I sat up until morning in the parlour. I didn't bother with the poker. I must've dozed off because I was woken by the melody of church bells. They were ringing for me on Easter Sunday. I continued to put it off the scent by wearing some old clothes of Father's. I know it's not done to wear a jersey to church, so I sat at the back, out of the way. The service didn't capture much of my attention; I attempted to fix my spirit on prayers of my own — for Mikey and Ruth and, finally, for the whole congregation who were shortly to be plunged into lamentation when the Lord pinched His salt of the earth and gave the world over to the rotten dispensation of the Beast. And verily I was struck with terror at *knowing* and yet being unable to save them, or myself.

'I'm afraid Dr Noble is in session at the moment. He can't be disturbed.' The young male nurse looked sorrowful.

'But he is treating Harry?' Ruth asked again.

'Oh, yes. He's treating old Harry.' The nurse leant back in his chair and tapped his crooked teeth with a pencil. Then he leant forward and, with his elbows on the desk, added in a confidential tone: 'Dr Noble's rather old-fashioned. Ninety per cent of psychiatry these days is drugs. But he likes to do a lot of talking. Makes a lot of tapes.'

'Yes. I see,' said Ruth absently. 'Harry told me he was an outpatient.'

'It's policy to return patients to the community as soon as possible. That means about seventy per cent of them. Of course, most of the drugs have side-effects which are not all that pleasant, so a lot of patients drop them as soon as they're out of here – and that means a lot of them come back. Harry'll probably be back before long, poor old sod.'

'You mean . . . ?'

'He hasn't been in for a while. Our Social Services woman – sorry, person – has been round to his house more than once. You can have a go if you're that keen. I've got the address on file.' He pulled a folder from a filing cabinet behind him and extracted a small index card. 'Nice old bloke, Harry. No harm in him. Not many patients actually ask for ECTs. But he must've felt better because he never followed up the idea. My guess is, he might make it out there. He didn't strike me as the dependent sort.' Ruth had already edged away from the garrulous young man and was halfway through the door. 'Tell him he's a naughty boy,' laughed the nurse. 'Tell him "Come back, all is for-given"!'

Ruth walked very fast, bent forward and red in the face. One or two passers-by on Station Road gave her curious looks. She was so positive that Harry would be waiting for her that she was momentarily thrown when her knocking at the door of No. 1, South Road went unanswered.

She walked around to the back of the dingy little house and peered through a grimy window. She could just make out a room containing piles of pamphlets, some of them coloured, interspersed with old bits of cheap furniture. There was no sign of life. She tapped on the window.

'Harry! It's me, Ruth.'

She wondered if she ought to break in. Perhaps Harry had injured himself and was lying inside, unable to speak. But that was a ridiculous idea. He was strong as an ox.

His absence was a blow. Her scheme — if that's what it was — depended on his help. Who else could be trusted absolutely? It had not crossed her mind that Harry wouldn't be ready and waiting for her word. It had seemed ordained. Now she'd have to go alone. She was surprised, even faintly amused, that thinking counted for so little — her legs were in charge, obeying the gentle urgent whisper. They were marching her towards St Michael's Hill. Her direction was clear.

Dorothy watched the policeman receding down the drive. She turned away from the front door and returned to the drawing room. The first thing that caught her eye was the glint of steel. Klackan's knife was lodged where he had let it drop between the arm of the sofa and the cushion. The departure of the policeman, like an abdication of responsibility, entitled her to the knife. It wasn't something you took up lightly. It was Klackan's instrument. There'd be no going back.

The knife fitted neatly in her hand. The sturdy blade was exquisitely pointed and seemed much sharper than a mere vegetable-slicer. She could almost feel it twitching like a diviner's rod with its own momentum and goal. With the knife held in front of her, Dorothy ascended the stairs. She felt clear-headed and practical. She had shaken Klackan, shaken him off. He was fallible, after all; he was flesh and blood.

It was no good storming Mikey's room and endangering him. She'd take Klackan off his guard in her room. The secret was to appear as listless and obedient as ever. She changed quickly into her grubby dressing gown and lay on the bed. As an afterthought, she selected one of Rex's tapes at random and pressed it into the video recorder with the sound off. It would be an added distraction. He'd find her slumped harmlessly in front of some film; perhaps he'd even congratulate her on her performance with the police. He'd be sure to punish her for her brief moment of insolence. She would wait until he was practically on top of her and then— She gripped the knife hidden in the folds of her robe and mentally enacted the spring and thrust and twist.

The door was closed as he would expect it to be. She was ready to wait for as long as it took. You didn't rush these things. The scene on the video looked familiar, but she couldn't quite place the film. A large double bed dominated the screen. An attractive young actress, also familiar to her, appeared and lay on the bed. She was naked and smiling nervously at someone off-camera. The smile froze on her face. She made an adamant gesture of refusal and made as if to get off the bed.

Her performance was rendered rather touching by the unprofessional naturalism of the static camera.

A naked man stepped into view and pushed her back with one hand. He was concealing something behind his back with the other. He kissed the girl several times and stroked her long black hair. He was coaxing her with caresses, teasing her. She was smiling again in spite of herself, still nervous.

Dorothy forgot to listen for the footfall outside the door. She leant forward, interested. Surely she'd seen the wallpaper, the bedside lamp and – yes – even the girl before? Surely she'd seen them somewhere other than on the screen. And the man – didn't he look a bit like Paul Newman?

Grateful for the moist darkness, Rex didn't bother to strike a match or light the candle, but sank weakly on to the jumble of newspapers. His clothes felt heavy and unnatural. Oblivious of the cold, he pulled them off. The scratching in his head was very loud. 'Not a cat,' he reminded himself. He gently probed his afflicted genitals with forefinger and thumb. 'Am a man.' He licked his fingers and began to masturbate.

He broke into his hoard of memory-tapes and replayed them for the reassurance of his manhood. There was no pleasure to be had. The women slid dutifully before his closed eyes. The more he drummed up, the fewer he could hold in focus. His longing for them grew diffuse and chaotic. They whirled past, faster and faster, jerking through him like fleeting phantoms in the swarming dark. Rex gasped, flinging out tendrils of desire to pin them down; but the women flashed out of sight before he could trace their lineaments. A series of red sexual organs wove around him a vest of flame that burnt and burnt and brought no warmth.

He drove himself on until the tape looped and snagged on the unknown girl whose red high-heels had clicked down Station Road, her gold ankle-chain bobbing up and down. He briefly gunned the engine of his powerful car, then switched it off and followed her through the scrubby bushes of the heath. She looked round once. He sensed the thrill of her fright. He felt her thin blouse, warm from her body, tearing under his fingers like skin. But she was running, one red shoe abandoned in the green thicket, running away and melting out of sight, out of mind, into the undergrowth.

Rex thrashed his legs among the newspapers and rolled his head from side to side to free it from the scratch and itch he couldn't reach. 'Puss, puss,' he whistled between his clenched teeth. 'Pussy pussy, puss puss.' The claws bit deeper into the invaginations of his brain.

In desperation he flogged up his latest memory, still fresh in his mind. He scanned it in slow motion, terrified of squandering it . . . . He was nearly home when he picked her out in his headlights on the dark road. She was already running from someone he couldn't see. He was out of the car; his blood was up; the chase was on. She was a bit of luck at last. He put on the hood, like an executioner, to exact impersonal justice on Andrea and all those other tarts. He was near enough now to inhale the sexy smell of her fear.

He took her on the damp baize of the ninth green. His loins drew strength from the strength of her struggle. The claws scraped out morsels of grey meat. The flagpole rattled in the centre of the green. The rhododendrons rustled in the wind. The blood was loose in his brain. Her face was a mask of fright, much younger under the make-up than it looked. Younger than any of them, even María. The sky was a shower of stars. She opened under him like a chasm. Her stifled scream was hot on his ear. She was powerless under his humped muscles.

Vistas of limitless desire encircled him. He struck out towards the lurid horizon. But the shadow on the green began to elude him. He could get no purchase as she drifted dreamily into the shape of Dorothy. Rex beat a tattoo between his legs, trying wildly to launch himself on his wife. He saw only himself, as in a third-rate film, gagged and bound and stripped of the hood that hid the weakness in his face. Dorothy groaned as Klackan, the black folds of the hood thick on his neck like a mane, covered her. Rex groaned, his impotence mingling with hers; the faceless darkness pressed him down; he shuddered under the mighty chop of Klackan's foam-flecked haunches, shuddered and jerked. Dry spasms tightened him like a vice. There was no release to be had in the world. His desire spilled over the edge into space. Rex clung on like grim death. Craving cut into craving; he clung on to nothing except his own clinging. The claws stopped their scratching. He breathed out and lay still. He seemed to hear a mewing sound, pitched higher and higher until it passed beyond the range of human ears. He turned his face to the wall.

THREE

I DIDN'T NOTICE the vicar or the people leave. I just found myself alone in the church with the musty dusty smell as it'd always been. I was sleepy. A bird was trapped in the church, which worried me. I could hear it fluttering around. There'd be a silence, and then a sudden flurry of frantic wings, then silence again. The sun was streaming through the stained glass, warming my back and throwing rainbows on the polished wood of the pew in front. I stayed on my knees, but there didn't seem to be anything left to say except 'Lord, Lord', calling on His Name over and over, 'Lord, Lord', rolling up all my hopes and fears into the one word 'Lord' until I was beside myself.

Far away the bird swooped without a sound across the high space of the church. Three ripples of air stirred against my skin in time to its wingbeat. A shadow passed in front of the sun. The rainbow faded from the pew. There was a voice, oh God, in my ear. . . . And the voice spoke.

'Harold. I am the Angel of the Lord. Why do you flee from me?'

The voice was very serene and beautiful, but sorrowing. I was sorely amazed. But, mindful of the deceit of spirits, I determined to examine the voice (as it is written) to see whether it was of God.

'Do you believe in Jesus Christ?' I asked boldly.

'I believe in Jesus Christ,' came the reply, 'who shall come in clouds of glory to reap the wicked and gather the blessed.'

Well, at the sound of these words my heart began to beat again; for an evil spirit can't pronounce the name of Our Saviour.

'Let me look at you,' I asked.

'None may look on my face without courting madness or death,' said the Angel, as I knew him then to be; for a demon loves to be looked on that he may mesmerise his prey. I couldn't hold back tears of gratitude and relief.

'What do you want of me?' I asked clumsily.

'Not what I want, Harold, but what the Lord wants.' The Angel's voice, low as a whisper, was like a breath of wind blowing in the centre of my head. 'Are you ready to do whatsoever He commands?'

'Yes, yes, I'm ready – but I fear my own weakness.'

'The Lord gives strength for what He commands. You have only to consent,' the Angel reminded me.

'I consent with all my heart,' I said. 'Let His will be done.'

'Praise the Lord. You've spoken well, Harold,' said the Angel, and he whispered the Lord's command, of which I'm forbidden to speak.

I trembled with the power of his word, burning like ice. And the word was like a two-edged sword, cleaving me in half. I moaned aloud, begging for mercy. 'Let me die rather than do this,' I cried; but the Angel had spoken and was silent, only breathing his displeasure on me. And I was bound over in the shadow of his wrath, and led out of the church, and sent to do the bidding of the Lord.

Yes, you can look sceptical. But I tell you frankly, not since the days of Abraham, the father of faith, has a man been so tested. But the question remains: why am I here? Am I cruelly deceived and hell-bent? I tell myself that God's love is not our love and – who knows? – its strange Face may be fiercer than we imagine. But I wonder, I wonder. . . .

I hardly like to mention this . . . . You're not a doctor at all, are you? It doesn't matter. As long as it all gets said. Then maybe we can find some peace. Do I know you? You knew I was going to ask that. You know my thoughts almost before I say them. I sense that you'll help me. The Lord knows I need help. You see, I can't remember things from one moment to the next. Out there it's a nightmare of deceitful spirits. It's only real in here. I'm not dead, I know that; but I don't feel exactly alive, either. If I'm asleep, who will wake me? And why do I fear waking as I fear death?

Listen. Can you hear it? The whisper of his breath, the beat of his heart? Angel or devil, he's coming nearer, for better or worse. I must finish quickly, quickly. What happened? Yes, I remember the warmth of the day outside the church. I remember going to . . . to the Unit, yes. Where's Ruth? Where's *Mikey*? Gone, gone. I set off again, up to the hills. The Angel is hovering invisibly at my back. I'm looking at all the big houses. I can't find the one I want. Where is it, where? I'm trembling with the power of the word. Oh, Lord, where is he?

And the Lord gives me a Sign. It is in the ditch by the road outside the great house on the high hill. The Sign is telling me I've reached my journey's end. I grasp the Sign and brush the mud from its face. The Sign is a yellow cat. *Yiaou*. He points with his paws. I follow the pointing. I'm coming, Mikey … coming.

A long black car slid past her. Three Arab women in the back seat turned their heads in unison to look at her. Their kohl-rimmed eyes were stone-cold above their yashmaks. A solitary young policeman stepped on to the grass verge as the car passed; he watched it for a moment and then returned to studying his large clipboard. Ruth examined the hedges to avoid catching his eye.

The essence of her plan was to have no plan. At the back of her mind she thought that perhaps she was meant to kidnap Mikey. That was chiefly why she had taken it on herself to contact Harry. Between them they could sweep all obstacles aside. But apparently she was to tackle the Ballantines alone. It was an unnerving prospect; but it wasn't her business to worry about it. She'd know what to do when the time came.

The house on the hill was partially visible from a distance. Its top windows caught the light of the dying sun. Ruth walked on, breathing hard. When she reached the gates, she did not hesitate, but passed through them and began the ascent of the long curved drive. She felt calm and happy with anticipation, equal to any task.

Once she was in full view of the house, Ruth slipped into the bushes and skirted round to the back. She had to get to Mikey undetected. She peeped cautiously through each downstairs window in turn, certain that one of them would be open. Some of them were curtained, others revealed uninhabited rooms; all of them were closed. Ruth found that she had returned full-circle to the front door.

Undaunted, she assumed that she had to ring the bell and take the consequences. But as she raised her hand she noticed that the door was not locked. It yielded to her exploratory push, and she found herself standing in a wide panelled hall, facing the staircase. She listened carefully but could hear neither occupants of the downstairs rooms nor the rustle of her internal voice. Her nerve was on the point of failing her. She wanted to run away from the house. She should never have come in the first place.

The overwhelming realisation that she was going to see Mikey again forced her on. At the foot of the stairs, an attack of vertigo made her hang on to the banister – any minute now she would be holding Mikey in her arms! She tiptoed up the stairs. Every creak sounded like a pistol shot. She breathed as quietly as she could in quick shallow gasps.

On the first-floor landing all the bedroom doors were shut. She stretched out her hands as if to divine what lay behind them. Without faltering she walked down to the end of the passage and turned into the east wing. In front of the last door on the left she suddenly stopped. The door was ajar. For a second she fancied that she could hear a man's voice coming from inside, an urgent mutter as though he were swearing or praying. She put her hand to her ear in a theatrical attitude of intense listening. She must have been mistaken – she could hear nothing.

The man had produced leather bracelets from behind his back and had slipped them around the girl's wrists. She shook her head violently, no longer amused, as he tied the thongs to the brass bedstead. The girl was visibly distressed; her thin arms, stretched behind her head, looked stringy as she strained at her bonds. The man disappeared from view. The girl bit her lip and looked distractedly into the camera.

Dorothy saw that the girl wasn't an actress at all. She was familiar because she was María. The room was familiar because it had been her own bedroom in the London flat. The bedstead was the same one she was now lying on. She realised that of course she'd known all along who the man was, but had refused to accept the evidence of her eyes.

The man reappeared. The handsome face which Dorothy had vaguely mistaken for Paul Newman's was hidden by a black woollen mask. He stepped on to the bed and stood over María, his jutting penis out of all proportion to his body. He held it in his hand like a blunt instrument. Dorothy didn't flinch as he plunged it into the motionless frightened girl, but narrowed her eyes, missing nothing. She watched the man mechanically stabbing over and over again. María went limp, closing her eyes; a few fat tears squeezed out from under her thick lashes.

The screen went dark. The performance was over. Dorothy felt very sorry for María. She was touched by the girl's annual letters from the Spanish convent, enquiring after Mikey; she was puzzled by their apologetic – even shame-faced – tone, which she attributed at the time to poor grammar. In the end, unwilling to write about Mikey any more, she had referred María directly to Ruth Maier at the Unit.

She felt a deep sorrow for Rex as well. Was it her coldness that had driven him to act out the sad little pantomime? She experimented with emotions of anger and jealousy, but could only raise pity and disgust at his bullying of a young unprotected foreigner. Dorothy felt defiled and at fault: if she hadn't been so wrapped up in herself, she might've forestalled the whole miserable business.

The sound of creaking floorboards outside the door roused her. Footsteps paused, and moved on in the direction of Mikey's room. Squeezing the knife tightly, she crossed silently to the door and opened it an inch. She peeped out. The passage was empty.

She was seized by sudden panic. Anything could be happening while she waited; she'd done nothing *but* wait, all this time. Waiting was her weakness. If she didn't do it now, she never would.

She made no sound as she slipped down the corridor in her bare feet, avoiding the creaks. She couldn't imagine why she hadn't plucked up the courage to act before now. It was intoxicating to be doing something at last, glorious to be saving her son. 'Don't worry, Mikey,' she repeated to herself. 'It'll be all right. Mummy's coming. It'll soon be over.'

I hide in the bushes for a while. I go into the house through the tall windows. There's an unclean guardian spirit in a man's likeness. I catch him unawares. I don't need – not yet – the bottle of holy water in my pocket. For he's no match for the strength of the Lord in my arm. I brush him aside and store him away in the cellar with the rubbish. I find in his den the disguise for his face. I veil my own face that the child may not know me. In the kitchen I take up a knife in great fear and trembling, for it is written that if any man shall kill with the sword with the sword must he be killed. I climb the stairs with heavy heart and tread the passage, testing the doors, until—

Sweet Jesus! It's here, in the room; I can feel its breath. Why is it so stale and laden with death? The darkness is pressing down on me ... it's filling my head. I can't see you properly. What's that crouched in the corner? Shadows, only a shadow. I must hurry, God help me, I must finish.... Its breath is on my neck. What happened next? *What?* Yes, it's coming back to me ... yes. Mikey.

He is sitting in the chair, waiting. The room is dark ... as dark as this room. The Lord's command is tearing me. In bitter anguish I call on Him who stayed Abraham's hand even as it was raised over the beloved child of his old age. But the Lord and His Angel hide their faces from me. I walk up to the precious child who is dearer to me than life itself. The blade is shaking and sparkling in my hand. I can see his face now ... I look into Mikey's shining face ... his eyes are jewels of joy — he knows, he *knows*. Forgive me, Mikey, forgive me; it's the Lord's work. I give him the Sign. YIAOU, he cries. He holds the yellow cat who beckons me to be swift. I can't, I can't . . . I can't obey the Lord. I can't defy Him. Mikey moves his head back, he smiles, he shows me the white flesh of his neck. . . . *Thy will be done* . . . . DADDY, he whispers, NOW. I bring my hand down. The blade sighs through the air.

It is finished.

Did I, too, die at that instant? I remember feeling the cold steel as the scorpion its own sting. My eyes were blinded by the sight; my heart was turned to ice. But, no, I'm still alive — and yet not I; but another liveth . . . ?

I have to wait, wait among sinful spirits until the fullness of time. I stretch forth my hand against them, and smite them, like the Lord whose anger was kindled against His people. I'm charged to bind them, as I am bound, until the Lord comes in Glory — and yet not I . . . ?

I feel . . . I feel that I'm waking up. Is the nightmare ending? Have I reached the end at last? Look! There's a crack of light at the window. Perhaps it's not so dark in here.

Where am I? Why am I holding this? Poor Father, I never did slice off the head of his Worm. It's getting clearer. Why don't you move or speak? Help me.

Mikey, Mikey. Oh. What's become of you? Surely not I . . . ? Oh. So it's true.

And who's that? Who are you standing so tall in the corner? I'm beginning . . . to . . . see . . . you've shown yourself at last. You've come for me. Are you Angel or Devil? Unveil your face. I'm not afraid any more. Let me look on the light or dark of your countenance. I've woken from my dream. I want to know why . . . I want the whole truth.

I know that smile. I know. . . . Oh, Lord, *Lord* . . . I know your face. Why are you looking at me like that? *Why have you taken my face?* You never were an angel. It's all been for nothing. Yes, go on — smile, smile. Nothing can save me now. I'm mad. My name is . . . we live at number one. . . . Your name is— *No.*

My name is Harry I live at number one South Road Wyebridge Surrey the World etcetera, yes, yes, keep smiling this'll wipe it off — you'll do no more harm, damn you, *damn you.* When it pops its head out, said Father, chop chop — slice it off. Oh, Jesus, Jesus, Jesus, Jes —

TWO

RUTH PUSHED THE DOOR OPEN and, slipping into the darkened room, swung it to behind her. There was an appalling smell. Ruth wrinkled her nose and held her breath. As her eyes adjusted to the darkness, relieved only by a crack of light between the drawn curtains, she detected the shapes of furniture. 'Mikey . . .?' she said softly. 'It's Ruth. I got the message.'

She took five quick little steps towards the wide table in the centre of the room. Much of its surface was covered with bowls and plates of uneaten food, some of it days old. The expensive high-backed chair in front of the table was empty; the other, behind the table, was occupied by the small huddled figure of a boy.

'Mikey,' said Ruth. She walked around the desk and bent over him. It wasn't easy to recognise him at first, owing to his putrefaction. His flesh was puffy and very white, his eyes had all but liquefied, and his pyjamas were rusty with the blood that had once flowed from the wide black smile across his throat. He'd clearly been dead for a long time.

Ruth gave a little jerk backwards as though a bottle of smelling salts had been thrust under her nose. She had difficulty breathing through her open mouth. Averting her head from the boy in the chair, she noticed a second body lying on the floor in front of the full-length mirror in the corner of the room. Closer inspection showed that it was

Harry Klackan, his blood – a surprising amount of it – still warm on the carpet. One hand clasped a sort of black woollen Balaclava helmet; in the other was a razor whose blade was still bright after its quick clean cut across the strong neck. Ruth sensed that any further attempt at breathing would be to invite suffocation; and, noticing that the room was closing in on her at an alarming rate, she lunged towards the doorway.

As she burst through it in a breathless rush, something pointed and hard stopped her in her tracks. She was standing face to face with Dorothy Ballantine. Ruth formed the irrational impression that Mikey's mother had thrust a taloned hand inside her ribcage and was tearing at her lungs. A wave of pain swelled up, toppled and broke over her.

'Oh,' she said, or tried to say, for the word had too little air to leave her throat. Her lungs bubbled, filling up with liquid. She realised she was drowning from the inside.

The icicle of pain in her heart and lungs drove her to her knees. Her body was slipping away from her, sinking into numbness. She struggled to keep her head above the surface, but when she inhaled she only choked on the salty fluid in her mouth. A powerful undertow pulled her down and sucked her into the swirling dark.

The cloying oppressive atmosphere, as dense as another element, bruised his body which seemed to be made of some spongy, hyper-sensitive substance. The natural light he shed around him painfully pushed aside the fog-like drifts of gloom. Nevertheless, he felt extra-ordinarily *well* and extremely wide-awake. With some effort he brought his light to bear on the ceiling which, once he had cleared a channel, he saw to have been peeled back like the top of a sardine tin. A brilliant canopy of stars scintillated through a shaft in the dark shifting clouds.

In a single willed movement, Harry stood up. The action was delightful, effortless. He gazed dispassionately at his conquered spirit, lying full-length at his feet like a shadow. Half in wonder, half in supplication – perhaps out of habit – he pronounced the name of the Lord.

The walls of the room were hidden by, or possibly dissolved into, a greyish mist. The chair appeared to be a matter of feet away. But when the boy climbed out of it and moved towards Harry he grew rapidly in size as though he had in fact been seated at an immense distance. Harry was a little afraid of the boy whose brightness eclipsed the surroundings; he was even inclined to kneel in his presence, but

Mikey prevented this by kissing him on the cheek. Only then did Harry realise what an age they'd known each other.

'Harold,' the boy seemed to say, 'as good comes out of evil, light out of dark, so you have overcome your own darkness and brought yourself to light. Divided, your courage has reunited you; being one, you are one with me whom, through your faith, you set free to become reunited with myself. I'm saved through you, Harold, and you through me.'

At first he was apprehensive of the sensation — its strength threatened to burst him. But he found that he was able to expand comfortably under its inward pressure, easily overflowing the room, growing so big that he almost touched the stars. He'd never known anything remotely like it, and had to ask Mikey what was happening to him. Mikey's laughter pulsed in lovely beams of healing light. 'You're happy,' the boy explained. 'That's all.'

It was time to leave. Mikey entrusted him with a bag of provisions for the journey. Inside the bag, glowing in all the colours of the rainbow, and more, was (Harry calculated) several years' supply of gobstoppers. He popped an exquisite gold one into his mouth and, savouring its refreshment, clasped his arms around Mikey's neck. Smoothly, as if attached to an invisible cable, the two were drawn up on a slope of calm air into the clouds. Harry knew that, were he to fall, Mikey would catch him. As they rose faster, breaking free of the clouds, flying into the blue, he surveyed the extent of his joy, stretching across the heavens.

The milk-white stars grew denser, compacting like snow crystals, gathering him in. The crisp chime of silver-voiced children, singing hosannas, welcomed him home. His heart swooped and soared, lifting him over immaculate valleys. Around the ringing mountains, a heart-rending echo sounded: the plaintive whistle of the six-fifty to Waterloo.

Dorothy thought that, on the whole, she'd like a cup of tea. Drifting towards the remote region where tea could be found, she was aware of moving in a strange way as though she had dreamt she was asleep and, waking, found herself on the far side of sleep where a different, more vivid order of reality prevailed.

The kitchen was untidy. Dirty crockery lay scattered over the various surfaces; on the pine table a mound of deep-frozen food had thawed and was now decaying. Dorothy was touched by Klackan's unexpected domestic ineptitude. She regretted never having met him face to face – his features, beautiful and youthful in death, had already assumed a new mask, smooth and white.

She turned on the cold tap and was immediately lost in contemplation of the wonderful silver water. Tentatively, she surrendered a hand to the satiny liquid's exquisite agonising gush.

Love, she considered, was a puzzle. It had taken so long to unloose it, learning the hard way, that she'd imagined it infallible; in its name she had taken the knife to cut Mikey free. But the shape had come out of the darkness in a frightful rush. The impact jarred her arm up to the shoulder. The staggered look on Ruth Maier's face matched her own. She leant forward politely as Ruth seemed to clear her throat. But instead of speaking the woman tottered backwards, the knife caught up under her ribcage; her wide eyes flashed once and rolled up into statuesque blanks as she dropped. Like a practical joke, Mikey had been beyond love all along.

What on earth was she to do with her love now? With nowhere to go, still it wouldn't go away. It coursed over and out of her in a stream as simple and impersonal as water from a tap. It was a puzzle.

She remembered Rex. He seemed very far away. But tea was out of the question until something had been done about him. She splashed some water on her face and scooped a few drops – all she could bear – into her mouth. Then she turned off the tap and headed purposefully towards the cellar.

Ruth whizzed silently through the pitch-black tunnel, airless as a vacuum tube. She was sitting in a narrow open carriage which ran like a roller-coaster on frictionless rails. As she wondered whether she was destined to travel for ever, a dab of light appeared in the distance and rapidly enlarged. She longed for a gust of cold wind to blow through her punctured body. The patch of light opened wider and wider like an eye.

Dazzling light broke around her. Standing quite still, she let its liquid gold penetrate every part of her until she couldn't tell where the light ended and she began. She felt at home, perfectly. The landscape was as she knew it would be – sky, sun, mountains, snow, all laid out like a glowing banquet. From the smallest snow crystal to the grandest mountain, from the sun's bronze disc to the lapis lazuli sky, she was joined to every atom by intelligent filaments of light as fine as spun gold.

To look was to touch, taste – good Lord! – *eat*. Her eyes feasted on the preternatural sweetness of crisp snowfields; drank in beams of honeyed sunlight; gorged on the rich fruity minerals of rolling peaks, consummately iced. She brimmed with delight.

At the brink of the ravine, so profound that even she could never fathom it, Ruth nerved herself to scan the sheer north face where the dead lay encased in eternal ice. As she raised her eyes, the forbidding mountain was brilliantly lit up and she saw a thousand souls, arrayed like rainbows, dallying along paths and through archways delicately carved like lace.

'Ruth!' They called out, smiling and waving. 'Hello! Ruth!' She could see every detail of each dear familiar face and, dearest of all, Mama and Papa, whose transparent gladness was like her own. She understood that her chosen path prevented her from joining them, but that they were in any case always with her. They reached out their hands and shot from their fingers two silver rails which landed at her feet, forming a solid bridge across the chasm. A strange whistle stirred the surrounding mountains.

When she was five years old, Dorothy used to watch the boys fishing in the canal at the end of her street. One of them showed her his bait-tin. Peeking inside, she saw a seething mass of bloated maggots feeding on themselves. Horrified, she couldn't tear her eyes away from the obscene spectacle: their naked lust for survival at all costs possessed an infernal fascination.

She was reminded of this sight when she looked into Rex's eyes. They'd be better off empty, she guessed, like the six empty eyes in the charnel house upstairs. He was curled up naked among the newspapers on the cellar floor, staring at the pile of coal. He was a dreadful weight to haul to his feet, and it was all she could do not to shake him off when he clutched her dressing gown. However, the rapacious movement contained nothing human; it was simply the battening of maggots.

But when all was said and done, he was part of her failure, her partner and, yes, her accomplice. She doubted whether her superfluous love could do any good, but it was at his disposal – it wasn't as though it had much to do with her. She guided him up the cellar steps and, steering clear of the unhappy drawing room, led him up the stairs to their bedroom. She chose to shut her ears to the deathly sound of his shuffling feet. His hand hung on for dear life to the shoulder of her robe. When she threw open the curtains, gasping at the sudden shock of light, he shielded his face with his arm.

'Forgive me,' said Dorothy. She was addressing herself as much as Rex; and, more than either, some half-forgotten juvenile deity who by its very absence, deeply felt, was made manifest. Rex fumbled at the lapel of her dressing gown. She saw with absolute clarity where her duty lay. It wasn't after all such a great penance to pay for reviving (if that were possible) his spirit, now sunk so low. Gathering up her rags of love, she enfolded her husband in her arms and drew him down on to the wide bed. One last effort of atonement was required and then, with any luck, there'd be forgiveness.

ONE

THE SPANKING GREEN STEAM TRAIN, caparisoned in gleaming brass, chuffed over the silver rails. The open carriages were chock-a-block with laughing children. Ruth clapped her hands. A large yellow cat came ramping and pirouetting over the snow, showing off and falling over his own floppy legs. Smiling slyly, he rubbed his flannel cheek gently against her hand.

The tall straight-backed engine driver strode majestically towards her, encircled by cheering children, his noble face lovely to look upon. Speechlessly she took Harold's hand, wanting never to let go. A carnival of rejoicing people, streaming over the bridge, gathered around them, making merry.

Suddenly, an expectant murmur rippled through the throng and swelled to a great cheer: 'He is coming!' The people parted to form a reverential avenue. Ruth craned her neck to glimpse the regal personage; but a hubbub among her neighbours distracted her.

Amid exclamations of astonishment, a small person was pushing through the legs of the assembled company. He broke free, running and jumping towards her. He was her own darling, but older perhaps, as Harold was younger – both of them ageless, and bright as the sun. In a single movement she swept him into the air and then clasped him tightly. Her heart was full, full.

Harold spoke softly: 'He is here to honour you.' Ruth glanced around wildly – she could see no one but Mikey. Harold nodded, smiling. She gazed into the boy's tremendous face. Mikey waggled his ears modestly, making her laugh.

They waved goodbye to the joyful company, who withdrew across the gulf to the infinite brightness beyond. Mikey took her free hand.

'Your love gave birth to me,' he seemed to say, 'and I, complete at last, called you from another realm to complete yourself. Mother, you are the daughter of your son, for I am your own true self . . . .' He took Harold's hand. 'He and I and you, here we are complete at last, a single Soul. . . .'

Hand in hand with them, moving in a measured round, Ruth breathed freely at last, breathing in them as they breathed in her, with love transpiring as easily as air.

The completed circle turns; we who died live; yet not in ourselves, but in each other. Heart to heart, we beat in unison, beat as one. . . . *I whirl towards the fathomless abyss. . . .*

The sun hung in flames on the horizon. Rods of crimson light beat on the window-panes. Dorothy's compassionate hands tugged at her husband. His body was heavy; his unlimited hunger was burning inside her. Redness broke into the room. Her aching bones effervesced. Jets of warm foam shot up her spine. His face was nuzzling her breast. 'Mikey,' she breathed. His name was drowned by the ecstatic crash of blood-red surf in her skull.

. . . The sad blue world hangs on the black horizon. Gladly I submit to the grave-deep darkness. Faster than light, I fall like a red dart, straight to the heavy heart of Earth.

PART THREE

The Seventh Stair

SLEET-LADEN SQUALLS rattled the window-panes. The fire flared in a sudden draught down the chimney. She stretched her legs towards the flames and warmed her stockinged feet. The small house came into its own in winter. It was cosy, easy to heat, altogether more like home than she remembered it.

The final episode of 'Book at Bedtime' had just finished on the radio. Dorothy reached over and turned it off. On the floor above her father was getting ready for bed. She heard his comforting leisurely step with gratitude. Against expectation, he had been rather wonderful: not only had he protected her in the early days from intrusive reporters (guilty of manslaughter, she'd been discharged immediately), but he had also accepted her, in her condition, without fuss. He had even followed the coroner's tactful line in not pressing her for details of the long ordeal. The view was that she had suffered enough. The dead were to be left to bury the dead. Dorothy smiled into the fire and placidly took up her needlework. She'd put in a few stitches before taking up Dad's cocoa.

Time was, impatient of imperfection, she'd have bought something pretty and neat from the toyshop. Now, despite her cack-handedness, she was wholly absorbed in the process – partly planned, partly fortuitous – by which the animal took shape under her inept but loving needle. She had vaguely had in mind to make a comical orange monkey. It had turned out instead as a marmalade cat. By a series of happy accidents its face was charming. A botched eye, for instance, gave the cat a saucy wink which she couldn't bring herself to correct. It reminded her of the other cat which, prised from Mikey's hands, had been incinerated, just as its master had been. The baby would laugh when she made the marmalade cat say silly things and waggle its floppy legs. They had suggested, of course, that she have it out; but, whatever they might say about its genesis, the child was hers alone. Eight months gone, Dorothy lugged herself out of the armchair and, laying her cat aside, walked to the kitchen where she put on the milk to heat.

Four months ago, Rex had closed his eyes and passed away. It was no euphemism. The surprise was that, immobile and mute, he had hung on for so long. They'd had to wash and dress him, even force food down him. She recalled the dismay on the face of Constable Steve Richardson (he was praised for his initiative in returning to the house after a routine enquiry). She poured the hot milk into the mug marked 'A Souvenir of Tralee'. It was about the only thing she had cared to salvage from the house which, sold to offset Rex's debts, now lay bare and empty of everything but echoes.

On the seventh stair, Dorothy pauses for a rest as the baby stirs inside her. Its weight is second nature to her now; she loves the feel of her feet square on the ground. Waiting, she counts the tiny shamrocks on the mug, breathing in the milky steam and absent-mindedly stroking her swollen belly. An involuntary flick of the head, as if to toss an invisible pigtail over her shoulder, makes her smile at herself.

Tomorrow she will go to early Mass, as she sometimes does these days, partly because she still dreams of Rex just as the young policeman found him, face to the wall, dragging his feet leadenly round in a tight circle. Life is doubly precious to her now, knowing that without constant attention the soul can lapse into mortality.

But mostly she goes to give thanks for her second chance, for another birth; and, in default of anyone more specific, she likes to thank God. She guesses that God has forgiven her, as she has forgiven Him. But there remains a tiny stone-cold part of her, left behind where it died in that dark house, which prevents her from forgetting. The child curls up quietly in her womb once again. Heavily, she climbs on to the eighth step and carries the hot cocoa to her father.